She did not know it or when it came to kissing. She thought she didn't know what to do, but instinctively she did, and that made the kiss almost painful in its perfection. She tasted so good that he growled low in his throat, pulled her mouth up tighter to his, and then licked her between her lips.

She was startled by the introduction of his tongue. She had seen others kiss in such ways, but seeing it and doing it were two very different things. It somehow seemed far more intimate than what had just transpired had felt. Her heart was clamoring in her chest from the riot of emotions and worries that were stampeding through her.

"Enough!" he said on a low rumbling huff as he gave her a little shake. "Your taste tempts me and I will have the whole of it." His mouth sealed to hers again and this time he thrust his tongue past her teeth. She was prepared to hate it, prepared to be repulsed . . . but she was shocked to find she liked his taste as well, and the way he tangled their tongues together was so very hot and erotic to her. Illicit. Temptingly forbidden.

As she absorbed all this, she went completely boneless against him. The softening of her body only heightened her awareness of the hardness of his. He stood strong and dominant, feet braced apart, and his mouth devoured her in demanding sweeps of his tongue.

"There's a sweet girl," he breathed against her lips. "Ah, you have a fine flavor and I can feel the heat buried inside you." He drew back and looked down into her eyes. "Yes, you'll do very nicely," he assured her. "And then some."

think it, but she was a natural.

CURSED
by
FIRE

Books published by Random House are available at quantity discounts on bulk purchases for premium, educational, fund-raising, and special sales use. For details, please call 1-800-733-3000.

CURSED
by
FIRE

The
IMMORTAL
BROTHERS

JACQUELYN FRANK

BALLANTINE BOOKS • NEW YORK

A Ballantine Books Mass Market Original

Copyright © 2015 by Jacquelyn Frank

Excerpt from *Cursed by Ice* by Jacquelyn Frank copyright © 2015 by Jacquelyn Frank

Published in the United States by Ballantine Books, an imprint of Random House, a division of Random House LLC, a Penguin Random House Company, New York.

BALLANTINE and the HOUSE colophon are registered trademarks of Random House LLC.

This book contains an excerpt from the forthcoming book *Cursed by Ice* by Jacquelyn Frank. This excerpt has been set for this edition only and may not reflect the final content of the forthcoming edition.

ISBN 978-0-345-53493-4
eBook ISBN 978-0-345-54990-7

Cover photograph: Claudio Marinesco

Printed in the United States of America

www.ballantinebooks.com

9 8 7 6 5 4 3 2 1

Ballantine Books mass market edition: March 2015

For all my kids.
Furry though you may be,
you still mean the world to me.

CURSED
by
FIRE

CHAPTER
ONE

The heat was unbearable, searing and constant, burning his skin until it crisped. He could smell the aroma of cooking flesh and knew it was himself that he smelled. It was all too familiar, singeing and sinking into his nostrils, a vile stench he would never forget. Would never be allowed to forget. As usual, the metal around his wrists burned first, glowing a hot red . . . as though it could melt away or be smelted along with his flesh. But it never melted away; it held true time and time again. He had torn at his manacles, strained against them. Every time the fire came, he prayed it would melt his hands away first, allowing him to slip free.

But that was not how things worked here. There was never going to be freedom for him. His was an eternal damnation. He had sinned against all the gods and they, who usually warred amongst themselves, had come together to see him punished. That was how deeply he had sinned.

Dethan and his brothers had been chained, entombed in these forsaken caverns, and their immortal lives, the ones they had dared to wrest from the secrets of the gods, were now their curse as they died again and again. Death by fire. Or rather, as near to death as was possible for an immortal. Dethan suffered and singed and crackled to a crisp until his lungs could no longer breathe in the flames, until his marrow boiled within his bones and until his chains held only a desiccated corpse turned mostly to ash.

And then the flames would subside, and slowly, ever so excruciatingly slowly, his body would heal. Flesh would rebuild itself along the lines of his bones, cell by cell, one healing piece of sinew after another. Immortality repairing itself, birthing him new again, making his skin supple and whole, and preparing him to be fresh and healthy, and ready to be burned all over again.

The chains he wore went around his forearms in gauntlets from wrist to elbow, and for good measure a bolt had been shot through them, spearing through the flesh and bone of each forearm from one side to the next, making certain there was no way he could slide free. Not that it was necessary. These were chains forged by gods. If you were dressed in the chains of the gods, there would be no freedom from them until the gods decided to set you free.

He laughed, the sound hollow in the echo of the abated flames. But the flames were growing again; he could hear them with his newly healed eardrums. He had long ago ceased begging the gods for mercy. They had not heard him, although he had screamed it for hours. For days. For turnings. For ages. He no longer knew how much time had passed, and it had ceased being important to him. Nothing was important to him. His lot in this existence was merely to burn and to suffer. Again and again, over and over.

You thought you deserved eternal life. Now see what your ambition has won you. See it. Feel it. Deserve it.

No. No one deserved this. True, his crimes had been brash and arrogant, but they had been crimes of hubris, not unabashed wickedness. He had never been evil incarnate.

But he dared not think that he was blameless for his lot. No. Nor did he dare blame the gods. Oh, he had cursed them. Screamed their names and damned them. Renouncing them one moment and yet pleading to them with utter devotion mere hours later. Such was the nature of torment like this.

But he had not tried to bargain for his release or promised to be the most devout of men should they set him free. No. He knew that freedom would now be wasted on him. His mind was so scorched, so torn, it was nothing but a wasteland.

No. He would simply sit here and burn. He did not even think of his brothers any longer. How often he had wished he could turn back time, wished that he had heeded Garreth, who had tried one last time to recall them from the task they had set for themselves. But by then they had almost reached the mountain's pinnacle. By then they had already fought and killed two manticores, vile powerful creatures with the head of a Sholet lion, the torso of a man, and a powerful cat below the waist. Its tail was that of a Bytwyte scorpion. Its massive arms were capable of great strength, and each of its wings was tipped with savage talons meant to rip the flesh from a man.

But more alarming than the frightful creatures Dethan and his brothers had faced was that they had almost frozen to death, exposed on the face of Mount Airidare. Garreth had been dying at their feet from the crippling cold, and the only way to save him had been to continue onward in hopes of finding their prize.

At the heart of it all had been nothing but selfish desire for the power of immortality. As warriors, they had faced death every day and without fear, but what they had wanted was the glory of being invincible. Like the demigods, the gods' own children, or the special heroes that had been awarded immortality as a prized gift for their service to the gods.

They had first tried to obtain the gift through their deeds—winning battles and waging war, overtaking heathen lands and building monuments to the gods, teaching their ways to the untaught. They had converted land after land into the lands of the shield goddess or the god of peace and tranquillity. But the gods had been unimpressed and had offered no reward for their service.

And now he knew why. He knew it was because they had never really done any of it in the name of the gods. They had done it for their own ends and no other reason, and the gods had seen through them.

The four brothers had grown tired of waiting for the gods to get around to rewarding their so-called faithful servants and instead had researched a tale, told to them all through their lives growing up, about the hero Gynnis, who had climbed a great mountain and had found atop it a fountain of gold and gems, and within that fountain had been the waters of immortality. One sip of these waters and they would be gifted with youth, health, and life everlasting. The waters would heal all wounds, new and old, they would erase the hardest years from face and form, and again . . . bestow life everlasting.

And through much work, much research, much capturing of holy scrolls from holy cities, Jaykun had finally concluded that the fountain was on Mount Airidare. It could not be anywhere else, for all other mountains had reportedly been conquered by other men and there had never been tales of success of finding the fountain. No mortal other than Gynnis had ever gained immortality by drinking its waters. So by process of elimination and by the use of many signs and landmarks in those holy scrolls, they had known it would be there.

After days of deadly progress, days when they could have and should have failed dozens of times, they had seen the pinnacle and there, running free and gleaming of gold and gemstones, had sat a fountain where water should've been frozen solid, but was not. They had been in the thinnest air the world had to offer—that was how far up near the field of heaven they had climbed. They could barely breathe, it was so thin.

But laying eyes on that fountain had been like a bolt of pure oxygen and exhilarating, revitalizing energy. Just from the sight of it.

And still Garreth had tried to stay them. Upon seeing it, he had hesitated and asked them to rethink this, had claimed a sense of foreboding. But they had ignored him and had pressed on, and in the end all four of them, even Garreth, had drunk deeply of the fountain's waters.

It had truly been the most miraculous thing Dethan had ever known. His battle-scarred and weather-frozen body had healed before his very eyes. Frostbite that had claimed at least three of his fingers had reversed itself, revealing warm, pink flesh once more. Old battle wounds, like the one that had nearly dismembered his left leg from the rest of his body, had healed, the tightness and pain he had dealt with every day since evaporating with alacrity. The scar had disappeared from beneath his many layers of clothing. He had not needed to see it because he had felt it. And in the reflective surface of the fountain's waters he had seen the years melt away from his face, until he looked as he had looked fifteen summers past, a younger man in the prime of his life, no more than thirty, no less than twenty-five, from what he could see. Garreth, previously near death, had sprung to his feet, laughing and full of life once more.

And then . . . then the gods had come. With a mighty storm of fury, clouds full of lightning and thunder, snow driving them down to the ground, the ground itself hauling and shuddering with rage. Oh yes, they had come.

You dare steal this reward when you have not deserved it in our eyes? You dare to do so without permission, without honor? You will pay for your folly, foolish, arrogant worms. You will pay for your immortality with blood and bone and flesh. We cannot take this gift back, but we can see to it you wish you had never dared to think you could push the hands of the gods to your will and your liking.

Then Dethan had been thrown down from that mountain and into the deepest chamber in the eight hells and had been left there to burn. He did not know what had become of his brothers, Garreth, Jaykun, and Maxum. He could only assume they had been thrown into similar caverns and were suffering similar fates. He had been alone ever since, day after day, with nothing to keep his interest and nothing but the fire for company.

So Dethan was not prepared when, just as the fires were about to roar to life once more, the softest waterfall of sparkling light appeared before his eyes. It started small, with just a falling dot of light, then two, then twenty, then hundreds. The sparkling bits of light began to form into the shape of a woman. Then, in a flash, a woman of dark hair and blinding beauty was standing before him.

He blinked hard several times, trying to rid himself of the vision. It would not be the first time he had hallucinated under the stress of his torment. But there she stayed and there she stood, wearing a dress so glittering and beautiful it refracted the firelight like diamonds might do. Or perhaps kitomite, which was harder and more brilliant than diamonds. Yes, that was it. The dress, he realized, was a suit of chain-mail armor, fitting her form with perfection and looking as stunning and impervious as it must be if made from kitomite.

That was when he knew it was Weysa, the goddess of conflict. The shield goddess. He had erected statues of her above her altars, where spoils of war were frequently laid in homage to her when an army or fighter was victorious. He had prayed to her before every battle and he had seen her fury when he had drunk from the forbidden waters and subsequently banished him to this place in the eight hells, so it was no wonder that he recognized her once he had seen past the blinding brilliance of that armor. He shuffled about on his hands and knees, rolling himself into obeisance, his forehead touching the scalding hot rock, his palms doing the same, his flesh searing against the stone like a cut of fresh junjun beast being seared in a pan.

She regarded him in silence, and as she did so, the fires remained completely abated for the first time since he had come there. He was grateful for the reprieve, no matter what the reason, no matter what further curses she might rain down upon his head.

"Low beast," she said after long moments.

"The lowest," he agreed with her, fearful that she might grow angry with him for speaking aloud to her.

"What have you learned here, in your time spent?"

He did not know how to answer her. He did not know what she wanted to hear. So he fumbled for the most honest of answers he could come to. "Never to cross the mighty gods, for their will is the only will."

"Do you beg for mercy?"

"No, mistress," he said, "For your will shall be done, and there is nothing I can do to change it."

"Good, because we have been merciful thus far. Your fate could have been much worse, but we took into account all that you have done in our name."

Merciful? This torment had been the gods' idea of mercy? Dethan felt a wash of rage overcoming him, and he struggled to fight it back. What if she could divine his thoughts? He would anger her and then she would show him what it meant for a god to be unmerciful.

"So," Weysa said, "your time here has not cowed you completely."

Dread filled him. Surely she would become angry with him now. What would she do with him?

"Good," she said then, surprising him. "I need a true warrior. A man loyal to me who will fight in my name."

She wanted him to fight for her? Yes. He would fight for her. Anything. Anything to be free of this hell.

"Fortune has told me that you are my one true hope in this matter. And so you will be. Rise."

He did so, leaving strips of his flesh behind, burned to the floor, all the while keeping his eyes cast downward. Partly to honor her, partly because her armor was too brilliant for his eyes to bear.

"I have grown weak," she said, again surprising him. "Things have changed greatly since the times when you fought for me. My strength lies in those who worship me, and so many have fallen by the wayside, worshipping false gods instead or . . . following my enemies and giving them the strength I need. You see, the gods have split into two factions, low beast. We war. We war violently. But we cannot win or find advantage unless we have devotion to us. I need you to find me that devotion, to win over those who do not believe and those who would choose my enemies over me."

Dethan remained silent as she relayed this, but all the while his mind was racing. A war between the gods? This did not surprise him. They had always been a contentious lot. But things must have grown desperate if she was coming to him for help.

"I will give you these gifts and you will not squander

them or you will pay dearly for it," she said. And suddenly a suit of plated armor appeared at his feet. It seemed to be made of hedonite, a black, shining stone known for its lightness of weight. It was far too fragile to be of use in armor.

"Do not let the look of it deceive you, for this is godmade armor, forged by my own hands and imbued with my strength. It will protect you against any weapon. It will make you invulnerable. Invulnerability coupled with immortality will make you nigh invincible. But be warned: You can die if your head leaves your shoulders by way of a god-made weapon, and my enemies will make gifts of such weapons to stop your progress. Do you understand?"

"Yes, mistress," he said.

"Good. Then there is this." A sword also appeared at his feet. It too seemed to be made of the black hedonite. "This is a mighty weapon. In your hands, be your intentions true and just, it will cut down your foes, of which there will be many. It can pierce god-made armor, no matter how strongly imbued. This was forged with the strength of six gods. All of our faction together."

"Mistress, may I ask which six gods?" he asked, knowing there were twelve gods in all and this meant they were split exactly down the middle.

"Our faction consists of Hella, the goddess of fate and fortune; Meru, the goddess of hearth, home, and harvest; her brother Mordu, the god of hope, love, and dreams; Lothas, the god of day and night; and last is Framun, the god of peace and tranquillity."

"So you war with Xaxis, the god of the eight hells; Grimu, the god of the eight heavens; Diathus, the goddess of the lands and oceans; Kitari, the goddess of life and death; Jikaro, the god of anger, deception, and storms; and Sabo, the god of pain and suffering." He swallowed. That Kitari had sided with five of the darkest gods did not ring true to him; she was the queen of all the gods and demanded much respect.

"Your thoughts do you justice, low beast. Kitari has been swayed by these other gods. I believe she is held hostage more than she has sided with them. They together have the power to subdue her in spite of her great powers. And that is part of your goal. You will be gaining worshippers for me and the other gods who side with me. By doing this I believe I will be able to rescue Kitari from their influence. Such a coup would no doubt turn the tide of this war. And there is something else . . ."

"Yes, my mistress," he encouraged her. His mind was racing. If she was rescuing him from this fate worse than death, then things were as dire as they appeared. He would fight for her, as he had done in the past. This in spite of the rage he felt toward all the gods for the suffering they had subjected him to. Especially if it meant freedom from this torment. It was the only choice, really, because there was nothing he could do in the face of their power. But perhaps . . . perhaps he could convince her . . .

No. He would not try to manipulate his goddess. That was a slippery slope and he would not risk angering her. But he would ask . . . he would beg . . .

"There is a great weapon that can be used against Xaxis's faction."

So it was Xaxis leading the faction, Dethan thought. That figured. Xaxis had been trying to wrest power from the other gods for time immemorial.

"This weapon is surrounded by a great city, a city that guards the mouth of the eight hells."

"Olan?" he asked.

"Olan," she agreed. "I need you to conquer this city and to wrest control of this weapon."

Suddenly she looked over her shoulder, as if she heard someone coming. She turned to him quickly. "This is

Xaxis's territory and he is beginning to sense that I am here. I must leave before I am captured by him. But you are freed. I will take you above the hells and you must begin your work. But be warned: You do not go freely. You are cursed ever after, to make you remember where you have come from and where you will return should you fail me. Every night, at dusk, you will conflagrate and burn until the juquil's hour. If you perform well for me, I will consider lifting the curse. Do you understand?"

Dethan's fists clenched in anger, but he controlled the emotion with an iron will. So he would be made to suffer this same hell again and again, even while he worked for her honor and ends. But the rest of the time . . . the rest of the time he would live in reprieve, and that was far better than what he suffered now.

"Yes, mistress, I understand. But . . . if your humble servant might ask . . . my brothers are great warriors. If you were to rescue them from this torment as well, they too could fight for your faction."

"Your brothers, unlike you, are not here in the hells. However, like you, they are made to suffer in the territories ruled by the other faction. I have risked all coming here and cannot do so again. The only reason I was able to come at all is because the others have distracted Xaxis in order to free me to do this. Your brother Garreth is chained to the very mountain where you found the fountain, freezing solid again and again. The territory is controlled by Diathus. Jaykun is chained to a star and, like you, burns again and again. This is Grimu's territory and I have no access to the heavens. Maxum . . . I do not know where Maxum is. He was given to Sabo to be dealt with and Sabo never shared with us the punishment he meted out." She looked over her shoulder again and this time Dethan saw true anxiety on her features. "I must go now. Fight, warrior, as you have never fought before. Find an army. Fight to take my name to the people. Fight until the day I deem your worth restored. And never forget who has set you free and who can set you down again."

"No, mistress. Never."

"The fires will see to that. Remember, dusk every day. It will do you well to make sure no others are nearby when this happens or they will be consumed by the flames as well. Now, we are off."

CHAPTER
TWO

In a flash of speed and burning light that sickened him, Dethan found himself standing at the mouth of one of the four entrances to the eight hells, easily recognizable by the dragon's head carved into the massive stones surrounding it, the mouth of the creature leading downward to the fiery pit. He could assume this was not the entrance in Olan. Weysa would not put him in the heart of the very city she wished him to conquer. So it was one of the others placed upon the face of Ethos. One he knew was underwater. One, like the fountain, was set high on a mountain. And since it was not cold but more summery climes around him, that left the largest opening, the one in Hexis. His armor rested at his feet and he hastened to pick it up. He was still seared and wounded, and he had no clothing, so he stood naked, knowing nothing of the world around him.

He could have hidden back within the cave, but he could not bring himself to step toward it, his muscle and sinew screaming in fear of moving toward the fires below in even the smallest of increments.

Luckily the closest thing to the mouth of the cave was an altar upon which sacrifices to Xaxis were made. He hurried over to it, hiding and skulking behind it as he looked around with wide, wild eyes. The altar was laden with all manner of things, from fruits to dead beasts. Things going to rot and waste. And thanks to that, the first thing he realized was that he was starving—famished from who knew how long without food. But to steal from the altar might mean an insult to the god it was meant for, so he touched nothing there, not wishing to incite any further wrath from the gods. Especially not Xaxis. He was to be working covertly for his goddess's interests. He could not draw attention to himself until it was time to begin to war in her name.

But she had given him no army. She expected him to find one on his own. It had taken ages for him to build the forces he had once used to march across the world. But what of those lands he had once defeated? Would they still be his to command? How long had it been since he had been locked away?

No. He could not hope that any of the people of those lands would know who he was. None but perhaps . . . home. Perhaps where he had once sat as warlord and master they would know who he was. But it did not follow that they would accept him. And he was a very long way from the massive walls of Toren, his home. It would take travel across a desert, a lush living valley, and an ocean before he could get there.

It felt strange to use the term "home." His home for so long had been that fiery cavern. His home had been a pair of chains.

That was when he looked down at his arms.

Free. *Free.* His skin—raw and ragged as it was; pale, damp, and weak it might be—was in the open air for the first time since . . . well . . . since. Naked in the cooler air after being in the scalding heat, he was shivering so hard his teeth clacked like heavy sticks knocking together.

There was no one nearby. That did not surprise him.

The cavern was located well above the sprawl of the city. Xaxis was not the sort of god one wanted to spend too much time on or get too close to. He was worshipped out of fear. He was worshipped whenever someone died, the idea being that he could be convinced to turn a blind eye to the departed, allowing them to bypass the eight hells and be lifted up to the eight heavens, where they would reside in brightness and glory. Kitari, goddess of life and death, worked hand in hand with the goddess of fate, Hella, to decide the moment and manner of death one might face, but if one led an impure life, that person would be brought to the attention of Xaxis, and then he would decide whether the person deserved the chains of the hells. It was key that one did nothing to attract such attention. But often Xaxis was worshipped by those who dealt in death, who thrived in the causing of it—warriors looking to send their enemies to the hells. Dethan had been mistaken to be a worshipper of death because he had dealt in war. In war there was always death. But in truth it had been Weysa, the goddess of conflict, who had earned his devotion, and that was probably why she had come to him and none of his other brothers.

They were all warriors, but each in his own way. Garreth had not even been a part of his forces, preferring to take on quests of honor. Maxum was a gold-sword, selling his sword for gold and going wherever the money was best, whether the cause was good or bad. And yet Maxum had his own set of morals, his own limitations, his own rules. That left Jaykun. Jaykun had been Dethan's right arm, his first lieutenant. His successor, had it come to that. But it never had. They had taken on the folly of finding immortality, in spite of all the riches and glories they already had in the world.

Riches. *Yes,* he thought with sudden elation. He had hidden caches of wealth all over the Red Continent. All he needed to do was get to one of them, hoping above all that they had not been discovered. He could buy an army if he had those monies. Or at least he could start to buy one. The one thing he had learned in his days as a warlord was that war was an expensive undertaking. Tactics and planning were all well and good, but without the funds to support one's troops, the effort would come to a standstill.

But one step at a time. He needed clothes. And then a horse. With a horse and some proper provisioning, he could cross the Syken Desert and see if one of his largest caches was still intact.

He looked around and found some thick shrubbery to the side of the opening to the eight hells. He grabbed his sword and the armor and dragged it all behind a bush, hiding it well. The weight of it was light, but it was still cumbersome. He hid it as best he could, looking around furtively to make certain no one was watching. But set so far from the town, he was alone.

Once he was free of encumbrance, he crept toward the city. A piece of fruit had rolled down the hill, presumably from the offerings above, and he snatched it up greedily. He ripped through the thick skin, shoving his entire face into the sweet, pulpy heart of it. He devoured it as he moved, but it was gone all too quickly. He threw the skins aside and wiped his face.

It was daytime—late afternoon, by the position of the blue sun. It was told that the sun burned blue because that was the hottest part of the flame . . . although the songs of the gods said that the sun was the blue of the eyes of Atemna, the mortal woman who captured Lothas's heart, the heart of the god of day and night. The moon and sun were his to command, and he had the power to change the color of the sun in remembrance of his love.

Of course Atemna had met a tragic end when Diathus, Lothas's wife and the goddess of land and oceans, drowned the girl in a fit of jealousy.

It wasn't the first story of mortals suffering because of the tumultuous whims of the gods. But Dethan knew that better than anyone. He wondered if he and his brothers were now one of the songs of the gods. A cautionary tale for those who reached too high.

The worst part of Hexis was closest to the entrance to the hells. After all, who wanted to live nearest to the hells? The children who ran in the muddied streets wore tatters and rags, the stench of poor sewage reeked heavy on the air, and the noise was more overwhelming the closer he got to it. The stench was harsh in his singed nostrils, but welcome after ages of smelling nothing but soot and crisping flesh. He had crept well into the edge of the mess of it without anyone taking notice of his lack of clothing. They had stronger worries, these impoverished people, and no doubt he wasn't the first naked beggar they had ever seen.

But he would not beg. No. Not that he was above it. He was not above anything anymore. But beggars would be cast down on, would earn nothing but negative attention. Especially one like him, who looked so vulnerable on sight. Begging would not get him what he needed.

Thievery would.

The first order was some kind of clothing. He snuck down a back alley, and immediately he could see clothing lines had been drawn up high between the buildings. But they were a good two stories up.

This did not sway him from his course. He found a strange metal pipe that ran from ground to roof, water running out of the opening in the bottom. He wrapped a hand around it and pulled, studying the fastenings that held it to the stone. With a shrug, he began to climb it. After all, if he fell, he would not die. Oh, it would hurt . . . it might slow him down, but he would heal, and then he would walk away from it.

Because he could walk. Because he was free.

Only . . . the sun was lowering. If the fires were going to return . . .

The thought lent him speed. Because his muscles were still burnt and shriveled, it took all his strength to climb the pipe up to the nearest line and the clothing he found upon it. There was a pair of pants, worn and barely patched in places, but clean and ten times better than nothing. A hundred times better. He snatched them from the line, and like a rat that steals a sliver of cheese, he scurried back down the pipe and slipped into the late-day shadows of the alley. Scrambling, he shoved first one leg and then the other into the pants and then held them clutched to his body, for he had no belt and they were meant for a much stockier man. But now he was clothed and could walk around freely. What he needed now was to find a horse. He would observe barns or smithies, places where horses could be found, and when night fell, he would come back . . .

After the juquil's hour, he reminded himself. Because from sunset to the juquil's hour he would burn. And he had to find a place where he could do so and not bring danger to others . . . or notice to himself. And the only place he could think of that would fit that need was . . .

Just thinking about the entrance to the hells made him break out in a cold sweat. The idea of voluntarily stepping into the mouth of the hells all but paralyzed him with fear. He had not been well acquainted with fear during his life as a warlord. He had even been called fearless in bard song. But he was well acquainted with it now. And he didn't dare step back near the hells and Xaxis's territory. What if Xaxis could sense him then? What if Xaxis came for him and dragged him back down and chained him once more?

The thought of it made him shake with terror. Bone-chilled, flesh-scorched terror. He had to stop, sinking down onto his haunches in the shadows of the wet, smelly alleyway, huddling into himself and trying for all he was worth to remind himself of who he had once been. A man of courage. A warrior. A warlord who had ruled with an iron fist.

But he was not that man any longer.

After a minute he rose up again and then made his way out into the open streets. The deeper he went into the city, the thicker the traffic. Pedestrians and horses, carts and coaches, lined the roads, kicking up mud and grinding it down again until Dethan found himself sticking in the sludge as it sucked at his feet and ankles. It was a wonder anyone managed to get anywhere at all. The wheels of one of the heavier coaches must have sunk a good four inches or better into the muck. It was only the team of stout ginger merries that kept it from slogging down. And beautiful horses they were. A perfectly matched set of four ginger-colored steeds with white manes and tails. They were called ginger merries because of their sweet, playful dispositions. They were usually women's horses, and indeed the coach was full of highborn women.

At least that much was the same. The rich still lived better than the poor. Ginger merries still existed. But already he was seeing things he'd never seen before. Like the metal pipe he had climbed. It was a clever thing, he realized. It kept water from accumulating on the roof of the building.

The buildings were another thing. They were well made, not just of stone but of wood and some kind of plaster. Some of the buildings he was now passing were whitish in color, while those he'd just come from had been brown. Still others were made even better with wood planks nailed to the sides. He couldn't help himself. He stopped and pulled at one. The wood shingle held fast. He could not comprehend its purpose, so he simply let it be and left. He had many other things to accomplish. Although he understood that he could not hope to conquer a world he did not understand. So he would pay attention as he went.

Dethan found a stable after a short while and within it a horse of fine flesh. If his fortune ran well, the horse would still be there come the juquil's hour.

"Beauteous Hella, look upon me this night, so I may aid your cause," he prayed with fervor to the goddess of fate and fortune.

He turned away and heard a loud shout. Fearing someone had noticed him, he cringed. He turned just as the sound of a cracking whip cut through the air. There, not too far down the partly cobbled road, was one of the fine coaches . . . this one led by dark stallions with shining coats that showed the musculature and fine breeding of the foursome. Now, there, he thought, was a horse worth stealing.

The whip cracked again and a man cried out. Dethan moved a little closer so he could see better because it was very clear the whip was not being used on the team of horses. The coachman raised his arm again and Dethan could see a man, wearing little better clothing than he wore, cowering away from the coming blow, two stripes of red showing through the mud on his skin where the whip had struck before.

"Dog! Foul thing, you dare interfere with his lordship's horses?" the coachman yelled.

And then, when Dethan looked into the open coach windows at who was within, he could see a pair of dark eyes watching the exchange rapaciously. The man within did not intervene, did not stop the abuse. It was more like . . . he hungered for it. Was eager to see it. The smile that touched his cruel lips only solidified the impression. Dethan had known men like this before. Wicked men. Cruel men. He had fought both with and against them in the wars he had engaged in. Though he had had no tolerance for it in his own camps, there were those who had a thirst for such cruelties.

Dethan did not know why he stepped forward, did not know why he thrust his hand out, blocking the next strike of the whip's tail from hitting the man, letting it wrap around his wrist instead. He yanked as hard as he could, testing the strength of his healing muscles to the maximum. The coachman had such a grip on the whip that Dethan ended up yanking the lot of them, man and whip, from high above down into the wet of the mud. The coachman spluttered and spat, getting to his feet in a state, his face mottled red with fury.

"How dare you! Do you not see the sigil on this coach? It is the lord high jenden's vehicle! You will be whipped for your insolence!"

"Would that be with this whip?" Dethan asked, rolling the whip up slowly in his hands. His manner might appear mild on first glance, but anyone who looked a bit harder would realize what the coachman realized: that Dethan, for all he wore baggy rags and a thick layer of mud, was the one fully in charge of the altercation.

"You there! You let my man go or you will find yourself without a head!" barked a man leaning out the window of the conveyance.

"Oh, I'll let him go," Dethan said. "Only not with his whip. The whip is mine now."

"How dare you commandeer anything of mine! How dare you interfere with—!"

He broke off suddenly when a delicate, gloved hand appeared from the darkness of the coach and rested on the hand of the man within. The glove was white with a sprig of flowers ringed around the wrist.

She, for it was obviously a woman, must have said something—Dethan could not hear what—because the angry man subsided somewhat, though it was very clear he was not happy about it. He looked to the left and right, seeing the crowd they were beginning to draw.

"But . . . my dear . . . he is an upstart of a peasant and we cannot abide—"

"Is this truly worthy of your time?" she asked, this time loud enough for Dethan to hear, though in no way with strong emotion. More like she might scold a puppy. Then she finally appeared in the window, and Dethan felt his breath lock up in cold shock in his chest.

She was the most beautiful woman he had ever seen . . . save the goddesses themselves. Her only flaw, immediately noticeable, was the burn scar along her lower cheek and jaw on the left side of her face. But he hardly saw it because the rest of her face was stunning, her eyes dark and bottomless, her nose small and delicate, and her lips lush and smiling over perfectly white teeth. It was a shock to him that she had all her teeth. Women of his time hardly made it to her age with all intact.

Her hair was dark and curly, piled high on her head with a jaunty little cap set amid it. The teal cap had a stiff veil, which dropped down over the left side of her face, presumably to hide the scar, only it had been pushed back, either by accident or design, and she could be seen quite clearly. She had the longest of necks, the whitest of skin. Her gloved hand was graceful on the man's.

"Can you not see how out of line your carriage driver was, Lord Grannish?" she asked him gently. "This man was only doing what was right. Those with power should not use it to press down those without," she said, almost pointedly. No. It *was* with a point. Something Dethan did not fully understand was being passed between them.

"Very well," Grannish groused, his narrow face with its curling moustache looking a cross between angry and deferential. Whatever it was, he was not happy about the situation. "Driver!"

"Sor." The lady addressed Dethan. "The driver cannot drive without the whip."

The implication was clear. She was trying to manipulate him the way she had just managed the other man. But he had no intention of being managed.

"A whip should not be applied to such fine horseflesh, woman. If he cannot control them with reins alone, then you are in need of a better driver. And I am in need of a belt." With a sharp movement he whipped the whip around his waist, effectively belting up his pants, and tied the end tightly to his body, the long, hard handle dangling down against his upper thigh.

"This is a woman of the highest born blood," the man Grannish hissed. "You will refer to her by her title—!"

She cut him off. " 'My lady' will suffice."

"Your pardon, *my lady*. I am a foreigner to these lands and things are different here than where I come from."

"Then it is understood. Truly, you are forgiven. Driver, ride on!" she said in loud command.

The driver had since climbed out of the mud and back up into his seat, Dethan having kept a sharp eye on him the entire time. He made a sound to the horses and they drove on with a jolting start. Dethan watched them go, his eyes on the woman and hers on him the entire time. It took him a minute to shake himself free of the trance in which he found himself, and then he questioned why he had done what he had just done. He should be worrying about his own skin, his own tasks, and not what happened to a lone man in the filth of the street.

"Thank you!" the man said then, coming up to him and grabbing his hand. He touched the back of his hand to the back of Dethan's, pressing them together. "I owe you much. Come, let me reward you."

"I have no need of reward," Dethan said. He eyed the other man. The man was tall and gangly, full of long, loose limbs and a corded sort of lean strength. It was clear he knew what a hard day's work was. He had a mop of dark curly hair and warm, laughing brown eyes. "And you have little to give, I think."

"Any other day that would be true, but today is the fair and I have been saving my silver to go. I think I might find me a wife today, if I can be so lucky."

"You intend to buy one?" Dethan asked.

"Oh well . . . I suppose I could. From one of the slavers. But my money is so little that I wouldn't be able to buy any woman of passing health. It takes a strong woman to be a mud farmer's wife."

"You might be surprised," Dethan said. "A sickly slave might be made well with good care. I've seen it done."

"It might be cheaper at that!" The man chuckled; it was a low raspy sound. He ran a hand back through his hair, obviously a habit because there were streaks of mud in various stages of wetness from the times before. "By the time the courting is done a man can be begging in the streets. Your idea has merit! To the fair, then? I'll buy you a roasted gossel leg for your trouble, though I wish it was more."

"A gossel leg is more than fair and will be more than welcome."

"Very well, then." The man pressed the backs of their hands together again. "My name's Tonkin. You are new around here."

"Yes. Why does that matter?" Dethan said uneasily.

"Well, no one who knows would step in to interfere with his lordship the high jenden's business. He's a cruel bastard, make no mistake about it. If I hadn't fallen, I would never have come close to that vehicle of his. He rides it round here all fine and fierce-looking, making sure all us drudges know our place."

"Jenden?" Dethan asked cautiously. He didn't want to seem too strange to this individual. But by the look the man sent him, he could tell he was very much so strange.

"Advisor to the grand. You know, advisor to the *king,*" Tonkin stressed when Dethan's expression remained blank. "And anyways, that was the grandina, the grand's daughter, with him. I guarantee you had she not been with him the whole business would have gone much differently. It's rumored that once the jenden killed someone right in the middle of the street. And the grand is so enamored with all the jenden says and does he can do no wrong. I suppose that's why the grand has given his eldest daughter and heir to the jenden to marry. Though some say the jenden's getting the raw deal, what with her being so ugly and all."

"Ugly? That's ugly?" Dethan asked incredulously, cocking a thumb in the direction the coach had disappeared. "She's nearly as beautiful as Kitari. And I do not make that case lightly, for I've seen Kitari with my own eyes!"

He regretted it the minute Tonkin looked at him as though he'd grown boils all over his face. After all, what manner of man claimed to have seen the unattainable queen of the gods? But then Tonkin's face relaxed and he chuckled.

"Oh aye, she is a beauty at that. *I* agree with you. But round here that burn makes her ugly to most. Some say she will be unfit to rule after her father's death . . . no doubt some like the jenden himself. Jenden Grannish wouldn't be marrying her, you could wager, if he could think of any other way of becoming grand himself. As it is, the grand's children have been cast a sad eye by

Hella. Misfortunes have fallen on the royal family in terrible ways. The grand's sons dying like that. And his two youngest daughters taken by the plague just this past summer. That leaves only the grandina Selinda and grandino Drakin. But the boy prince is only two and of poor health." Dethan's companion tsked his tongue and shook his head gravely. As though to say that was the whole of it and there was nothing to be done about it. But surely anyone could see that there was something dark at play in the grand's household.

Of course Hella was as capricious a goddess as any and she had been known to toy with entire families, entire bloodlines, especially if she felt slighted in some way. It was hard to say what moved her and why her whims fluctuated so wildly. There were those who said Hella had gone mad, her mind crazed by the many things she could see and feel unfolding in the world. From all the choices she had to make every day that could save a person or bring about their demise or worse.

But fate could be changed or altered under the right conditions. One just needed to know all the elements at play.

CHAPTER
THREE

None of this was any concern of Dethan's. He had much more important things to tackle and trying to comprehend the whims of fate was a waste of his energies. He had to stay focused on his goal. Get a horse. Get to his cache. Get an army. It was as simple as that, and yet in his present circumstances it was also hard.

He and Tonkin moved into the fair and Dethan found himself feeling on edge. He didn't know why at first, because there was nothing at all threatening about the happy people milling about, enjoying the vendors' wares and eating the large quantities of foods available. Everyone was relaxed and having a good time.

After a while he realized it was the crowd itself that was the problem. He had spent an untold amount of time chained up alone in the hells, with no one but himself for company. Here he was thrust into the mix of hundreds of people, packed end to end in some places where the crowd bottlenecked between two vendors or where there was an attraction, such as the dancing gossels presently taking place. The six-legged beastie was better served up broiled and salted, in his opinion, but to each his own.

Dethan's best bet was to get out of there as soon as

possible. But there was one other thing he needed before he could go, and this crowd might help him to get it. There were clothing vendors all about and possibly he could nick a shirt to go with his pants. Once he did that he would be able to wear his armor. Without underpadding it could be painful . . . but he would suffer the pain and chafing if it meant getting on with his journey.

He was keeping his eyes open when he saw an opportunity. But before he could move toward taking advantage of it, his companion grabbed him around one of his arms and dragged him toward a raucous uproar of shouting.

"Shivov fights!" his companion said with no little amount of glee.

The more things changed, the more they didn't. How many centuries had it been since he had been dragged into the hells? And yet shivov fighting still existed. He had won four shivov matches in his time. He could not have afforded to lose. No one could, for it was a death match. There were winners and then there were corpses. There was no ground given, only ground that was taken.

Unable to help himself, he was drawn toward the arena. The crowd was even thicker here and his apprehension ratcheted up to a new level. He struggled with himself. Forced himself to shove down all the anxiety clawing through him. He tried to remind himself that he had once been one of the most renowned and most feared warlords of his time. But with a body still burned and barely healed, he was hardly more than a shadow of who he had once been.

Tonkin, for all his slight build and undernourished state, had surprising strength in him as he dragged Dethan to a place right at ringside, shoving into the space for all he was worth and receiving some angry epithets in the process. Right away Dethan could see the two fighters, seeming at first glance unevenly matched. One was burly, no more than three straps tall, by the look of him, but carrying a good two hundred rocks if he carried one. His opponent was closer to four straps tall, the same as Dethan, and also like Dethan—when healthy—was about a hundred and seventy-five rocks, give or take. It would be a fairer match if Dethan were in the ring rather than the stockier man. But it was obvious right away that each had their strengths.

And as soon as the first blow connected, something else was very obvious as well.

The weapons were blunted.

"How do they expect them to fight to the death with blunted weapons?" Dethan asked his new friend. "Are they forcing them to do this more brutally? Forcing them to kill each other with their bare hands?"

Tonkin gave him another one of those looks.

"They aren't trying to kill each other! They haven't done that since my father's father was a boy! No, here it's to the edge of the ring. Whichever fighter can toss the other out of the ring is the winner."

"You must be joking," Dethan said with a scoffing laugh. It had to be a jest. Shivov was the most glorious test there was of manhood and of a warrior's skills. "What do your youngbloods do to prove themselves men?"

"A shivov test. This same here," Tonkin said, indicating the fight. "That's right, Willem. Give 'em what for!" he yelled at the top of a pair of mighty lungs. "Keeps us from losing some fine young men," he said to Dethan.

"How fine can they be if they lose their fight?" Dethan muttered. Training for one's shivov fight took every moment of every day; it forced a man to make a weapon of himself. Learn or die. Improve or die. Without that goal, what force drove men these days to better themselves? To make them reach the pinnacle of performance?

The fight was over a moment later when the shorter man used his low center of gravity and exploited his opponent's overreaching swings, catching him under his ribs and sending him flying backward over the barrier of the ring. With a roar, the barbarian claimed his victory, showing off to the adulating crowd. Then he moved forward and made a kneeling bow to someone in the stands on the far side of the ring. The minute Dethan saw the teal coloring of her cap and the darkness of her veil, pulled down over her face, he knew it was the grandina. Seated beside her in the position of overseer was the jenden she was engaged to.

"I, Jjanjiu, am your champion, woman!" the warrior called out rudely to her. "Give me my reward. Give me my gold and give me my kiss!"

A kiss? That was what the victor got for winning? And now she had to give it to this overbearing and obviously unclean oaf? He wasn't even that worthy an opponent, all bluster and strength and no finesse. Even across the way from her, even with the veil, Dethan could see the discomfort on her features.

"That's the jenden's doing," Tonkin confided. "Offering her up to a commoner like a prize. She's too good for us lot, and so she should be. But he does it to embarrass her. He does a lot of things to her to get back at her for being in a more exalted position than him, if you ask me."

"Are there no other challengers?" the grandina asked in a loud, clear voice, but Dethan could hear the quaver of discomfiture in her tone.

"Give me a weapon and I will challenge him, Grandina."

Had those words just come out of his mouth? It must

be the press of the crowd. It must be the heat of the day. No, it had to be for the gold, he told himself, satisfied at last with that reasoning. That and the offensive idea that this piece of ill-skilled trash could ever consider calling himself a champion. It was probably better the battle wasn't to the death because it would be unfair, since he was now immortal. Not that his opponent would know that.

He stepped into the ring, making certain the grandina could see him clearly, and he could tell immediately that she recognized him, and that she was relieved beyond words that he had stepped forward. Why she thought he, with his burn-scarred body, was anything better than the other oaf was beyond him. But he would not be burn-scarred forever. His body would eventually heal . . . although not for a while, because by the time he healed enough for it to show, the curse would be upon him again at dusk and he wouldn't be any more healed then than he was now. But he had to realize that anything would appear better to her than a lumbering man with rotten stumps for teeth in his mouth. Gods only knew the type of kiss the lecherous hecka was seeking to have. The very idea disgusted him, just as much as it must disgust her.

He would not be asking for a kiss, he thought. Gold was enough at this juncture.

When he reached the center of the ring, he bent to pick up the blunt wooden practice sword that the previous contestant had been divested of.

His opponent turned and, upon seeing him, let out a raucous barroom laugh. "This is the best the stinking city has to offer me? A gnarled, scarred stump of a man?"

Dethan looked down at his hands, thinking he wasn't all that gnarled and his burns were nowhere near as bad as they had been an hour before. In fact, it was the best he had looked or felt in eons. The truth was he had been immortalized at the peak of his physical prowess, and so he would always be, once he had the time to heal. But even as injured as he presently was, he was more than a match for this man. The shape of his body was one thing; the cunning and skill earned on the battlefield was something that could never be removed.

Dethan stood still, watching the other man carefully as he hefted the weight of his wooden battle-axe in his hands, swinging it threateningly every so often. The man growled and made a violent lunge for Dethan in a sudden rush, barreling into him, a tactic he had used to haul the previous opponent over the barrier of the ring. Dethan allowed himself to be picked up, and then he rolled over the man's shoulder, down his back, and back onto his feet, leaving Jjanjiu to stumble without resistance, face-first, into the mud of the ring. The crowd erupted into laughter and Dethan supposed it was a hilarious sight. Just as the idea of this low beast besting anyone of any real skill was as big a joke as was ever told. If he was the best this city had to offer, then perhaps Dethan would make this city his first conquest. There were certainly spoils to be had, he noted. And since this city seemed to worship Xaxis, it seemed a good place to start. To take away worshippers from Xaxis while gaining them for Weysa would double the impact in Weysa's favor. Without a doubt it would please her. And there would be a certain amount of irony in the idea that the grand's gold would be funding the city's downfall. But he would not oust the grand entirely . . . if he were worth anything as far as management and political skills were concerned. Dethan needed others to run his cities as he went off and conquered more cities. And since all his former generals were no longer alive . . .

He was missing his brothers even more now. He could have used them by his side. As it was, he was very much a man alone.

His thoughts did him a disservice. They distracted him from the roundhouse blow of his opponent's axe and he caught it in his right ribcage, the blow taking him off his feet and sending him flying aside and into the mud, his sword flinging free of his hand. He pushed to his hands, but a powerful, weighty foot on his spine shoved him back down into the mud. But here the mud worked in his favor. He rolled beneath that foot, the friction completely nil around his thoroughly lubricated body, grabbed the heavier man's foot, and jerked it forward hard. Rolling just far enough to get out of the way as Jjanjiu fell onto his back in the mud.

Once the man was down, Dethan kicked at him, forcing him to roll, making certain he was equally covered in the slick mud. He wouldn't wrestle with the man—mud wrestling was exhausting and pointless—but it would put them on equal footing if they were both covered in the stuff. Holding on to a weapon while muddied up like this was tricky, and he wanted his opponent to struggle with it just as much as he would.

While Jjanjiu was sputtering, spitting out mud and obscenities, Dethan scrambled for his sword. Really, it was useless. What he needed was something with weight and power, something to countermand the weight of his opponent. Something like that battle-axe Jjanjiu was sporting.

Jjanjiu was back on his feet, angry now, letting his emotions take over his fight. It was yet another flaw of many. He so arrogantly thought he was undefeatable. Dethan would prove otherwise and he would do so with a cool head. Emotion had no place in a shivov contest. He had watched many in his day, and it was always the fighter who became frustrated, insulted, or angry who lost the battle. Emotions made you do things wrong. It served you ill no matter how skilled you were. It was why he never let emotion color his battles. Or anything else, for that matter.

By the time Jjanjiu hit the mud again, he had been completely divested of his battle-axe and the weapon was seated firmly in his opponent's hands. Adding to the embarrassment, Dethan threw the sword down in front of the other man, as if to make it very clear that he was simply toying with the brute. Enough to be unconcerned about giving the man a weapon to replace the one he had just lost.

"Would you like to try again?" Dethan asked archly.

The fury in Jjanjiu's face was all too obvious. It was reflected in his roar as he grabbed up the sword and charged Dethan. Dethan sidestepped him and swung the battle-axe down hard on the back of his opponent's neck. Had he been paying attention, he would have heard the crowd audibly wince. But all his focus was on Jjanjiu. The man might be clumsy and enraged, but underestimating him would be foolish. And still, Dethan had to get him closer to the edge of the ring. They had been traveling that way since the beginning of the fight, moving from the center toward the edge closest to the grandina's viewing box. Dethan looked up, easily finding her because of that brightly colored cap, so blue in a sea of muddy browns and blacks. Their eyes locked, and while it didn't distract him from his goal, he felt something, something charged and intense, pass between them. There was something in her eyes . . .

Gratitude. It was gratitude. Because she knew he was going to win and somehow, in her eyes, he was the better choice of the two of them. She would not mind giving him his reward, however muddy and burn-scarred he might be.

Jjanjiu charged a second time, and once again, Dethan sidestepped him, this time grabbing the man by the back of his pants, and with a tremendous hauling movement Dethan used his own momentum to send Jjanjiu over the ring barrier.

The crowd roared in delight, the shouting beating at him from all around. He kicked the wooden sword away and held up the axe, eliciting yet another roar of approval. Then he walked the final steps to the viewing box and said, "You have your true champion now, most beautiful lady." He bowed to her, putting his fist to his heart. But, again, he did not take his eyes away from her. As she moved down the stands, he thought of how brave she must be. Knowing that her immediate fate rested in the hands of a mud-slung vagrant of obviously no breeding and maybe only a little skill to speak for him in her eyes said more about her bravery than Jjanjiu's self-boastings had and with far more honesty.

When she stood before him, he became aware of the dead silence at his back and that hundreds of eyes were straining to see what was about to pass between the mud slug and the grandina. But more than that, he became aware of the softest cloud of scent drifting toward him, something sweet and clean yet lush and rich at the same time.

It was her perfume. And like her, it was beautiful and bold. In her hands she held a velveteen purse, the weight impressive for such a simple contest. It made him realize just how wealthy this city was, that sums like this could be awarded for child's play.

"Your purse, champion," she said, keeping her voice raised, even though he could tell by the trembling in her fine-boned hands that it was taking a great deal of effort for her to keep up her appearance of calm and graciousness. She handed the purse to him and he took it carefully with a single palm. She let go and could have withdrawn, keeping herself free of contact with him, but he felt her fingertips suddenly running along his forearm, through the mud caked and dried there like a damp and crumbling shell.

"You are burned," she said softly, the words meant for their ears alone.

He didn't think before saying, "As are you." He regretted the words almost instantly, but instead of taking offense she simply nodded. Now that he was up close, he found himself realizing that her eyes matched her hat almost perfectly. A brilliant, glorious teal. As if the great dye makers had come up with the color for only two purposes: first, her eyes; then, her hat. And beyond that, there would never be anything to match. Her hair was black, as pure a black as ever there was, the gloss of it shining like well-oiled leather. It was all pulled up away from her face so tightly, leaving her corkscrew curls covered by her cap and only a single sprig, and that was curled into the tightest of natural curls, let loose in front of her ear. Oddly enough, it wasn't until just then that he realized almost every person he'd laid eyes on that day had had blade-straight hair. His own hair, a brown like the darkest of nuts, had a curl to it also though nowhere near as tight as hers were. It was true of all the brothers.

"Forgive me. That was rude," he said hastily. Awkwardly. In his time, women who were not in service to the gods were not given places of prestige. But he was aware that he was not in his time and he tried to act accordingly. He had never seen a woman who looked like her, other than a goddess, and he had learned the hard way not to cross a goddess.

"Not at all," she soothed him gently. "I believe I started it."

Yes. Of course she had. He should stop acting so foolishly tongue-tied. No matter what the time, what the place, he was a warrior and he would behave as such!

"I have my reward and I will take my leave," he said briskly, turning to do so. But her sudden grip on his wrist stayed him as the shackles of the hells had stayed him.

"But not all of your reward is given," she said. And this time it was she who seemed awkward.

Ah. The kiss, he realized after a moment.

"I have no interest in your other reward," he said brusquely.

She looked as though he had slapped her, and he became aware of the murmur, the unkind murmur, of the crowd.

"What? You insult your grandina in such a beastly manner?!" Dethan looked up to see the jendan surging to his feet from his seat in the viewing box above them.

"She is not my grandina, for I am not from here," Dethan barked back at him. He turned to look again at the woman before him. "And I would not debase her so by asking her to kiss one such as I."

Understanding lit her features as well as a sort of relief. That was when he realized she had thought he had found her offensive. But everything the opposite was true. He merely found her to be . . . untouchable.

He did not deserve this woman's beauties. He had much sin upon his head and much filth upon his body. He would no sooner kiss a priestess of Kitari, the goddess who was considered to be the most beautiful and demanded her priestesses be of rivaling beauty.

"Then you must be rewarded in some other way," she spoke up. She seemed to cast about in her mind for a solution, but then she smiled. "You will dine at table with me tonight."

"My dear!" The protest was meant to be cajoling, but the jenden had barked it out with too much force. He corrected his tone when she shot him an acidic glare. "Your grandness, you will forgive me for saying so, but this man . . . He is little more than a beast covered with filth and mud. Are we all to suffer over our meals?"

"Yes," she hissed. And that was all. One sibilant yes and the jenden paled a little and backed down, but he did not look happy about it and his eyes were filled with an unholy sort of hatred. But no sooner had the impression registered on Dethan than it was gone and the jenden was smiling with acquiescence.

"Anything you desire, my dear."

"Yes. Anything I desire," she said. These were not the words of a spoiled, childish girl, however. Merely the powerful words of a woman who knew what she wanted and what she had the right as grandina to ask for. "You will come with us. Grannish, I wish to return home now."

"But we only just arrived. You were so looking forward to coming," he hedged.

"I have seen all I needed to see for today. The fair will be here for a week, and tomorrow is another day." Then she spoke to Dethan, whom she had never turned away from during her exchange with Grannish. "Since it is clear you do not come from here and do not know the way, you will walk behind us and we will go slowly. You will rest, wash yourself, and we will find you some proper clothing." She brushed her hand absently down the front of her gown, drawing his attention to the long length of her brown skirt. The bottom hem, which settled just above her toes, was made of brown leather for a full forearm's length before the bottom. The rest was of a much finer and softer fabric. One could see the intelligence in the design, for the leather was spattered with the mud that seemed so prevalent in the city. The rest . . . It made him wonder what she had hidden beneath so much fabric. More burns perhaps? In his time, in his city, clothing had been short, light, and much less cumbersome than this was. Everyone could see what was to be seen on others they met. Then again, he could understand the design of their mode of dress, for it had been cool and wet the entire time as the day had worn on.

He wanted to turn her down. He had far more pressing things to attend to. But the sad truth was that he was hungry and he was dirty and he was in need of proper clothing. It was true he could have bought all those things now, if the weight of his new purse were anything to judge by, but he had other provisions to think about and there was no knowing how far his new coin would stretch. The journey across the desert promised to be an arduous one and he needed to be careful. He might be immortal, but he would feel every moment of the suffering being stranded in the desert would heap upon him, and he'd had his fill of burning and suffering.

Thinking of that made him look at the lowering sun once more. He had maybe two hours before it set entirely, by the look of it. Two hours to get fed and get out of reach of anyone else.

"Very well, lovely grandina," he said, touching his fist to his heart. "But I cannot stay long, for I have a long journey ahead of me."

"A journey?" she asked with some amount of incredulity. Then she waved off the reaction. "Rest assured, we will eat within the hour," she guaranteed him. "Then you are free to do whatever it is you will. Come. Follow us to the fortress." She turned away from him and, lifting her skirt in one hand, she began to walk away. When she turned back to see if he was following and saw him standing still, she laughed at him. "Come. I promise I will not bite you," she said, holding out her hand blindly, as if she knew someone was going to take it for her. And surely someone did. The jenden was there to grasp it like a well-trained gormlet. She waited until Dethan took his first step, and then, with an expression of pure satisfaction, she let Grannish lead her away.

CHAPTER
FOUR

Dethan followed the coach and four in the mud, but he didn't really need to. As with many cities, the castle fortress was at its center. However, this was poor planning, in his opinion, because the city was situated up against a mountainous section of land. It would have been wiser to build the castle fortress into the mountainside, giving it the high ground and letting the city in its entirety act as a buffer against any invaders. However, the entrance to the eight hells was located on that rock mountain face and the city had been built a more comforting distance away from it. Hexis had no doubt been built so the idea of the mouth of the hells being at the city's back would quell any raiders trying to commandeer it.

After all, who really wanted ownership to a mouth of the hells? The city had probably once been ruled by barbarians, worshippers of Xaxis. But it was clear the rulers, from what Dethan had seen, were not of that hulking, warmongering, crude bent. If Selinda was an example of the leadership here, it was elegant, refined, and had impeccable manners.

It was exactly the kind of leadership and the kind of city he would have attacked and overthrown in his time.

Perhaps this would be his first target once he had his wealth and an army. Then that would make the royal family—make Selinda—his captive.

He jolted. It was horrifyingly, outstandingly shocking to his whole system and psyche when the very idea of it made him hard with anticipation and excitement, his cock drawing tight to nearly full attention. Why would such a thing—why would *anything*—excite him? The physical needs of his body had long ago been burned out of him, and even before then he had not found delicate women at all appealing. To be honest, he had been a little bit afraid of them. Afraid of hurting them.

Then again, she wasn't exactly delicate. She had stood up to the jenden with a quiet sort of ferocity. She was very well acquainted with her own power, and perhaps that was what he found appealing.

And then there was her beauty. She was well formed, a tall woman with an unbelievably erect posture. She had been wearing something, some sort of restrictive garment that had pulled her waist in tightly, making it narrow and small yet allowing the swell of her hips to curve freely, provocatively. He wondered what the point of such a garment was. Maybe she had a deformity of the spine that required the garment to keep her from slouching forward.

No. He noticed other women wearing similar garments as they traveled into the finer parts of the city, the part where the mud was less because there was a series of grated holes in the streets that appeared to allow water to run off rather than sit in the dirt and be churned into mud. The runoff no doubt let out into the poorer sections of town, he thought with a shake of his head. He had never seen the point of allowing one part of a city to fall into disrepair and poverty while another part flourished with wealth and fine things. The poor of one's city were just as needed as the wealthy when war broke out, and they had to have reason and loyalty in order to fight their best. Burdening them only defeated their desire to defend their home. That made for bad soldiering. And one must always be prepared to use the members of the city for war. It was the only way to be certain the city remained properly defended.

The fact was the grandina's beauty had captured his fancy, and it was a distraction he could not afford. At the same time . . . it was good to feel alive again. He had been so dead, burned again and again into a rotten carcass, and this was so different. So much like life again. Even if that life was conditional. But Weysa was watching him. He was certain of it, and she would not be kind if she thought he was being distracted from the purpose she had freed him for. If he wanted to remain free from the fires of the eight hells, he would pay homage to Weysa and no other.

It was this thinking that allowed his desires to wane long before they had reached the fortress. Fortress. He laughed to himself. It was hardly that. Open gates, people milling about so thickly inside and outside the low walls that the gates couldn't possibly be shut in a hurry if necessary. It appeared that anyone would be able to walk right up to the house of the political seat, just as he was now doing.

He waited in the courtyard as the grandina alighted, her escort helping her down from the carriage. She immediately turned to one of the attendants standing nearby and reached to draw Dethan closer with an inviting hand gesture.

"Page," she said to the attendant. "This man will be my guest. See to it he is washed, properly clothed, and brought immediately to the dinner table." She turned to Dethan, raising a brow. "I am assuming this is what you would like. If you prefer to come to table as you are, you will still be welcome."

"No, Grandina," he said. "I accept your generous hospitality."

Dethan saw her smile, and with a nod, she turned to go. The jenden reached to take her hand and lead her inside, but she withdrew from him, the rebuff marked. To say he was not pleased with the rejection was an understatement, but he seemed to stiffly keep his composure and moved away from the grandina as she entered her home.

"Follow me," the page said.

Selinda was tired of pretending to enjoy the jenden's company, so as soon as they were out of the general public eye, she withdrew from the attentions of her intended. It sickened her every time she thought of herself being bonded for the rest of her life to that grasping, twisted man. She was not deluded as to what kind of man the jenden was. The trouble was her father was completely fooled by the jenden and would hear nothing against him, not even from his own daughter. She had tried on countless occasions to open her father's eyes, to make him see that all the jenden wanted was her father's seat on the throne of Hexis. She did not underestimate the avarice that motivated Grannish. She feared for her father. Feared that shortly after she was forced to wed Grannish some horrible accident might befall her father, just as it had befallen her brothers and sisters. She had not always been heir. Now she was and wished for all the world that she wasn't. She wished her brother Jorry was still alive. He had been so strong and so assured. He would never have allowed his sister to be sold to a man like Grannish.

But Jorry was gone now and her father thought he was securing his city by pledging her to Grannish.

She moved quickly through the halls of the fortress,

heading directly toward her rooms. Her days had been reduced to the untenable boredom of being waited on and kowtowed to by a man she despised. All of it a display when she knew, could feel in her soul, that he hated her almost as much as she hated him. He was cruel and there was something wrong inside him. And for the life of her, she could not understand why a man as bright as her father was could not see it for himself.

She sailed into her rooms and her pagettes came out of the woodwork like busy little bees, divesting her of her walking dress and bringing a tub of water for her to wash her hands and feet in, scrubbing away the mud of the city. The pagettes took her clothes away and would do the same with them, making them clean again for the next time she would wear them. Meanwhile, they brought in the fresh dress she requested and redressed her long, curling hair into a less severe upswept style that left a waterfall of curls tumbling down her back. She did not like to wear any part of her hair down when in the city. It seemed to just accumulate mud and dirt when it was left that way. But now that they would be within the confines of the fortress, she could wear it freely.

She also changed into an evening corset, a more formal corset that was longer, smoothing the lines of her body into a very correct and straight silhouette. The dress came next, a dove-gray velveteen that dropped straight to the ground, without the typical leather mud guarding that trimmed the bottom of all her day and walking gowns. She held out her hands and they were gloved. She arched her neck and it was bejeweled with a stunning minx-fire necklace, the red of it, it was said, redder than the deepest fires of the eight hells. Her teal-blue hat was replaced by one of gray, the veil on it longer than that on the previous one, the stiff netting covering the entire left side of her face. She had grown quite used to seeing the world through the threads of a veil and would probably feel naked without it. It might be considered silly, she supposed. Everyone knew what was hiding beneath the camouflage. Everyone knew she was burned and scarred, and ugly because of it.

But . . . but that man. That strange and strong man who had defeated the brute in the shivov fight, who had taken a purse but not the humiliating kiss that Grannish had offered as a prize . . . In spite of his rejecting the kiss, he had somehow made her feel as though she were . . . beautiful.

He had no courtly manners, had no grasping desires. And if she allowed herself to think it, it was possible he had joined the shivov fight . . . *for her*. Simply so she would not have to kiss a pig of a man.

"Foolish girl." She tsked to her reflection. "Romanticizing a man covered in mud."

But he had not been just any man. He was big, as tall as any man she'd ever seen, towering above them all. He'd had tremendous muscle definition underneath all that mud plastered to his skin. She found herself eager to see what was underneath the crust of it. As it was, two things had stood out to her. One, that he had eyes as green as the greenest clover in the fields. She had never seen such a green on a person before. Her people, they were dark of hair and dark of eye. She was one of the few in the city with eyes of blue, and she had them only because her mother had come from a land apart from this one. But her mother was dead. Her eldest brother, also blue of eye, was dead. Now only she remained, her youngest brother dark-eyed like their father, and if the trend continued, he too would soon be dead. It seemed she was cursed with fine health, she thought fatalistically.

The other thing she found startling about the man were his burns. She had never met anyone of such strength and vitality before, and somehow it was as though his burns did not even exist for him. He had not let them hinder him. She couldn't tell just how extensive his burning had been—she hoped to see more clearly once he was divested of all that mud—but somehow . . . with those eyes and that full head of dark hair, he was still amazingly handsome. More so than Grannish, that was certain. Grannish had a narrow sort of pinched look about him, as though he were constantly smelling something that was a little bit off.

Then again, compared to Grannish she would find anyone to be more handsome, possibly even that pig at the shivov fights. Her vision was colored by contempt for the jenden. Whether it was deserved or not, whether it was fair or not, she hardly even knew anymore. The whole business had made her weary and endlessly unhappy. She had come to realize her future was a bleak one unless something extraordinary happened. The future was bleak for them all unless something extraordinary happened.

She refused to dwell on that just then. She had found a diversion in this man and she was determined to use it to its fullest extent. She needed some activity, some excitement for her mind. Even if it was just an exercise in curiosity, it was a distraction from the painful responsibilities of her life.

"Hanit, color my lips. I wish for them to stand out."

Hanit stood and blinked for a moment, looking as though she were unsure she had heard her mistress correctly. That made some sense of course. Hanit had been trained to play down anything and everything that might draw attention to her mistress's face. Selinda could not have explained the desire even if the pagette had found the voice to question it. Instead Hanit went in search of a coloring pot and brush, appearing with them shortly and proceeding to paint her mistress's lips the colors of the setting sun, from blue to lavender to violet. Selinda's mouth glistened with color.

"A beautiful job," Selinda complimented Hanit with more than a little wonder in her voice. "I did not know you could do this."

"You never asked before, grand lady," Hanit said in a low, deferential tone. Hanit was relatively new to Selinda's rooms. The pagette had replaced an old and dear friend who had fallen ill and died in the summer plagues a full turning of the seasons past. The curse of this wet city was its plagues. No one could get dry, it seemed, and illness festered in the wet, muddy mess. Even in summer, when the sun baked the mud and made it hard, all it took was a single day of rain for everything to be wet again. Then illness would come in the wake of it.

Selinda did not want to think of death when she was looking at her sun-streaked lips. She wanted for once to act as though there were no troubles in her world. That she was not ugly and burned. That she was not going to marry a vile little worm. That her city might not last long enough for her to inherit.

No. Tonight, all she wanted to think about was a stranger. A man. Someone . . . different. That was it. He was somehow just . . . different. Maybe tonight at dinner she would be able to figure out just what that difference was. And then later, after the sun dropped and let night reign, maybe she would speak with him or play games with him or find some way for him to further entertain her. Maybe if he was truly interesting she could convince her father to let him stay on in the castle for a day or two. Not for long. Just . . . for a little while.

Eager now, she arose from her dressing bench and hurried to the door of her rooms. The pagette opened it as she approached, and Selinda came up short when she saw Jenden Grannish standing in the doorway. For all his leanness of form, he had a presence to him that could not be ignored, no matter how hard she might try. It was like a malevolent cloud that darkened her days and nights constantly, one that would not move away no matter how hard she tried to escape it.

"My dear," he greeted. Then he drew himself up short, his dark eyes narrowing on her with a frightening ferocity. He reached out, his hand like a sudden viper around her arm, his strength unmistakable as he jerked her closer to himself. "What is this?" he hissed into her face. With his free hand, his thumb smeared across her colored lips. "Are you mad? You paint yourself like a brightly colored whore?"

She gasped and tried to push him away before he ruined Hanit's lovely work. "The highest ladies in this court wear similar!" she protested.

"The highest ladies of this court are not monstrously scarred. I would think you would avoid drawing attention to the fact that you *are*."

"Stop it," she cried as he continued to smear his fingers over her lips.

"Off! Remove it this instant! I'll not have my future bride parading herself around as though she had some sort of beauty to be proud of. Accept what you are, Selinda. Just as I must do my duty as asked by my grand. I have promised to wed you in spite of your deformities, but I will not have you drawing attention to them and making a laughingstock of yourself!"

The whole of his palm smeared across her lips, bruising the flesh both outside and inside, where the sharpness of her teeth cut into the tender skin he was mashing against them. The color, she could feel, was not just being wiped away. He was streaking it over her skin. But when his hand touched the scar at her jaw, she cried out and struck him away, shoving at him with all her strength as tears of shame burned in her eyes. She fought to keep herself from crying, however, unwilling to give him the satisfaction.

"Very well, I will wash it off!" she spat out.

"I have half a mind to drag you to table looking as you are, like a painted, grisly little doll. Your father would be humiliated and the court would laugh to see such a disgusting sight. But I will spare your father the shame of it. Wash up. I am impatient to go to table. I want to see them seat the stinking, mangled mud farmer at your side. The two of you should make quite a pair."

Tears hovering in her eyes, Selinda shrugged him off one last time and went back into her room, where Hanit, bless her kind soul, was ready with a damp cloth to help her wash the sunset away from her lips.

CHAPTER
FIVE

Grannish led Selinda into the main dining hall. As usual, it was abustle with noise and activity. Servers abounded, bringing in great trays of foods, their rich smells wafting throughout the room. Courtly guests milled about their chairs, chattering and gossiping about one another, creating a sort of noisy hum in the air.

Grannish had Selinda's right hand grasped firmly in his own, the twisted pair of them raised elegantly high. When they entered, the room came to immediate attention. Those who had been seated stood at once. Grannish knew it was not for him that this respect was being given but for this mangled little harlot. But soon, one day soon, he would be grand and they would be coming to attention for *him*. They would be respecting *him* in this way. The way he deserved to be respected. After all, who was she but the imperfect get of an idiot king? He had no respect for either of them. Especially not this intemperate little girl. She took great delight in setting him down in public, knowing he had to defer to her in all things by law and in the eyes of the masses. But he would make her pay for each and every slight she thought to cast in his direction.

Tonight's guest, for instance. He had made sure she

would be seated next to her muddied guest. Grannish himself would sit across the table as far from the stench of him as was possible, but she would be made to suffer for her folly. Inviting a lowborn to table. The very idea of it was repugnant to him. No doubt it would be to her father too. Grannish would let the grand witness his daughter seated beside a pig of a farmer and he would see for himself why his daughter should not be allowed to make decisions for herself. Then Grannish would be able to exert more control over her. Then he would be able to keep her in her place.

Oh, how he wished he did not need her at all. But his blood was not royal. It was barely even noble. A fact he worked hard to have everyone forget. Only by the grace of his ability to advise the grand had he been able to rise so high in his esteem. High enough for the grand to offer his heir's hand in marriage. But Grannish wished he could be grand without having to saddle himself with the wretched creature. He would wed someone very different if he had a choice in the matter.

His eyes immediately tracked to Likessa. As always the perfect beauty was surrounded by courtiers, the center of all attentions and affections. A true grandina if there ever was one, in everything but title and blood. She was deserving of the position this carcass now possessed. Beauty like hers should be revered and celebrated. And beyond beauty, she was of perfect grace and manners. Every movement, even the lightest floating of her hand to her dinner fork, was a thing of elegance and refinement. He watched as one of the lords hastened to pull out a chair for Likessa, whom Grannish had seated next to him. At least he would have the joy of her company, even as he enjoyed his fiancée's humiliation.

Ever the perfect escort, he guided Selinda to her chair, noting that her companion for the evening had yet to arrive. That meant everyone would already be seated by the time he arrived, and that would make him the center of attention and even more of a delightful spectacle. Oh yes, this promised to be quite a diversion.

The grand entered the room and everyone nodded their heads in respect, palms pressed flat against their stomachs. He sat down immediately, barely noticing the crowd around him, as was usual. No, the grand's attentions were never concerned with the court undercurrents. He had no interest in them unless they ran counter to his desires. Yet he did not consider himself an oblivious man. He trusted his advisor, the jenden, to keep him apprised of any situations that needed his attention, which left him free to pursue other fascinations. Such as hunting and, upon occasion, charming a young woman. He had not strayed from his wife in all his years of marriage, but once he had finished mourning her, he had found himself feeling newly free to enjoy the attentions of the women of his court, and enjoy them he did. But any woman with the idea that she might actually become granda one day was simply deluding herself. The grand had loved only one woman and would forever love her. The man would never choose to follow her with anyone subpar. The grand would never insult her memory in such a way.

But taking a mistress and practically fawning over her at his end of the table, seating her directly to his right, where she could hold and fondle his hand, where she could occasionally lean toward him and draw his attention to her young, healthy breasts, well, that was entirely in the realm of possibilities. Gwynn was a spicy little redhead who barely came up to the grand's shoulder, but she had all the curves in the world to make up for what she lacked in height. She was also quite beautiful, with her pale, flawless skin, her long elegant neck, and her pretty fey features. But there was calculation in her eyes. Yet another thing the grand could not see. But it was clear to all that she had quite a shrewdness to go with her sparkling wit.

As everyone settled into their seats, the grandina kept her head down, self-consciously tugging her veil into place and rubbing at her bruised lips. They were a little swollen and red from the jenden's rough treatment, and her eyes were wet from continually filling with tears, which she fought back. She would not give Grannish the satisfaction. She sat up ramrod straight and looked longingly toward her father. The jenden was on his immediate left and Gwynn was on his immediate right, leaving her at Gwynn's right, the woman between them. And anyway, she could not tell her father of Grannish's treatment, for he would not hear it. He would make up some kind of excuse or accuse her of blowing things out of proportion. If she called Grannish out in front of him, it would only anger the jenden more, and the next thing he did would be even crueler. Oh, Grannish would never leave distinctive marks on her. No cuts or bruises she could point to as proof to her father and make the grand honestly question him, but there were other things he could do. And over time Grannish had proved to be quite *creative* when it came to his cruelties.

She was not in the mood to eat, but a quelling look from Grannish had her reaching for some bread and some meat and cheese. She could make the pretense of eating these things, perhaps feeding them to her father's hunting dogs, who were seated attentively around the edges of the room. If they saw so much as a crumb drop, they would dart forward to gobble it up, then move back to their places. They were not allowed to beg, but they would sit and drool in anticipation of a guest possibly calling them forward to feed them a treat.

She had just called the wine steward forward to fill her glass when a man entered the far end of the room.

She froze in place, putting down her glass before the boy could fill it. She shooed the boy back when he blocked her view of the man.

He was tall. So very tall. He had a square, beautiful jawline, hair as brown and soft looking as a fru's winter coat, and there were those stunning green eyes. If not for those three things, she would never have recognized him as the mud-caked man of earlier. She would swear on her father's life that she had never seen shoulders so broad or arms so well muscled. Someone had given him leggings, ones that molded tightly to every well-muscled contour of his legs and snuggled close to . . . other large portions of his body. If not for the leggings being black, they would have been truly obscene. Selinda found herself swallowing back a strange and unexpected dryness in her throat, her face flushing hot as she thought of what he might look like without those leggings on. She shocked herself. She was not the sort to think such things. In fact, wondering about men was something she simply didn't indulge in. She had neither the luxury nor the inclination. She had her unhappy life to attend to; there was no room in it for sexual flights of fancy.

Yet her mind was drifting into that particular sky. He wore a tanned leather vest and no shirt, leaving his powerful arms and defined chest and belly bare for all to see. The fact that his arms bore the scars of burns meant very little. It was impossible to notice the scars when there was so much beautiful flesh to see everywhere else.

He looked hard and capable, and Selinda wondered what it would feel like to be held up against such an undeniably powerful and male body. What would it mean to be a woman in that man's arms? A real woman. One with the luxury to indulge in such a very real sort of man.

Apparently everyone agreed with her stunned surprise at his appearance, for a deadened silence fell over the room, the sound of movement and action ceasing. All were seeing him for the first time, save for Selinda and Grannish, but Grannish looked just as shocked as she must have. Instantly that gave her pleasure. Grannish no doubt had been certain she would be humiliated by the presence of the mud farmer. It would explain why the only chair left empty was the one by her side, instead of one farther down and closer to the end of table where those of lower rank would sit.

One of the dinner stewards brought the tidied-up man to the seat beside her and she watched with obvious amazement as he came to the chair, nodded his head to her, and then sat down as though there was nothing at all unusual about the situation. As though he sat at the table of the grand all the time. If Grannish had been hoping the man would be awkward and out of his element, he was being rudely divested of the notion.

"Sor," she heard herself saying, marveling within herself that she had found the wherewithal to speak. "I was so rude as to not ask your name earlier. Now I do not know how to address you."

"My name is Dethan," he said carefully, almost as though he weren't sure he wanted to share the information. She found herself feeling honored that he had.

"Sor Dethan, this is my father, Luzien, the grand of Hexis. He welcomes you to his house and table."

"Indeed I do!" the grand spoke up, surprising Selinda. She had thought him too wrapped up in Gwynn to have even taken notice, but how silly she was to think anyone in that room had not taken notice of Dethan. "My jenden tells me you defeated the city's champion two years running at the shivov fights!"

"If you wish to call it a shivov match. Where I come from, the shivov is a fight to the death. With real weapons."

"And where is it you come from?" Luzien asked.

There was a slight hesitation. "I was born in Toren."

"Toren! That is at the very southern edge of the Black Continent! That is very far from here. Two deserts and an ocean away. The Grinder Mountains stand in between as well. How is it you come so far over such treacherous territory?"

"Just traveling the continent, sor," Dethan said.

" 'My lord,' " Selinda corrected him gently. "Here men of rank are referred to as lords or your lordship. Men without titles are sors."

"And women?"

"Women of no rank are called 'sora'; women of rank are 'lady' or 'my lady' or 'her ladyship,' " she informed with a smile. She felt everyone's riveted interest at their end of the table and she nervously tugged her veil into place, though it had not moved an inch. He reached out and took her hand, pulling it away from the nervous gesture. The whole table audibly drew in its breath. It was not allowed for anyone to touch a member of the royal family without his or her express permission. She could have been utterly offended, could have called him out on it, could have—

"Do not do that," Dethan scolded her with a grim frown. "There is nothing for you to hide, unless you seek to hide your beauty from this table of unsuspecting men, lest they all fall in love with their grandina."

The idea was so ludicrous that she laughed out loud in a startled burst. The entire table tittered in response. She flushed at that, knowing it was mocking, just as his words must be mocking her. But it had not felt as though he were being cruel. The words had felt . . . serious.

"Is there some reason you should not believe me?" he asked, divining her thoughts.

"You mean other than the fact that you are the only one who thinks so?" she asked in a low voice, a touch of temper to the words. She was being embarrassed . . .

She was being paid attention to and she did not like it. She withdrew her hand from his, dropping it into her lap. He frowned but did not press the matter.

"It is a wonder you were able to come here at all, what with the Redoe. You certainly will not be leaving anytime soon unless you know of any tricks that we do not," the grand said.

This brought a stiffness to Dethan's spine, his whole body tense and taut as a bowstring. "Redoe?" he asked slowly. Carefully. As if he needed to make himself perfectly clear.

"Yes. The enemy at our walls. The Redoe have always been a thorn in our side, but with this latest siege, they are proving to be heartier and more serious than ever before."

"The city is under siege?" he asked. Again, very carefully.

"Why, yes. How can you be here and not know that?" Selinda asked him, genuine curiosity in her features.

"I have only . . . just arrived."

"But surely you passed the Redoe at the gates of the city. They have been camped there for ages."

"I came from . . . the other direction."

"The other . . . You mean the Death Mountains?" The jenden scoffed. "No one comes in from the Death Mountains. He is a liar."

Dethan shot the jenden a look. He did not take kindly to being called a liar, but he did not press the matter. Mainly because in a way it was a lie. He had come from that direction, but not necessarily from the mountains themselves.

"You are very brave and a warrior besides. Perhaps a skilled fighter such as yourself has an idea of how to fight back these Redoe," the grand said.

Dethan frowned. "I would begin by not having a fair in the middle of a war," he said darkly.

The entire table went quiet.

"But the harvest fair is a tradition," the grand argued. "We always . . ."

"And apparently the Redoe laying siege is a tradition as well. If you want to be free of your enemy, you must defeat them once and for all. And defeat them soundly to relieve any other enemies of the notion you are weak and vulnerable. You might start by moving the heart of your city to the plateau at the leading edge of the Death Mountains. It would give you the high ground and leave you naturally defended on three sides. A good sound wall on the fourth will make it nearly impossible for the fortress to be penetrated. I would create a series of walls . . ." He stood and reached to the center of the table, grabbed up a candle and blew it out, then turned it upside down. He used the softened, colored wax to draw on the white linen tablecloth a rough sketch of the city. It was a circle, with the mountains on one side, the city wall on the other, and the city between. "A wall here, here, and here," he said, bisecting the city and then splitting those halves in half again, "and you will buffer the entire city. Should your enemy breach one of the walls, you could pull the inhabitants and resources of the city behind the next wall . . . and then the next. This will exhaust the enemy's energy and supplies as they try to get at you again and again. If you must be on the defensive, make certain you have a defense in the first place."

Dethan dropped the candle onto the table, sat back down, and began to grab food off the serving plates in front of him. He ate as though he had not had a meal in decades. He savored it all, ate it all. And all the while he seemed completely oblivious to the fact that he was being stared at.

"I say . . ." the grand said after several minutes.

"Were you . . . How do you, a simple mud farmer, know how to do something like that?"

"Who said I was a mud farmer?" Dethan asked, his brow lifting. The grand looked at his jenden acidly.

"You are not a mud farmer?"

"No, your lordship."

"Then . . . what are you?"

"My trade you mean? I am a general. I once commanded a great army."

Grannish scoffed. "You barely had clothes on your back and you expect us to believe—"

"I do not expect you to believe anything, nor do I care if you do. I do care if you call me a liar once more, Jenden Grannish, so I would use caution if I were you."

The jenden paled and grew angry all in the same breath. Selinda opened her mouth to say something to diffuse the situation but she was disrupted when Gwynn suddenly leaned toward her, her buxom chest nearly dumping into Selinda's lap as she leaned eagerly toward Dethan.

"So you are used to commanding leagues of men? Are they all as powerful as you?" She practically oozed the word "powerful," leading everyone to believe she meant something else entirely.

"Yes, but I have been on my own for some time," he said carefully. "I have taken a sabbatical for some years. I will be returning to Toren as soon as possible, though. I must lead my armies once more."

"Armies?" Selinda asked, marking the plural.

He seemed to catch himself. "I misspoke. I will lead one army. One is enough."

Selinda believed him. She believed without a doubt that all it would take was one army for this man to conquer worlds. Apparently her father did as well.

"You must advise my general of the army. Perhaps your ideas can end this conflict with the Redoe."

There was a choked sound from down the table. Firru, a relatively short, stockily built man with a curling, grizzled beard and no moustache, clearly took offense at the idea of a stranger giving him military advice.

"Your most honorable," Firru sputtered, "the matter is clearly in hand. We are weeks away from a solution. You know the Redoe. They will tire of this nonsense outside the walls and they will retire to their nomad tents, content to have stolen a few supplies for the winter days. The temperature will soon drop and they will be gone."

"Only to return again next spring," Selinda said with a scoffing sound. "And again. And again. Until one day they finally make it beyond the walls and win the city for themselves."

"I will never let that day come," Jenden Grannish said.

It was clear to Dethan that Selinda wanted to say something, something very bitter tasting, but for some reason she bit her tongue and backed down from the jenden's claim. It was also clear, however, that she had no faith in his abilities to back up that claim. So if she outranked him, if she did not believe him, why would she not call him out on it? Dethan wondered. She had seemed so strong earlier. So able to take control of a situation. But now she was deferring. Now she was hiding behind her veil as if she were something to be ashamed of.

"And what will you do to stop them?" Dethan queried, his tone hard and dark. He didn't like what he was seeing. He liked what he was feeling even less. None of this should matter to him. None of it did matter to him, he insisted in his own head. "Because once they get beyond the walls, the end of your city follows quickly after, and no doubt your lives."

The observation cast a grim pall down the length of the table.

"Well," Gwynn said brightly, "I daresay this isn't the topic for proper dinner conversation. You've put us all off our meals. Come, tell us a funny little story to chase away this doom and gloom."

"Why tell a different story when this one is already so humorous," Dethan said, his frown anything but amused. "You sit here dining, joking, going to the fair, posturing, and preening, and all the while the beasts outside are whittling away at your defenses. I have hardly heard of anything funnier." Dethan moved to get to his feet, disgusted with the lot of them. "I'll take my leave before your barbarians make it to the dinner table," he said.

"No!" To everyone's shock, the grandina came out of her seat and grabbed on to his arm. She leaned so much of her weight into her grasp that his biceps bulged to a heftily rounded mass of muscle. "Please do not give up on us. We are not as ignorant as we seem. Surely we are not as unworthy. Please, I beg of you to stay."

"Selinda!" Grannish snapped, his tone appalled and his expression aghast. "A grandina does not beg anything from such common filth!"

"Quiet!" she hissed at him, that defiant fire Dethan had seen earlier rearing its head with a vengeance. It raced over her features beneath the veil, causing every muscle in her body to stiffen. It was as though it took every ounce of the energy in her body to stand up to that man. Because it obviously cost her so much, Dethan let himself be detained. He looked through the crosshatching of her veil down into her eyes, their vivid teal so full of her desperation. It was such a powerful thing. She made it a powerful thing. As though her entire life hinged on him staying. Him. A stranger of no fame and no fortune, only the words on his lips to recommend him, and yet she was willing to throw weight behind him. "He has spoken more truth in these past minutes than has been spoken at this table in years," she said fiercely. "Father, if you do not see the wisdom of his words, then . . . then . . . then you are not the grand I thought you were."

"Sit down!" Grannish spat out, leaping to his feet and leaning across the table as though he wanted to grab hold of the grandina and shove her into her seat. "You are making a spectacle of yourself!" For some reason this made the redhead on Selinda's left snort out a laugh, as if to say, What do you expect from *her*.

"Daughter, he is a stranger," the grand said, but it was with a thoughtful gleam in his eyes. His daughter seized hold of the hope to be found in that fleeting expression.

"Perhaps we need a stranger to look at this from the outside. Perhaps we have been sitting in the middle of it for so long that we no longer can think of a new way of dealing with the situation."

"Selinda. Please." The grand gestured to her chair, and after a moment with her jaw set in resistance, she slowly regained her seat. A pointed look from the grand put Grannish back in his seat as well. "It will do none of us any good to become hot tempered about this business. If we tear one another to shreds, it will make it all the easier for the Redoe to pick over our remains. Sor, if you would be so kind as to confer with my general on the morrow, perhaps you can lend insight to—"

"No. I cannot."

The grand's last word hung suspended on his lips even as his eyes widened a little at the understanding that he had been both interrupted and denied.

"You cannot?" the grand echoed.

"I have pressing business and have no time to waste," Dethan explained, though he did not know why he was making excuses. He had never done so before. He saw a thing, wanted a thing, and he took that thing. He did all of this with little regard for the collateral damage it would cause. And even now, he saw no reason to be concerned with any other details . . . save one.

He did not know why, but the undercurrent to the way the grandina was being treated, to the way she was regarded with so little respect, irritated him. Perhaps it was because where he came from women were strong and powerful. They had to be to give birth to sons and then send them off to be trained as warriors. There had also been those women who had become warriors themselves, standing shoulder to shoulder with the sons of other women, all of whom looked up to them, knowing just how hard they had had to work in order to be considered the equal of a man, often being tested twice as hard as the men simply because they bore breasts and bore children. Some men thought this made them weaker. Dethan knew better. It made them lighter. Made them faster. Made them more cunning than their male counterparts. They compensated in wits for what they were short of in strength.

Dethan saw these strengths in the grandina. And yet he saw weakness in her as well. He saw vulnerability. Why that should matter to him, he did not know. It simply . . . did. Perhaps, he thought, it was a test. Perhaps his commitment to his goal was being tested by this distraction. Or perhaps she was a test of his honor. Had he learned humility and respect as he had burned in the hells? Had he learned to think of others before himself? Weysa *was* the guardian of women.

No. He would think himself into circles trying to figure out the wishes and whims of the gods. He had been given a clear assignment and he must stick to that plan.

But perhaps gaining the grand's respect could secure him an advantage. Perhaps it could also secure him resources. Both of which, he thought with an internal grimace, he was apparently going to need if he was going to get past the Redoe.

"Your most honorable," Grannish began in protest, "it is not worth your time to deal with the disrespect of this mud farmer. Allow me to purge him from this fortress entirely and—"

"It would require all your substandard army to achieve such a thing if I do not wish to go," Dethan said softly. Dangerously.

Then the strangest thing happened. The grandina's hand, which had dropped beneath the tablecloth, reached to lie atop his thigh. She very gently squeezed the muscles of his legs. It was a message of some sort, though he could not understand if she was warning him to tread carefully or supporting him in delight for his strength in standing up to Grannish.

But it wasn't either of those things that mattered to him. What mattered was the way it felt. It felt like . . . like . . . like something he had not felt in so long he was afraid to even consider it. Did her warm, strong hand on his thigh actually make him feel . . . aroused? As a woman arouses a man? It could not be, he thought with all due haste. It should not be. His body was not his own to give. It was not allowed to feel the heat that bled insidiously up the inside of his thigh and into the seat of his groin.

Was this on purpose? he asked himself next. Was it her design to arouse him, to use feminine lures on him in order to win him over? He wanted to reach out and grab her hand, shove it back into her lap, but he did not. He let it linger there, let himself feel the illicit pleasure it gave him, even though he knew with every fiber of his being that he should not.

"Now, Grannish," the grand chastened with an amused tone in his voice. "This man is still a guest. My daughter has invited him and we will respect that invitation."

"Something she should not have done," Grannish hissed.

"I did not need or want your permission," the grandina said, barely leashing the contempt in her voice.

"Allow me," the grand said over the exchange, "to implore you to stay. It will be your decision and it will be difficult for you to leave anyway. Perhaps if you can help us, if you can help resolve the issue with the Redoe, it will make it easier for you to be on your way. And I say to you now, if you have success at this thing, then you will be appropriately compensated."

"Gold?" Dethan asked with sudden interest.

"A great deal of gold if you are instrumental in the resolution to this problem."

"I see," Dethan said. "I will consider your offer and give you an answer at dawntide." Although a heavy part of him thought he might not even be here come morning. But this problem with the Redoe meant he would need a few more days to figure his way around them. One thing he knew from all his time laying siege to cities was that there was always a way for sneaking in and out of a city. There was always some enterprising individual willing to slip beyond the walls to get supplies, which were then sold on the black market or for an exorbitant sum. All Dethan needed to do was find such people.

"Meanwhile," the grandina hastened to add, "you will stay here tonight. In comfort. As a guest."

"That is not necessary or an appealing idea," Grannish said, his disdain even more evident.

"I agree with my daughter. A night of comfort and hospitality may sway you to help us."

"A night of the discomforts of war would more effectively persuade me," Dethan said. "Nothing compels action more than being faced with discomfort." He found them all too comfortable for a city that was supposedly under siege.

"Are you declining our hospitality, then?" the grand asked, amusement in his eyes.

"No, of course he isn't," the grandina said hastily. "You would not insult us, surely," she said to Dethan pointedly.

"No. I will not insult you. I will thank you for your comfort. First . . . I must go elsewhere. I will return shortly after the juquil's hour. Only . . . I do not wish to return too late and disturb the household."

"No matter," Selinda said dismissively. "There is always someone on guard. We will notify them to expect you, that is all."

Selinda looked down when Dethan took hold of her hand and moved it back into her lap. She flushed hotly as she was removed from touching all that hot, virile muscle. She had not realized she had left it there all this while. There had been something very comfortable about being in contact with him, and yet very disturbing. He had such strength and energy about him. She had felt that strength in the muscles of his leg, had felt them moving and flexing with his tension. It was a tactile experience that left her strangely hot and uncomfortable.

She should have been more cautious. He could very well have gotten the wrong idea. She could easily see how he might. It was very forward of her to have done such a thing. But she had been desperate that he not alienate her father and that he not leave. She didn't fully understand why, but she felt a desperation within herself that he *could not leave*. And she had learned long ago, from listening to the words of the magesses, that feelings as strong as that one were not to be ignored. The magical women of the gods had, over the years, encouraged her to heed those feelings. And heeding them had served Selinda well over time. She was not about to change her habits now.

The rest of the meal passed with little contribution to the conversation from their guest. She noticed that he kept looking out the window, and with every passing minute, he seemed to grow tenser and more agitated, though only someone paying close attention might notice it.

"I must go," he said suddenly, lurching to his feet, his chair scraping hard across the stone flooring.

"Surely not. You haven't—"

"I must go," he said even more harshly, setting down all remaining protest from her. She silenced and nodded, fighting the urge to come to tears. She knew . . . knew very well that she was going to pay dearly for standing up to Grannish. Somehow she thought that if Dethan stayed, maybe his presence would delay the inevitable. Or at least lend her strength. But with a deflating sigh, she knew that wasn't to be.

Her own father had ignorantly refused to see the abuse she suffered at Grannish's hands. What led her to believe a total stranger would make any difference? But she never knew when or how Grannish's retributions would come. Sometimes he would simply ignore the slights she could never seem to keep herself from delivering. Other times he stored them up and found ways to pay her back when she was least expecting it. In fact, that was his favorite torment. To wait until she thought she was free of punishment. To wait for when she was most relaxed. It was because of this that she endeavored to never let her guard down. Yet somehow he always managed it. He seemed to know the very moment she began to enjoy herself. Almost as though he were a carrion bird, sitting high on a branch, watching and waiting for when it would be best to pick the meat from her bones.

If only she could convince her father of his poison. She had given up almost all hope of ever doing so. Until tonight. It suddenly occurred to her that the only way her father might begin to see Grannish's flaws would be if someone else came along and did his job better than he did. Someone like Dethan.

There had been others in the past. Other up-and-comers who might have contested Grannish's power, but they had all met terrible ends: transferred into dangerous positions of ambassadorship or abjectly humiliated or even . . . death under mysterious circumstances. By encouraging Dethan to stay and play this role, she knew she was painting a target on his back, and at the first opportunity she needed to warn him of that fact. But now he was going and she would not see him again until morning . . . unless she waited up for him until the juquil's hour when he returned. She needed to catch him alone as soon as possible. She knew the look in Grannish's eyes all too well.

She hastened to stand as he moved away, something that was highly inappropriate. It was a sign of respect for someone to stand when others were leaving, and looking down the table, she saw only a few had stood—those of no real rank and therefore equal to their guest. Had her father stood, all would rise . . . just as they soon did after she had risen to her feet unthinkingly. Realizing what she had done, she awkwardly held out her hand to her guest.

"We look forward to your return," she said quietly, trying to sound measured and not as desperate as parts of her were truly feeling.

Dethan looked at her offered hand for a moment, finding himself feeling gauche and unsure. Clearly she was expecting him to do something. To show her some sign of respect. But not being from Hexis, he did not know what it was.

Evidently she understood his dilemma, and with a smile she leaned in and whispered to him, "Take my hand and kiss the center of my palm."

Finding himself grateful for her assistance and irritated with himself for even bothering with such trivialities, he took her hand and brought it hastily to his lips. He kissed her hand so quickly that the only thing he took away from it was the scent of a soft, seductively sweet perfume. It almost compelled him to linger, but he had no time. The sun was setting and he had no idea when the curse would begin. As soon as the sun touched the horizon? Halfway set? Once it was fully below? He had no idea. All he did know was that he had to make it through the city and back up into the mouth of the eight hells before it took place. He could not allow anyone else to be harmed, and he knew he could not allow anyone else to see him suffer. One, because they would know he was cursed and it would make a target of him. He did not need any undue attention. He needed to be on his way with little or no disturbance. And two, because his shame was absolute. It was bad enough that he must face the humiliating lesson at the hands of the gods, worse still for it to be witnessed. The one blessing all these decades was that his punishments had been suffered in solitude.

And as he looked down into the fair teal-blue of her eyes, the blue silkflower the only thing comparable in his estimation, he knew he never wanted those eyes to look on him in abject horror or disgust. He may deserve both and more, but from her . . . He would have her be ignorant of who and what he really was for as long as it may be allowed. Yes. He would take a small pleasure for himself in the idea that at least someone in the world who had touched him thought better than ill of him.

But he also saw hope in her eyes. A desperate sort of hope. He knew he should squash it, crush it under the grinding of his boot heel. It was better for her if she put no faith in him. He had nothing to offer her. He was no source of hope for her. She was looking in the wrong direction and with the wrong eyes.

He turned away from her and quickly made his way from the room.

"Selinda, do sit down!" Grannish snapped out to her. Then he must have realized what he sounded like and plastered a small smile on his lips. "I mean only to say these others are waiting until you do before resuming their meals."

"Yes," she said absently, slowly lowering herself back into her seat. *Why*, she asked herself, *do I feel as though my survival just walked out that door?*

That was the feeling that would keep her awake and awaiting his return at the juquil's hour. She would pray. Pray to her god for his safe return.

She would pray to Kitari.

CHAPTER
SIX

Dethan reached the cave with barely enough time to spare. Oh, how he despised the act of walking into the eight hells. How he feared it. He broke out in a sweat right at the threshold of the cave and found he was trembling from the exertion it was taking to simply face what was coming. He wished he were ignorant of it. Wished it would take him by surprise so that his suffering would not start until the very last minute. But he knew that it was better this way. This way no one else would be harmed or have to suffer along with him. If he was going to burn the way he had burned before, such a conflagration could bring the entire city to its knees. Certainly it would deliver it a wound that might mean life or death in their battle with the Redoe.

And what of that? Oh, he knew he could be of help, knew that his head for strategy would allow them to win against the Redoe, but the question remained: Should he bother? What ends would it serve him? Or, more concisely, what ends would it serve Weysa?

Wait, he thought suddenly. Weysa was the goddess of conflict. Here was a conflict. Perhaps not the mightiest of battles but a conflict just the same. And if he and the people of Hexis could defeat these barbarians, they could do so in Weysa's name. It could be the start he was in need of. If nothing else, it would gain him gold. Gold he would need in order to gather an army. There was no guarantee that after all this time his cache would still be there. So much time had passed; so many things had changed. He would then have traveled across the desert for no reason. Here there was an assurance of victory and gold. In the desert . . . there was a big question and insecurity.

No, he realized. It was better to stay. Better to work the king and his daughter to his advantage. He could see it would be fraught with troubles and would not be smooth going, but what battle ever was?

With that thought, his body suddenly seared hot. The shock of it, the pain of it, brought him to his knees. Before, he had been chained to the ground, so he had not been upright for the burning; it had never occurred to him to lower himself to the ground in preparation. But he was on the ground now, hands and feet against the stone, his skin rippling and blistering wherever it was exposed.

Suddenly he realized his clothing might burn as well. He would come from this and find himself naked again. He forced himself to rip at the clothing he wore, trying to get it free of his body. But it was too late. Flame slammed through him, rupturing out of his palms first, then the sensitive flesh of his groin, the flames licking along his cock like an acidic lover's tongue. That was what made screams break out of him. He felt his hair burning, his skin melting and crisping. The fire raced over every inch of him, and he went from hands and knees down to the floor on his face. Fire melted his eyes in his head, and he thought it was worse this time. After having known tranquillity and a life without the fire, coming back to it was worse than when it had been ever present. He breathed in flame, scorching his lungs. On and on it went until his flesh was a melted puddle around him and he was just burning bones.

And so it would be. Until the juquil's hour. And somehow knowing there would be an end; knowing there would be a reprieve; knowing there would be teal eyes and a soft, delicious scent, and rich dark hair, made it a little more bearable. There was a snake, the krunada snake, a black furred creature of such sleekness, glistening and sinuous, beautiful in its own way—nothing in the world could compare to it . . . save the hair of a grandina.

He quieted the strength of his thoughts. Clung to them but savored them quietly, lest they become known to the gods and the gods sought to take them away from him or punish him further. He couldn't imagine what would be worse than this, but if this torment had taught him anything, it was that the gods were creative in their punishments.

He had to keep focused on his goals. For as much as getting an army and defeating cities were his goals in Weysa's name, there was another goal—one closer to his heart—that drove him. He would win wars for Weysa, give her the power to defeat her enemies, and then he would ask for . . . would beg a reward from her. And it would not be that she permanently remove his curse. This was nothing. This suffering could be borne. No. He would ask for something else entirely.

He would ask for his brothers.

CHAPTER
SEVEN

The grandina of Hexis had sent all but her closest pagette to bed. She was sitting in the window well, amongst the cushions and pillows that had long ago been placed there for her comfort, staring through the glass. The view from the window was twofold. Its height allowed her to see over the entire city, all the way to the massive wall that surrounded them in a curving arch, each end of the wall built into the impenetrable stone of the mountains at the back of the city. Sheer rock shot up all around the city, with no known passes through for miles, although the nomads had tried time and again to find a way to sneak in from behind. But the mountains were too steep and too wild, and Xaxis, the god of the eight hells, protected them, if in no other way than by deterring those who feared the opening to the eight hells. She had her doubts that Xaxis actually paid attention to Hexis at all. He certainly had never shown himself to the city, not even in the most ancient of lore. That was probably why worship for him had fallen by the wayside over the years. There was habit but no strength behind the city's respect for the gods. The second benefit to her window was that it directly overlooked the bailey of the fortress, allowing her to see every coming and going through the gates. There was no other entrance to the high-walled fortress, so she knew he would be coming that way.

She didn't know what she would do once she saw him return. Perhaps she would just take comfort in the knowledge, then go to bed and wait for the morrow to speak with him. However, the more compelling idea was that she would wait for his return and sneak down through the castle to confront him before he retired for the night. She needed to beg him once more to stay and help them. She also needed to make it clear the danger he would be facing if in fact he did stay. She did not want to do this. She was afraid it would put him off the idea of becoming involved in the political machinations of their court, and it would be highly understandable if it did. But she would beg him to her last breath, if necessary, to change his mind. She didn't even know him, but he was strong and unafraid of Grannish, and she desperately needed someone like that. Someone her father might one day come to respect above Grannish. Someone who might listen to her when she explained the things Grannish did to her.

She had no guarantees that Dethan would be that someone, but it was better than doing nothing at all. And she believed with the last shred of her heart that could potentially trust another that he was worth supporting. That he would speak favorably about her.

Foolish girl, she whispered fiercely into her own mind. *A man makes you feel pretty for two seconds of time and you parlay that into a reason to trust?* But as small as the hope was, it was her last hope. She had to exploit the opportunity. It was the only choice left to her.

And so she remained fully dressed, looking fixedly out the window, staring so hard her eyes dried out and then burned when she blinked.

"Memsa," her accented, soft-voiced pagette said, addressing her with the affectionate term her people used to express love and respect. Hanit was from the foreign city of Siccoro, a city far beyond the Syken Desert outside the Hexis walls. She was a sturdy woman in the beginnings of her third decade, at Selinda's guess. Selinda had never asked her pagette how old she was. Hanit was strangely blond—a sort of silvery blond, the coloring of her people—with grey eyes to complement. She was no great beauty, but she was pretty in her own unique way. "Memsa, if you will not come away from the window, may this one bring you something to eat or drink? This one needs to see to memsa's comfort."

"Very well," Selinda relented. "Something to drink, then, Hanit. But you must not let anyone see you. You must make certain no one knows I am still awake." She would have denied her pagette entirely, but she knew that to deny her too long would make the pagette highly agitated and stressed. The woman lived to serve her, to see to her every last whim or need, and when she was thwarted from that it seemed to almost physically pain her. They had grown close very quickly in the full turning since Selinda's former pagette had died. Now Selinda could not imagine her life without her trusted servant.

But Hanit's agitation was rubbing her own nerves raw. She was anxious enough as it was, going back and forth in her mind about what she must do next. She must somehow convince Dethan to stay in spite of the danger it would present to him.

Oh, but why would he? she thought with dismay. Why would he want to willingly entangle himself in a mess she prayed daily to be delivered from? Many thought she was so fortunate, so lucky to be the grandina, living in comfort and wealth in a big fortress at the very hub of the city, able to look down upon them all in safety and security.

Or so they thought. But they did not have to live every day knowing they were promised to Grannish, a man who clearly despised her. Since she could not think of any slights or arguments prior to their engagement that she might have perpetrated against him, she could only assume it was because he did not want to marry her. Or so she had thought at first. Until one day, before she had truly understood who and what he was, she had pulled him aside into the privacy of the grand's council chamber.

"My lord Grannish, I wish to speak with you," she had said hastily, her hands nervously twisting the ends of a long red silken scarf she had been wearing to protect her throat from the chill of the first flush of fall.

"What is it?" he had asked her impatiently once he had checked to make certain none could see or hear them.

"I wanted to make an offer to you that should make you very happy. You see, it is very obvious that you do not like me and that you do not wish to marry me. My father must be pressing you into doing this and I can see how unhappy it has made you. I truly do not wish for you to be unhappy. I am certain you are loath to wake up to this every morning." She reached a shaking hand to touch her veil where it lay over her scar. "I thought that if we went to him together, as a joined force, and convinced him that we would be much happier otherwise, he would have no choice but to release us from the commitment and find other solutions if indeed he seeks to reward us."

"Really? Is that what you think we should do?" he asked archly, one thin brow lifting in abject curiosity. Then his hand came out like a shot, grabbing her around her arm and jerking her forward, against his body. "Yes," he hissed into her shocked face, "it is true I have no desire to wake up to the horrifying visage you bear every morning. In truth the very idea disgusts me to my soul. But as repulsive as you are in the flesh, you are three times more contemptible in your sniveling weakness and your sheer idiocy. You think I want to give up the chance to be grand?" He laughed then, a rolling, overloud sound that echoed off the high ceilings of the chamber. "I have wanted to be grand all my life and now it is here in my grasp." He looked down at his hands, where they were locked around her, and gave her a shake. "I have known all along what it would take, that it meant I would have to marry in order to achieve it. I have worked and slaved, catered to your *father*"— the way he said "father" was an utter sneer—"putting up with his moods and maneuvering him away from his ridiculous ideas, all the while keeping other vipers in their place. Truly, it is an exhausting job." He sighed, as if under the strain of a mighty weight. "And you think I am going to throw it all away because *you* don't want to marry *me*?" He laughed again, this one even more derisive than the first. "As if you have so many options! Even with the opportunity to become grand, your hideousness has put off anyone of decent noble blood. There have been no suitors—not a single one has applied to your father because yes, as you say, they are loath to wake up to your mangled face every morning. I am all you have. So you will shut up and you will be a dutiful wife. I will piss my seed into you and get you with my progeny and try to forgive them for the inferiority of their mother. I will build a dynasty on you and you will take them to breast and see they grow up strong, then I will take them from you before you can warp idiocy into their impressionable little brains. And all the while you will smile and wave to the crowds"— he grabbed her hand at the wrist and waved it, the limp appendage flopping about—"and you will shut up. Maybe if you perform your duties sufficiently I will not kill you once your monthly woman's blood stops and you can no longer bear me children. And if you think," he said, his hands tightening on her until she cried out and almost sank to the ground in her pain, "that you will run and cry to your father and tell him all that I have told you, I will deny everything and I will remind him what a flighty, fanciful thing you are, that you merely mistook something I said. And you know what? He will not even care. Oh, he loves you, that much is true, but he does not respect you any more than I do."

He shoved her away and she went stumbling back, stepping on her long skirt and tumbling to the hard stone floor, skinning both of the palms she put out just in time to protect her face from hitting the stone.

"If I hear one word from your father about this, I promise you, you will not enjoy the consequences. So do yourself a favor and do not even try it."

She had not heeded him then. She had known in her heart that her father did love her, that he would never marry her to such a cruel and odious man if only he could see the truth of it. She had run and told all.

He had laughed.

"Darling girl," he had said, patting her fondly on her cheek. "Surely you are mistaking the matter. I know Grannish well and he is an honest and honorable man. I think that you are afraid of your upcoming nuptials and are beginning to make things up in your mind. Grannish is as polite and even tempered a man as I know."

"Father, please! I am not mistaking anything! Look . . . look at my hands where they were scraped upon the floor from when he pushed me down!"

Her father barely glanced at her hands, but he frowned and she took it as encouragement. "In a few hours' time the bruises on my arms will also be visible. Please, Father, do not make me marry him!"

"Daughter," he said grimly, looking her in the eye, "I trust Grannish with my life and yours. With the lives of all in this kingdom. He has served us very well and deserves to be grand. And you should know . . . there have been no other suitors, nor are there likely to be any. I love you and therefore find you beautiful, but this"—he reached up and stroked a thumb over the ridged scar on her face—"has kept any other decent man away. I'm sorry to have to be truthful to you. No one else has asked for you."

"I don't care," she said, tears in her eyes. "I will serve as granda alone, and when I die Drakin will become grand and his children his heirs."

"Your youngest brother is sickly and will not live beyond his maturing years," her father said grimly. "I have come to face that. If I want my dynasty to continue, I need you to bear children. And before you say it, you know that any child born outside the marriage bed would be constantly called into question."

"Why?" she demanded to know. "It is my body that has our bloodline within it and a child will be born of that body, married or not! In fact, it is more possible to assure a bloodline from a woman than it is from a man! A woman grows the baby of her blood, expels it from her womb, but no one can ever know who the father truly is, marriage or no! Why, it is said that Lord Harkness has fathered none of his children, that all were gotten by the affairs of his wife! And yet they will inherit his titles and his lands." She scoffed. "It's foolish and ridiculous."

"Be that as it may, if you want a respectful life, you will marry and bear your children legitimately. If you do not like Grannish . . . well, you must find a way to like him. He does you a great honor by taking you into his arms and his house. Try to remember that."

"More like it is I who do him the honor," she said acidly. "He wants nothing more than to be grand."

"Well, who wouldn't?" her father asked with a low chuckle. "Everyone wishes to be grand. You cannot hold that against him. Now, give me a hug and a smile. I will talk with Grannish and we will clear the matter up between us."

"No!" she cried, in a sudden panic.

"Well, then what do you want me to do?" he asked, clearly exasperated.

"I . . . I just don't want to marry him," she said quietly. Dejectedly.

"I'll speak with Grannish and have him come to you in my presence and reassure you. Now off with you. Go and do those things you women always do to pass the time. I'll hear no more about this."

And he had sent her away.

He had been true to his word, calling her into the room with himself and Grannish, and Grannish had smiled and simpered, had said all the right reassuring things, but all the while she had looked in his eyes and she had seen the rage boiling just beneath the surface. So she had meekly accepted his words in front of her father.

And she had feared.

Within hours she had been stricken with sickness, her stomach in flux, with painful cramps, nausea, and vomiting. She had been thoroughly sick, sweating violently one moment, then chilled the next. Was it a coincidence, or was it Grannish's retribution? She was convinced it was the latter. She had been sick for three days and it had taken seven more before she had been up to her usual health. She had been poisoned. She was sure of it. And suddenly she saw her brother's illnesses in a whole new light. What if Grannish was poisoning her baby brother in an effort to make certain she was the only heir? What if the illnesses and accidents that had taken the lives of her older siblings had not been accidents? Jorry had been heir first and promised from birth to a beautiful and sweet-natured young woman named Glenna. But Jorry had died while swimming, a strong swimmer somehow drowning in a shallow pool. It was believed he had hit his head on a rock, rendering him unconscious in the water. But what if the strike on his head had been deliberate?

And then Kyna, who became heir after Jorry had died. A strong boy suddenly stricken with illness, taken from the world in less than two days in a vicious, suffering form of death.

Leaving her as the next heir. The first female in line for the throne. The first access to grand available to Grannish. But that did not explain her younger sisters' deaths by plague. If she so repulsed him, he could easily have had her murdered as well and taken one of her younger sisters to bride. Indeed Arra had been lauded as a great beauty and had been much sought after in spite of her young age. But that beauty had withered and died.

Or maybe Grannish had planned on Selinda's death but had been waiting until it would not look so obvious on the heels of Kyna's death . . . only the plague had taken her sisters naturally, thwarting that possibility.

She would never know the truth unless somehow she got him to confess it to her. Even so, he was perverse enough to admit to it freely, then watch her flail about trying to get her father to listen to her, all the while stroking her father into believing her emotional or even mad. Gods above, perhaps that was his eventual goal. To make everyone think her mad. Selinda shuddered at the thought, knowing that rich or poor, lowborn or highborn, those with madness found true equality in treatment, and it was not a pretty life to lead. Indeed she would wish herself penniless and worse disfigured before she would wish herself to be proved mad. The asylum . . . it was outside of the city walls, the belief being that madness was contagious. Outside the walls, the asylum was largely undefended. The Redoe sacked it regularly, doing what they willed with the inhabitants and their keepers. And she had heard stories . . . such horrible stories . . .

Her thoughts had brought her breathing to panicked levels, her fists clenching so hard that her nails were digging into the soft flesh of her palms. She licked the sweat off her upper lip and stared all the harder out the window. Soon. He would come back soon. He *must* come back.

Oh my beloved goddess, please let him come back. I ask you for so little, and even this is in relation to the prayers I most frequently send up to you. He is your instrument to aid me. I know it. I see it! I swear to you I will not let this gift go to waste. I will—

Her prayer froze in her head as a body appeared in the light of the bailey. He walked in, his gait off center and almost . . . staggering. Drunk, she thought bitterly. He had taken some of his gold and gone off to carouse. She should not be shocked; indeed she was not shocked. She knew of men and their fallibility. But it made no difference to her. He had earned his celebrations tonight. She would have thrown a party for him herself had she been able to.

Selinda hastened to her feet, stumbling when she realized her legs had cramped up from sitting so long in one position. She shrugged off her shawl, bent to look quickly into a mirror, and made certain to arrange her hair so it fell over the left side of her face. Then, feet bare upon the cold stone, she flew out of her rooms and down the back stairwells. She was cautious enough not to be seen, knowing Grannish had spies around every corner, but she had to risk this . . . or the opportunity would be lost. He might leave if she didn't do something, and she desperately wanted . . . no, *needed* him to stay.

She headed through the back corridors toward the rooms she knew he'd been given. She was just around the corner from it when she saw a light coming in her direction. She ducked into the thick arch of another doorway, squeezing herself into the shadow and cover it provided her. He was wearing a hooded cloak and being led by a page boy.

"Do you need any other assistance, sor?" the boy asked.

"No," came the rough reply. His voice sounded more harsh than it did drunk, she thought. His words were not slurred but were hoarse. "Go," he commanded of the boy. She could not see him in the shadows of his cloak, but she could hear the dismissal in his voice. As could the page no doubt because he departed quickly after that, leaving him the lantern he'd used to provide light along the way. Dethan then moved into his rooms and shut the door behind him. Selinda silently crept up to the door.

Dethan barely managed to place the lantern on the rickety little table the room provided before stumbling toward the bed. He should have waited longer, he told himself. Should have let himself heal more. Instead he had crept into town, stolen a cloak, and headed back to the fortress, driven by one thing and one thing only: the idea of a bed. He had not known the comfort of a bed in hundreds of years. Or at least it had felt like hundreds of years. He still did not know how long he had lain chained in torment. He had already seen many strange new things in the world. Building materials alone in the finer parts of town, this fortress included, set things apart. Not all the stone was the harsh gray of unmatched rock hewn from the ground, but there were large matching slabs of it in wondrous colors polished and smooth. There was also the carriage the grandina had traveled in. And the finely tooled tack on the horses.

But none of that mattered to him right then. All he cared about was that the bed was sturdy. Whatever the comfort level, it would be more than he'd had before.

That was when he heard it. The creak of the door on its hinges. Another difference. In his day hinging had been with leather. These were metal and squeaked noisily. He waited until the door shut, pretending he had not heard it. He waited until the person came closer, then, just when the bastard reached out to attack him, he whirled about, grabbed the outstretched arm, and swiftly moved to snap the assailant's arm in two at the long bone by yanking it hard in a lever of counterforce and the drive of his elbow.

But at the very last instant before his elbow struck down he found himself looking into frightened eyes of stunning teal. Shocked, he stopped himself from further injuring her. As it was, he may have already dislocated her shoulder. He placed a hand on her breastbone and shoved her away from him. She stumbled back, tripping on the hem of her gown, the sound of the fabric tearing filling the room as she struggled to regain her balance.

"What are doing you here?" he demanded roughly of her. "Do you realize I could have ripped your arm off?" He found himself checking to be sure she hadn't had a weapon after all. She had none that he could see.

"I'm sorry, but I needed to talk with you," she said in earnest. "I did not mean to startle you, but I was afraid to knock and someone was coming down the hall. I could not afford to be seen."

"Yes, you would not wish to be seen with one such as me," he said bitterly.

"It is not my honor I am worried about. Although I

am expected to be chaste until my wedding day, I promise you I do not care about that. In fac—"

"Chaste," he said incredulously. "A woman is expected to be chaste until she is wed?" He scoffed. "I have never heard anything so ridiculous in my life. What has chastity to do with honor? Either you are true or you are not. That is where your honor will lie once you are wed. As for chastity, why would you not want to know if your lover can perform to your satisfaction? You cannot know this unless you try him out to begin with. To be ignorant of that until you are wed and saddled with the man is ludicrous."

"It does not matter. Women rarely have the choice of the man they are going to marry anyway. Highborn women at least. Sometimes I think it might be better to be poor and without a title. Then one might choose freely about . . . many things."

"You only say that because you have never been poor," he said in a rumble of irritation. "I think the mud farmers of your city would wish otherwise if it meant constant food in their mouths and fine clothes on their backs."

"Listen to me, I did not come here to argue the merits of being wealthy," she said with exasperation. "And will you please pull back your hood? I cannot see you!"

Before Dethan could stop her, before he even knew what she was doing, she reached up and shoved back his hood. All it took was one look at him and she released a horrified gasp. She stumbled back, catching herself on the rickety table.

"My gods! What happened to you?"

And that was as long as her horror lasted. The next instant she was near him again, her lithe body and full skirts pressing against him and causing him pain, but at the same time they felt so good that he bit back the sound of agony brewing behind his lips. Her delicate fingers flew near his face, as though she would touch him; yet knowing she would hurt him if she did so, she kept an inch of distance between her fingers and his face.

"By the queen goddess, you must be in agony!" she cried on a fierce whisper. "Come, you must sit." She tugged at his cloak, urging him toward the bed, and he found he had little choice but to obey her. He had longed for that bed for hours. Had dreamed of it while his body burned over and over again. Had dreamed of her in it with him. But that had been a thought brought on by the madness of pain. Brought on because he had needed anything to keep him from thinking about how badly it hurt.

"This is nothing," he told her, his voice low and rough. His throat still burned from the fire. And it *was* nothing. Nothing compared to how it had looked an hour ago.

"Sit!" she commanded in her grandina tone of voice, the one with which she was denied nothing by anyone. He obeyed her once more and sat down on the bed. "Stay here. Take off that cloak. The roughness of it must be killing you."

She reached out and shoved the cloak from his shoulders, exposing the full horror of his burn-riddled body. His very naked body. He could have stolen clothes, he supposed, but the idea of putting them on was just one pain too many.

"Oh. Well . . . never mind," she said, her fair cheeks flushing in the lamplight as her eyes stumbled over his dormant cock. Dormant because it was barely regenerated from being burned to near ashes. Otherwise, just the touch of her pretty blue eyes on him might have given him temptation to rise and greet her. Funny, that thought. It was as though becoming erect was second nature . . . and it was not. Not any longer. He had not reacted in the ways of a man for much longer than he had been alive originally. He had been thirty summers when he had become immortal and had first been thrust into the hells. He must have been down there nearly ten times that long.

"I'll be right back," she said softly to him. "Do not move from this spot. Do you understand me?"

Her tone made a smile twitch upon his lips. "Yes, madam. I am not a child. I can follow a simple command."

"Good. I will have many more commands of you before the night is through, so it is good you are well versed in heeding them."

Selinda stepped back from him and with great reluctance turned to the door. She opened it and passed through with stealth, leaving the light behind and using only the lamplight from the kerosene lamps that burned low in the hallway alcoves every thirty feet or so. It made for slow going, but the shadows helped her. She hurried to her rooms first and found Hanit within. Hanit startled at her entrance.

"My goodness, your ladyship gave me a fright!" the older woman said, fanning her cherubic face with her hands.

"Never mind that. I need your help. I need you to run to the kitchen and fetch these things." The grandina whipped a piece of finely milled stationery from the short shack of it on her desk, wetted her pen, and began to scrawl in a florid script the things she wanted. "Do not let anyone see you if it can be avoided, and under no circumstance is anyone to stop you. If you are challenged, just say these items are for me. That I am not feeling well. Gather these things, then take them to Sor Dethan's chambers. I will meet you there."

"Your ladyship!" Hanit gasped. "You cannot go into a man's rooms unchaperoned! It is not seemly for you to be alone with him. Your honor will be called into question."

"Good," Selinda muttered. "Maybe if it is Grannish will no longer want me." But even as she said it, she knew it wasn't true. He would merely find a way to punish her for the infraction. "Go! And hurry!" she said to Hanit, shooing her out of the room. Then she rummaged in her closet of fine linens and pulled out two voluminous underskirts, the white fabric soft and limp, without starch to make it straight and crisp. They were among her older underskirts and she scarcely wore them any longer, so they would hardly be missed.

She hurriedly rolled them into a fluffy, rustling ball and then, grabbing a pair of scissors at the last minute, she slipped back into the hallway. Her heart was pounding more than ever, the bundle of white she held negating any effect the shadows might provide since they practically glowed in the dark. But she somehow made it into Dethan's chambers without being seen. She turned and found that he had not moved so much as an inch, as directed. She dropped the underskirts on the bed and immediately went to work cutting them up into long strips.

"What is that for?" he asked.

"I should think that would be clear. Bandages," she said at the shake of his head.

"That isn't necessary," he told her.

"It is," she argued. "If you leave the burns open, you are bidding infection to enter them."

"They will heal. Very soon. I'll not get an infection."

"Not if I can help it," she said. "I have to go to the common bath down the hall for some water," she said, picking up the chipped porcelain pitcher from a table in the room.

She did not appear to want Dethan's input, because she was gone a second later. She was back in a flash and came straight to his side. She stopped then, all her energy seeming to still for a long moment as she folded her arms beneath her breasts and drummed her fingers against her arm. She was thrumming with impatience, he realized. Waiting for something, though he knew not what.

The answer came a minute later when there was a light scratching at the door. Selinda hastened to let in a slightly plump woman, who appeared to be about a decade older than the grandina. Still in her young years, if not in her youth. It made him realize just how young the grandina really was. No more than twenty summers, he reckoned.

"Over here, Hanit," the grandina beckoned to her.

"No!" he protested, pulling away as if to hide, but there was nowhere for him to go. He was trapped by a pair of women. The truth was the more exposed he was in this state, the more questions there would be later on when he healed. He didn't exactly know how long it would take for him to completely heal—he had never gotten that far before being burned all over again. It was possible he could heal completely before next sunset. There was no way for him to know. This day would be the first day he would have a chance to learn.

"I trust Hanit completely," the grandina said, making sure his eyes met hers as she spoke. "And believe me when I say there are very few who can make that claim of me. Now, you must trust me. Let me help you. And, to be fair, know that I will be seeking your help in return."

That surprised him. Usually people were not so up front about ulterior motives. Especially women, in his experience. They tended to wheedle and manipulate, working the world around them like soft clay. But not this one. No. Everything he had seen of her thus far had been direct and, he sensed, honest.

"And if I told you I do not need your help?" he asked her.

She briefly looked down, watching her own hands as she set out a basin and began to pour liquid into it from a variety of flasks the serving woman had brought with her.

"I would help you anyway. I will ask your help, but it does not follow that you are beholden to me. You have as much right to say no as any man has."

There was a tone in her voice . . . not bitterness, but more like . . . resignation. She was resigned to the fact that the men she knew had power over her. But she was not defeated, he thought. She wanted his help. If she were defeated, she wouldn't have even bothered to ask.

He relaxed as much as his pained body allowed and let her work on him. She tore hunks of white linen from what he assumed was her own clothing, saturated each piece, and then carefully began to wrap up his limbs in the fabric. The first touched him and he hissed in pain as it stung him, but quickly after that his burns began to feel cooler, then slightly numb.

"The juice of the funi root has anesthetic qualities. It will ease your pain," she explained to him.

She bent to wrap his left leg and her hair slid forward off her shoulder. It was a thick black snake that coiled in a single large curl at its end. It shone in the lantern light, full of deep, rich darkness and maybe even the faintest touch of brown. It was scented. He could smell the sweet sensuality of it and he racked his brain trying to figure out what the scent was, but he had to concede it was like nothing he could remember. Then again, it had been so long since he had smelled anything other than fire and burning flesh, how was he to even know?

"I am not worth your efforts," he found himself telling her.

"It is fortunate for you that I disagree," she said,

shifting to begin on his other leg. She touched him high on his inner thigh, a signal to get him to lift his leg so she could wrap it. It felt strange to have her touch him there. To have her touch him anywhere, really, but there it was so close to something almost . . . sexual. Surely only from his perspective, but he could not help himself. The craving that washed over him so suddenly took his breath away far more thoroughly than the pain he'd been feeling. *What is this?* he asked himself. *I am not a man. Not as defines any free man. So I cannot allow for any feelings of . . . any feelings at all, never mind those of a sexual nature. And it is clear she has no purposeful intention of engendering them.*

"Does that hurt?" she asked him.

"No," he replied. *Not at all.* "You have helped me," he said as she straightened and began to smooth wet fabric over his back. He was nearly mummified at that point. "Now, tell me what I might do for you."

"I . . ." She hesitated distinctly. "After I do your back you will lie down and rest. My demands can be made after you are better. Thank you, Hanit. You may go to bed now."

"But . . . your ladyship, it's not—"

"Seemly. Yes, yes," she said with exasperation. "Honestly, Hanit, the man can barely move from pain, not to mention how we've bound him up. I hardly think my honor is under any threat. It is within my duties as mistress of this household to see to the health and wellbeing of all those under this roof, and that is what I will be doing tonight. Is there anything wrong with that?"

It was clear by her tone that there was to be no argument even if Hanit could come up with one. The grandina had spoken and that was the end of it.

"Of course, grand lady. But you will need help undressing," she pointed out. "So I will stay awake and wait for you."

And so Hanit had spoken. She would not allow the grandina to spend the entire night with him even if to do it she had to make Selinda feel guilty for keeping her awake.

"Very well," her ladyship relented. "I will be up shortly."

"Of course. Fare well, Sor Dethan," she said. Then she glided out of the room as quietly as she had entered, moving with surprising stealth for someone so obviously on good terms with good foods.

Left alone, Selinda helped him to lie down and then wet the remainder of the fabric and slowly laid it over his chest. She gently smoothed the white linen over the large pectoral muscle on the right side of his chest. She pulled her bottom lip between her teeth, worrying at it a little as she tried to decide what to do next. Any plans she'd had regarding him had just been dashed to the ground and broken into bits. In this shape, what good could he possibly do her? But then again . . . she only needed him for his mind. His body may not be sound, but it was his intelligence and his cunning she needed most, and his words at dinner tonight had proven him to have an abundance of both. But like this, how could she expect him to protect himself against the machinations of an animal like Grannish?

"Go on. Say it. Tell me what you need," he said.

She met his eyes with surprise. Then she sat back with a sigh. "It's just that . . . I had very much hoped . . . But of course it is foolish to put your hopes in one place. And for that place to be a stranger as well . . . It makes me a very foolhardy woman."

"Probably," he agreed. "But let us begin to look at the problem before we assume its conclusion. You are skipping steps."

"Very well. My father is under the sway of an evil, odious man and I need someone to make him see his judgment in this matter is not sound." Dethan watched her deflate a little with another sigh. "He is not a stupid man, my father. And he is not a bad one. He is merely a blind one." She looked at him then, earnestness in her eyes. "But if you help us to win this war, it will be a chink in the wall of his perceived perfection."

"I take it we are talking of Grannish. Or perhaps the general?"

She scoffed. "The general is merely one of Grannish's many well-placed lackeys. Grannish has his hooks dug deeply and all around. Never trust anyone. Never speak in public places of things you do not wish him to hear because it will be reported to him."

"And this is why you give your trust so sparingly."

She couldn't seem to help herself from wringing her hands together, Dethan noticed. She was at a very high point of anxiety. He could smell the fear on her. And the determination.

"Yes. You must see . . . Grannish is running our city into the ground. It begins with the Redoe, but it doesn't end with them. The siege is starting to take its toll. The poor are beginning to starve and the wealthy are hoarding whatever they can. They stock up all they can before the Redoe come back in the summers. Every year the farmers outside the walls plant their fields and every year the Redoe make off with about half the produce. It's gotten so that we are feeding them more than we are feeding ourselves. Please, I'm begging you to stay. Help us stand against the Redoe. Help us be rid of them once and for all and show my father that Grannish is not an expert in everything. True, Grannish has insulated himself and will let the general take more than enough of the fall for it, but the general was appointed by Grannish, and if we prove it a crucial poor decision . . ." She trailed off, her eyes searching his face frantically for signs he would agree with her and help her.

"And what do I get in return?" he asked.

Her pretty eyes widened slightly. "My f-father will pay you gold."

"Your father has already offered that to me for routing the Redoe. You are asking for something else entirely."

"I-I was hoping my kindness tonight and my loyalty into the future would be—"

"I told you I did not need, nor did I request, your assistance tonight. It does not follow that it is not appreciated, however. I am far more comfortable and it has made me grateful for the reprieve from the pain. But that does not parlay into a reason for sticking my neck out. And I *will* be sticking my neck out. Grannish isn't the sort to sit by and let the house he has so carefully constructed fall down around his ears. He will retaliate. But you already know that, don't you? You experience it firsthand every day."

Again that widening of her eyes. "Yes, it is true. All of it," she confessed quickly. "And more. It will be very dangerous, and I will not lie to you about that." Which impressed him. She could have struggled to pretty the whole thing up in order to make things more appealing to him, but she did not. Again that honesty. A rare trait. One that could and probably did make her a target. She swallowed then and rose to her feet. She stood almost regally, ever the grandina, save for the fact that she was trembling and her eyes were bright with unshed, frustrated tears. "I have nothing to give you. What do you want from me? Tell me and it is yours."

He was quiet for a long minute.

"You will warm my bed for as long as I am here."

"*What?*"

What? he asked himself in shock. *Where in the eight hells had that come from?*

"Those are my terms," he said, digging the hole even deeper with impetus. But the more he spoke, the more the idea developed in his brain. "You will sleep at my side every night."

"Sleep? Only . . . sleep?"

"No. Not only." Dethan knew this was the very last thing he should be doing. He had an agenda to satisfy and bedding the grandina of Hexis was not chief among his tasks.

Then again . . . what was gold when there might be a city to be had? Perhaps the first city to be conquered should be Hexis. If he could find a way to rule over Hexis, not only would he be giving a city to Weysa, he would be taking one away from Xaxis. It would be a dual blow to the enemies of Weysa's faction, making her stronger and them weaker. Yes. If he could rout Grannish and put himself in his stead, put the heir of the city in his bed and in his hands, then he could win the city without raising an army. Then it could serve as a base of operations as he defeated others . . . like the Redoe. Two peoples to be converted right within his grasp. All he need do was negotiate the pitfalls of a court and government completely controlled by Lord Grannish.

And it would start with the woman standing before him.

"What you truly want, besides what you have already mentioned, is an escape from your impending marriage to Grannish. Is that not correct?"

She was shaking hard, her eyes brimming with unshed tears. She gripped her hands within each other so hard the skin had gone white with interrupted circulation.

"That does not mean I will shame myself or my father by . . . by becoming a kickskirt to the type of man who would ask such a thing from an innocent woman!"

"See now, again you are speaking as though sex with a man is something you should be ashamed of. This is an attitude I disagree with. I will have you test me as a lover. I will have you certain that it is I you want in your bed. I of course will also be judging you. You will be my reward in this endeavor, as valuable as any sack of gold. With you comes a great city and all its wealth and forces."

"A-and if I do not please you? Will you not take me anyway? Grannish says he will force himself to tolerate my deformities in order to get what he wants. Would you not do the same?"

"I want a wife. A lover and a helpmate. A ruler and a caregiver. If you cannot give me these things, then there are other ways of seizing this city that will not include saddling myself with an incompatible wife. But it will not come to that, I think. I will destroy Grannish for you utterly, leaving you free to marry whomever you choose, and should I please you, you will choose me."

Shock finally stilled her shaking body as she absorbed the full impact of what he was saying. "You mean . . . you don't wish to treat me dishonorably? You . . . you want to *wed* me?"

"I want to wed the heir to this kingdom. I will not romanticize it for you. This is a transaction. I will take Grannish's place in this house and this city. It will satisfy both our needs."

"But I thought you wanted to leave," she whispered.

He smiled gently. "I have been tempted to do otherwise," he said to her. "I will ask only two things of you: your utter loyalty to me and that you will be true. Any children you birth will be mine and no one else's. I will not tolerate being made a cuckold."

"You . . ." Selinda was absolutely floored. She had never thought something like this would come of her visit with him. Her desperation was profound and she would do anything . . . anything to spare her father, her city, and herself from Grannish. There was nothing she would not do. But . . . here was a wild card. She knew nothing about him. How was she to know if he was any better than Grannish? She could literally be getting into bed with an even worse sort of tyrant.

If that was possible. No, she told herself, Grannish was the worst. There was no conceiving anything more vile. And she knew he was capable of much more. Once he was wed to her . . . the only thing holding him back would be her father's life.

Goddesses above, *no*! Oh, how easily Grannish had poisoned her; it would be just as easy for him to do the same to her father!

"If he feels things are slipping out of his grasp, then he will lash out," she whispered to him, hearing the fear in her own voice. "My father and I are protected because right now he needs us, but my young brother a-and most of all *you* will be in the gravest of danger. I already suspect him of—"

"Killing off your older siblings in order to manipulate his way onto the throne."

She blinked, staring at him. "How did you know that? You're a stranger. You said yourself that you know nothing of our ways and politics . . ."

"Sometimes," he said in the quietest but strongest of tones, "an outsider can see things more clearly than those who are in the mix."

She was still for a very long minute, turning his proposal over in her mind. Then she absently lifted her hand to the burn on the line of her jaw. She looked over his burned and mummified body. "How can you accomplish any of this in the state you are in?"

"You will simply have to invest trust in me when I tell you I will be more than able. But think on it. Go to Hanit. When we come face-to-face in the morning, you will see what you need to in order to have more faith in me. Me *and* the goddess I worship. She will bring you the solution you need in the form of this man before you. It is up to you to accept Weysa's gift."

"Weysa? The goddess of war," she said. Then she nodded. "I will think on it and provide you with an answer in the morning."

With that, she moved away from the bed and toward the door. Before opening it, she turned back to him and said, "I'm not sure if you are my salvation or my destruction, Sor Dethan. But I am sure you are one or the other and you are about to change my life. I can only pray it will be for the better."

"If you pray, pray to Weysa. You will need her strength and skill to help you through what is to come."

"Of course you would say that. You are a warrior." She nodded to him. "You pray to your god and I will pray to mine. With two such resources, perhaps we will find what we need."

She slipped through the doorway, shutting the door in total silence in her wake.

Dethan remained there for a while, looking at the door in the flickering lantern light. Then he exhaled a sigh and let his body sink into relaxation. As he lay there, knowing the fire was not going to come for him for another whole day, he felt tears of relief pricking at his eyes. It didn't matter that he was still in a significant amount of pain. It was nothing compared to the worst he had suffered. This was pure luxury and he dared, for just a moment, to sink into it.

And for the first time in an untold number of ages, he knew the peace and beauty of sleep.

CHAPTER
EIGHT

Selinda was feeling no effects of a largely sleepless night. Her adrenaline and anxiety were at an all time high. She was hurrying down to the morning meal, her hands locked in laced fingers, palms pressed against each other.

He would expect her answer this morning. She was going to have to choose between certain evil and uncertain possibilities. To an outsider it might have seemed an easy choice; it was anything but. She had been suffering under Grannish for so long with no one to hear her cries and protests . . . If she got into bed with this warrior, literally and figuratively, what danger would she be beckoning in and who would there be to hear her cry for help? No one heard her now. She was so utterly alone. She had been ever since her elder brothers had died. They had listened to her. When they were alive Grannish had not been cruel to her. He had played the game well, seeming even tempered and charming. What if the even temper she saw in Sor Dethan was just another cover over pure evil?

No. Even when he had been at his kindest she had always known something was off about Grannish. She had sensed it. The sisters at the temple said it was her knowing showing itself, that her knowing was very strong. But they had also said she would wield great power one day. And while the sisters of Kitari seemed to hold little power in their lone temple in the roughest part of the city, some considered them to have great powers. Indeed Selinda had seen them do some amazing things in the name of their queenly goddess. But all the mems in all the various temples seemed to have their own special kinds of gifts.

But the only power Selinda would ever have would be the power of her throne, and right now, as things stood, that meant very little. She was being bartered like a captive slave with no regard for the conditions she was being sold into. All the terms had been negotiated and never once had anyone cared enough to ask her what she wanted.

Selinda took a deep breath, trying to cool the emotions her thoughts were churning up. If she struck this bargain with Dethan, she would regain her power over herself and her crown. At least that was what she hoped. She could simply be throwing herself into the same situation only to find herself still a slave but to a new master.

No. No matter how this unraveled, she was never going to find herself in a position of power. She was still merely a pawn, something for Dethan to use to get what he now wanted. But wasn't that the whole point of her going to him in the first place? How could she fault him for doing what she was asking him to do? Who could fault him for wanting the power and position marrying her would offer up to him? She would take it for herself if she could manage it.

She should feign illness, she thought in a sudden panic as she neared the doorway leading into the dining chamber. Go back to her rooms and sleep her life away, freeing herself of all choices and potential pain.

No. She would not be ignorant and weak. She had already done enough of that. Today she was taking charge of her life, for better or for worse. And even if she did choose Dethan, there was no possible way he could be physically up to the challenge. He would be lucky if he could even make it down for the morning meal.

The thought froze in the center of her mind as she stepped into the room and saw him, standing at least a full head over everyone else in the room. He was . . .

Healed. Almost completely. There were still scarred burns on his neck and arms similar to the ones from when she had first met him, but there was nothing else. Nothing to show that last night he had been burned nearly to the bone in some places. It was as though the injuries had never happened at all.

He looked up abruptly, almost as though he had sensed her entering the room. She found herself suddenly afraid that he had the ability to do exactly that. If he had the power to heal in such a way, who knew what other powers he possessed?

His eyes met hers and he arrested her gaze, making her feel like they were alone in spite of the crowd of people between them. He had been standing apart from everyone, leaning back against a wall, looking so dark, silent, and beyond powerful. He had somehow procured a new set of clothes for himself and he looked dominant in the breeches and linen shirt he wore. Over the shirt he wore a finely tooled leather vest.

Considering his station, he should be the least powerful person in the room, yet he commanded it like a warrior chieftain. As he came toward her, her heart hammered in her chest with the power of the strongest of blacksmiths, banging against her ribs so hard she wondered why everyone couldn't see it. Couldn't hear it. He came up to her and stood before her. He said nothing, merely looked down into her eyes with expectation on his face.

She swallowed, trying to think about what she should say first to him. He looked at her with this expression like he knew what she was seeing was going to change everything, wipe away her doubts.

And it did, she realized. Not all of them, but the ones about whether or not he was the right choice . . . the strongest choice. A man made of such breathtaking magic was a man she wanted on her side. It was an advantage against Grannish she could never have dreamed of.

She opened her mouth and only one word came out. "Yes."

He gave her a little smile, reached to pick up her hand, and placed it on his arm as he turned to lead her into the room.

"My bed. Tonight and every night."

"Why?" she asked him in a nervous whisper. "In the end I have no choice but to marry you. There is no need for me to, as you say, test you out to find out if you are a sufficient lover."

"I will make you a contract," he said, one of those almost grins toying at his lips. "If you find me insufficient as a lover, then you may refuse my suit for your hand."

She stopped and stared up at him incredulously. "You would do that? What will keep me from denying you your prize at the end if all this succeeds?"

"Because I will know if you are enjoying yourself enough to fulfill our bargain."

His words made a hot flush sweep across her cheeks and face. She couldn't meet his eyes again.

"Besides, being in my bed serves a dual purpose. From what you say, Grannish is expecting a chaste bride. If you are no longer chaste, if there is a possibility that you are about to bear a bastard heir to the throne, it will ruin all his plans far more soundly than anything else I might do." At her horrified gasp he chuckled. "But rest assured, I have plans far more overt than getting you with child. Let us consider that my secondary plan. My main efforts won't take as long in any event, and from what you have told me, it would not be above Grannish to find a way to expel the child from your body or kill it once it's born. And since it will be my child, I am wholly against the idea."

Selinda didn't know what to say. He was right, and yet it was all so wrong. What was she doing? This was utter lunacy!

And yet she knew his ideas were very sound. If these were only his secondary plans, she wondered what his main tactics were going to be.

He turned, cleared his throat, and said, "The grandina has arrived." He did not shout it—he did not need to—and yet everyone in the room heard him and fell into respectful silence. He led her to the head of the table, and immediately the crowd broke apart and headed to their chairs.

Oh, how nice it would be, she thought, to have such power of mere spirit. The ability to command respect without titles or position to back you up. Her power was just a shell. She was powerful over most of her people, and yet powerless where it counted most. Powerless to save her family, powerless to make her father see, powerless to command her own life and do with it what she would.

But none of that disturbed her more than the idea of walking willingly down the stairs from her rooms tonight and into his chambers.

No. She could not risk that long course night after night. She would be seen. It would be reported. And as much as he might like the idea of Grannish hearing about it, she did not. If Grannish thought he was losing his power over her, he would not hesitate to gain it back by any means necessary. She had no wish to be ill again or, worse, to die. She would have to be careful never to take any food in her chambers. She would have to be satisfied with these common meals, where it would be impossible for her to be poisoned without risking poisoning the entire table. Or so she hoped. She did not put it past Grannish to kill others in his quest to get to her.

She barely paid attention as she was led to her seat. Her father entered the room moments later and everyone sat down, Dethan at her right elbow and Grannish boring holes into her from across the table. Gwynn was in her seat to Selinda's left, a point that had irritated her a great deal when it had first happened. She should have headed the table with her father; instead, his mistress was given a position above her. Yet another way she was made certain of the strength of her father's respect for her, she thought bitterly.

She caught herself in the thought. No! Her father was being misled and manipulated. By Grannish on the one side and Gwynn on the other. She should not be angry with him for trusting the wrong people.

"Your most honorable, I have reconsidered your offer," Dethan said baldly after their first course was served. "I will help you with the Redoe. It is in my best interests because I cannot leave without it and because I can always use the gold. Provided the sum is correct."

"And what sum would you ask of me?" the grand asked. "We are a small city and our coffers suffer from the Redoe."

"Are you withdrawing your offer, then?" Dethan asked. And Selinda knew a moment of sheer panic. No. That could not happen!

"Father, I would gladly give up half my personal jewels if it will help us to be free of the Redoe. They can easily be replaced once the city is thriving again."

"Nonsense," the grand said with a chuckle. "You see my daughter, Sor Dethan? She always jumps in with both feet before thinking of the consequences. It is why she could never be grand in her own standing. She reacts too emotionally."

"Better that than with no emotional sensitivity at all," Dethan argued. Her father may not have been aware of it, but that was a dig at him. She was sure of it. She frowned at Dethan, but he wasn't looking at her. She suspected he wouldn't much care even if he was.

"True," the grand agreed. "Very well. Ten thousand gold pieces," the grand said magnanimously. The sum was tidy and it elicited murmurs of surprise up and down the table.

"A large sum for such a poor city," Dethan said. It was another dig, Selinda thought. But why should he care if he was getting what he wanted. The gold should have been enough for him. And yet she sensed that his respect for her father was very low indeed and she didn't know how to feel about that. She prayed she had not released a viper in her father's house. Then again, she thought as she looked over at Grannish, there was already a viper at her father's neck, poised to strike at any moment.

"You will be worth your weight in gold if you can achieve what we have been trying to do for nearly five decades. Before then the Redoe were just raiders who came in occasionally and stole from the outlying farms. Now they are two thousand strong and organized like we have never seen before."

"What else do you know about them?" Dethan asked.

"I'm afraid that's all we know," the grand said.

"Have you no intelligence? None at all?" This remark Dethan aimed down the table, toward the general.

"It's not as though a spy would blend in," Firru snapped.

"The Redoe are red-skinned," Selinda whispered to Dethan.

Dethan smiled internally. It pleased him that she wasn't willing to just sit aside and dry her tears while he took over and fixed the mess of her life. He had not deemed her to be so weak from the ways he had seen her stand up to Grannish in public, all the while knowing she would pay for it later. That reminded him. Tonight he would have to remember to ask her just how far Grannish had gone against her. He suspected he'd made more than a little impression; otherwise, why would Selinda have sought him out?

"And it did not occur to you to find a spy of their coloring?" Dethan asked.

The general sputtered, "You know nothing of what you speak! The Redoe are not to be trusted. Not a single one of them! They would simply hand us false information and it would be a waste of our time!"

"Then I see where I am to start," Dethan said, turning his back on the general. "I will begin immediately. If all goes well, I should have the problem resolved by turntide."

"Turntide!" the general spluttered, his face turning a mottled red. "Sor, I but live for the time! Then my liege will see what a liar and a deceiver you are! What say you, your most honorable?" General Firru said to the grand. "The Redoe routed by turntide or this . . . this *liar* thrown into the dungeons by turntide!"

"Sor Dethan, turntide is only sixty or so sunsets away."

"I am aware of that," Dethan said with a respectful nod. "These are *your* conditions, your most honorable? Because I face them without any fear if they are."

The grand fiddled with his fork for a long minute as the table awaited his words in near total silence. Everyone had ceased to eat.

"Very well. The Redoe routed by turntide or you will reside in my dungeons until I say otherwise. I do hope you know what you are doing, Sor Dethan, because I would hate to see you in the cold, dark belly of this fortress."

"Believe me, your most honorable," Dethan said, "I have been in far worse places."

"Very well, then. And since you will be working hand in hand with General Firru, you will have the same benefits afforded to him. Your chambers will be moved to the main level of the fortress. You will be given a page of your own."

"Of my choosing," Dethan said quickly. "And I would have you leave General Firru to the city watch and me to my own troops. It will work better, since we have such differing opinions."

"As you like. Although Grannish is much better versed in the workings of this castle and the day-to-day abilities of its staff. You might do well to ask him for a suggestion as to a page."

"Thank you, but I think not," he said, the smile he shot the jenden acidic. "I have someone else in mind and I wouldn't want to put any undue strain on the household by depriving it of a regular servant."

The grand accepted his answer, completely oblivious to the undertones going on across the table. Or at least it seemed as though he were. Perhaps he was choosing to act ignorant. Either that, and he was as sly as a fox for doing so, or he was truly as blind as his daughter had said he was.

"Very well. So tell me how you plan to tackle this matter."

"If you would like to know, I will be happy to tell you so . . . in private and with your promise not to speak of it with anyone else. The success of my plan hinges on secrecy. I do not trust others when it comes to matters of war, and neither should you." Dethan dulled any sting that might be perceived by his words with a lazy smile.

"Too right," the grand said after a moment of deciding exactly how he should take the idea of a total stranger of low station telling him what to do. If he had been worth the throne he sat on, he would have taken umbrage, would have at least questioned Dethan. But he did not. He did what Dethan believed was an all too common habit for the grand. He accepted the word of another at face value and left it at that. And this before Dethan had even done anything to prove himself. Dethan's hand closed into a fist on his thigh. This was why the man's daughter had been driven to all but sell herself to a total stranger, thinking her lot could not possibly get any worse. Fortunately for Dethan she didn't really see that things could *always* get worse. In fact, he was rather an expert in worse.

If he had any say in the matter, he would see that she experienced nothing worse than she already had.

No. Wait. He could make no such promises. If anything, his experiences had taught him that he was not in control of fate, his or anyone else's. Only the gods could truly do that. The gods had the final say in all things . . . and the gods were not known for championing mere mortals. They were better known for punishing them. But there were rewards too, weren't there? There were stories of great people, mortals, who fought through great ordeals and were then rewarded by the gods. It was these stories, however, that had led him to his folly. He had believed that by following in the footsteps of another great mortal he would deserve the same great reward. But while the gods had been impressed by the first mortal to find the youthful waters, they had taken Dethan and his brothers' actions as an assault. A raping of their goodwill and power. And they had been right to punish the men for their hubris.

But did it have to be for so long and in such a way?

Yes. It did, he realized. Even now, he was fighting the temptation to do the wrong thing, to let himself be distracted from his course. He could not lose sight of his goal. He must win cities for Weysa. To give her power meant an opportunity for her to achieve her ends. And maybe . . .

He closed his eyes and forced away thoughts of his brothers. His motives needed to be pure and concise. He could not wallow in undue emotion or get mired by others.

Unfortunately by entangling himself in the politics of Hexis he was doing exactly that. But he was in the unique position of being able to conquer a city without need of an army and he would be a fool to pass up that kind of opportunity.

He looked to his left and watched Selinda. There was food on her plate, but she was not eating. She was merely poking at the sausage with the prongs of her fork, stabbing into it again and again very slowly, each puncture allowing the contained grease to bleed out onto her plate until the sausage was swimming in a small lake of its own juices. He could easily imagine her desire to stab that fork into her true enemy, sitting merely a table's width away from her.

That brought his attention to Grannish. Grannish was staring hard at Selinda as well, as though he were trying to divine her thoughts for some reason. Dethan knew the very moment she became aware of the jenden's regard. Her entire body went tense and she dropped her fork to her plate. She forced both her hands into her lap and stared hard at her butchered sausage as if it were the most interesting piece of meat she had ever seen. Dethan decided that he did not like seeing her so afraid. He did not doubt she had cause to be that fearful. But she was braver than she thought. He had seen her stand up to Grannish, had seen her manipulate him in public, where he dared not immediately retaliate or gainsay her. That took courage. Especially knowing the consequences. Grannish was a bully, Dethan surmised. He had a cruel streak—Dethan had seen it when Grannish's man had been whipping Tonkin. There had been an appetite for the suffering of others in his eyes.

So in what ways was he making Selinda suffer? Dethan wondered. And no sooner had he thought it than a sickened feeling crept low into his gut. The idea of her being under the thumb of someone like Grannish . . . No wonder she was scrabbling for something, anything, to save herself with.

He had known others like Grannish, and they had earned nothing but his contempt. A man made his way in the world using his intelligence and his skills of battle, compensating with one where he was weak in the other. Yes, it was true that innocents fell in battle alongside those who were not so innocent, but the cities Dethan had taken had been in dire need of taking, in dire need of someone at the helm who could manage them and make them flourish. Very often the innocents that died in the taking of the city were outweighed by those already dying from disease or starvation or any number of other things that a mismanaged city was prone to.

That was exactly what he was facing here. A city so mismanaged it was dying a slow, agonizing death. Perhaps a quicker death with the Redoe outside its walls, sitting and waiting for them to collapse in on themselves. The Redoe were far cleverer than Grannish and the general were giving them credit for. They were whittling away at Hexis more and more each year and their patience was beginning to pay off. They could afford to sit and be patient. They had all the crops they could want at their disposal and no one was challenging them . . . so why not sit and wait? Dethan's task was to make it as uncomfortable for the interlopers as possible. But that would require discomfort for those behind the walls as well.

"I should like to go about inspecting your troops later today," he said to the general.

"What, all together?"

"Yes. All together."

"The city guard protects the walls and those within the walls. I can't just call them all together. It would allow for mayhem in the streets."

"They will be called together and will do so in shifts afterward at least once per day. Otherwise, how do they know what is expected of them, what direction you wish them to take?" He grimaced. "Or is it that you don't give them any direction at all?"

The general coughed, bits of eggs flying from his lips, his face mottling in fury and indignation. "Your most honorable! I refuse to take such insult from a lowborn piece of—"

"Be warned," Dethan said quietly, "I do not take kindly to insults."

He did not raise his voice like the general did. He did not have to, Selinda thought. The entire room quieted in response to his warning because they could all feel the coiled threat that he was, like a serpent ready to strike if he was poked or irritated.

"It is no insult, only truth!" the general hissed, although there was a sudden caution in the lines of his stocky body. "I have been his most honorable's general for fifteen years! You are hardly old enough to be called a commander, never mind a general. And we still have no proof you are anything but a wastrel off the street, taking advantage of his most honorable's need and graces."

"Are you saying the grand is so weak that he would not be able to see through a simple charlatan, if indeed

I was one?" Dethan asked archly, one of his dark brows lifting high.

"I . . ." Firru hesitated, looking away from Dethan to see his liege lord's expression of interest in his response. "I-I just meant to say . . ." he stammered.

"Your grand has hired me to find out what is wrong with his army and to use that army to get rid of the Redoe. I can hardly do that if you plan on fighting me every step of the way," Dethan said. "If indeed there is an army." He frowned as he thought on that. "A city guard is not an army. The city guard's focus is to protect the city while your army's focus should be beyond the walls. Do you have an army?"

The general's gape-mouthed, wide-eyed silence was telling, even if Selinda didn't already know the answer. There was no army. Firru had always said that the city guard was more than enough to keep the city safe.

"We have no soldiers and nowhere to find them," Grannish spoke up, discomfited irritation in the lines of his body. Firru was *his* man. He couldn't afford for his man to look bad in front of the grand.

"That is peculiar, for *I* saw a mass of soldiers in the center of the city square yesterday."

"There were no soldiers in the city square! The only thing taking place in the square is the fair!" Grannish said.

"Yes, and there were hundreds of healthy men able for battle if properly trained. Many of whom, as I understand it, are idle and starving as their farms are squatted upon outside the walls."

"Mud farmers? What do mud farmers know about fighting?" Grannish scoffed. He laughed and many at the table laughed with him.

"Not much, I am certain, but it is their farms out there, so they will fight passionately for them. They are strong from backbreaking work, tilling muddy fields. A little training and they could be a force to be reckoned with."

Grannish laughed again, but there was an uneasiness in his tone that had not been there a moment ago. "And you will convince them to fight how? They will resent conscription."

"I disagree. I believe they will readily volunteer. But there is only one way to prove which of us is right."

"You are correct. I welcome the opportunity to be proved wrong. The aim is what is best for Hexis," Grannish said, suddenly magnanimous. He leaned back in his chair and smiled at his grand. "That is all we want. You work for gold, but we work for the love and well-being of our city."

"That remains to be seen," Dethan said sotto voce. But Selinda heard him well enough. She also felt him. When she would have spoken a moment ago, leapt into the conversation, he had stayed her the way she had tried to stay him the night before, with a hand on her thigh and a gentle, insistent squeeze. She very rarely got to speak her opinion on matters, and in public in front of her father was one of the few venues she had. Sure, she might pay for it later, but at least she was able to openly speak her mind to her father, invest her opinion, and hope it somehow reached him on some level. At the very least it would cause Grannish to dance and bow and scrape a little faster to undo whatever damage she might have done. It was a small victory, if it could be called that, but it still made her feel a little better. But now Dethan was holding her back, trying to control her just as Grannish tried to control her.

No. That wasn't fair, she thought hastily. He had not proved himself to be anything close to what Grannish was. Only time would tell on that score and on many others. For the moment, she had many other things to be worried about that were far more serious than a missed opportunity to join a conversation.

For instance, the fact that he expected her to come to his bed tonight. The very thought of it had her feeling nauseated. Not that she was repulsed by him—she had to admit he was exceptionally appealing in a rugged sort of way, with his dark hair left free down to his shoulders and curling at the ends and the thick black of his lashes a perfect framework for his clover-green eyes. He was mind-numbingly tall, and that was to say nothing of his well-muscled body. She had seen all of it, but what she had seen had been covered in burns and scarring, dead flesh and ashes. Yet here he was today and she could see the meat in his biceps, the ropey veins running down and over his forearms. His hand on her leg was large and warm, and it was that touch that made her feel small in comparison to him. His palm nearly engulfed the whole of her thigh and she could feel his strength in his fingers. That strength seemed to seek out an unknown and secret part of her, making her highly aware of the imprint of each finger on her thigh and just how close those fingers were to a place where no man had ever touched her before. To a place that seemed to be . . . craving his touch, as scandalous as that sounded. Almost as if it were calling out to him. Selinda flushed hotly at the wanton sensation, confusion overtaking her as heat burned her cheeks. Was he doing this on purpose? Or was it just her own cravings making it seem so?

She suddenly had the idea that he was measuring how much strength he was using to get his message across . . . yet not hurt her, as if to say, *I have the strength to rip the world to shreds every moment of every day, but at this moment I choose to do otherwise.* But was that all he was saying? Was he perhaps asking for more? Here? Surreptitiously but in front of everyone? The idea sent wicked, shocking chills down her spine and a wet heat appeared in secret places.

Selinda swallowed noisily. She wanted to push his hand away, but she found herself ridiculously fearing the skin-to-skin contact. She imagined it might burn her. Why she was suddenly imagining him to be all these dangerous things she could not say, but there it was all the same.

She stood up suddenly, causing a ripple of similar movement to occur down along the table.

"Please sit. I find I am not feeling well." Although she found she felt better now that the pressure of his touch and all its possible meanings had been lifted. "I am going to rest awhile."

"I will escort you to your rooms," Dethan said immediately, talking over a similar offer being delivered by Jenden Grannish.

She couldn't deny them both, and the hidden command in Grannish's eyes made her decision for her quickly. "Thank you, Sor Dethan," she said, lightly placing her hand atop his and letting him lead her away. It was a new experience, having two men vying for her attention, and she found it a horrible position to be in. To think some women actually enjoyed such things! She supposed it might be different were the suitors men one wanted to have the attention of, but one could never really choose these things, could one? Men would do what men wanted to do, as was proved at that moment. The very man she had sought to avoid was right now walking her up to her rooms.

"Thank you for remaining silent just now," he said to her once they were out of the hearing range of anyone, surprising her greatly. She wasn't used to being thanked for her behavior . . . or lack thereof.

"You are . . . welcome. Why would you not let me

speak?" she asked in honest curiosity, amazed to find she was no longer irritated by his silencing of her.

"Although you have not told me the whole of it, I have gathered you pay for your opinion in some way or another at Grannish's hands. You will be tempting fate enough with your actions these coming weeks. I'll not have you hurt over this."

"He won't hurt me," she hedged. "He needs me too much. There are no other women for him to wed in this family. He has seen to that."

"So you truly do believe he murdered your family. I had suspected it was someone, but I did not know who until you put forward Grannish. After all, it is obvious he was the only one left to gain by such a thing."

"Yes. Before me were my two elder brothers and after me my two younger sisters. Though I suspect he was not responsible for Arra's and Gia's deaths. They were taken by plague. Arra was considered the greatest beauty of her time. It was more likely that I was the one in the way of him marrying her . . . until she died and left him with no option other than to marry something ugly and scarred." She touched the ridged scarring on her jaw.

Suddenly she felt him grab hold of her. She was dragged into a dark alcove, out of the way of foot traffic, and pressed up against the wall. She gasped, looking up into his fiery green eyes.

"And that is the last time you will refer to yourself as ugly in my presence. You will not even think it and I will know if you do." He gave her a little shake. "You are one of the most beautiful women I have ever laid eyes upon, and believe me when I say I have seen the most beautiful women in the eight heavens and beyond. You are not the sum of this scar and it is not the only thing on your body worth seeing!"

Then, instead of pushing her away, Dethan drew her closer, his hands opening and closing again on her upper arms, almost as though he was fighting himself for a moment over what he wished to do with her. She found herself pressed to the full length of his body, feeling his strength through the density of her corset and her skirts, as though she were not wearing them at all. The thought made her flush hotly and she knew it colored her face because he smiled a little as he looked down on her. Then he reached for the veil that covered the damaged half of her face and pulled it up and away. She gasped and tried to pull it back into place but he grabbed hold of her wrist and held her tightly until she stopped struggling.

"And this is the last time you will wear one of these while you are in my sight," he said, pulling the cap completely from her head. It was pinned in place so it dragged at her hair, ruining the delicate chignon it had been sculpted into and Hanit's hard work. He dropped the cap to the floor, and now that he had started, he finished pulling the rest of the pins free, letting the black mass dump down over her shoulders and back, letting it fill his hungry hands, where he stroked it and fondled it eagerly.

"Y-you don't understand. I-I have never gone without my veil! Grannish will be very—"

"And," he said as if she hadn't spoken, "I think I should like you to wear your hair down as well. It makes the blue of your eyes stand out, and I find I like that. I noticed your eyes from the very first and find them stunning."

"My eyes are not the first thing most people see when they look at me," she said, her tone bordering on bitter. She tried to pull free of him but he tightened his hands around her head.

"They are the first thing *I* saw. And since I am to be your husband one day, I should think my opinion would be the only one that matters to you."

When he put it like that, she stopped fighting him and relaxed in his hold a little.

"You are only marrying me to get to my father's throne," she said in a soft whisper, afraid her words would anger him, daring much by calling him on it. But instead of getting angry with her, he surprised her by chuckling.

"Only? You know very little about men if you think that is the only reason I want you as a wife, when you will warm my bed with this body for the rest of your days." His hand filtered out of her hair, his large knuckles drawing along the skin from her collarbone to her breast. "But then again, in a world gone mad, where *this* is considered ugly, I can see how you might be twisted about." He reached the swell of her breast, where it met the conservative line of her corset, and frowned. "What is this? Why do you bind yourself up in such a way?"

"I-it's just a corset," she stammered, her face on fire as he touched her in a way no one had ever touched her before.

"Yes. I gathered this is the fashion, for I saw it on other women at the table. But unlike you, they swelled over the top of theirs, showing off the plumpness of their breasts. And while I find it to be surprisingly bold, I wonder why you are not so daring. In my day no one wore these . . . corsets. Women left their bodies free. But still, you are bound tighter than most."

"Some of the women are wearing underbusts," she explained, "and others are . . . I just . . . I'm not allowed to flaunt myself."

"Not allowed?"

"Yes," she whispered. "Grannish has forbidden it. I am not even allowed to wear makeup in the court fashion. If at all."

"I had noticed that too. And while you do not need such embellishments, it wears ill on me that he should prevent you from expressing your looks as other women do or as you might like to. We will have to change this."

"Oh no!" she cried, sudden panic winging through her. "I cannot! You must not make me! Please! He will become enraged. He will—" She cut herself off and swallowed hard.

"He will what?" Dethan demanded to know, his expression turning thunderous. "What will he do to you?"

"Nothing," she whispered in a lie. But knowing he would see through it, she hastily added, "Nothing serious. I'm sure I make more out of it than it really is."

"And I'm sure his attitude and behavior in this matter set the trend for your other interactions with him. It set in motion your need to come to a complete stranger for help, bartering yourself to him freely without knowing a damned thing about him."

His words made her swallow hard. "It had to be a stranger," she whispered. "Grannish knows everyone else. Has them all afraid of him or in collusion with his goals. I knew, listening to you at the table, that anyone who understood the first thing about Grannish would never challenge him in such a way. His ego would not tolerate it. It is not just that he believes he's not wrong; it is that he cannot tolerate a world where he might be deemed as being wrong. I do not think you understand what you are putting yourself into."

"But you were hoping for that," he mused, his glittering eyes searching her face. "And you do not believe I will succeed."

"I did not," she agreed breathlessly, "until I saw you this morning." She quickly dared to ask, "Why are you not burned? You are a little, but nowhere near what I saw! You have healed almost completely in comparison to last night!"

"First, I must ask you, will your girl talk of this to

anyone? Is she in Grannish's pocket? It seems to me she would be the best way to keep close eyes on you."

"No. Hanit has been my servant only a short while, but . . . but I believe in her. Grannish approached her shortly after my sisters died and threatened her if she did not work for him, then cajoled her by offering her money. She agreed to both but immediately told me. She knew if she had refused she would have been replaced. So we have it worked out that she will tell him only a little. We sometimes invent things to make her believable . . . but the important things she keeps secret. In a world where I cannot afford to trust, I believe and have total faith in her."

"Very well. I will accept your estimation of the matter." But Dethan was not entirely convinced. He realized the risk she would be taking by coming to his rooms each night. But still . . .

Dethan reached to touch the soft, supple skin of her long throat. He had never seen such a graceful neck that had not been on a goddess. She wore a sheer shawl over her shoulders and tucked into the top of her corset—yet another way of covering herself up. Why would Grannish want to hide her rather than flaunt his ownership of such beauty? Dethan would most certainly be proud of having a lover who—

"Have you been intimate with him?" he asked suddenly, sharply, before he realized he was even going to say it.

"What? No!" She sounded suitably horrified and the expression of disgust on her face convinced him that she had never had any desire toward Grannish, that this wasn't just some ploy to make him jealous. He had not read her to be that way, but it wouldn't be the first time he had misjudged a situation.

"He has not forced himself on you?" he asked more gently.

Color crept up her neck, chin, and cheeks. "No. Not yet," she said softly. "But if he thinks there is a danger of you getting me pregnant before he can—"

"Nicely attempted," he said with a chuckle, watching her color deepen, "but you will still be coming to my rooms. You must simply be careful so he doesn't find out. And you will return to your rooms before the household awakens in the morning."

"If that is what you want, Sor Dethan, then I will honor our agreement."

"Every night, after juquil's hour."

"Very well," she said.

He studied her for a moment, then touched her chin, using the connection to tip her head back and pull her gaze up to his.

He did not know why, did not fully understand the pull in those teal eyes of hers, but he found himself drawn to her. Found himself studying the softness of her lips. Had he ever seen a mouth so lush? How could she expect him to notice that small patch of burned skin on her lower cheek and jaw when she had such a pretty mouth to look at?

"How did it happen?" he asked, an attempt to thwart himself from the urge to kiss her. He would kiss her. Soon he would kiss her and claim those lush lips as his. He angled her head to the side and studied the scar up close. Upset, her hand immediately fluttered up to cover her cheek. He grabbed hold of it instantly and pulled it away. "The more you try to hide it, the more you try to cover it up, the more you draw attention to it," he told her sternly. "Now, tell me. How did it happen?"

"My . . . my sister and I were playing and she pushed me . . . I fell into the fire and my hair caught fire. Nanny was quick to put it out—it could have been much worse— but the damage was done, and then it became infected and . . ." She swallowed hard and he saw tears shining in her eyes. That strength he saw in her showed itself, however, as she straightened her spine and met his eyes and refused to shed a single one of those tears. "I learned very young to hide it however I could. It makes people uncomfortable to see it. Please don't ask me to not wear my veils. I need them—"

"To make other people feel better?" He made a scoffing sound. "Let that be on them. Let them figure out how to deal with it. You are grandina of Hexis. Hold your head high and your face bare and remember that you possess all the power over them. If your father died tomorrow, you would be heir to the throne and would be granda in your own right."

"Please," she said softly, "do not speak of my father's death. I have already lost so much of my family. More than half of it. As it is, I am afraid that as soon as I marry Grannish my father's life will be in jeopardy." She reached out and grasped at his shirt above his heart. "Please promise me you will not let that happen."

"Your marriage or your father's untimely demise?"

"Both," she said, and he felt her tremble in his hands.

"My promises will mean nothing to you," he said gently. "You do not know me, nor do you know my capabilities. All I can do is promise you to do my best to see to it none of that happens. My motives, as you know, are not altruistic or emotional. I will have my gold, will be head of your army, and I will have you to wife. Those are my goals and I rarely fail to achieve a goal. Take from that whatever comfort you can."

"It gives me a great deal of comfort," she said, opening her hand against his chest. "More comfort than I have known in turntides. For I believe you can do what you say you can. I would not have thrown my lot in with you otherwise."

"Your bet is well placed, my lady," he said with a cocky smile on his lips. Oh, it felt good to smile again.

To enjoy the company of another. Of a woman. Dethan had to admit he found the idea of marrying her more than a little appealing. He took in a breath and enjoyed the clean, floral scent of her. He pulled long waves of her ebony hair into his hand, brought it closer to his nose, and breathed even deeper of her scent.

"Oh, how I've missed this," he said, his words low and fierce.

"M-missed . . . ?"

He regained himself, letting her hair filter through his fingers and back onto her shoulder and breast.

"I have not been . . . I have not been close to a woman in a very long time. I look forward to your company tonight."

She flushed a deep pink and looked down at his chest. They were standing too close together for her gaze to touch the floor. She went suddenly stiff in his hands and against his body.

"Wh-what if I do not wish to . . . to test you. To experience . . . you."

He chuckled at her, unable to help himself. "Oh, you will want to," he assured her. "But I will not force you, if that is what you mean. I will not have to force you. I assure you all will come very naturally."

"I just don't see how I could ever willingly . . ." She had begun to pull hard for breath and he could feel the upset in her with every fiber of his soul.

"Enough," he said, lifting his fingers to her left cheek and brushing his thumb over her bottom lip. "You will like whatever we do," he said on a low, compelling whisper, his head dropping until his mouth was but a breath away from hers. Her eyes were wide, her breath heaving out of her. There was so much fear in her that he could practically taste it. And he simply would not have her that way. Unlike Grannish, he did not need to control her. There were better ways of winning loyalty from someone other than fear and intimidation.

Dethan swept his mouth down onto hers in a sudden rush, his hands around her arms tightening as though he feared she would escape. But she was too stunned to make any attempt at it. So few had dared to kiss her . . . and those who had tried had been resoundingly rebuffed. Mostly because they were horribly unpalatable or horridly inappropriate. So, outside of her family members, she had never been kissed before. She had never known the astounding feel of a strong male mouth rushing up against her own.

The kiss was followed by the feel of that strong male body going tight with strength and tension. His heat all along the front of her body was overwhelming and it radiated his barely leashed power into her. And yet his mouth was soft . . . strong but soft. He slid his hands up from her arms and cradled her head between them, tilting her chin up so that she met with him better, so that she meshed more perfectly.

She did not know it or think it, but she was a natural when it came to kissing. She thought she didn't know what to do, but instinctively she did, and that made the kiss almost painful in its perfection. She tasted so good that Dethan growled low in his throat, pulled her mouth up tighter to his, and then licked her between her lips.

She was startled by the introduction of his tongue. She had seen others kiss in such ways, but seeing it and doing it were two very different things. It somehow seemed far more intimate than what had just transpired had felt. Her heart was clamoring in her chest from the riot of emotions and worries stampeding through her.

"Enough!" he said on a low rumbling huff as he gave her a little shake. "Your taste tempts me and I will have the whole of it." His mouth sealed to hers again and this time he thrust his tongue past her teeth. She was prepared to hate it, prepared to be repulsed . . . but she was shocked to find she liked his taste as well, and the way he tangled their tongues together was so very hot and erotic to her. Illicit. Temptingly forbidden.

As she absorbed all this, she went completely boneless against him. The softening of her body only heightened her awareness of the hardness of his. He stood strong and dominant, feet braced apart, and his mouth devoured her in demanding sweeps of his tongue.

"There's a sweet girl," he breathed against her lips. "Ah, you have a fine flavor and I can feel the heat buried inside you." He drew back and looked down into her eyes. "Yes, you'll do very nicely," he assured her. "And then some."

She thought she should be offended, but she wasn't. She was panting hard for breath and trying not to slide to the floor in a weak little pile of flesh that seemed to be suddenly absent any bone.

He seemed to understand her dilemma, because he slid his hand down to her back and used the press of his body to jog her more upright.

"Come, let us bring you to your rooms where you can lie down. I think you need some sleep."

"But . . ." She looked genuinely puzzled.

"Unless there was something more you wanted?" he asked suggestively.

Another blush flamed across her cheeks and she fell all over herself to blurt out, "No!"

He threw back his head and laughed at her. But it wasn't a mocking laugh or even a patronizing one. She knew the sound of those all too well. It was the laugh of someone who was honestly amused. She was so used to everything in the court being measured or manipulated, she couldn't remember the last time she had experienced such genuine, unfiltered emotion.

"Come, sweet silk," he said, running his fingertips

down the left side of her face before taking her hand and pulling her back into the hall. "Show me to your rooms so I will know the way."

The very idea of him knowing where her rooms were and what he might use that knowledge for had her breath quickening in her lungs and her heart racing all over again. Only this time she was pretty sure it wasn't fear she was feeling at the prospect of meeting him in the dark of night. She didn't exactly know how to define it, but there it was just the same. She hesitated only a moment but then realized he could easily find someone else to show him the way if he so chose.

She stepped forward and led the way.

CHAPTER
NINE

After leaving Selinda in her rooms, Dethan began the task of getting to know his way around. The fortress was heavily populated and extremely busy. Finding himself alone in a hallway was nearly impossible. It was a wonder he had been able to have those few private moments with Selinda. It also concerned him because if he insisted she keep her part of the bargain and come to his rooms every night, it would be easier for her to be seen and potentially get caught. He could have let her out of that part of the agreement, but the fact was this whole venture might endanger her, not just that aspect of it, and he needed her to be there every night if he was going to make any headway in his tasks. And his tasks were monumental.

And now of course there was something else . . . there was a kiss. A fierce, hotly innocent kiss. She so clearly knew nothing in the way of a man . . . or in what it meant to be a lover. That she was untouched only solidified this insanity, running rampant through these people, that she was somehow ugly. Were they all blind? Her father was apparently blind, but was everyone else equally blind? The idea was staggering. Like some sort of mass delusion. But he had seen a lot of strange things in a lot of alien cultures in his time as a conqueror so it really ought not to surprise him.

Yet it did.

And that was the least of his worries. The rest of his goal loomed before him at a tremendous incline. But that had never stopped him before, and after learning how to endure under fiery, constant torture, navigating a few hiccups and bumps in this court seemed like child's play. Or it would be if it were only himself at stake.

No. He shook that thought off. He was a conqueror. Whether the grandina lived or died, whether she wed him or not, he would conquer this city in Weysa's name one way or another. He had to. He had to give Weysa everything she needed if he ever hoped to find himself in the position of being granted a favor by the goddess. Knowing that every day his brothers suffered as he had suffered drove him to find some way to see to their release from their curse. True, Weysa had risked much to free him, but if she could risk that much for him, then surely she could do so again. She would need good warriors, and if he did well, maybe he could convince her that they were worthy of saving and would only aid her cause.

But first things first. He reached out and stopped a passing page. "Where is the king's coin handler and who do I speak to about having my rooms relocated?"

"The grand's coin handler is just down the hall. As for your rooms, that be the head mistress's duty," the young boy said with a sniffle. He rubbed the back of his hand under his nose. "She has an office right off the kitchens," he offered, anticipating Dethan's next question.

"Very well. Which way to the kitchens?"

After a brief visit to the grand's coin handler to procure some gold for his pocket—he was happy to hear that the coin handler had been expecting his appearance—he took only one wrong turn before he finally found the kitchens. It was a madhouse of bustling energy and noise. Shouting and good smells filled the air, along with the clattering of copper pans and chopping knives. The head mistress showed up at her office door after only a minute's wait.

"Change your rooms? What for?" she asked suspiciously.

"Because all the grand's advisors have rooms on the level below the family and that is where I am to be placed." It was not a suggestion and he made certain she knew it.

"Well," she said hesitantly, "I've not heard anything about a new advisor."

That was a lie, he realized. He knew the one thing that flew fast in a household of this size was news and gossip. One was usually true and the other was just as often not. She surely already knew and was hemming and hawing for a reason. He suspected he knew what it was. If he were Grannish and he wanted to keep tabs on what was going on in the house, this was the woman he would use to do it.

"Your awareness of the situation does not change the fact that it needs to be done. I will have suitable rooms by one hour before evening meal."

"Very well, Sor Dethan," she said, her whole demeanor changing when he used the tone he would use with any of his lieutenants. "I'll have it done right away and they'll be ready by noontide or I'm not head of this household!"

"Well done," Dethan said gruffly and took his leave.

The next task was to find a page—a trustworthy one. No mean trick in a household full of Grannish's spies. And as though thinking about him made him appear, there Grannish was. Since they were just outside the kitchens, Dethan knew immediately that he had been followed. The kitchen gangway was not exactly common territory for the jenden of Hexis.

"Ah! So glad I found you," Grannish said amicably. "I was wondering how you wished to go about implementing this drafting of the commoners."

"I have a few ideas," Dethan said vaguely. "But if I need your help, I am certain I'll be able to find you not too far away." Dethan moved to go past Grannish, but Grannish stepped into his path.

"I fear we've gotten off to a bad start," he said, his tone still amicable. "I'm not opposed to you. I am merely protective of my city. And believe me when I say we have tried everything we can with the Redoe."

"Obviously not everything or you would have succeeded. And we have already set the tone for our relationship, Grannish, and it is a tone I like. Also, it isn't your city. It is the grand, the grandina, and the young grandino's city. They are the ruling family, and they are the first word and the last word in this city."

"You will find," Grannish said, his voice dropping a full octave, "that this is also my city. You will shortly discover that there is nothing in this city that I do not know about. Nothing I do not control. I do so in the name of the ruling family, but the fact remains it is very much *my* city."

"I see. Thank you for the warning. Now, let me deliver one of my own. I will be watching over the grandina just as closely as you watch over this city. If she comes to the slightest bit of harm, if she so much as breaks an eyelash, I will come to you to answer for it. You are after all her fiancé and therefore her protector. Are you not?"

"Yes, but . . ." Grannish spluttered, his face coloring as his temper rose. Good, Dethan thought. He has a temper that he cannot always control. *Already that makes him weaker as an opponent.* The more he got Grannish to show his temper in front of the grand, the better it would be.

"So much as an eyelash," Dethan reiterated, leaning in to the man and towering over him by at least a head. Grannish didn't like this, so he was forced to step back. A retreat. Dethan hoped that set the tone for their entire relationship, but he knew it would not be that easy. He walked away from Grannish, who was silent, probably trying to control his outrage. For the moment, Grannish was keeping his true nature hidden from Dethan. No doubt because he didn't want Dethan reporting bad behavior to the grand. Not until he was in a better position to denounce Dethan. Dethan was the grand's new pet pastime and Grannish would have to work to undermine him. Better to do so while touching his hand, smiling to his face, and working with deception behind his back. But they had just drawn their lines with each other and that was the end of it.

For the time being.

Now, to find a trustworthy page.

Dethan found him around noontide. "Tonkin!" he called out when he saw the muddied peasant. Today he was in nothing but a pair of baggy pants, much in the way Tonkin had first found Dethan.

"Well, my friend! Are you come to claim that gossel leg at las—" He broke off, his eyes widening a moment. "More like you could buy me one!" he said, eyeing the mode of Dethan's dress. "That vest alone . . . hand-tooled leather, gold embossing in the grooves . . . Why, that'd be a month's rent for me!"

"Then you will have it," Dethan said, shrugging the vest off and handing it to the stunned man. "And a job as well that pays real gold if you want it. Be my page, and all I will want in return is utter and absolute loyalty. There will be food and clothes, new lodgings. Any comfort you need."

Tonkin took the proffered vest with shaking fingers, as though afraid to touch the fine thing with his muddy hands. "My lord, you must be some kind of night fairy come to give me all my wishes in one fell swoop!"

"I am not your lord," Dethan said firmly. "I am 'sor' to you and others."

"No, my lord. If you give me all these things, then you will be my lord. And I will be your page. Though before you put me in any clothes, a bath might be in order. And not just a mud bath, no! With water. Imagine that!"

Dethan chuckled. "You shall have it, my friend. Come, let's get you some clothes. Then that bath while we discuss the details of your duties."

"Who would think Tonkin Mudskin would be a page in the grand's fortress! It pays to be kind to a stranger!"

"I suppose it does," Dethan said. But he made sure his tone was dark when he said, "But you may find this all a curse instead of a blessing before long, so be careful in your adulation. I have powerful enemies in the fortress. To be specific, the jenden. You will become a target as my page. He will try to buy you first, and when he cannot do that he will try to use force to have his will done with us."

"Well, he can try to buy me all he likes. He won't succeed. I've been on the brink of starving for too long not to know a good thing. And all I need you've already offered. Got no family, no desires to have all the things others seem to want to gather. Only thing I ever wanted was my farm back. And peace from the Redoe."

"Be loyal to me and I will see you have both," Dethan promised him. "That and a little bit more."

Tonkin chuckled. "I will be loyal to a fault, my lord. And I ain't afraid of the jenden. He might be the most powerful man around, but the people know his heart is black as sooted mud. In whispers people talk about the tragedy of it."

"The tragedy?"

"Of the grandina being forced to marry the likes of him."

"So . . . the people are against the marriage?" Dethan found that very intriguing.

"Them that's not afraid to talk about it. The jenden's reach is far. That's what we say. 'Careful, the jenden's reach is far.' But it doesn't change true feelings, and true feelings are that the grandina is a kind and gentle bird and he's a black cloud she's being forced to fly into. If that happens, the jenden will be grand one day, and that's a downright scary thought."

"Indeed it is. Come. Clothes, bath, and the gossel leg is on me."

"Well, I won't complain! Let's be off!"

Selinda awoke sometime in midafternoon with a blazing headache. She got them sometimes. Horrible, awful headaches during which even the light burned pain into her brain. Usually they coincided with one of her encounters with the jenden or some other time of spiked stress, so it shouldn't surprise her that she was suffering. Sor Dethan had brought a great deal of stress with him. As well as a great deal of promise. As she fretted about going to his rooms that night, she wondered which she would find there: stress or promise.

She had Hanit pull all the drapes, darkening the room to almost night. She lay back in her bed quietly, trying to shed the pain in her head. There was too much going on for her to spend the day lounging around in bed.

Or maybe this was the better idea. To stay out of the

line of fire. She dreaded her next private encounter with Grannish.

And she didn't have long to wait for it. He came to her rooms, pushing his way past Hanit. She jumped to her feet with a wince as he took in the darkness and sneered at her. "Sick again? Is that why our new general feels the need to protect you? Although I shouldn't bother to call him a general. I know he has no such qualifications."

"I do not know what you—"

"Or is there another reason?" Grannish stepped up to her, his very presence beating her back until she butted up against the bed. "I warn you, little princess, do not cross me. You know well enough what I am capable of, and do not think your crown protects you."

"What will you do?" she railed back at him suddenly, spurred on by recklessness and pain. "You may despise me, but you *need* me. Until we are properly wed, and even after, you need me."

A fact he obviously did not care to be reminded of. That was why he raised his arm, ready to backhand her across her face. But something stayed him. For a moment she thought it was her words, that he'd seen the truth of them, that she had suddenly found traction in her ability to deal with him.

Until he smiled. Grannish angry was a force to be reckoned with, but when he smiled . . . Oh, the terrible things that could happen when he smiled.

"You are, unfortunately, correct," he said, his arm lowering. "I do need you. And until we are wed, I need your father. But do you know who I do not need?" he asked, leaning farther forward with every word until his hot breath rushed over her ear in a whisper. "Your little brother."

Selinda's eyes went wide and she sucked in a shocked breath.

"Yes, oh yes," he hissed against her ear, his hand coming to caress her now along the scarring at her jaw. "And he is so sickly to begin with. Since more than half the city believes the royal family is cursed, this will just be further proof of it. More tragedy. So sad. That is, until I wed you and put *my* blood on the throne. Now, there will be a strong bloodline. A worthy one. I see it all, a future I can almost grasp." He grasped at the empty air in front of her face. "And just like that the curse on your family will be lifted. But until then . . . until then . . . Well, there's no telling what further tragedy might befall them."

By the time he finished she had fast, fearful tears running down her face and her head was screaming with agonizing pain as she contained her sobs. She knew from experience that he liked to see his female victims cry . . . to a point. It all depended on his mood, how much he was willing to extract at the time. Apparently her silent tears were enough to satisfy for that moment.

With a satisfied chuckle, he stepped back from her. Hanit didn't dare come to her side until he was halfway across the room, and as soon as her pagette touched her, she collapsed against her, sliding them down onto the cold stone floor together. She didn't let out her first heartfelt sob until he was well out of earshot. Then she lay there, her face pressed to a cold tile, her head throbbing with blinding pain.

She was weak, she thought. Weak and utterly useless to her family. All her hopes were pinned on an unproven stranger. She was weak and she was *foolish*. She was going to end up giving her innocence to Dethan, and he would walk away satisfied, while she was left with . . . with Grannish.

But if Grannish was all she could look forward to, then she would give herself gladly to another man. At least he seemed . . . That is, he was not an unhandsome man, she thought. He had many good qualities a woman might enjoy in a lover. Though she was far from being able to judge. Perhaps she should confide in someone better able to judge than she was. Still . . . that kiss . . . It had stirred her in ways as nothing had ever done before. Had she not been in so much pain she would have flushed hotly in memory of it. Indeed she did, but there was too much pain to explore the sensation.

She turned onto her back, which Hanit had been stroking soothingly, and looked up at the other woman.

"Hanit?"

"Yes, my sad little juquil. What can I do for you?"

"Can you fetch me a mem from Hella's temple?"

"Yes, my juquil, I can get her right away, but only if you promise to get back into bed and rest."

Selinda nodded and gave Hanit a little smile. Hanit always called her her little juquil when their class differences didn't seem to matter. The juquil was a beautiful shining black bird that only sang at night. That was why it was known as juquil's hour . . . the high point of the night when the juquil began to sing. It was always perceived as a sad little bird because its song seemed so lonesome. Selinda liked moments like these, when it didn't matter that she was grandina and Hanit was just her servant. Although she didn't care for the things that had to happen to make moments like these come about. Her head pounding, she let Hanit help her into bed, and then Hanit went in search of a Hella priestess.

"My lady," came a murmuring voice through the miasma of a pained sleep some time later. Selinda cracked open her eyes and saw a mem sitting beside her on the bed.

"Oh, Mem, my head," she said, closing her eyes again.

"Come, look at me." Selinda did, taking in the visage of a strong, beautiful woman, about Hanit's age, with a straight tail of hair falling down from where it had been pulled up to the top of her head, and it was every color of brown in the spectrum. It shone and was among the most beautiful hair in their world, Selinda thought, matched by her equally beautiful brown eyes. They would have been pure gold, only they had just enough brown in them to keep them from being so. She was wearing her priestess's shawl over her shoulders, the corners knotted together just above her breasts. Selinda knew that on the back of the shawl was the symbol of Hella, a circle with three stars in its center: one for fate, one for fortune, and one for healing. A very powerful sign and very much deserved by the goddess of fate.

"My lady, what can I do for you?" the mem asked quietly.

"My head hurts. I can barely open my eyes." Selinda knew the mems of Hella were healers, some astoundingly so. But she had never met this mem before. She hoped the woman was of significant enough talent. She must have been, in order to be sent to care for the grandina. "Are you new . . . ?" she said, trailing off.

"I have only just arrived . . . just before the Redoe set in. My name is Josepha."

"Why would you come here, to our little city with all its troubles?" Selinda asked curiously.

The mem laughed at that, a warm, enriched sound. "I did not know what troubles the city had when I came. But I am certain if I had known I would have come all the faster. I must go where I am needed, not where I wish to. Hella guided me here. Maybe she guided me to you and you to me, and that is our fate. Although those who are faithful seem to be faithful to Xaxis in this city. If not for our healing, there would not even be a temple to Hella here, I think."

"No one really worships the gods anymore. There is little faith."

"And yet you have faith in us?" the mem asked with amusement touching her lips.

"I have faith in your ability to heal," Selinda said, returning the other woman's smile.

"This is very true. I am a great healer . . . and portender. Perhaps, once we give you relief, I might read your runes?"

"I do not think I will need you to do that," Selinda said with a sigh. "I already know my future."

"No future is truly known, Grandina. Not by us. All we can know is what we should do in order to shape that future."

"I never know how to shape my future," Selinda said with a frown. "It just seems to . . . happen to me."

"Well, we shall have to fix that," the mem said with another smile. "But first, your headache." The mem sat forward and enclosed Selinda's head in her hands. She hushed a soothing sound, her sweetly scented breath spilling over Selinda's face.

"Now, tell me why you think you have this headache."

"I have . . . There is much stress in my life," she said vaguely. She certainly wasn't about to trust a stranger with details. True, the mem was new to the city and probably had not slid into Grannish's grasp as yet, but once he knew the mem had visited Selinda, that would all change. And he would know. He always knew.

A studied, almost pained look crossed the mem's lovely face, and then she closed her eyes. "I do not think this is from what you think it is from," she said quietly, the concentration on her face deepening. "There is something inside you . . . something building up that needs release. If you do not release it, the pressure becomes too much and the headache comes."

"Something? Like what?"

"I wish I could tell you," she said, opening her eyes

and sitting back. "I'm not certain I can help you," she said, biting a full lower lip. "Perhaps if I read your runes I will get a clearer picture. Do you mind?" she asked, jiggling the bag of runes hanging from a pretty braided belt low on her hips.

"Go ahead," Selinda said with a pained sigh. "For whatever good it will do."

"Now, my lady." The woman tsked like a scolding mother. "You must not be that way. You need to open your soul to the runes or they will not work."

"All right," Selinda agreed. Her headache seemed to be lifting just by the mem's presence, and at the very least the runes would distract her from the mangling pain.

"Now, lie back completely. No pillow. There now. Perfect." She opened the bag and dumped all the runes out on Selinda's belly. "Now, do not look at them, but one by one pick up a rune when I ask for it. Start with the first one."

The mem called for a rune and then took it from Selinda's fingers. In the end, there were six runes. The first she laid on Selinda's forehead. "The mind," she said. Then her chest. "The heart." Then her solar plexus. "The soul," she said. Then one on each wrist. "The past and the present." And the last she placed just above Selinda's pubic bone, above her womb. "The future," she said. Then she scooped up the remaining runes, put them back into her bag, and with a concentrated frown began to study the six runes.

"You are a victim. To your life," she said. "But you are not to blame, so do not think that you are. You have made every effort to shape the future to the better. In fact, recently you have taken a great step toward the future. Very recently."

"Is it . . . is it the right choice, this step?"

"Hmm. Perhaps it is. Or perhaps it is not about right

or wrong. It is about better or worse. You will not have made anything worse," she said.

"Encouraging," Selinda said wryly. She would have rolled her eyes if she weren't afraid of it hurting her head.

The mem chuckled. "Now, now. Sometimes that is the best kind of future. One that does not get worse."

She had a point. Right now Selinda would settle for things not getting any worse. After Grannish's threats today, things could very easily get worse.

"What else do you see?"

"Well, it is the soul and mind and heart runes that have me most intrigued. This heart rune, it is the symbol for fire and light. And the mind rune is a very powerful rune. But the soul rune is blocked. It is as though . . . as though what you really are is being kept inside. Yes! I have seen this combination before! It was in a young man who used to have these terrible chest pains . . . like your head pains . . . and it turned out that he was a latent mage! He needed to tap into his power and release it. Once he did, he never had pain again. Does magery run in your family?" she asked quickly, seeming to grow very excited.

"No! And everyone knows you have to have a mage bloodline in order to be a mage!" Selinda sat up, shoving the runes off her body. "What trickery is this?" she demanded to know. "Did Grannish send you? Is this his idea of a joke?"

"No! Your ladyship, no! I promise you this is no joke," she said imploringly, holding out a calming hand. "I would not joke about something so serious. A magess who does not use her gifts is a waste of an important talent, but it is also highly dangerous to her. Please . . . I beg you to listen to me. If you do not believe me, then at least try to do something . . . try to use your magery on something."

"Like what?" Selinda asked suspiciously.

"Well . . . here!" Mem Josepha hurried to the table nearby and poured water from the pitcher into a crystal glass. "Water. It is as pure an element as you can find, and in some way every mage has the ability to bend water to their will. Take the glass in your hands and focus on it. Concentrate all the pain in your head into this glass of water."

Feeling foolish, Selinda did as the mem said. Of course she didn't believe she was a magess for even a second, but she would entertain the mem.

As expected, nothing happened. The glass of still water just remained a glass of still water.

"Well done," the mem said with satisfaction.

"Well done?" Selinda asked incredulously. "I didn't do anything!"

"Nothing?" the mem asked archly.

"No! Nothing! And this isn't funny anymore."

"How does your head feel?" the mem asked persistently.

"It feels . . ." Better. Significantly so, Selinda realized with surprise.

"You see? You were able to release some of your power after all!"

"But the water didn't do anything," Selinda said with confusion.

"And you expected to go from nothing to casting fire or ice in the blink of an eye?" Mem Josepha chuckled. "Dearest, you did not walk without crawling first and you did not crawl until you learned to roll over."

"Do not be so familiar with me," Selinda snapped. She didn't believe this. Not any of it. And she certainly had more important things to worry about. It was already coming around to the evening meal, and soon it would be juquil's hour and she would be required to go to her new lover's bed. "Thank you for your services. You are dismissed. Hanit, see her out," she said shortly.

"Very well, my lady," the mem said graciously, gathering her runes back into her bag and giving Selinda a respectful bow. "If you need me further, you may call on me any time, day or night, and I will come to you. And my lady?"

"Yes?" Selinda sighed in a cross between irritation and exasperation.

"I am yours," she said. "I am true to only one other person above you and that is my goddess. You need never fear my loyalty. Serving you serves my goddess and that means everything to me."

The statement of devotion did much to soften Selinda's irritation toward the other woman. She wasn't sure she believed her, but just hearing the statement made her feel better.

"Very well. Good night to you, Mem. Hanit will see you paid."

"Thank you, your ladyship."

With another bow, the priestess slipped out of Selinda's rooms.

CHAPTER
TEN

The difference in how Selinda felt by the time she went down to join the others at table was remarkable. Especially considering she ought to be more concerned about the impending encounter come juquil's hour. But that was some time away and she allowed herself the luxury of not thinking about it.

There was nothing relaxing about their meal. She felt the ominous presence of Grannish seated next to her—he had since switched seats with Dethan, seeing him settled across the table and down a few seats, as was befitting his station. But she felt it was more to make a point. Grannish held all the power in that household and he was making sure she knew it.

Still, she found herself looking over toward Dethan often. He looked haler and heartier than she had remembered from earlier. Had he grown even more muscular? Was such a thing even possible? She could see the massive width of his shoulders under his shirt and, she noticed, the vest he had been wearing earlier was gone, only to have appeared on a page now seated at the servants' table, which was set aside from the masters' table. The body servants, personal pages and pagettes, were allowed to dine at the same time as their masters because it made them readily available at all times. The household servants were another matter entirely. Like their masters' table, the servants' table was arranged by rank. Hanit sat close to the head of the table and Selinda could see that her pagette's interest strayed often to the new page. Almost as often as Selinda's attention drifted to his master.

Was it her mistaking or did he look almost completely free of his burns and scarring? She remembered them being more prominent that morning. They had been nearly bone deep the night previous. None of it should be possible, and yet it was. She wondered if anyone else had taken note of the difference between day and night. Then again, by morning he had appeared mostly healed . . . though the differences might not be noticed unless one was obsessing over his appearance as she was.

It was still light out, sunset an hour away. The main dining room was dark and shadowed for the most part. It was lit brightly by lamps, but lamps cast shadows and played tricks on the eyes. Perhaps she was seeing it all wrong to begin with.

But she didn't think so.

Once again Dethan did not make it entirely through the evening meal before he was hastily excusing himself. His page, after some urging by Hanit, immediately followed. *Strange. What kind of page needed to be told how to behave?*

Dethan had procured horses for himself and his page earlier that day from the stables, but it was only his horse he had made certain was saddled and ready to go half an hour before dusk, giving him thirty minutes to make the ten minute ride to the cavern, which allowed plenty of time for potential holdups or trouble.

He had no intention of telling Tonkin what was about to happen. He had come prepared this time with a cloak, intending that the darkness and the folds of the

garment would hide the worst of his punishment's results from any curious eyes.

"No, Tonkin. Go finish your meal and find your bed
in your room adjacent to mine. I will not need you anymore tonight."

"Are you certain, my lord?"

"Most certain. Good eve and good night."

He urged his horse onward and headed out of the bailey at a gallop.

Juquil's hour came too soon, to Selinda's thinking. She
had Hanit clasp a cloak about her shoulders and she
pulled the hood up to conceal her face. She had worn
dark clothing, one of Hanit's gowns cinched tighter
than the slightly rounder woman wore them. The fine-
ness of her own gowns would be easily recognizable.
This way she would pass for any pagette.

She had braided her hair and pinned it decoratively to
her head. Then she'd found herself fussing. Primping in
other ways. This time she had painted her lips, although
in a more subdued fashion than the brilliant sunset colors. She didn't want to look too eager. Then she'd per-
fumed herself—not too heavily like some women did,
choking anyone in range, but lightly. Sweetly. Using her
most delicately scented perfume.

With a touch of lotion to soften her hands, she deemed
herself ready and presentable. But just as she was about
to go, her stomach sickened with nerves. She reached
out and grabbed on to Hanit, in whom she had confided
everything.

"My lady, perhaps you should rethink this bargain. If
he should get you with child . . ."

"I believe that is partly his purpose in this," she said
in a soft, heated whisper. "And it is not an idea I am
adverse to. I'd rather a bastard child than one of Gran-

nish's. But the child would be in danger every day of its life as long as Grannish remained in favor. It would need a strong father and protector."

"Strong or not, nothing can defy poison. Grannish's favored weapon," Hanit reminded her with disgust.

"I know. I think the only reason my brother lives is because he is a backup plan. Grannish cannot marry him, but he could control him. Be king by proxy."

"My lady, that would require your father's dea—No! He would not dare!"

Selinda looked at her hard. "Wouldn't he?"

"I . . . I suppose he would at that. I forgot about his earlier threats."

"How could you? I never will. I am thinking of them even now as I ready to do this thing." She took a deep breath. "I am to be off, then," she said shakily and moved herself out the door.

Once she had left the safety of her rooms, she moved with haste through the fortress, terrified with every minute that she would be seen. Earlier a page—not Dethan's new one—had been sent to tell her that Dethan's rooms had been moved. She was grateful for this because it meant she had a shorter distance to go. However, it took her past the rooms of those who would recognize her. Luckily most of them would be safe in their beds by now.

She stopped in front of his door, nervously hoping she had the right rooms. She was about to push in on the handle when a sudden hulking presence came up behind her, covering her hand with his. She squealed a short, crisp sound of panic and jerked about . . . only to look up into the burned face of the man she was supposed to be meeting. She gasped in horror at the sight and smell of him. He looked even worse than the night before and this close she could smell the burnt flesh on his body; he overwhelmed her with his presence. He hushed her gently, then used her hand to open the door. She hurried into the room and he staggered in behind her. The first thing he did was drop his cloak from his shoulders and skim out of his pants, all the while gritting back sounds of torment. The feel of the clothes must have been agonizing.

Selinda leapt into action, helping him toward his bed-chamber and into his bed. He could only bear to sit up on the edge of it, gritting his teeth and breathing hard through them.

"What is this?" she demanded to know. "Why does this keep happening to you?"

He remained stubbornly close-mouthed. With a sound that was a hybrid of frustration and anger at him, she marched back through his sitting room and banged on the door to the opposite suite room, raising the page from his sleep. He came to the door looking grouchy and tired.

"What's this, then? Can't a man get some sleep?"

"You are a page," Selinda reminded him. "You are beholden to your master at any time of the day or night."

"Well, if I'd known that, I might not have taken the job!"

Selinda stared at him incredulously. "Your master needs you direly and you are *complaining* about having a job most would kill for in these times?"

That brought him up to his full height, which was not inconsiderable. He rivaled his master in both height and build. He had stood out amongst the prettier page boys that night at supper.

"Right. Sorry, my lady." Then he seemed to recognize her and his eyes went a little wider. He hastened to bow to her, but she stopped him impatiently.

"Enough of that. Go to the kitchens and fetch me a bottle of hyaita juice, some kettle greed, gloaming goat, and juni beet juice. Do you know where the kitchens are?"

"Found them first thing," the man said with a pat on his belly and a chuckle. "Will anyone be there? How will I know where all these things are and what they are?"

Selinda sighed with impatience. "You are right and I am sorry. Go find my rooms and fetch my pagette. Tell her what I need and you can go together. Now, be quick about it!"

"Yes, my lady. Right away, and I don't mind seeing that pretty Hanit again, I do say!" And he was off like a shot before she could say anything further in reprimand. "You could have put a shirt on," she said to the empty room. No doubt the page was going to shock her conservative Hanit.

She moved back into the bedroom.

"Now, you are going to tell me what is going on right this very instant," she said sternly to Dethan, her hands on her hips. "And I will not accept any dithering about it. The truth. Right now!"

"It's a curse," he said after only a moment in which she was certain he was considering arguing with her. "I'm to be burned, every night, from dusk to juquil's hour."

"Oh my sweet merciful gods," she breathed. That was why he left in the middle of dinner!

"The gods are anything but merciful, I assure you," he said bitterly. "It is they who have cursed me. And rightfully so. I was a man of much arrogance and am made to suffer for it."

"And the other part?" she asked.

"What other part?"

"The part where you heal with incredible rapidity."

He laughed bitterly. "Another part of my curse, although this was self-inflicted. I am immortal. I cannot be killed."

She gasped with disbelief. "That's impossible!"

"Oh, it is quite possible, I assure you. I have been burned to the bone, chained in the eight hells, every minute of every day for the past . . . What is the turning, anyway?"

"The turning? It's twenty and twenty-two."

"Gods, it has been nearly two hundred full turnings."

"Two hundred full turnings!" she cried. "You've been . . . But that is . . . Oh my gods." She knew it was true. Every last bit of it. She knew it because she could see it in his face.

"I don't want anyone to know. Not even Tonkin."

"Someone is eventually bound to notice. I have. And it would be best if your man was by your side for this. Where do you go every night?" Understanding rushed through her. "You go to the mouth. You go back into the hells."

"Not fully. I can barely make myself cross the threshold of the mouth."

"I can imagine why." Sympathy tugged through her.

"Do not feel badly for me. I am not an innocent victim. I am made to suffer because I deserve to suffer."

"No one deserves this," she said harshly. "And certainly not two hundred full turnings of it. How did you get out? Did you somehow escape?"

"Weysa set me free. Not entirely, as you see. But she gave me my days back and I am grateful for that."

"So . . . you knew that every night you would be weak and injured?"

"Yes," he said.

Understanding dawned in her eyes and she sagged into a sitting position on the bed beside him. "You knew. You knew you couldn't touch me in this condition! You made me worry and fret, and all this time . . ."

He reached out then, snagging her wrist and pulling her eyes to his with the action. "I will not be this injured the whole of the night. I will heal. And you are mine until just before dawn. I promised you that you would be able to test my abilities as a lover and I intend to deliver on that promise." But the moment he saw the anxiety clawing its way up into her eyes, he eased. "But only when you are ready, my lady. You think little of me if you think I will force myself upon you."

She cleared her throat and looked down at their connected hands. "And if I never want to . . . to . . . ?"

"Oh, you will want to. I promise you that."

"I could easily say I don't. Whether I mean it or not."

"You mean you would lie. Somehow I doubt you will do that. You are not the lying sort."

"How do you know what sort I am?" she asked softly, looking down again. "You barely know me."

"I know enough. I know enough to know you are honest. That you are strong and brave, that you are a champion of those less fortunate than you are. I know you would have kissed that barbarian had I not stepped forward, because he had been promised a prize and you were willing to live up to that promise however repugnant you found it. Tell me . . . was that one of Grannish's ideas?"

She flushed and lowered her lashes, but not before he could see the fire of anger entering her eyes.

"He loves to humiliate me at every opportunity. He probably paid that barbarian to win. It is just the sort of machination he likes to take part in."

"That sounds a little paranoid," he mused.

"With good cause," she muttered.

"No doubt. Tomorrow I am to inspect the city guard and I wish to begin to accept volunteers of additional troops. Conscription will come later."

"It seems a sound plan," she said.

"It is, but I was wondering if you could help me gar-ner volunteers. It is one thing for a soldier to ask, quite another for the beautiful grandina of Hexis to ask her people to help her fight off their enemy. The people look up to you. They think good things about you. They want to help you."

"Well, I don't know if all that is true. But I will help you. I will do anything you need. Tomorrow I will go to the fair, in the square, and make a public address."

Just then Hanit and Tonkin arrived back at the rooms.

"Thank you, Tonkin," Selinda said dismissively. "You may go back to bed and you will speak of this to no one."

"My lady, I'm not the speaking sort, I can promise you that. Does my lord need me?" Tonkin hedged when he saw Hanit moving into Dethan's bedroom.

"Not anymore. Good eve and good night."

"Good night," the man said, although he didn't seem to want to go to bed and not be a part of whatever was happening beyond the other door.

Selinda went back into the bedroom, and with Ha-nit's help, she once again dressed Dethan's burns. He was able to sit back in bed in a certain amount of relief, the numbing agent in the herbs she used doing wonders.

He pulled a blanket up to cover himself from the waist down but she stopped him.

"I know the weight of it will be uncomfortable. Do not worry about my discomfiture. It is twice now I have seen you naked. It's rather becoming a habit."

"Speak to me again in a few hours when my vigor . . . and other things . . . are restored. In fact, I insist you stay around for that. You will sleep beside me. I would know the feel of your warmth in my bed. Up against me," he said, reaching to touch a finger to her temple, to the right side of her face, and drawing a line down along it to the very tip of her chin. The touch was so personal, so connecting, that she almost didn't comprehend the meaning of the words accompanying it. She felt incredibly drawn to him, more so with every passing minute, and she knew it was because he was the better choice presented to her. He had to be, and she had to accept that . . . and everything that went with it. If these were his demands in order for her to be free of Grannish, then she would submit to them.

"Now come, sit beside me, and let us get to know each other."

"Gods above," Hanit said softly, fanning herself with both hands and blinking rapidly. "If his lordship knew what you were doing . . . gods above."

"But he will not know," Dethan said sharply. "If he does, then we know exactly where it has come from, and I promise you I will not take kindly to my lady being put in danger."

Hanit gasped, then clenched her hands into fists and jammed them onto her hips.

"Oh dear, you are going to regret that," Selinda muttered quickly.

"Now, you listen here, Sor Baked-and-Roasted, I have been taking care of this girl for a year. Certainly longer than you have. She means the world to me, and I should matter. And who are *you* exactly? You are no one of any significance."

"Hanit . . ." Selinda tried to stop her. "Please forgive her. She's overprotective—"

"No! I'll speak my mind, and why shouldn't I? I don't like what you're into, your ladyship. I know I shouldn't have an opinion on the matter, but I do. I worry this vagabond is going to compromise you and leave your life in ruins . . . or worse. You heard Grannish today. That man would just as soon kill you if he had another way to get onto the throne!"

"Wait. Grannish came to you today?" Dethan asked

harshly, taking Selinda's chin in his hand and forcing her eyes to his. "What happened?"

"Nothing. It was nothing," she said, trying to reassure him. Her instinct was to placate the source of anger she was faced with at any cost. Of course she would react that way. It was the only way she knew how to survive, and it sickened Dethan when he thought about it.

"I am not angry with you, Selinda. And Hanit has every right to feel the need to protect you. There is much around you from which you need to be protected. But, Hanit, I promise you I am not one of them. We have honesty between us. I make no claims at romance or play at fanciful emotions and ideals. This is a contract between your mistress and me. I will fulfill my side of it and she hers, and nothing will muddy it up in between. Now, I am pleased to see how loyal you are to your mistress and I hope her trust in you is well justified, but we are all strangers in this room, so you will understand my mistrust ... especially when it could mean your mistress will be in danger."

This speech seemed to mollify Hanit somewhat, for her body relaxed a little from its steadfast, bristling pose.

"I do not care how big or how dangerous you may be. If you hurt her, you will have me to answer to, make no mistake about that!" Hanit reminded him sternly.

"And you have my permission to do so. Now, head back to your mistress's rooms and make certain no one finds her missing. This will be your task every night."

"After dressing you, you mean," Hanit said. "If you will be coming in each night looking like this"—she indicated his burned body—"she will need help dressing your wounds. Then I will head back. And if you do not mind me saying, your man is going to notice something eventually. You either have to tell him yourself and scare the silence into him or risk letting him tittle-tattle it to others in household gossip."

"You are right," Dethan said, mollifying her once again. Hanit nodded and then turned with a wide swing of skirts and left the room.

It wasn't until she shut the door that Selinda felt truly alone with Dethan.

"Now . . . come and sit and tell me all about you."

The request still surprised her, and it must have shown on her face, for he chuckled at her.

"Did you think I wouldn't want to know more details about the woman who will become my wife? And I am certain you have questions as well."

She nodded silently.

"Well, go on, then. Ask me something. Ask me anything, and for this time tonight I will answer all your questions."

"Did you have a wife?" she blurted out. "I . . . I mean before," she finished more tamely.

"I had two wives," he said. "Although not at the same time," he felt the need to add, knowing it was going to be her next question. "Both were very young when they died. After my second wife died there was no need for another."

"Did you . . . did you love them?" she asked, knowing she sounded foolish and childish for asking about it. Marriage was rarely about love. It was about gains and land and women used as bargaining chips.

"I . . . I married them for power," he said predictably. "They were the daughters of two rulers of two different cities I had acquired. My marriages were about establishing a foothold in the regency of each of those cities."

"Like what you are doing with me," she said quietly.

"Would you prefer I pretended otherwise?" he asked.

"No," she said hastily. "Please don't. I prefer honesty. I prefer to know where I stand."

"Then you will have honesty. I swear it to you."

"Do not make me a promise you cannot or will not keep," she said sternly. "I do not think I could tolerate another deceptive snake of a man in my life."

"He will not be in your life for long if we have our way."

"I would like that very much," she said with great feeling, making him chuckle. Then he reached for her, touching his thumb to her lips, running it gently over them.

"Was this for me?" he asked her, and she knew he meant the color she had painted there. She flushed hotly, but she nodded and looked down at her lap. "I like it very much," he said, and she found herself looking up at him with surprise before she could quell the reaction. He frowned then. "But you do not usually wear it because you are trying to keep peace with Grannish. Better to keep peace than satisfy a desire for a small indulgence, yes? I think you make many such sacrifices."

How strange, she thought, that he should notice such a fine detail. And that he should understand why she did not do it normally. "He does not like me to draw attention to . . ." She lifted her hand and brushed her fingertips over the scar on her jaw.

"I don't see why. The scar is not so very big. Why does everyone treat you as though half your face were engulfed in it?"

"I . . . cannot answer that. They just do."

"A simple accident. I am sorry. I am more sorry that people deem it a reason to find you anything but the beauty you are. And I thought so even before you made me an offer that might make me grand one day." He said it to cut the brewing thought off at the knees and she had to smile. How was it that he could anticipate the things she wanted to hear and know?

"Do . . . Have you ever had children?" she asked him.

"I did. And I often wondered what became of them. My two sons. They were ten and fifteen summers when I left them. Hopefully old enough to still become good men after I was lost to them. I think there is little I regret more than that. They should have had a father to raise them. Instead I was off on a fool's quest. One that ended very badly."

"I should think so," she agreed. "And I am glad—or at least I hope—that you have learned something from your errors. I would not wish to lose my husband to such an end."

"You should know," he hedged, "that I will be leaving you to rule in my stead once this is established."

This meaning their marriage.

"What do you mean?" she asked a bit numbly.

"I have a purpose, Selinda. I have a contract with the goddess Weysa. I must go forth and conquer cities in her name. I cannot do so from here."

"But . . . to conquer whole cities would take years! How would you be able to . . . I mean," she hastily covered a flushing cheek with her fist. "How do you think to have children if you are not here to father them?"

"I hope to leave you pregnant with our first child before I go," he told her baldly.

She was so upset by his news that she lurched to her feet.

"I-I will go with you!" she blurted out before she could stop herself. "You cannot leave me here with Grannish to win back his favor over my father, if indeed we can ever break my father's loyalty to him. I would come with you. Then I-I—"

She knew how desperate she sounded. Knew how desperate she must look. He reached out to her, taking her hand in his and pulling her back down beside him on the bed.

"Hush, little one," he soothed her, touching her on her face again in that reverent way. "I will not leave you until you are safe. And a campaign trail is no place for a woman. Not a delicately bred woman, in any event."

"I am not delicately bred," she said stubbornly, though they both knew it was a lie. "I am far tougher than I seem."

"You would have to be," he agreed, "in order to face Grannish every day and then dare to throw your lot in with a stranger in a wild effort to undermine him. That takes incredible strength and fortitude. Do not doubt it for a second. But a campaign is rough living. With rough men all about you, doing very rough things. Campaigning is not glamorous, nor is it as full of glory as the bards and recruiters would have you believe. Very often armies are less decimated by one another than they are by living conditions, illness . . . starvation. Desertion is the highest casualty rate in a poorly run campaign."

"But you would not run a campaign poorly," she said with remarkable assuredness.

"Ah no, that I would not," he said with a chuckle. "But you do not truly know that I would not. You have never seen me proved in battle."

"I wish I didn't have to at all," she said, and he could feel the fervor behind her words. He didn't fool himself into thinking her recalcitrance had anything to do with him. She was afraid for herself and for her family. Even for her people. All these things would come well before a damned former general with no army, no future, and very few prospects at present. In fact, it was probably very unfair of him to saddle her, young and beautiful as she was, with someone as damned as he was. For all he knew, tomorrow Weysa would come find him and drag him back down into the eight hells, where he would burn and rot once more.

The thought made his skin, formerly burning hot,

go ice-cold. He made himself laugh as a way of shedding the terror that might otherwise paralyze him. He couldn't afford to let fear get under his skin. It was his fearlessness, he believed, that had made him the general he was.

It had also gotten him into the position of being damned. Perhaps there was a better way of dealing with the world, but if there was, he was not aware of it. So . . . courage, purposefulness, and ruthlessness would have to be enough. They were all he had to offer her, and considering her circumstances, it would have to be enough for her as well.

"Come, lie down beside me and sleep for a while," he invited her, moving aside to make space for her, though she would have to climb over him to get to that space. He could have moved in the other direction, but for some perverse reason he did not. He enjoyed the color that flamed across her face.

Selinda's panic rose higher when he reached out and patted the bed beside him, asking her to join him once more. She must have looked stricken, because he chuckled and reached to touch that finger to her face again, the touch so soothing and disarming.

"I cannot make a nuisance of myself for a few hours yet. I want you to lie here and sleep. I do not expect for you to attend to me all night. I'm not a sick child, and besides, your weariness come the morning would start to tell. You must not appear to be anything different than you were before."

"All right," she said with caution. She slowly, gingerly began to climb over him.

"No. Not like that."

"Oh! Am I hurting you?" she asked with hasty worry.

"No. I meant you should take off your dress."

"But I—" She gasped.

"I will redress you myself. And you may leave on your undergarments. I assume you have some."

"Why, yes, an undergown. But it . . . it is plain and unattractive. Surely you do not wish to see it."

"I wish for you to sleep beside me. You cannot do that if you are laced tightly in a corset. The purpose of this fashion is clear, but the practicality of it falls very short. I only want you to be comfortable, little juquil."

Her face registered surprise. "That is what Hanit calls me."

"Rightly so. The juquil is an extraordinarily beautiful bird. Yet it is fearful and mistrusting. It is said that a man who can tame a juquil can tame the world. I used to keep juquils as pets, taming them into my hand."

"Really?" She was duly impressed by that. It took a sensitive, patient person to do such a thing. Something he was proving to be in spades.

"Do not be so impressed. I did it to prove I could tame the world. Highly selfish intents, I promise you. Now, let's be on with it."

She stood up from the bed and moved amusingly out of his reach. She didn't yet realize he was already well enough to move freely. He could lunge for her if he wished to and there would be nothing she could do to stop him. The thought made him frown. It also made him realize just how reckless it had been for her to strike this bargain, just how desperate she had been.

She began by unlacing her sleeves. They were long and went from the edge of her shoulder to the seat of her palm. He had noticed the daring bareness of her shoulders when she'd doffed her cape earlier. He had no doubt she would never have worn such a dress publicly for fear of inciting Grannish. But it stood to reason that if she had a gown like it hidden away, then she had defied her harsh master yet again, in another small way. And yet she did not think herself strong. It was very

clear to him that there was a steely spirit within her, but
it was on the verge of breaking. Grannish would have
her completely if Dethan did not achieve his promise to
help her. The idea sat very sickly in his stomach.

She next pulled the ties of her dress until it had
dropped to the floor.

"Do you need help?" he asked at that point.

She shook her head and reached back for the bow of
her laced-up stays, pulling it free. She pushed on her
chest, then pulled, doing so several times until the corset began to loosen and finally she could draw it over
her head. But first she hesitated and then shyly turned
away from him. He was just about to tease her when
he realized this was the very first time, no doubt, that
she had ever disrobed in front of a man. He needed to
be kinder to her. He was taking her far outside what she
normally felt comfortable doing and he would be patient with her as she found her footing in the situation.

And yet he could not let the moment simply slip by,
unnoticed and unremarked upon. Not only was it her
first time disrobing for a man, it was her first time disrobing for him. There would not be another and he would
not let it slip past unappreciated.

"Turn back to me," he said, his voice rasping lower
upon the request.

She went very still and turned her cheek toward him.
He could see the high color brush across it.

"Please . . . I cannot."

"You can and you will," he urged her gently. "I wish
to see what will come to me in my part of this bargain.
And I wish for you to see the appreciation in my eyes
when I do."

Her hesitation lasted a good long minute as she thought
about his request. Then slowly, bravely, she turned back
toward him. He could see the tautness of the bone corset, the ice-blue color of it and satin material seeming

somehow decadent on her finely shaped body. She had plump, pretty breasts and they were obviously at the edge of the corset, even though it was somewhat conservative. There was no hiding such delights. Men may try, but other men could always see the charms of a woman if they really wanted to. All it took was a decent imagination.

At last she slowly pulled the corset over her head. This left her in a thin chemise and a lighter underskirt, which was meant to add body and fullness to the skirt of her dress. It was still as heavy as the dress itself and it made him wonder exactly how much weight in clothing she must wear all day.

But an instant later all such thoughts flew away. An instant later he realized the chemise was near to sheer and he could see the dark tips of her nipples through it. His mouth went dry and his healing body grew tense. He tried to will himself into relaxing because there was a measure of pain involved, but he could not be convinced.

She was erotic and lovely even without trying, and he realized he wanted her. Wanted her in a way he had not wanted a woman for over two centuries.

He saw her hesitate in her disrobing, her finger toying with the bow at the back waist of those skirts.

"Do you mean I should . . . ?" she hedged.

"Does this chemise reach your knees?" he asked, somehow managing to sound unaffected. He had no desire to scare her away. Not when he was dying to see more of her. To feel her . . . even if it was just the feel of her weight and her warmth next to him in his bed.

"It reaches my ankles."

"Then, yes, I mean you should take off all but the chemise."

Her face colored again, something he was realizing he found delightful about her. She was so innocent, so delicately bred. No, he thought, she is not the sort of woman who would do well in a battle camp. Not that he would ever even want her there, he thought with haste.

Selinda swallowed hard before pulling the ties to her underskirt. Her heart was pounding so hard she was surprised he could not hear it. Or maybe he could but he just didn't care about her nervousness and fear. Did he not even realize what she was risking by doing this? Everything was on the line at that moment. Everything.

And yet all she could worry about was if he would find her ugly. She wasn't even wearing one of her prettier shifts. It was plain with no lace. Plain and thin, she realized as the cold of the room hit the warm fabric, making her feel just how exposed she was. *Foolish girl,* she thought. She had known it was possible he would see her in her underclothing. Why had she not thought to wear something prettier?

She felt his eyes on her and she dared to look at him. As mottled and burned as his face was, she could easily read the expression in his eyes. He craved the sight of her. He was waiting for more. And suddenly she felt as though she were standing fully naked in front of him. Her breasts grew heavy and felt obvious. Her belly grew taut with anticipation. Or was it fear? She didn't know. She had nothing to compare this experience to.

The moment her skirts hit the ground she hastened to the bed, crawled over him, and burrowed like a frantic little drivet beneath the cover on the bed. Although Dethan was quite certain she would not enjoy the idea of him equating her to a small, burrowing rodent, so he would adhere to thinking of her as a beautiful, wary juquil.

"Now relax and sleep," he said, even though both relaxation and sleep were far out of his own realm. "I will wake you before dawn so you can return to your rooms."

She couldn't hide the surprise on her face. She was so certain that he would do his worst to her. She probably didn't even remember the last time a male was kind to her. And, yes, he included her father in that. A man who would not listen to the fears of his daughter, who would not take her reports of abuse seriously, was very unkind indeed.

"You said . . . that I should . . . that I would . . ."

"Try me out?" he offered, chuckling when she gave him a shy nod. "Aye, and that you will. But not tonight. Now sleep. I will watch over you."

She snuggled down deeper under the covers, and he could see she was comforted by that idea. And as he watched her, slowly, surely, she finally drifted into sleep.

CHAPTER
ELEVEN

Selinda awoke to the gentle sensation of something stroking along the side of her face. It reminded her of what it felt like when Dethan touched her like that.

Dethan!

Selinda awoke suddenly and sat up like a shot, so that Dethan had to quickly dodge her to keep them from cracking their skulls together.

"Easy, little juquil. No need to be so startled. It is only me."

And that was what had her so startled, Selinda thought worriedly. She came awake enough to run her eyes over him and she realized with no little shock that he was healed over again, only white scarring in some places to mark where he'd been burned the worst. She knew this because he was entirely bare chested and bare legged and bare . . . everything! Before, when he had been so severely wounded, it had not mattered to her that he was naked. Indeed he had been so badly burned it was almost as though he weren't even a male. But he was very much a naked male now. The huge expanse of his chest, the thick strength of his thighs, the flexed muscu-lature of his abdomen all told her very clearly that not only was he male, he was a powerful one. He had been very gentle with her so far, but there was no mistaking the potential for brute force should he so desire it.

And then her eyes drifted to the narrowing of his hips and the sturdy hanging flesh of his penis. In fact, it was very sturdy. Very hard and sturdy.

She cringed away from him, scuttling back toward the wall. But he was having none of that. He locked a hand around her wrist, clamped another on her hip, and drew her closer to him.

"No," he scolded her. "You need not be afraid of me. We've talked about this."

"B-but . . . I did not expect you to be so . . . so . . . healthy," she finished lamely.

Dethan followed her wide eyes to where they were fixated on his body. He found himself laughing before he could help himself.

"Know you nothing of men?" he asked her. "No, of course you do not. But trust me when I tell you that even your own brothers awakened in this state, without any provocation. It is only nature that makes it so, all things natural and good."

"Good for you," she said dryly.

"And for you," he promised her. "But not until you are ready. I am not going to force you, Selinda."

"S-so if I say I don't want to make sex with you . . . you won't push me?"

"I did not say that," he said, his low voice dropping an octave lower. His hand drifted up her arm and his fingers caressed the bareness of her shoulder where the shift had fallen off it. "I am going to do everything in my power to push you, to coax you, into letting me inside you."

His frankness made her gasp and she tried to pull away again, but again he held her where he wanted her.

"This is for you," he reminded her, "not for me. And

while I get great benefit from it, this is for you to see if
we are compatible as lovers. And I promise you if you
do not find pleasure in my arms, I will let you out of our
agreement. I will do away with Grannish and let you be
free of us both." At her wide eyes he continued. "But if
you do find pleasure, then you will make me yours. Are
we agreed on that much?"

It seemed like a more than fair agreement, Selinda
thought. In fact, she could pretend not to feel anything
at all and she could potentially be rid of both men entirely! Oh, what would she do with such freedom, she
wondered, her body going soft with the wistful idea. To
be free of all the men who sought to control her would
be the answer to all her prayers.

But that was never to be. Not as long as her father
was alive and in control of her fate. And as difficult as
that was, she wouldn't wish him gone for anything in
the world. She had already lost too many of her family.
She couldn't bear losing any more.

But in the short term, it would not be so hard to act
as though she felt no pleasure. Honestly, she did not
understand how the act, described to her by her mother
shortly before her death, could in any way be considered pleasurable. Though her mother had assured her
that it was . . . with the right person.

The idea of Grannish doing that to get his children on
her had horrified her no end. Had her mother lived, she
would have put a stop to her father's blind plans for her.
But her mother had died two years earlier in childbirth.

Oh, why couldn't Selinda have been taken by the
plague like her sisters? Then none of this would worry
her. She would have gone to the fields of glory, chosen
one of the eight heavens, and broken bread with Kitari,
and all this would have meant nothing . . . would never
have happened.

"I know what you are thinking," he said, jerking her

back into the present moment with anxiety. He couldn't possibly know! "You are thinking you will not feel anything of great import," he said, that touch on her face once more. "But I am here to prove otherwise, and I will." His touch fell onto her lips, brushed there briefly, and continued down to her chin. Then, using his fingertips under her chin, he tipped her head back and made her look into his eyes. "You are so beautiful," he remarked with something almost like awe in his tone. "And you were made for loving."

"H-how so?" she wanted to know, trying for all she was worth to break the spell his deep voice and soft words were weaving. She felt herself being drawn to him, and it frightened her how strong a sensation it was.

"The beauty of your face is meant to please the eyes. The beauty of your body is meant to please another body," he said simply.

"Oh," she whispered. The truth was she was not used to being called beautiful by anyone other than Hanit, and she dismissed Hanit's praises as loyalty. There was something comforting in hearing it from the lips of another. Something compelling.

"You do not believe me," he said knowingly.

"I believe you have an agenda," she said, her voice more than a little bitter.

"I do, but that does not change the degree of your beauty. Think you I would want this throne so badly if it meant having an ugly wife? There are other thrones, other heiresses out there in the world who could be much easier to obtain. Easier, yes . . . prettier . . . no. I do not think so."

"There are. Prettier and unflawed," she said, with more bitterness in her words and the hard brush of her fingertips over the scar on her face. "My sister was much more beautiful than I ever could hope to be. She would have been an example of a potentially more beautiful heiress."

"Since I never met her, I cannot agree or disagree. But you forget I have been married for power twice before . . . Ask me how beautiful my wives were."

"Were they very?" she asked, unable to prevent herself from doing so. Her curiosity was too great.

"Quite. I would not have married them otherwise. So you see, I will not marry an ugly woman; therefore, you must be stunning."

She couldn't help but laugh at his reverse logic. "I still think you have an agenda," she said, only this time with a smile.

"You already know that I do. But that agenda does not include lying to you. I can achieve my ends without any pretty talk. So any pretty talk you receive you can be assured is truthfully meant. But do not get too used to it," he warned playfully. "I am a coarse man with no manners and very little prettiness to my talk. You may never hear me say such things again."

"Oh, but that would not do at all. If you wish to *please* me, you will have to talk prettily to me constantly."

Dethan laughed at her sly remark. "So that's the way of it, then? Well, good thing that I find you beautiful."

She smiled at him, the expression lighting her features and making her so much more attractive. In fact, it made him realize how unhappy her expressions truly were throughout the day. But he would be unhappy in her situation as well.

He found his gaze drawn to her smiling lips. She had colored them for him and the color still held, even after sleeping. It made them seem a darker, richer magenta color against the backdrop of her white teeth. Her breath smelled sweet, he thought. A scent he knew and yet could not place. Yes, she had endeavored to attract him to her tonight, and she had succeeded famously. The very idea that she had engineered herself to please him was something he found lighting a fire in his blood.

He used his touch on her chin to tip her head a little farther back, and he fixated on those lush berry lips. She looked as though she would taste as delicious as she looked, and he was determined to test the theory.

His mouth moved to only an inch away from hers, their breath mingling, his slow and deep, hers fast and short. He could see the anxiety crawling through her, so he did not drag it out any longer than need be. The longer he waited, the longer she had to make mountains of fear inside of herself.

His mouth touched hers.

He was infinitely gentle. Letting her adapt to the feel of his lips. At least he was at the start of it. He had not intended to overwhelm her, had had the very best of intentions, but it had been so long since he had known the taste of a woman.

So very damn long.

And the taste he'd had of her before, he found, was not even close to enough. Remembering how she had reacted so hotly to their first kiss had him dragging her even tighter into this one, his arms wrapping around her in fervent bands of need. She resisted him, her hands flattening against his chest and pushing against him for a very long moment. But then, after that moment, she softened, relaxed . . . welcomed.

She was his first woman in a very long time, for almost ten times as long as she had been alive. He told himself that this was the reason why he felt so suddenly impatient.

She was warm against him, so very warm. Without her outer clothes, she was soft and supple. He had felt her against him before, but the rigidity of her corset had kept him at a distance. He wondered then if it wasn't so much a fashion statement as a method of men keeping their women all the more chaste. For who would want to be intimate with the feel of metal rods?

But here and now she was lush and young, and it made him crave so many things all at once. He hardly knew what to do first. He was struggling with himself, trying to keep a rein on his arousal. She was fresh and innocent. He could feel it . . . smell it on her. She positively reeked of it. And somehow that made her even more desirable to him. He marveled at the craving. He had never wanted innocents before. He had found them trying. He preferred skill and experience far and above the idea of being the first one there.

Oh, but there was something intriguing about the idea of no one having touched her before this. Of no one having kissed her. Yes. Intriguing and delightful and oh so delicious.

That was nothing compared to the actual flavor of her, however. A flavor he dove more deeply for the next instant. With the touch of two fingers on her chin, Dethan coaxed Selinda's mouth open.

Nervousness clenched around her heart. They had kissed like this before, but they had not been closed away in a room . . . she had not been lying beneath him in a bed. He could do anything he wanted to. Anything at all, and there would be nothing she could do to gainsay him. He had it over her in sheer size and in more than obvious strength, not to mention that he, who had been penniless in the mud a mere day ago, had far and away more power over his fate than she did. And that was saying something, seeing as how he was cursed by the gods.

She wanted to worry about that. Wanted to tell herself she should be afraid to throw her lot in with someone who had the gods' swords at his throat. Life was difficult enough for her as the powerless female heir to a country . . . Would she really wish to incite the wrath of the gods as well?

Yes.

It was better to give herself to this man, like this, in the face of all those gods, than the alternative. At least this way it made it her choice. In this she would whole-heartedly defy that tyrant who held her in such a vise-like grip.

That didn't change the fact, however, that she didn't really know what to do next. She found herself cursing the chastity she had previously been so proud of. She knew other women of the court gave their favors freely, to one man and the next, but she had kept herself above that . . . above even the most pious mem. Selinda had remained perfectly chaste. She, the first lady of the court, had set a perfect example. A reputation she had used as a shield from the advances of others . . . including Grannish. Before he had shown his true colors he had tried to coax her into kissing him or letting him hug and pet her, but she had kindly rebuffed him, using her honor as her guard and chaperone.

Now she feared there was nothing she could do if he decided one day to come after her in earnest. Luckily he thought her so repulsive that the idea apparently wasn't crossing his mind.

Thanks be to Hella.

Selinda drew in a soft breath right before Dethan's tongue slipped inside her mouth. The sensation, the in-vasion, was still so strange that she pushed away from him, breaking their mouths apart. His response was to give her a reproaching expression, then he gently wrapped his hand around her head, his big palms en-gulfing her and making her feel so small as he pulled her mouth back against his and reintroduced the feel of his warm tongue in her mouth. It was a gentle invasion. A dip, just far enough to touch their tongues together, then he pulled his tongue back so only their lips clung together. He did it again. And again. Until she was moaning softly from the steady growth in the heat of the kiss. She could feel it, the energy of his leashed desires, just a little below the surface. It was like a beast in a powerful cage. But he was the strongest cage there was and he would not let the beast get to her, she thought.

Not yet.

She jerked away from him with a gasp.

"Please!" she cried, the word jolting out of her purely on instinct. He seemed to know that was the case, for he smiled at her, the expression lightening the darkness of his features. She liked it when he smiled. She had come to understand that he had so much weight on his shoulders, so many things trying to press him down. She liked the idea that when she made him smile it was almost like pushing that darkness aside. Lifting the weight off him.

"Please? Go on. Tell me what you please. Tell me what pleases you, little juquil."

"I . . . I wish . . . I-if it is all right . . . I should like this to stop. F-for now."

She was testing him, Dethan realized. She was testing him to see if he would grant her request or if he would grow angry with her for thwarting his attempts to be passionate with her.

"Do you wish to stop?" he asked her, turning it back on her. "Or are you afraid to continue? There is a difference between the two."

"I-I do not understand," she said, clearly casting about for what would both fulfill her wishes and keep him from becoming incensed. She was so used to volatility that it did not occur to her that it should be absent. "Do not be angry with me. I am just not used to such familiarity."

"I am not angry," he assured her in a low, steady tone.

"Nor will I ever be with you. I am not a man prone to temper. No, wait. That is untrue. I can have a great deal of anger within me. But as long as you are honest with me and keep faith with me, I will never direct that anger toward you. Do you understand?"

"Keep faith?" she asked shakily.

"I understand what it must take for you to trust me or anyone right now, but I will prove myself to you. Once I do, I expect your true loyalty to me. Unquestioning. Putting no other desires before those that you know would best represent and please me. That does not mean I do not want you to have your own voice, for you are of no use to me without a voice and thoughts of your own. I can get a womb anywhere; what I need is a mother and wife and political ruler. That is why I have chosen you. Just as you have chosen me to be a warlord, a husband, a provider, and a protector. If we keep faith with each other, we can become an unstoppable force together. I will be able to leave you in charge of the city while I conquer other lands in Weysa's name. I must know that you can be trusted to fill that role."

After a long moment of staring up into his eyes, a long enough moment to make him question whether or not she had heard him, she looked away, shook her head gently, and laughed.

"There must be something wrong with you," she insisted before looking back into his eyes. "My fortunes are not this good as a rule. There must be something wrong with you."

He chuckled at her. "There are a great many things wrong with me. Do you forget I am cursed?"

Her frown was instantaneous. "Is there no way to cure you from this curse?"

"None," he assured her. "My only goal is to fulfill Weysa's demands of me."

"Perhaps if you perform well she will forgive you your crimes entirely and set you free."

"I would not presume such a thing. It serves no purpose to exercise false hopes, so please, I wish you to stop thinking on it. All I need from you is to come be by my side each night and help ease me."

She lowered her lashes at that remark, color spotting her cheeks. "I will do whatever I can. Whatever you ask."

"Little juquil, you are not a slave to me," he said sternly, lifting her chin up with his hand and making her look into his eyes. "Do you understand? I have seen the fire in you. The defiance you show. I want to cultivate that fire, build it until it burns so brightly others will have to look away from its powerful beauty. Do you understand?"

"Are you certain that's what you want?" she asked cautiously. "Most men prefer their wives cowed and dutiful."

"Dutiful, yes. Cowed, no. Feel free to test me. In time, you will understand. Now it grows light. You need to get back to your bed lest you are caught."

Dethan rose from the bed and she flushed furiously, looking away from him as he stood gloriously nude and held out a hand to her.

She scooted out of the bed, lurching to her feet. She hastily slid on her corset, adjusting herself and trying to reach her own laces. She jumped a little when she felt his hands settle over hers and then push them away. He took the ties into his hands and slowly, learning how to do it with a few queries, he laced her into her corset just as well as Hanit would have done, if taking a little longer in the doing of it. His hands kept drifting along the length of her torso. Caresses she did not feel through the stiffness of the corset yet was still very aware of.

Next, she stepped into her dress and pulled it over her

arms. He helped her lace this together as well where it was needed. Then he reached for her cloak as she stepped into her slippers. He cloaked her and then turned her to face him. There she was, fully dressed in contrast to his utter nudity, and she still felt as though she were nude with him. She felt far more exposed than he was as he tipped up her chin and gave her one more gentle kiss on the lips before sending her out into the hallway.

CHAPTER
TWELVE

~~~~~~~~~~~~~~~

Grannish was studying his adversary hard.

He sat in one of the empty household chambers that looked over the fortress bailey. In the bailey were the usual comings and goings, but there was something very distinctly different today. There was a line of men leading away from two tables that had been set up. A very long line. Apparently this Dethan had posted notices and paid for criers to announce that Hexis was forming an army, that troops would have bread and a bed within the week. All they need do was volunteer.

Grannish had thought perhaps fifty men would respond to something like that. It was not glamorous, did not promise glory and personal fulfillment. Just a bed and bread and a little joining silver. And yet there it was, a long line of men leading out of the bailey, down into the streets, and as far as the old High Post. Perhaps beyond that. Where Grannish was he did not have the proper perspective to see. But there were well over two hundred men waiting and fifty others had already been given their joining silver and the papers they would need to gain a bed in the barracks, once the barracks were done being built.

Grannish smiled. He wondered just where and how these magical barracks would be built. Grannish had instructed the master of the king's purse to be very stingy when it came to the army's needs. He was going to make this as difficult to pull off as he possibly could. After all, it would not do if Dethan were somehow able to actually succeed at this attempt to free them from the Redoe's siege.

No, it would not do at all. Grannish refused to be upstaged by some upstart peasant who was promising solutions to problems that had none. Grannish had tried raising an army himself before, and the results had been lackluster. He had been reduced to forcing men to become soldiers, forcing them to fight, the lazy bastards. But the army, such as it was, had fallen apart and their attempt to cure the Redoe plague had failed.

Well, it would fail again, Grannish thought. He would see to it. Volunteers or no volunteers, Dethan would be forced to call up a draft eventually. It was the only way to get the numbers that would be needed to set the Redoe down. Then they would see what a waste of time it was.

There were two clerks at the two tables taking down names and giving out papers. Behind the clerks stood Dethan, his arms folded over his chest, his calculating, dark eyes taking in the goings-on with an almost evil air. Often he would step forward and say something to the new soldier.

Soldiers were all well and good, but it took a chain of command to run an army, which meant lords of high houses. And Grannish would see to it that not one lord of any of the high houses stepped forward to offer command. If they did, they knew Grannish would make them pay for it. One way or another, they would pay. He would bide his time so it did not look so obvious, but eventually he would poison the grand against that particular lord until he was no longer a lord, his lands and titles stripped from him at the command of the grand. Grannish was a very, very patient man with an excellent record as far as these things were concerned. His reputation would ensure compliance. All the lords knew not to cross him.

He had already begun to make it clear to them that they were in no way to help Dethan's cause. The trick was how to do it while seeming to be supportive of it when in front of the grand. He could puppet the grand only so far. The grand was still under the illusion that he was in control of his own city. There were times like this, like with Dethan, when the grand went completely off in his own direction without seeking any guidance from Grannish.

But that was okay, Grannish thought serenely. It had become a little boring of late, to be honest. Manipulating that regal idiot and his whiny little daughter was sometimes so easy he could cry with the boredom of it.

At that moment the little bitch herself walked out into the courtyard. Everything ground to an instant halt and everyone bowed to her respectfully.

Everyone save Dethan. Dethan merely watched her, those dark eyes looking at her with . . . with what? Grannish wasn't certain. He needed to figure out how to get into the man's head. Needed someone to pay very close attention to him.

"Your lordship, *Page* Tonkin," his page announced, the disdain he felt at being forced to call Tonkin "page" all too clear.

Tonkin was as big and oafish as could possibly be imagined. He actually had to duck to keep from hitting his head on the top of the doorframe. Where in the hells had Dethan found this fellow? Grannish thought he was familiar somehow, but he could not place him.

"Ah, Page Tonkin. Good of you to join me," Gran-

nish said, turning his back on the window and his all-
seeing view of the courtyard.

"As your lordship likes," Tonkin said deferentially.
The page's cap was in his hands and he was mauling the
fabric in great pawing twists. He was nervous. Good.

"Sit down, my good man," Grannish invited, indicating a nearby chair.

"If it's all the same, I'll stand. My lord Dethan will be
wanting after me soon."

"*Sor* Dethan is no lord," Grannish bit out.

"He is *my* lord, begging your pardon."

Grannish frowned but decided he had better things
to do with his time than teach the lumbering ass about
etiquette. "Page Tonkin, I will get straight to the point.
You know who I am, correct?"

"Yes, your lordship. Everyone knows who you are."

"Very good. I am here to make you an offer. And before I make the offer, I want you to take into consider-
ation what I might do if you choose to refuse the offer."
Grannish smiled when Tonkin went suddenly still, like
a deer in the woods that had heard a sound and knew
something dangerous was lurking about. "I know you
are a farmer, with lands beyond the walls. I also know
you have not cultivated your fields this year. That is a
direct violation of your deed agreement with the grand.
Technically I could default your lands right now and
you'd never be able to set foot on them again."

"B-but I . . . I didn't have the money for seed this year
'cause the Redoe took all my crop last year. They took
a lot of the crops last year. I'm not the only one—"

"I really do not care about any of that," Grannish
said, trying with difficulty not to yawn in the other
man's face. "The law says a farmer must farm his fields
or he will be in default. You are in default."

He let Tonkin stew on that a moment.

"What's your offer?" Tonkin ground out. It was clear

the man was trying to rein in his temper. There was anger in his eyes and tightness around his mouth.

"You are angry. Good. I want you to be angry. And I want you to remember that had your new master not singled you out and made you his page, I would never have known about your farm. Now, while you think on that . . . my offer is thus: You tell me anything and everything of significance your master does and I will not only overlook your breaking of the rules but I will give you enough money to buy seed for next year's crops."

Grannish truly wanted to laugh. It was all Tonkin could do to keep his jaw from dropping open. So easy. It was all so easy. All it took was knowing where they were most vulnerable and where they were most greedy.

"So? What is your answer?" Grannish asked needlessly.

Selinda was not an idle grandina, Dethan thought as he watched her from a distance. When he had left her this morning shortly after breaking their fast, she had been called aside to handle a domestic squabble of some kind. Then before noon meal he found her in the common room presiding over matters of law and arguments between the commoners or general grievances. She listened to every one very carefully and her quick mind always seemed to come up with the perfect solution. She was fair but stern when necessary. Kind and altruistic when it was called for. A ruler to her very core. This was a proceeding her father should be officiating over, in Dethan's opinion, and a remark questioning that made Tonkin tell him that it was indeed supposed to be the grand's duty, but he was dealing with other matters of state. It was often the case, it seemed, for the grandina was usually the one presiding on any given grievance day.

Later on, she came into the courtyard, and as Dethan stood behind the drafting tables, he watched her stop and have a conversation with nearly every commoner in the bailey. She had ordered kitchen wenches to bring water to the men standing in line in the sweltering sun, then she walked slowly down the line greeting them, many by name, and thanking them for their service to the crown. Telling them how vital they were and how appreciated they were. It was by far the best thing she could have done. *There she is, the grandina, reaching out, touching, and feeling gratitude toward me . . .* What man alive wouldn't want to be touched by something so ethereal in both station and actual beauty. She believed they thought her ugly, and that may be, but it was just as clear they were readily willing to look past that fact and see the inner beauties she had to offer.

Yes, he thought, she would be a phenomenal ruler in his stead. Oh, he had his doubts that so kind a heart had the toughness needed to keep a city safe. He would have to leave a proven and trusted lieutenant behind to support her rule. But who? As it was, he was in need of captains to marshal all these men. The men needed to be organized into work details, put to the task of building their own barracks. They needed to know there was a watchful eye above them. Until they proved themselves together, there would be little cohesion. Right now all that drove them was the promise of a hot meal and a roof. Providing those things would take time, effort, and, more important, money.

And that was why he was standing in the office of the grand's coin handler, fuming at being made to wait a full twenty minutes while the coin handler tallied a seemingly endless amount of numbers.

"Now, what is it you want?" he said at last, peering

down his nose at Dethan from his raised dais. Behind him, behind a significant guard detail—one that Dethan hadn't noticed the first time he had come here—was presumably the vault holding the grand's coin. It was a massive metal door surrounded by thick stone. It was locked in no less than five different places. But the coin could be under a thousand locks and it wouldn't be any safer from the potential invading force outside the gate. Once the castle was overrun, it would be nothing at all to get at a vault.

"I told you," Dethan said, impatient from having stood under the hot sun all day. His burn scars, what few were left by then, had not liked the heat at all. "I will need significant coin in order to build the men's barracks and pay them their first wages."

"Pay wages? What for? They haven't done anything yet!" the man scoffed. "We don't have the money to cast at every lowborn piece of trash out there on the promise of what they *might* do."

Dethan stepped forward, his expression dangerous. "You do your job your way and I will do mine my way. Let us agree on that."

"I do agree. And my job is to hold the grand's coin as tightly as possible! I will not allow it to be spent frivolously."

"But the grand has charged me with this task and this task requires money," Dethan said, his fist clenching as he resisted the urge to climb up the dais, grab the pinched-nose little fiend, and shake the wax out of his ears.

"That may be, but until Jenden Grannish tells me to release a specified amount of coin, I am not able to do so. As it stands, the jenden has allowed for . . ."—he peered at a piece of paper—"twenty gold sovereigns."

"Twenty—! That won't even pay for the building of the barracks!"

"That is the sum allotted. Do you wish it or not?"

Dethan ground his teeth. Grannish. He should have realized. The entire household, the entire granddom, was run by Grannish, held hard in his fist. He would have to tackle this another way.

"Very well. Twenty sovereigns. It is a beginning."

He stood there waiting while the coin was doled out to him and then he turned to Tonkin. "I'm in need of many things and have no idea how to find them. I will need your help most of all in these matters."

"You can count on me, my lord," Tonkin said.

"First, I need a ledger. I wish to track this coin as closely as possible."

"A wise idea," the coin handler said, suddenly eagerly interested in Dethan. "I have an empty ledger for you." Something resembling a smile touched his thin lips. "Perhaps if you show the use of your coin thoroughly the grand will issue you more."

As Dethan accepted the ledger he could tell that the coin handler had acquired a sort of respect for the new general that had not been there moments ago. As though he was impressed that Dethan would be keeping books on his expenditures. But why wouldn't he, Dethan thought in puzzlement. Any good army was run with good bookkeeping. Without well-managed coin a campaign could fall apart. It was one of the many underpinnings that held an army afloat. Food. Coin. Leadership. Strategy. These were key. And Grannish knew this as well, Dethan realized. Grannish was going to attack his efforts by attacking his underpinnings. So not only was he expected to battle the Redoe, he was expected to do it while Grannish kicked away as much of Dethan's support as he could.

Dethan would have to figure a way around this, and the key to that would no doubt lie in completely winning over the grand.

But wait. If Selinda was acting in her father's stead in matters of state, then clearly she had the ability to delegate coin. But should he use her in this way? It might draw unwelcome attention to her by Grannish.

No, he would need to do this another way. As he left the room, he drew Tonkin beside him.

"I need lieutenants. I can second some from the city guard, but I would much prefer an untapped resource."

"Well, usually the nobles lead the forces of an army," Tonkin provided.

"Why? Are they better skilled at it?" Dethan asked sharply. "Birthright does not make for the best generals. The man in charge of the forces at present is a fine example of that. No. I need strong leaders that the men will want to follow. Men with brains enough to handle strategy and direction, who are not slaves to impulsivity."

"Then I know just where to find them," Tonkin said with a toothy grin.

Selinda moved down the hallway, just a few rooms away from her own, to the nursery. She pushed into the room and found her young brother sitting on the floor in the sunshine playing with a rag doll.

"Linda!" he cried, reaching his arms up to her. He still couldn't quite get her full name right. But that hardly mattered. It was one of the things that endeared him to her. She hastened to kneel beside him and gathered his frail little body into her arms, pressing him close to her heart.

"So, Drakin, how are you feeling today?"

"Oh, he's having a good day, my lady," the governess said fondly. She had been sitting in a rocking chair watching over the young boy.

Selinda didn't quite know if the nanny could be trusted.

Grannish had been the one to hire her, yet the nanny seemed entirely devoted to Drakin. She spoiled him, to be honest, and it was clear he was the apple of her eye. But Selinda couldn't escape the feeling that the nanny might be a viper in disguise, poised to strike the innocent child down at Grannish's command.

"Feel good!" Drakin confirmed. "Play wif me?" he asked, holding up the doll.

"Of course I will," she said with a smile. She sat him back on the floor with no little reluctance. She always felt he was safer while in her arms. But she couldn't watch over the child every single minute of the day. Had she been free of her duties as chatelaine she might have, but there was no one else and so many people depended on her.

She sometimes felt guilty for that. Even though she frequently snuck away to play with her brother, she still felt guilty that she could not keep better watch over him.

"Come, now. Let's find me a dolly and we shall play together," she said, scooting over to his toy chest.

She would play with him, and for a little while they would be safe and happy together.

"The grand sits up there in his pretty fortress eating his elegant food with his elegant daughter while we are down here starving! Our farms are overrun with the enemy. Every year the money we invest in seed is in danger of being thrown away should our fields be the ones the Redoe savage before they leave! And yet we are required to till and seed every year or we risk losing our farms entirely! Where is the fairness in that?" the lead speaker demanded, setting up a roar from the crowd stuffed into the large room.

Dethan stood in the back of the room with Tonkin,

leaning against the wall with his arms folded over his chest as he listened to the speaker. There were six of them altogether, standing at the head of the room. They stood on top of a table. So that everyone could see them, Dethan thought. And so that they were perceived as being bigger than they were. Very clever. As they spoke, reeling off points of why their lives were unbearable and who was most to blame, the crowd became more and more riled up. Shouting and surging as one. It was a powder keg, Dethan thought. It was the way revolutions were born. Was that the goal here? Or was this just a way of venting frustrations? Dethan knew of a sure way to find out. He took a step forward, drawing in a breath, readying to speak up.

"And the grandina," the man said suddenly.

Dethan stiffened, his words freezing on his lips. *What of her? What did they think of Selinda?*

"A good heart means nothing when trapped in a gilded cage," the speaker said bitterly. "She tries and we can all see it, but as long as she is controlled by others, she has no true effectiveness. And others *will* control her for the rest of her days. Her engagement to Grannish has seen to that."

Instead of roaring approval this time, the crowd fell deadly silent. A wave of discomfort rippled through the crowd and one of the other men stepped forward to say something with haste in the speaker's ear.

"I don't care," he said, shrugging off the man who was clearly warning him, his voice swelling over the crowd like a wave. "You see? I am not afraid to speak his name! Grannish! We all know he is the poison that is killing this city! We are just too afraid to do anything about it!"

"Kyran, please," the other man said, this time more loudly. "You know anyone who speaks against Grannish does so at risk of his life. We need you here, alive, not in Grannish's dungeons or dead from a mysterious illness. Grannish has the power to see into even the most hidden corners. You must be careful!"

"Let him come for me. Let them all cart me away. At least I will know I spoke my true heart and wasn't afraid to do so."

The crowd went absolutely wild, cheering in support, gaining courage from the man's blatant bravery.

"But can you temper that recklessness?" Dethan shouted above the ruckus.

The room turned as a single entity toward Dethan when he'd shot out the query.

"And who are you?" Kyran asked warily, eyeing the make of his clothes, which stood out in the crowd of mud farmers and commoners.

"A man looking for men who wish to make a difference," Dethan said.

"You mean you're a noble looking for peons to do your dirty work," the leader scoffed.

"I'm no noble."

Kyran narrowed his dark eyes on the man, seeing that his stance was strong and his lack of fear in the face of a rowdy crowd emanated off him in impressive waves. Kyran could believe the man was not a noble. Nobles were soft. Arrogant without cause.

"Then who are you?" Kyran asked when the man did not volunteer the information.

"I am Dethan, and I am to lead an army of men against the Redoe."

Kyran laughed and the laughter was echoed throughout the room.

"I heard something about this. Another folly led by the nobles, done half well and as ineffectual as ever."

"There will be no half measures this time," Dethan said, stepping forward into the crowd. The mass of men tried to bully him with their size and their discontent, but he paid them no mind. "I do not lose when I fight a war."

"Strong words. You think much of yourself."

"I do. I am a proven general. I have conquered many cities. A pestilence like the Redoe will be an easy matter . . . provided I can find strong and trustworthy lieutenants. Do you say you are up to the task?"

Kyran was floored and looked around him, as if to discover which of his fellow revolutionaries had set him up for a joke.

"He speaks with truth," Tonkin spoke up over the rising response from the crowd. "Are you all talk or will you put your words to action?"

The room fell silent, and they all looked up at Kyran. The leader swallowed as he tried to grasp how the use of the room had changed from being his sounding board to being a source of expectation to action. All with just a few words and the presence of a man.

"I'll not fight to line the pockets of fat nobles," Kyran scoffed.

"But will you fight to get your farms back? Will you fight to free the city of Grannish's grasp? For if we succeed in this endeavor, we will have done both." Dethan stepped up to the table Kyran was standing on. "You say you have no love of Grannish? Then help me to depose him. Every task I accomplish that he could not will elevate me above him in the grand's eyes."

"And why should I want you to be elevated? Why should I help you in your effort to gain power?"

"My power will be the people's power. I will only ever have as much as they will want me to have. I will prove myself over time and will gladly work to earn their trust. I am asking for you to help toward that end. Let us make a start by giving the mud farmers back their lands and freeing this city from the siege that hurts its trade and starves its people. Show me you have the skill and bravery to lead men into battle, and I will make you my second in command." Dethan gave the group an assessing glance. "Take with you those you trust most to do what you ask of them.

"You are standing here demanding power to change things and here I stand offering it to you. Will you accept it or are you just full of words?"

Kyran's jaw clenched as he realized he was being baited and manipulated . . . and that it was working. "How do I know you have the power to do what you say?" he asked, honestly wanting to know. He had been watching so many of his people suffer under Grannish's governance. He had longed for the opportunity to do something for them in the face of that known tyrant. But he had felt just as helpless as everyone else. They couldn't even plot a proper revolution because the Redoe had all movement out of the city completely blocked off. There was no way to gain munitions except through the black market, and the blockade runners charged dearly for their services. And no wonder, for it was a deadly business. Anyone caught leaving the city met a bad fate at the hands of the Redoe. They would not be moved until they wished to be moved.

"I'm awaiting an answer. The offer will stand for only as long as I am in this building. I do not have time to waste on prevaricators."

Dethan waited another few moments while the rebellious speaker struggled with what he should do next. Then he turned on his heel and began to walk toward the exit door. It wasn't until his hand was on the handle of the door that the man blurted out. "All right!"

Kyran leapt off the table and pushed through the murmuring crowd as Dethan turned back toward him.

"Very well, you say you are a general. You say you can do these things. I will be with you and I will watch you closely. The minute I see you are in this solely for your own gain while walking on the backs of others, so help me I will run you through myself."

"You can try. I am not that easy to run through," Dethan said with some amusement.

"That's good, because Grannish isn't going to stand for you. He will not let you show him up and he will use any means necessary."

"Including no doubt killing off my best lieutenants," Dethan noted.

Kyran narrowed his eyes a moment, then he chuckled. "He can try," he said. "I am not easy to run through either."

"I'm glad to hear it. Now come with me. Tonkin says you can duel with a sword as well as you duel with your tongue. Come show me. And bring with you the men you feel can swing one as well."

Kyran nodded and held out his hand. "Kyran," he said.

Dethan pressed the back of his hand to Kyran's.

CHAPTER
THIRTEEN

Selinda was being watched.

She ought to have been used to it. She'd been spied on constantly since Grannish had come into a position of power. But this was something very, very different. The dark eyes upon her were those of a tall, powerfully built man, one whose surety and confidence seemed to radiate into her even from the relative distance he was standing at.

Dethan didn't even flit an eyelash when she turned to meet his regard of her with a lifted chin. She wanted him to know she was aware of his disconcerting staring. She couldn't figure out why he was watching her so closely. Was he looking to see if she would somehow betray his trust? Was it just because he lacked Grannish's network of spies and therefore had to resort to doing the dirty work himself?

She tried to focus on her task at hand. She was in the main antechamber, sitting on the cold stone floor amongst a throng of children, all plucked from the lower quarter of the city. Their clothes and their feet were brittle with dried mud.

She was teaching them basket weaving. On other days she taught stitchery. On still others she taught cooking.

She stood up after a while, moved around the children, and encouraged or corrected them, then—unable to help herself—she left the circle of children and faced him, moving to the wall he had chosen to lean against. As she confronted him, she couldn't escape how much bigger he seemed. Taller for certain, but the sheer mass of muscle had increased considerably throughout the day. She was realizing that this was truly how he had once looked. The frailer man she had first met had not yet had the opportunity of a full day to heal. Now it was nearing evening meal and he looked . . . vital. So alive and so strong. It gave her hope that he really would be able to face the challenges he would be coming up against, and it also filled her with trepidation. There was no sense that this man might be tamed. When he gained traction in this world, there would be little to stop him. She would once again be ineffectual in the face of a powerful man should he choose to use that power against her.

Still, she would not let herself be tamed by him any more than she let Grannish tame her. Perhaps that made her stupid. She often argued with herself about it: Wouldn't it be better to just keep her head down, do as he wished, and not make any waves? It would be safer, but it would not be better.

When she reached Dethan he nodded to the gathering of children. "Why do you do this? Can your time not be better spent?"

She lifted her chin and set her jaw, and he could see the affront in her eyes. He knew he was about to be upbraided, and she did not disappoint.

"These children have nothing," she said. "They are poor, their parents barely able to clothe them." She nodded to one child, who was nearly naked. "These are skills that might one day be marketable. One day they might make a living . . . or at the very least they can provide things for use in their own homes. They cannot read, cannot do figures. I would teach them, but . . . there're just too many of them, and Grannish will not provide schools."

Dethan could see the regret swimming in her brilliant blue eyes. She had the blackest of lashes, he realized, a perfect frame for the stunning teal of her eyes. When strong emotion filled them, like it did right then, it made them seem so compelling to him. He found he had the hardest time looking away from them. From her. There was so much beauty to her. She was tall for a woman. Fair-skinned and held safe from the rigors of the sun. Pale and protected. At first glance her frame might seem too slender, too delicate, but the strength in her spine and in her heart defied the delicacy of her build.

Dethan's gaze dropped to the swells of her breasts at the reasonably conservative line of her corset. She wore deep purple today, the darkness of the color making the skin of her cleavage seem all that much paler. He found her breasts were also dusted with the lightest hint of freckling. It made him want to touch his mouth to that skin. To stroke his tongue over the little marks.

The thought took him by surprise, as did the sensation of excitement that slithered through his body. Then craving came quickly on its heels. It had been so long since he had felt true desire that it stunned him. The times he had kissed her had been almost . . . chaste. But now, as time wore on, he found himself unable to stop watching her. Watching how she moved, the way her long skirts swayed and brushed the floor with every shift of her weight or drift of her hips. She moved so fluidly. Almost sensuously.

Even better, he knew she was completely unaware of it. So that meant it came naturally to her. How rare and exotic that was . . . a woman born to sensuality. Oh, he had known many women who had tried to peddle themselves as sensuous creatures, but he had always seen through them, had always found them wanting.

There was nothing left wanting about Selinda.

"Grannish would prefer the poor remain ignorant and easier to handle. That's his theory. I do not think—Why are you staring at me?" she asked fiercely, a hand fluttering up to cover the cleavage he had been fixated on.

He looked up to meet her eyes and found himself answering her honestly. "Because you have the prettiest breasts I've ever seen, and just the sight of them has me thinking and craving things I am sure you could hardly begin to imagine."

She caught her breath and he saw color flush across her cheeks and then across her breasts. Her breathing increased in tempo.

"Wh-what a thing to say to a woman!" she hissed at him, clearly flustered.

He chuckled at her. "If you're offended by that, I won't mention what comes to my mind when I see those sweet hips of yours."

Selinda gasped. She ought to have been horrifically offended, as he said, but along with her shock at being spoken about in such a way came something else . . . something heated and quick that raced through her blood. Unable to help herself, she imagined the things he might be thinking . . . and found she was woefully unequipped to come up with anything.

"M-my hips?" Oh gods! Why had she said that? He was going to take it as an invitation! She didn't want to encourage him . . . did she?

"Yes," he said, leaning his big body in closer to hers. "I imagine what they would feel like nestled between my hands. I imagine touching you, guiding you . . ." He trailed off and his lashes lowered for a second as he took a deep breath. What was wrong with him? he wondered. She was so sheltered that she would find his remarks offensive, yet he couldn't seem to keep from speaking them aloud. It was as though something else was driving him.

That same driving force made him reach out to touch her, his fingertips brushing over the delicate, bare yoke of her collarbone. Her breath hastened, and he was surprised and delighted by the reaction. His words were not offending her, they were . . . they were . . . arousing her perhaps? Had it been so long that he was mistaking her reaction?

When Dethan touched Selinda it was like striking a match. His touch singed her like a flame, but this flame did not burn in bad ways. No. This was something else. Something so different. She felt heat rushing through her and became hyperaware of the fact that his hand need only drop a few inches and he could be cradling her breast in his broad palm. He had not touched her so overtly yet, so why did she find herself suddenly craving . . .

Blushing, she awkwardly took a step back. She had intended to break away from him, but instead, it made his hand drop briefly to the line of her corset. His fingers lingered there a long moment, the touch of his skin against hers burning like acid. But then he looked up and around at their surroundings and let his hand fall away. It took a great deal of effort, it seemed, not to lean into him with her body, not to chase his withdrawing touch.

"Easy," he murmured. "Were it not for the eyes around us I would very much be touching your sweet skin right now. But that is a pleasure I must save for later."

Breathless, she looked around and saw the children had stopped weaving and were watching them with interest. Flustered, she stepped back again and smoothed her hands down her skirt.

"You presume a lot," she whispered heatedly. "It does

not stand to reason that I would welcome that touch now or later."

That made him laugh, a knowing glint in his clover-green eyes.

"You would. And you would ask for more shortly after," he said with wicked confidence.

She gasped and her skin went even hotter than it already was. "Stop saying such things to me!" she demanded.

"Why? Do they offend you . . . or tempt you?"

Oh, they tempted her all right, but she wasn't about to admit to it, nor was she going to give it voice in public. He was right; anyone could be watching. If Grannish knew she was granting favors to another man . . . who knew what fresh hell he would deliver to her for it.

"Children," she said loudly, turning her back on Dethan in a silent end to their conversation, "it's almost time for the evening meal. Go to the kitchens and take your meals home with you. Cook will have prepared them all."

"So you feed them as well?" Dethan queried.

"It's only one meal," she said defensively. "Sometimes it's the only meal they will have for the day. As it is, they will take it home and share it with their families. And believe me, it isn't enough to feed more than two people. I try, but . . ."

"Grannish?" he supplied.

She turned to face him. "That and the Redoe. Supplies are limited, even for us."

"And yet you have a fair," he said with disapproval.

"The fair keeps people entertained and gives them a short amount of happiness in an otherwise unhappy city," she said defensively. "It helps tradesmen sell a little more and gives the children something to do."

He thought about it for a moment, then gave her a

nod. "Very well. What do you like to do at the fair, besides watch the fights?"

She frowned. "That was not my idea. Grannish likes blood sport; I do not."

"And yet you ask me to organize bloodshed. I find that contrary."

Exasperated by the conflux of emotions this man was flinging at her, she huffed out a sigh and put her hands on her hips. "Is there nothing I do that meets with your approval?" she demanded of him.

He looked at her. Really looked at her. As in touched his eyes to the top of her head, then dropped them ever so slowly down the entire length of her body. She was flushed all over again by the time he said "Yes."

"W-well, what, then?" she asked, even though she knew she shouldn't. But even though she might not like the answer, she couldn't keep herself from asking.

"I find you . . . to be as a ruler should be. Caring for her people. What's more, your people know that you care for them. But they also know you are powerless. I wonder, how is it that Grannish does not stop you from doing this?" He indicated the floor that was still littered with weaving materials. Servants had just begun to gather them up.

"He . . . he allows me these small privileges . . . so that he has something to take away from me. To punish me."

Dethan frowned. He frowned because he knew she was right. Because he knew it was an intolerable way to live. Every moment of every day she was negotiating a field of spears. Never knowing when she might slip the wrong way and allow Grannish to stab through her.

"It will get worse before it gets better," he warned her needlessly. "But I promise you it *will* get better."

She looked up at him, seemingly measuring him. "We

shall see. I hope you are right." Then she added, "I hope it with all my heart."

"Selinda." He moved forward again, reaching to touch his thumb to the corner of her lips, his fingers drifting over her jawline. She went to shy away when he touched her scar, but he wouldn't let her. He made her look up into his serious eyes. "You can trust me to do this thing. I have conquered worlds. I will conquer the Redoe and then . . . then I will conquer you."

Selinda's breath caught and an unimaginable heat washed over her at the very idea. He leaned closer to her and she found herself lifting her chin, realizing that she was craving his kiss, was hoping he would kiss her right then. But it was a dangerous desire. Not just because they were out in the open. She had to be careful. She could not allow her emotions to get tangled up in this affair. She would only be inviting heartache. He was a man of purpose. He had goals. None of them, she knew, had anything to do with romantic feelings. He did not seem the sort to talk of things like love and affection. She needed to be careful and guard her heart.

Not that she would have to worry about such a thing. She had never been in love. She had always been too levelheaded for such fanciful notions. She had known even from a young age that love would not be a part of her marriage. Her marriage would be one of political import. That was just the way it was for the children of the grand. Her sisters and brothers would have met the same fate . . . had they but lived.

The thought made her sad and made it easier for her to draw away from him. He dropped his hand, sensing her withdrawal.

"My words mean little to you, and that is as it should be. So watch my actions, little juquil. They will speak louder than anything I could possibly say. Now, I am to meet with your father before eventide meal."

She drew in a quick breath. "What will you say to him? You must be careful! He shares everything with Grannish. He trusts him so implicitly. It's not his fault. He simply—"

"It is his fault," Dethan said in a hard, harsh tone. "His blindness to the plight of his people is most certainly his fault. Not to mention the blindness to the plight of his daughter."

Selinda realized there was nothing to say to contradict him, and it hurt her heart to know it. She did not want to think ill of her father, had made up excuses for him all throughout, but deep inside herself she had been angry with him for his actions and his inactions. It angered her that she could not find any arguments to defend him.

"Do not judge my father too harshly," she snapped, even though she agreed with him. "He is a good man."

"A good man does not necessarily make a good leader. But I will not speak ill of him if it upsets you."

The kindness took her by surprise and took the stormy wind out of her anger. Once her anger abandoned her, she found a rushing sting of tears pricking at her eyes.

No, she told herself sternly, *you will not do this. You will not be some weak, emotional woman. Not in front of him. Not in front of anyone.*

"I only ask that you be watchful. Have a care for his safety. I fear what Grannish might do if he feels he is losing control of him. He . . . he favors poison . . ," She trailed off as a cold sickness ran beneath her skin.

"And you know this how?"

"Firsthand," she told him on a whisper.

"He poisoned you?"

"I have no proof, but . . . I was taken ill and he said things that led me to believe it was him. In my heart, I have no doubt it was him."

"You should trust your instincts. I will do the same. I

will do my best to protect your father and your brother, but I do not have the power to protect everyone. I am one man pitted against a man with a network of others to do his work for him. As it stands, protecting you is my main concern."

"Then you should not ask me to come to you at night," she said in a heated whisper. "At any moment I could be caught and I—"

"Are you reneging on our bargain already?" he asked, his tone serious, but in his eyes she thought she saw some kind of amusement. It frustrated her.

"No, of course not! I have made a promise to you and I will keep it!"

"Good." Again he lifted his hand to her. This time his fingertips stroked along the side of her neck. "I must prove my ability as a lover to you. You must give me that opportunity."

"What if I told you I do not need for you to prove it? That I am willing to take your word for it that you are . . . that you are . . ."

"A good lover?" he supplied helpfully.

"Yes," she said, her hand coming up to press against her blushing cheek.

"No, little juquil, you will not escape me that easily. Nor will you consign yourself to a lifetime with a man who cannot please you. And then there is the other side of the coin. I will not consign myself to a lifetime with a woman who cannot please *me*. So you will come to my chambers tonight and every night," he said, moving closer to her until her head was tipped back and his breath was mingling with hers. There was something in his eyes, something fierce and hot as he met her gaze. "I confess," he said softly, "I look forward to it more and more."

"Please." She gasped, broke from him, and stepped back. "If someone should see us . . ." She glanced around the antechamber, but everyone had long since left the room.

Dethan realized she was right, and he really knew better than to tempt Grannish with reasons to lash out at her, but he found it difficult to keep his distance from her. As time ticked on, this pull he felt toward her grew stronger and ever hotter. He did not understand it fully. Even though it had been such a long time since he had known the pleasures of the flesh, he remembered what craving and arousal felt like. But this went beyond what he remembered somehow.

No, he thought with an internal shake of his head. *It has just been so very long and you are newly rediscovering what it means to desire a woman. That is all.*

"You are correct. Forgive me the impulsivity," he said aloud to her. "I will curtail it in the future."

With that, he turned and left her.

And Selinda felt a wave of regret wash over her. She did not want him to endanger her with his advances, but the idea of robbing herself of them . . . In spite of herself, it made her feel cheated.

Yet another pleasure Grannish was taking away from her, she thought bitterly as she watched him go.

CHAPTER
FOURTEEN

As he headed for the grand's governing chamber, Dethan wondered what had gotten into him. He knew
how dangerous it could be if he showed partiality to
Selinda when they were in public, but it had almost
been as though he couldn't help himself.

No. He *could* help himself, he thought fiercely. He
was not the kind of man who was a slave to his whims
or emotions.

Not true. If your brothers are involved . . .

Yes. Then he was quite capable of rendering emotion.
He had always had a bit of a blind spot when it came to
his brothers. He had done many a heedless thing in
order to see to their well-being. Even now he was struggling through this with the ultimate goal of finding
some way to rescue his brothers from their torment. He
shuddered when he thought of them suffering as he had
done. It would be nothing to him to go back to his place
in the hells if it meant freeing one of them instead.

But that was not going to be the way of it and this
way he had hopes of freeing all three of them eventually. All he need do was stay focused on winning this

city in Weysa's name. That meant controlling his impulses when it came to the grandina.

He was wise enough to admit that it was not going to be a simple request to make of himself. For all his worldly experience and his iron will, she was an incredible temptation. It must be, he thought, because he had been so long without the comforts of a woman.

But comfort was just the beginning of it, he admitted to himself. As much as her ministrations in the night gave him surcease, it was what happened when he was in his full vitality that most compelled and tempted him. She was so fine a woman, in so many ways. She thought herself weak, but he saw just how strong she was. She was intelligent and caring of her people. And . . . and she was lush and beautiful and all too alluring. There was something about her, she of the fey, imperfectly beautiful face and slender and strong figure. She carried around a full weight of clothing with ease and grace, and yet there was something inherently sexual in her carriage. It worried him. If Grannish ever got over the flaw of her scars, he might see beyond it and realize just how desirable she was. She was full-breasted, full-hipped, and made for loving. He had seen and felt it all, and yet hadn't even begun to touch her.

And touch her he would. He would claim her body and, through it, her throne. That was the only reason, he tried to tell himself. She was a means to an end. His desire to protect her was his desire to protect the only avenue of peacefully gaining control of this city. He was not afraid of war, but he had always been wise enough to avoid it whenever possible. A man of intelligence could just as easily defeat a city as a man of war could.

He reached the chamber doors and thundered his fist against the heavy, carved wood. A page opened it, scuttling back quickly afterward. Dethan strode into the chamber and immediately saw the grand . . . and Grannish by his side.

Of course. Dethan had known it would not be so easy to extract the grand from Grannish's watchful eye.

"I thought we were meeting in private," he said immediately to the grand.

"Oh, it's all right. I trust Grannish with all information."

"Then we have nothing to talk about," Dethan said. He gave the grand a short, respectful bow and turned to leave the room.

"Are you afraid of scrutiny?" Grannish called out mockingly.

"Here now, return to me!" the grand commanded.

Dethan had no choice but to stop and turn around. "As you wish," he said, returning to a position before the grand. "But you will find me silent in the presence of others."

"I will only relate the information afterward to Grannish, so what difference does it make?" the grand asked almost peevishly.

"All the more reason to keep my own council. You said I could rout the Redoe in whatever way I chose. I will do so. But experience has taught me that sharing my plans of war with too many others can be as good as relating them to the enemy. There are eyes and ears everywhere. If you wish to be rid of the Redoe, then you must trust me."

"But you do not trust me? Or your grand? I wonder what it is I've done to have given you such a low opinion of me."

"Let's just say I do not trust anyone and leave it at that," Dethan said. It took a great deal of restraint not to list Grannish's crimes right then, but he needed to bide his time. Needed to earn the grand's good opinion.

"Then what did you wish to discuss with me, if not your plans?"

"My payment," Dethan said.

"You will have your gold."

"I have decided gold is not enough. If you want the Redoe routed, then you must pay me the price I ask."

"And that is?" Grannish asked, his eyes narrowing slightly.

"The grandina. I ask for her hand in mine. I want her to wife."

"What?" Grannish exploded, lurching forward, his hand going to the pommel of the sword at his waist. "You presumptuous bastard! That is *my* bride you speak of!"

"And how will you care for her when this city crumbles to dust under the boots of the Redoe? I have had more time to assess the situation. Did you know the Redoe are undermining your walls as we speak?"

"What do you mean?" the grand asked, suddenly alarmed. He sat up straighter in his seat. "Grannish, is this true?"

"No, of course not," Grannish scoffed. "He is trying to alarm you in order to get what he wants!"

"I can prove it to you," Dethan said mildly. "But if you'd rather continue this approach, in which if you pretend it isn't happening it might go away on its own, then by all means . . ."

"The Redoe never try to breach the city," the grand said hesitantly. "They simply take over the fields, and once the crops have matured, they take what they need for their winter stores and then leave for their dwellings!"

"Well, apparently they are tired of feeding off your lands and walking away. They want something more, and an apathetic city waiting to be overrun is a perfect target."

"Who in the eight hells do you think you are?" Grannish roared, stepping forward again and half drawing his blade, the unmistakable sound of it filling the air.

"I warn you, now," Dethan said quietly, "if you draw that blade, only one of us will be left standing at the end of it."

"You aren't even armed," Grannish scoffed.

"I will be once I take your blade off you," Dethan said, again that quiet menace in his words.

"Enough!" the grand said abruptly, lurching out of his seat and stepping between the two men. "Dethan, if what you say is true, if my city truly is on the brink of invasion, then you shall have what you want."

"Luzien! She is promised to me!" Grannish was tight with his fury. He did not want to sound like a whining, spoiled child being asked to share his favorite toy, but he couldn't seem to help himself. Everything, every last one of his plans rested on his marrying that gnarled hag. As unpalatable as she was, he would readily take her and all the power that would come with her. How could it be that in the matter of a mere couple of days his entire future, all his power, was under threat? And all because of this one man? This filthy beggar posing as a general? "You cannot simply break a betrothal!"

"Why not?" The grand stopped his progress suddenly and turned so he was barely a pace from Grannish's face. "If you recall, I am grand here and my word is law. My daughter is mine to do with as I please. Her marriage is to gain as much benefit for this city as is possible. Up until moments ago I thought marrying her to you would be that best benefit. However, if what Sor Dethan says is true, then I am forced to recognize that my faith in your abilities might be overzealous. I never thought I would see the day when I would say that. I have had many people come to me and try to undermine you in their jealousy of your position and power, and I have shut them all out. I have always felt that my faith in you has been well placed, and because of that you have been rewarded handsomely for your services. But if this city is in imminent threat and it has escaped the notice of you or your little pet general, then Sor Dethan must be tempted to stay and fight for our survival, and if Selinda is that temptation, then so be it. Now, Sor Dethan, if you would be so kind as to show me your proof of this . . ."

"You must change your clothing first, your most honorable."

That made Luzien hesitate. "Why?" he asked.

"Because I am afraid that to take you onto the walls in such conspicuously wealthy clothing will be like painting a target on you."

"The Redoe are not known for their archers," Grannish said dryly. "They do not even wear shoes."

"Still, I would rather not take the chance."

"Very well. I will go change. You will both wait here for me."

Grand Luzien walked away and left the two men alone. Grannish was fuming and Dethan could feel it radiating off him in furious waves of energy, even though he masked it well in outer appearance. Dethan leaned back against a near wall, crossing his arms over his chest, and began to whistle indolently, as if he didn't have a worry in the world. As if the man standing across from him wasn't plotting the best way to kill him. And, as Dethan had known it would, Grannish's control eventually slipped.

"You will not have her," he hissed at Dethan. "I see your game. You think to have it all. You think you can walk into this city and be this close to being grand in only a day's time! Well, I have been working toward this for most of my adult life, and I promise you I will not let it go easily, nor will I let it go to some filthy mud farmer. Were you my equal I might find a reason to respect you as competition, but you are not!"

Dethan knew it was all Grannish could do to keep from spitting at Dethan's feet.

"The problem with that statement," Dethan said slowly, "is that one would have to presume there is anyone out there you would deem to be your equal. But there is not, is there?"

"No, there isn't," Grannish spat.

"Not even the grand?" Dethan asked.

That made Grannish hesitate, and he looked at Dethan suspiciously.

"You think you are so clever," the jenden said. "You think this will be so easy for you to accomplish. The grand has been my puppet for years. He would not be able to function or govern without me. He knows that. He depends on me and he knows he would be completely exposed without me."

"I do not doubt it. That makes him weak. Where I come from, a weak ruler is a ruler who needs to be deposed. I conquer cities ruled by weak men, and they deserve to be conquered."

"You speak words of treason! Ha! The truth of your goals is in your own words! You seek to depose the grand!"

"I seek to put the strongest ruler at the helm of this city. The grand might yet redeem himself if he is willing to open his eyes and begin ruling for himself, rather than relying entirely on another to do the hard work. But look at it this way, Grannish," Dethan said with a smile. "You will finally be able to relax. You will not have so many duties and responsibilities. It must be so very taxing on you."

"Shut up," Grannish said with a growl, his hand gripping at his sword again. "You know nothing of my duties. You know nothing of what it takes to rule a city such as this!"

"Oh now, there you are wrong," Dethan said, again that quiet strength in his softly spoken words. "I know what it takes to run a city such as this . . . and several more besides." Again, that smile. "But if you play nice, perhaps there will be a few things for you to do when all is said and done. After all, you will still be a noble. You still have your wealth. And if that is not enough, there are many other cities out there with many more opportunities for you to advance yourself."

"This is my city," Grannish hissed. "And I will see you dead before I will hand it over to you willingly!"

"Good. Then we understand each other," Dethan said. He rested his head back against the wall and once again began to whistle softly.

"Can you see the long rows of canvas there and there, your most honorable?" Dethan said, pointing out the canvas.

"They are tents," Grannish scoffed.

"They are too long and too narrow to be tents. But they are enough to shield the city from seeing what is being done beyond them. But if you walk twenty paces farther down the wall, you will be able to see mounds of dirt hidden behind the canvas. The Redoe are tunneling beneath the ground, heading for your walls. When they get to them, they will simply dig beneath them until the weight of the wall causes it to collapse. Once the wall is breached, it will be impossible to keep out the raiding parties. This wall is the only thing protecting you right now. Look at the Redoe's numbers. With no standing army and a weak city guard, the Redoe will have this city in less than a day after the walls fall."

"By the gods," the grand whispered, all the color leaching out of his face. "Grannish! Why didn't you know about this?"

"I . . . I depend on General Firru to tell me these things!" Grannish sputtered.

"And yet he has not. I seem to recall you telling me Firru was the best man for the job! You pushed quite hard for it as I recall." Luzien cleared his throat and looked at Dethan. "Very well. I'll meet your terms. You defeat the Redoe and banish them for good from my doors, and you shall have my daughter as payment."

"I will not let you down, your most honorable. I have been watching the Redoe and I can see where they are weak. It seems to me they are only being so bold because no one has forced them to behave for many years. But that will change now. However, I do need to have gold in order to gird your new army"—Grannish scoffed at that—"and it seems your coin handler is under the impression that I am not to be trusted with large sums of coin. Now, I realize you do not yet know me well, so I do not ask the coin be put in my hand. However, can we not work with the smithies and builders and such in a way in which the coin handler can pay them directly?"

"Of course! I have already given orders that you are not to be curtailed. I do not understand what the problem is."

"Your most honorable," Grannish said, "I told the coin handler to have a care for your coin. I simply did not wish to see you robbed by a man we knew nothing about!"

"Well, you can see now that he is what he says he is," the grand snapped. "Give him his gold, give him his head, and let us be free of this Redoe pestilence for good and all!"

The grand shoved the telescope he'd been using to look at the Redoe into Grannish's chest, then stormed past him and down the tower steps that led to the top of the city wall.

"It seems to me," Dethan said to Grannish, "that you might be more grateful. After all, it is your city I am saving."

Grannish merely hissed at him and stormed off in his grand's wake. Dethan watched him go for a minute. Tonkin stepped up to him.

"He's rightly furious just about now, I'm thinking," Tonkin said with a low chuckle.

"Aye, that he is," Dethan said. But he was not amused. He was looking at the darkening sky. "Come, let's attend the eventide meal. Then I have somewhere to be."

"Sor . . . my lord, where is it that you go at night? And why was the grandina in your bedchamber last night?"

Dethan turned to Tonkin, one dark brow lifting higher than the other. "So curious all of a sudden?"

"Well . . . I didn't mean . . ." Tonkin stammered. "I mean your business is your business, and I'll shut up and not ask you again, my lord."

"No, it's all right, Tonkin. You can ask anything you wish. But I might not answer."

"Fair enough."

"I require your loyalty, Tonkin," Dethan pressed on him. "The grandina would be in a great deal of danger if it was known she came to my chambers at night. I will not have her harmed, and if anything you do causes her to be harmed, I promise you I will find out about it and I will seek retribution for it. Am I making myself entirely clear here?"

Tonkin swallowed noisily and nodded. "You can trust me, sor."

"We will discover that as we go, I suppose. You need only know to keep quiet . . . no matter what you see. Now come. Dinner awaits."

CHAPTER
FIFTEEN

"You little slut!"

Grannish backhanded her with complete violence, throwing all his weight into the strike. Selinda flew back, her body slamming into her dressing vanity. As much as she had come to expect the worst of Grannish, she had not been expecting this. Grannish had laid hands on her before, but always in small, concealable ways. Ways that she couldn't point to in order to show her father his true nature. But this time . . . She could feel the instant swelling over her eye, her eyes smarting and her nose stinging. Before she could gather herself back onto her feet he was on her again, punching her dead in the face once more.

He was a storm of rage. She could feel it vibrating off him. And even though his beating was terrible, she could tell he was holding back. She fought him when he went to grab her by the front of her dress, trying to shove him off her, but he was far too strong. Grannish was not some simpering fop of a statesman. No, he was in his physical prime, strong from his horsemanship and swordsmanship and gods knew what else he did to keep himself fit.

He lifted his fist as if to strike her again, his body bowstring-taut and shaking as he in turn shook her. If this was him curtailing his rage, she thought fearfully, then gods help her if he ever really let loose on her or anyone else. Dethan included.

"What have you done?" Grannish demanded of her. "I know you've done something to make him want you. What is it? Surely it isn't the way you've been going about unveiled, displaying this hideousness to all and sundry! Have you spread these flaccid thighs for him?"

His fist changed direction so he could shove his hand up her skirts. She fought him, trying to push and kick him away as she felt his touch on her inner thighs.

"That's it, isn't it? Even now his seed is festering inside you, isn't it?"

"No! I am innocent!" It was the only thing that came to her mind in her blind panic.

"Don't you lie to me, whore!" he spat in her face. "Here, then, let me be the judge of how innocent you are. If you are, then we'll make it my seed inside you. If I can't be grand through you, then my son can be! He might be illegitimate, but he will still be the son of the grandina!"

"No! I swear to you, no! I've done nothing!" She kicked at him, smacking him, fighting him any way she could. Then she connected somewhere it counted because he fell back with a grunt. He crumpled to the floor, and as she gasped for breath and straightened up, she saw him nursing a hand between his legs. Shaking, she stood up tall over him, sniffling and wiping her hand under her nose. It came away streaked in blood.

She wanted to kick him again, but she was not stupid. She knew he would recover eventually, and then he would make her pay. Somehow, in some way that was most important to her, he would make her pay.

"Hanit!" she cried out.

"Yes, my lady. What is it?" Hanit said, bustling into the room. The woman froze in place halfway across the room from Selinda when she finally took in what she was seeing and it registered on her. "Here now, what's this?" she demanded to know. And in true Hanit style, she threw herself between Selinda and Grannish. "How dare you lay hands on my mistress!" she blustered.

"Oh, do shut up," Grannish seethed as he staggered to his feet. "This isn't over," he promised Selinda. But his progress toward the door told her that it *was* over. For now. "You'll pay for this. He can't protect you, and you know I will make you pay."

"Yes," Selinda said wearily. "I know. I know you believe that is true. But you also know things are different now. *He* has made things different. I have done nothing to deserve it, but I am under his protection now. My father may not listen to me, but what do you think Dethan will do when I come to him looking like this?" She indicated her battered face.

Grannish changed direction and came back toward her with all speed, growling deep in his throat with rage. Hanit, bless her brave heart, threw herself in front of Selinda, using her body as a shield to protect her. It kept Grannish at a small distance, but not very much of one.

"You will remain in your rooms tonight and tomorrow . . . until you can hide your face under your whore's paint. If you show your face to him or your father before then, I will kill your brother. Do you understand me?"

Fear clutched at Selinda's heart. No. Not fear. Terror. For she knew he would think nothing of carrying through on his threat.

"I understand," she whispered.

"Good. Now, I have to figure out how to get your new champion to fail at his attempt to quash the Redoe invasion. As disgusting to me as it is, your hand in marriage is the one thing I have striven for these past years and I will not be denied it! You had better hope he does not succeed, because the very *instant* I believe I have lost you to him, I will destroy you and your entire family! And do not think for a moment that I will not do it!"

Selinda swallowed. "I have every faith that you will make good on your threats," she said quietly.

"Good. Then we understand each other. Do not let me catch you encouraging him, Selinda. And gods help you if I catch you in his bed. And you know I will know. I know everything that goes on in this castle. Nothing escapes me."

"I know," she said softly.

Dethan waited a full hour in his chambers before coming to the conclusion that Selinda was not coming. He was surprised when he found himself disappointed with her. She had shown reluctance earlier, but he had thought he had made his wishes clear to her. He had thought she wanted to come just as much as he wanted her to be there. Something had passed between them . . .

Dethan shrugged that off. There was no space for fanciful notions. This was a business arrangement, not an emotional one. One had value; the other did not.

So why did he feel his disappointment so strongly? It was almost as though it were a physical pang.

Nonsense, he told himself harshly. He was a warlord, not some simpering young lad with sonnets and notions of love running loose in his head. No, he was stronger and harder than that. And anyway, he didn't know her well enough to even consider . . .

But he had thought her to be a woman of her word. She didn't have much in the way of power, but she held dominion over her personal honor and actions. To break a promise and then not even send word of the why of it, it seemed beneath her somehow.

No sooner had he had the thought than there was a light scratching at his door. He went to it.

"Who?" he asked.

"Hanit, Sor Dethan."

He opened the door for her and she scuttled inside. He shut the door behind her.

"Please forgive me, I meant to come sooner," Hanit said in a fast, heated whisper. "But Grannish has put a boy in the hall to watch the comings and goings to your rooms."

"Then how did you . . . ?"

"Oh," she said, grinning like a contented cat, "well, young Bibby, as is his name, has a weak spot for the kitchen wenches. One in particular. A good girl who don't mind doing me a favor."

"Clever Hanit," Dethan said with a chuckle. "Grannish thinks he has total dominion over all things, but he underestimates you . . . and your mistress. And about your mistress. I assume you are here to tell me she won't be making it?"

"Well . . . no, she won't," Hanit said. "But believe me when I say she is sorry for it."

"What's wrong? Why won't she come? Why did she not come to dinner?"

Here Hanit hesitated. It was clear she wanted to say more than what she did. "She's not feeling well."

"She seemed fine earlier," he said, narrowing his eyes on her.

"And she was fine . . . but this came on her suddenly. A headache. She gets these fiercely bad headaches. The mem says it's because she has magic inside her, but if you ask me I think she's just trying to make my mistress feel better."

"Magic is very powerful and not something to be

taken lightly. It is a blessing from the gods. Laying false claim to it risks angering the gods," Dethan said with a frown.

"Which is exactly what I said," Hanit said with a snort of air through her nose.

"I will speak with her about it on the morrow," he said.

"Well," Hanit hedged, "these headaches ... They can last for days sometimes. Ask anyone. They have put my mistress to bed quite a bit since she was in her first blush."

"Then maybe there is something to what the mem says after all," Dethan mused. "It is said that a magess is born at her first blush. As soon as she bleeds the first time."

"Perhaps," Hanit said. "But I'll not be hanging my hat on the notion."

"Very well. Send me word when she is feeling better."

"I will, sor. You can depend on it."

He saw her out and then stood at the door thinking a moment.

So Grannish had a boy in the hall. That meant he would have to be more careful with his comings and goings. The cloak he used would hide the burned state of his body, but he would need to be careful just the same. He wondered briefly if Selinda was actually ill or if this was a ruse to keep her out of his bed. Then he discarded the bulk of the idea. She was more straightforward than that in his estimation. She would have fought with him rather than hide from him . . . wouldn't she?

No. He didn't know why he trusted her so easily and so quickly. He wasn't exactly known for his ability to trust, but he believed he had her measure and she would not play games with him. He had been unrelenting, it was true, but she had not balked with any great passion. In fact, she had seemed resigned to her course, a course she herself had chosen.

He would look in on her in the morning if she didn't come down to morning meal.

"Mem! Oh, Mem!"

It was early the next day when Selinda fell into the other woman's arms, and for the first time since Grannish had beaten her she dissolved into tears of both weakness and relief. She was angry with herself for her cowering behavior but could not help it. She was so alone. She had Hanit, but the poor pagette was just as afraid of Grannish as Selinda was. Standing up to him had taken just about all the courage Hanit had. But the mem. The mem did not even know Grannish, so she had no cause to fear him.

"Shh," the mem said softly, holding on to Selinda and petting her hair, letting her have her cry and rocking her with comfort. "Poor little princess," she said soothingly. "If only people knew what troubles you endured."

"But they do not. No one does."

"Now, that's not true. There is one who knows. One who can help you."

That made Selinda's tears stop almost abruptly. With a sniff and the repression of some last sobs, she sat up straighter and looked at the mem. Josepha was such a beautiful woman, she realized. Not a grand beauty, a woman of splendor like those in the court, but a smooth, mature beauty. A strong one. She was still in her prime, her shining black hair falling perfectly straight and loose down to her backside. She was broad shouldered for a woman but not gone to fat in any way. Actually the strength in her hands and arms told Selinda she was not a soft woman.

"What do you know?" Selinda asked warily.

"Only as much as you do. There is someone close to you who will be able to help you one day. All is not lost for you. You may yet prevail against . . . those who hurt you." The mem raised cool, gentle fingers to touch the horrible swelling around Selinda's eye. "You need me to heal you, yes? To hide this injury?"

"Yes," Selinda whispered.

"I will do it. And then we will practice your magic."

Selinda frowned, but before she could shake her head, the mem touched her chin to prevent it.

"I see things beyond what others see and I believe you know this. Let me show you what I see. What can it hurt to try?" she asked.

"It can give me hope where there should be none," Selinda said bitterly.

"Ah, but you already have hope," the mem said gently. "Otherwise, you would have given up entirely."

Selinda sighed. "I do not think I wish you to be wise just now. Perhaps I wish to wallow in my own misery."

"You speak many untruths today," the mem said with a chuckle. "For if you wished to wallow you would not have called me to you at all. You wish to be healed so you can go about your day."

"Yes. I do. And it must be hidden," Selinda said, touching her battered face.

"Though I know not why," Hanit said acidly. "I say you should tell Sor Dethan what Grannish has done to you."

"To what end?" Selinda asked in a snap of temper. "What if he sees and thinks the risk to me and mine is too great and then stops his efforts altogether? Then that means I will be forced to Grannish's bed. And we both know his unkindnesses will not stop at the bedroom door."

"Unkindnesses," Hanit echoed with a snort. "That's an understatement if ever there was one. And this makes no sense. He would stop helping you because of Grannish's cruelty only to send you into marriage with him?"

"He would not risk my life and the lives of my family! I would not want him to! Better I suffer as Grannish's wife than see my father and brother dead! It could be worse," Selinda said fatalistically. "It can always get worse when it comes to Grannish."

Hanit could not argue that point so she remained quiet. Selinda was grateful for it. She simply wanted some peace. Just a moment. Even if it was an illusion.

"Now, let's see to your injuries," the mem said kindly, helping Selinda to lie back in her bed.

It took only half an hour for the mem to finish her work. When she was through, it was clear the effort had taken energy. And in spite of it, when Selinda looked in the mirror, only the worst of it had been cured. There was still much discoloration. But the swelling was gone. At least she could cover what remained with Hanit's clever paintwork.

"Now," the mem said. "Time to practice, my little magess."

"I wish you wouldn't call me that," Selinda said in a hard tone. "I am not a magess."

"And you never will be with that attitude. At least try before you dismiss me altogether. And I mean an honest effort," the mem said with a stern look.

"Very well. I will try. What do you wish me to do?"

"Let us see if we can discover what sort of magess you are. Last time we used water. This time we will use fire."

The mem rose from the bed and retrieved a candle from a nearby table. She struck a match and lit the wick.

"But fire is the most powerful magic there is. I do not think—"

"You said you would try," the mem scolded her.

"Very well," Selinda said with a sigh.

"Fire comes from Xaxis, its creator. As I understand it, it is natural to those born in this region, for they have been guardians of the eight hells from before time was time. You are of the ruling class and so your blood runs deep in fire."

"The fire of the eight hells can be a curse," Selinda said, thinking of Dethan and how he suffered night after night . . . how he had suffered for ages. "Xaxis is the cruelest of the gods."

"Some say Sabo is, for he thrives on the pain and suffering of others. Sabo and Xaxis have always competed with each other for the crown of cruelty. Xaxis would be proud to hear you say so."

"The others are little better," Selinda said, thinking of the way Weysa had cursed Dethan.

"Have a care. The gods hear what we say."

"Most folk don't even believe in the gods anymore."

"But you do."

"Yes, I do." How could she not after seeing what Dethan suffered? What she couldn't understand was how he could be so accepting of his fate. Perhaps he had deserved to be punished for reaching too far and trying to force the hands of the gods, but after ages of suffering, why must he still be tormented?

"Look into your heart," the mem said softly to her. "Focus on the flame."

"What am I trying to do? Put it out?"

"No. It takes far more skill to draw fire back than it does to thrust fire out. Drawing fire back into yourself can burn you, scorch your soul, if you are not careful. For now, try to make the flame burn brighter."

Selinda tried, but nothing happened. The taunting little flame just flickered and danced in its own way.

"Do not give up," the mem encouraged her.

But after ten minutes of trying, Selinda began to feel foolish. "This isn't working," Selinda huffed.

"You must give it time—"

"I have given it time!" Selinda snapped.

"So impatient and so like a child. You are a mature woman who has borne many trials! Surely a simple flame is not going to defeat you!"

"Go to the hells!" Selinda spat.

And the candle belched a large flame upward, setting both women back with gasps.

"There!" the mem cried in triumph. "I knew it would be fire!"

"But I . . . I didn't do anything! I wasn't even trying." She narrowed her eyes on the mem. "Is this some sort of trickery?"

"No, my sweet lady. Your fire is directly tied to your most passionate emotions. Anger. Lust. Fear. All are aspects of Xaxis and all are a part of his flame. What you must do is channel those emotions into the flame. Try it again. Think of something that angers you and focus on the flame."

It was not hard to come up with something that filled her with rage. All she needed to do was think of the impotence of her situation with Grannish and she was filled with the emotion. She gathered the whole of it up and pushed it at the flame.

The explosion was massive. Flame bellowed from above the candle, singeing Selinda's clothes and catching fire to the edge of the mem's cloak. The mem cried out, whipping the cloak off her shoulders and throwing it to the ground. She stomped at the flames and Hanit grabbed a pitcher full of water and doused the burning fabric with it.

All three women were breathing hard, staring at the smoldering cloak in their shock. The mem looked back at the candle and saw it was nothing more than a puddle of melted, burning wax. All she could think was that she was glad she hadn't been holding it in her hands. As it was, the table was scorched all around it. She looked at the grandina.

"Grandina, this is . . . What you have inside you is a very great power."

"A very dangerous power," Selinda said, still breathing hard. "We are lucky I didn't harm you!"

Josepha could see the fear in the girl's eyes. It was so raw she could almost taste it on her. She did not blame her in the least. This had been very unexpected.

"You must not fear your magic," she said in earnest, reaching to cover the grandina's hands with her own, encouraging her to look into her eyes. "You must realize this magic has been trapped inside you all these years with no outlet, and you with no way to measure or control it. You have a store of it inside you that now needs only to be vented regularly. To be exercised as one might exercise a horse for riding. It must be broken first. Tamed. And then all that power can be at the rider's command. You will command this, my lady. You just need time."

"And what if I burn you or Hanit in the process? Or burn the city to the ground?"

The mem leaned back a little and chuckled. "You think very much of your power. One large flame a long time in coming does not mean you can level a city. But it is true that we must be cautious. And perhaps I am not the best choice of teachers. We can apply to the temple of Xaxis for a mem or magess there."

"No! No one else!" Selinda said urgently. "It will be you or no one. I . . . I don't trust anyone else. And anyway"—she touched the melted puddle of wax, feeling the burn of it on her fingertips—"we have no fire magesses here in Hexis. I would know if we did. Grannish would have used a fire mage as a weapon long ago if there had been one." Then she heard her own words and swallowed. "My gods. If he knew about this . . .

Hanit, he would never let me go. He would . . . never let me go."

"He's not likely to let you go in any event," Hanit said pointedly. "We'll just have to see if . . . Well, the gods may yet intervene."

"Forgive me, Hanit, but I will not place my life in the hands of—" She stopped then. If anything, her life these past days should tell her not to think lightly of the gods and their power. After all, had they not, after a fashion, sent her Dethan? Then there was the mem and her guidance. And now this power inside her. "But perhaps you are right. It will all be as the gods will it to be."

"So it will be."

"So it will be," Hanit echoed the mem.

"So it will be," Selinda said with a sigh.

CHAPTER
SIXTEEN

He was staring at her again. Or maybe it was better described as brooding contemplation while Dethan stood watching her manage the women of the household, holding meetings with each group of maids or laundresses or cooks as they came. Only this time she was twice as self-conscious because she was constantly afraid that he could see through the makeup on her face to the bruising beneath. She dreaded what he would do if he knew about Grannish's attack. She was terrified he might act rashly.

No, she comforted herself, he was not a rash man. It was clear he approached things free of emotion. The only thing he had shown any hint of passion for was his cause, and since winning Hexis in Weysa's name meant a great deal to him, she could take comfort in it being unlikely he would quit.

"You are feeling better?"

Selinda had not realized he had left his distant position and had moved over to her. She was sitting at a table, writing some notes to herself about things important to the household. As chatelaine of the fortress she managed all the household staff. To a degree. They might appear to be serving her and her father, but she knew most of them were actually serving Grannish and his best interests.

A household army of spies. Sometimes it made her feel suffocated. As if she could not breathe for fear it would be interpreted the wrong way. She had to fight with herself to remain strong in spite of it. If she were not, they would walk all over her. Grannish's treatment of her would give them permission to walk all over her.

"Yes," she said a bit awkwardly. It was not a lie, after all. She was feeling better. She only hoped he did not ask her what had been wrong. Then she would have to lie, and for some reason . . . she didn't want to speak untruths to him. "I am sorry I could not come last night," she said with the barest of whispers.

"As am I," he said, his deep voice dropping even lower. It made her catch her breath. It was almost as if . . . as if he really had longed for her to be there.

Of course he had. Her ministrations must ease him greatly. She couldn't imagine the pain he suffered every single night. And to think he had once suffered it continuously.

"It will not happen again," she promised him.

"Selinda." He moved, his lithe strength and incredible presence washing over her as he leaned nearer to her. "We have an agreement, that is true, but you are not beholden to it if you are too ill or if some other credible reason should make it so. I will not be cruel to you."

She looked up into the powerful intelligence of his eyes, wondering where this man had come from and why the gods had seen fit to send him to her when she had needed someone like him most. She could only pray that he had what it took to defeat Grannish with her family coming out of the situation fully intact.

"I . . . I thank you for that," she said softly.

"But please come to me tonight," he said, reaching out to pull her hair into his hand, letting the strands sift through his fingers. The intimacy of it took her breath away one moment, and the next she was remembering herself, remembering Grannish's warning, and looking nervously around.

"Please," she said, drawing away from him by moving back a foot. "If anyone should see . . ."

"Let them see," he said gruffly, moving closer to her again. "I have told your father that I want you to wife as reward for defeating the Redoe and he has agreed. It stands to reason I will woo you in the interim."

That explained Grannish's tirade yesterday. Her eyes widened as she realized what he had done, and what she had suffered because of it.

"Why would you do that? Don't you understand?" She was heated and angry. "If Grannish thinks he is in danger of losing me, he will lash out any way he can!"

"Grannish will lose you," he said firmly. "One way or another you will be mine. He will lash out regardless. This is what *you* asked of me. This is what *you* wanted."

"I know. I know, but I am afraid," she confessed, gripping her hands together to hide their trembling. "I am afraid for my family."

"I will see them safely through," he promised her. And, oh, how she wished she could believe him. "You must trust me."

He reached for her again, his fingertips gliding along the line of her jaw, on the right side, the unscarred side. Good, she thought. She didn't like it when he touched her scar. But she did like the feel of his warm touch against her. So much so that it outweighed her fear of being spied upon. She realized then that she craved his touch. Craved his nearness. He was so very kind to her, and she so very much needed someone to be kind to her.

And the next moment his kindness became something more, something heated, and the color of his eyes seemed to darken and his intent toward her seemed nearly predatory. His thumb slid under her chin and he tipped her head back.

"It's the strangest thing," he said to her, his tone so very rich and so incredibly masculine. "I find myself with this incredible need to touch you. No . . . that is a lie, for it is too tame. I find I want you, Selinda. It is a powerful need that drives me to you. I have much to do and yet I am here because I needed to see you. To be near you. To possibly touch you. Do not deny me your presence in my bed tonight, Selinda. I find I cannot do without it. I must have you in private, where I can . . ." He trailed off and she fully understood what he wasn't saying. It took her breath away, and an outrageous response of heat flushed throughout her body. As he leaned closer to her, his body a wall of barely leashed power and male strength, it was everything she could do to keep from grabbing hold of him, from running her hands over all those virile muscles so her fingertips could absorb the power lying just beneath his skin.

The desire shocked her to her core. She had never felt anything like that before. Not in all her life had she known such a powerful, carnal craving. It made her forget . . . it made her forget to be afraid of the eyes that were always on her.

"I would like to a-as well. Touch you, I mean," she confessed with a fast and hot whisper. Oh, where were these words coming from? Was this scandalous creature really her?

But it was all worth it to see the slow, sure smile that eased over his lips. When it touched his eyes she realized what a wonderful smile it was. It lifted the aged weight from his eyes—the glint that was always there, which told anyone who could see it that he had endured incredible hardships. And while a smile did not erase those hardships completely, it did much to ease them.

"Now you have vexed me," he said, leaning so close she could feel his breath against her lips.

"O-oh, I-I did not mean to—"

He silenced her with a single finger against her lips. "I am vexed because now I cannot decide which I want more . . . to touch you or to be touched by you."

"Oh," she breathed.

"So come to my rooms tonight and we shall have both," he promised her.

This time the idea of what he was expecting of her didn't paralyze her with fear and the weight of the choices she had to make. This time she found herself looking forward to their time together in a way she hadn't thought herself capable of. She should be ashamed of herself, she tried to tell herself, but when she thought of being alone in a room with so much power and grace, knowing it was hers for the taking . . .

"I see the thoughts in your mind," he said with a growl. "You must stop thinking them if you do not wish for me to grab you here and now and kiss you until you do not care who is watching."

"My m-mind? You mean you can read my thoughts?" she asked with an appalled gasp, trying to recall what her thoughts had been.

But he chuckled and shook his head. "I am not a mage with mind magic. I am merely a man who knows when a woman wants him. I can see it. I can feel it."

She lifted her hand to cover her face. Not to hide, but in remembrance of Grannish's rage and words. If Dethan could see such things, would Grannish see them as well?

"You are mistaken," she whispered, jerking her body back. Then, much to Dethan's bewilderment, she hurried away from him and out of the room. She was incredibly flustered by her own desires and it bemused him. The women he had known had always been so confident in theirs. He had to remind himself that women were different now. This woman was different. She was . . . Gods, how could someone be so fragile and so strong at the same time? Perhaps it was because she didn't see her own strength. Didn't see the bravery he saw. It puzzled him. It intrigued him. Everything about her intrigued him.

He left the room, his mind thoroughly preoccupied with Selinda. He actually found himself excited by the coming night. Just thinking about her in his bed had him growing hard for her. No more nearly chaste kisses for her. It was time she learned what true passion was about. And if he was not mistaken, she had a very passionate nature just waiting to be discovered. There was a kind of fire inside her, something deep that burned . . . but unlike the fires of the eight hells that tormented him, this time he would not mind being scalded.

It was these thoughts that allowed him to turn a dark corner only to find a dagger suddenly plunged into his belly. Stumbling back in shock, it was only his warrior's instincts that had him avoiding a second blade striking across his throat by a mere hairsbreadth. Dethan grabbed the dagger in his belly, and with a mighty effort he eased the painful blade out of his body and then shoved back his attacker. But the man was as yet uninjured and had the advantage, so he immediately lunged toward Dethan again. But this time Dethan knew he was coming, so he reached and grabbed his opponent's wrist and jerked the blade forward, past his own body, moving out of the way just enough for the blade to miss but driving the assailant onto the sharp uprising of his knee. He caught the man in the gut, striking so hard that he heard the breath leave the man's body in a rush. In a second swift move Dethan turned the man's arm hard about, dancing around him on quick feet to avoid the second blade as he yanked the man's arm back against its natural extension, slamming the wrist above his head, as well as the whole of the man's body, into the stone of the fortress wall. He slammed the hand into the stone again . . . and again . . . until, with a cry, his attacker released the blade, dropping it. Dethan caught it before it could fall more than a foot and flipped it surely in his hand before stabbing the man in the throat with it. He sent it all the way in, right to the hilt.

And just like that, as suddenly as it had begun, it was over. The man slid down the wall, gagging and clawing at the knife as blood erupted from his mouth and throat. Dethan watched dispassionately as the man died a gruesome death. It seemed fitting since Dethan had no doubt that the death was exactly the same sort the assassin had planned to deal to him. Dethan put a hand to his side and cursed. He might be immortal, but it didn't make him invulnerable. He could still be wounded and could still suffer the pain of it. It also took time to heal. The worse the damage, the longer it took. He looked up and around to make certain no one was watching him. It was a stroke of luck that the boy Grannish had set on him, who had been shadowing him most of the day, was missing for some reason.

Or perhaps he was missing under instructions . . . so he would not bear witness to what was meant to happen. It stood to reason that Grannish had been so confident in his assassin he had not felt the need to have Dethan shadowed after he was supposed to be killed.

And Dethan had no doubts it was anyone but Grannish who was behind the attack. He needed to take the attack out into the open. Ignoring his wound, he grabbed the dead weight of the killer and hoisted him over his shoulder. He made his way directly to the grand's hall, and brushing past the pages guarding the way against unwelcome visitors, he burst into the room, strode up to the desk and hoisted the dead body right onto the grand's desktop. The grand leapt up from his chair in shock, but it was Grannish's face that Dethan watched closely. He saw the jenden's eyes widen, then cloud over with a brief moment of fury before he masked it and cried out, "What is the meaning of this?"

"The meaning is that this man just tried to kill me," Dethan said, turning to look at the grand, dismissing Grannish now that he had his answer.

"What?! Good gods, man, you're injured!" the grand cried.

"It is only a scratch. A glancing cut. Luckily I was able to fend him off."

"An assassin from the Redoe, no doubt," Grannish supplied quickly.

"Yes, yes!" the grand agreed. "But how do they know of you already?"

"There are spies everywhere, I assure you, your most honorable," Grannish said.

"What . . . My own people?" The grand looked stricken by the very idea.

"Or someone closer to you who doesn't want me to succeed where they have failed," Dethan said pointedly.

"You mean the general? That's preposterous!" the grand said.

"I mean anyone," Dethan said darkly. "You have to be prepared to find out that someone close to you may be behind this."

"Very well," the grand said. "But I do not like it. I do not like the idea of mistrusting one of my own advisors."

"You are at war. You do not have the luxury of trust. Or of hiding from the truth. And you have to realize that your own life may be under threat."

"I think you are clearly dramatizing matters," Grannish said. "We are safe here. The grand is—"

"The grand eats, does he not? The kitchen cooks his

food, do they not? Do you know every worker in those kitchens? Is it so safe and your staff so trusted that no one could poison him? Guards can do nothing against poison. I suggest that, for now, you have someone sample all your foods before you do. Even so, that will only discover immediate poisons. It will not protect you against longer-acting ones."

"My gods," the grand breathed, fear apparent in his eyes. "My daughter! She must be protected. She is my heir and it stands to reason she too will be a target. My son as well. He is so young."

It heartened Dethan a little to hear the grand's first concern was for his daughter. Even, it seemed, above his own safety. How strange, then, that he could be so blind to her plight. But it made Dethan believe that when faced with irrefutable proof of Grannish's treachery, he could be made to see the light. That is, provided Dethan could manage it before Grannish took his revenge on Selinda or some other member of her family. He knew that the more Grannish felt them all slipping through his fingers, the more unpredictable he would become.

Selinda was walking down the corridor when Dethan had left the grand's offices and she gasped at the sight of him. His shirt and his breeches were soaked with his blood.

"What happened?" she cried, rushing up to him.

"It's nothing to be concerned about," he assured her. "I will heal from it just as I heal from the burns."

"It does not follow that it doesn't *hurt*," she said sternly. "Come with me."

She took his arm and led him away, her stride almost a march. She led him to his quarters and into his bedroom. She'd had Hanit bring large amounts of linens and bandages and healing herbs and potions to be stored in his rooms so she would not have to go looking for them in the middle of the night any longer. There was a cabinet full of them and she bustled over to it. She began to pull out bandages.

"Strip," she ordered over her shoulder.

Dethan froze. This, he thought, was a bad idea. It was the middle of the day and surely half a dozen people had seen her come into his rooms. And if he were to be completely frank with himself, he would have to admit that being without his clothes in front of her would be all too inviting an idea. If it were in the privacy of night it would be one thing, but in the middle of the day . . .

She turned and frowned when she saw he had not obeyed her.

"Go on, then," she commanded. "Take off your shirt and your breeches. Are you being shy suddenly?" she teased him then. "I have seen you naked just as often as not."

"Only then I was not in the prime of health," he said pointedly.

She missed the point. "You aren't in the prime of health now either. Come, come." She dropped her bandages and medicaments on the bedside table and moved to pull his shirt free of his pants. He winced when she touched his wounded side. She gentled, but she was not satisfied until his shirt was off his back. "I do not care if you heal fast or not," she said softly. "I can see how much this hurts you and how very deep it is. I saw wounds like this the last time we tried to fight off the Redoe." That gave her pause. "No doubt I will be seeing much of it again."

"It is war," he said simply. "And it is necessary."

"I realize that," she said, her tone grim but clearly accepting. She knew what had to be done and all the reasons why. He would not sell her short on that. "Take off those bloody breeches. After I dress the wound you can put on some clean ones."

"I think you will dress the wound first, and then I will change once you are on your way."

She lifted a brow at him in surprise. "But I—"

"Just dress the wound, little juquil," he urged her, taking up her hand and giving it a meaningful squeeze.

"All right," she said, though it was clear she didn't understand him. She prodded at the wound with gentle fingers. "I do not want to sew it closed. You would just retain the blood inside. We will leave it to bleed freely while waiting for your body's healing processes to take over. I do hope it will be soon."

"Soon enough," he said.

She moved away to put water into a pitcher, wetted a piece of linen, then came to clean the wounded area as best she could with it still bleeding. She then applied a variety of medicines to the area before pressing a thick padding of bandages to the wound, keeping it in place by winding a long strip of linen around his midsection. As she did this she moved around him, close to his body, her hand warm against his flesh and the sweet scent of her drifting up to fill his senses. Today she smelled of the jamberry flower, a sugary sweet, small flower that then turned into the most luscious of berries, which made the most divine-tasting jams. When he had been young a trader had brought jamberry jam in from this continent and Dethan had thought it to be the most amazing thing he had ever tasted.

All he could think of was how very much tasting her reminded him of the first time he had tasted that jam. An explosion of sweetness, every touch of it against his tongue a surprise and a delight. He had been innocent then, his palate inexperienced, but he had known it was something sent straight from the eight heavens. Now he was not so innocent, had tasted many things and many women since then, but still . . . still she was a wonder to him. A temptation, he thought as she drifted into his senses again, her touch like fire against him.

Her hand slid low across his belly, right at the edge of his breeches, and he hissed in a breath and grabbed hold of her hand.

"Oh! Did I hurt you?" she asked worriedly.

"No. Damn it, woman, stop touching me like that or you'll find yourself in my bed and beneath my body while I make yours sing to my touch," he said heatedly.

Her eyes went wide and she looked down at where he held her hand pressed to his body. She realized then how it might have felt to him, and she flushed a furious shade of pink and quickly snatched her hand back.

"I'm sorry," she stammered. "I did not mean to—"

"No," he said, moving closer to her and bending his head to . . . Was he sniffing her hair? she wondered as he took a very deep breath in, his eyes closing briefly. "You never mean to. It makes me wonder what you could do to me should you ever mean to."

The idea intrigued her too, she realized. He made it sound as though she had some sort of power over him. And for someone who held so little power over the men around her, it was an incredibly compelling feeling.

"You mean," she said softly, daring to reach a hand out to touch him on his chest, above the bandage she had strapped around him, "that if I touch you it gives me some kind of control over you?"

"Careful, little juquil," he warned her. "It is not the kind of control you seek. In fact, you have resisted me as often as not when it has come to matters of passion." He lowered his head and took another breath full of her. "A tamer tempts a beast at his or her own peril."

His words made her hand tremble against him, but she did not pull away.

"You are not a beast," she argued with him.

"More so than not," he corrected her. "I should think the one thing you have learned over time is that all men are beasts."

"Yes. I suppose that's true. But you have never been unkind to me." She slowly drifted her touch from one side of his chest to the other, and back again, from one nipple to the other. She had never felt anything quite like the muscled definition of him. Each muscle was rounded and shaped, strong and powerful, yet his skin was soft and warm as it covered the steel of his strength. She could feel his heart beating hard beneath her fingertips. Was that because of her? Over his left shoulder he was still scarred from his burns, but it was like her scar—white and simply . . . a part of him. She touched the ridges of it.

"Can you feel me?" she asked on the softest breath.

"Good gods, woman, I feel nothing else but you. I've been run through and yet all I can feel is the touch of those incredible hands on my skin."

He reached out then, grasping her about the waist with both hands, dragging her closer to his body. "I cannot take you like this, Selinda. I won't. Too many people saw you come in here. I don't want to bleed all over you. I'll not take you like this."

"Then let me go," she whispered.

His hands gripped all the more tightly at her waist and she suddenly felt the difference in their strengths. He was so strong he could snap her in two if he wanted to. It took an incredibly strong man to be standing on his feet after being wounded the way he had been. It didn't matter how quickly he healed; it was still a terrible injury and he had to be feeling it.

But that was not the feeling he was focusing on. She could tell by the possessiveness of his grasp. He went to jerk her up against his body, but she tensed away from him just as he remembered he was covered in blood and could easily transfer it to her dress. It would announce to the world that she had been in his arms.

"Damn it to the eight hells!" he swore viciously. She knew he did not use a curse like that lightly, considering he had been in the eight hells. His frustration must be incredible, she thought, and something about that understanding pleased her no end.

But he did not let her go. Instead he transferred his hands to her head and dragged her mouth up to his. His chiseled lips covered hers with outright demand and a hot brand of desire. He wanted to own her. To own all the rights to her and damn everyone else. He wanted to be able to prove to everyone that she was his and he deserved her.

But how had he come to this? he wondered as he devoured her mouth, stroked his tongue against hers, swallowed the erotic flavor of her. This was supposed to have been a simple business arrangement. He was supposed to be focused on a single goal. How had he become enmeshed in a desire for a woman who did not deserve to be burdened with a cursed man? She had enough men in her life who were like a curse to her.

And yet he could not stop kissing her. He conveyed that to her with silent intensity. He wanted her to feel the power she had over him. She deserved to feel powerful . . . if in only this one thing.

Dethan kissed Selinda until she could not breathe. The feel of his tongue in her mouth was so sultry, as if he wished he were using it like this somewhere else on her body. The thought made her knees weaken, and her spine simply melted. But she could not let herself fall against him.

Realizing how close she was to doing so, Dethan stepped back from her, disengaging their mouths in the slowest of disconnections possible. He did not want to go and she did not want him to go.

"Tonight, you will come to me," he said urgently.

"Yes," she promised him.

"Good," he said, taking her by her shoulders and turning her away from him. "Now go. Go before I forget myself and endanger you."

Slowly she walked out of his grasp, toward the door. Once there, she hesitated, looking back at him.

"Tonight I want to make love with you," she said. She didn't know where the bold words had come from, but with him they seemed to come so easy.

"That is good because I plan on doing that very thing as soon as I am able."

"Good," she said, raising her chin. "As long as we understand each other."

"Perfectly," he assured her.

She smiled and left him.

Dethan felt the strength ebb out of him the minute she left, as if she had taken it with her. And perhaps she had. He felt stronger when he was with her somehow. It was purely perception, he knew, but he felt it just the same.

His hand went to his side and he felt the bandages already saturated with fresh blood. He lay back in the bed, thinking it was probably best to give his body an hour to heal. It would take longer than that to heal with any perfection, but it should be enough to get him back on his feet.

He had to fight the Redoe and win. He had to do it because so much was at stake.

And in his heart he knew that winning the city in Weysa's name was no longer the top priority it should be. Which was very dangerous, he warned himself. He was there by the grace of the goddess and could easily be returned to the hells if he displeased her in any way.

But there had to be a way to achieve both goals. To

win the city and to have Selinda as his own. There had to be a way and he had to find it and keep her safe in the doing of it. It was like balancing on the point of a sword. One wrong move and all his plans could be completely run through.

And Selinda as well in the process.

CHAPTER
SEVENTEEN

Dethan got up and was moving around again after only a short time. Keeping still had never sat well with him. The worst of the bleeding was done with, so he changed his bandages once more himself before heading downstairs. It had been much easier when Selinda had been there to wind the fabric around him, and far more pleasant.

He put thoughts of her aside as best he could. It seemed she had taken up permanent residence there, in his head. He went to the city guard barracks, which were also acting as a temporary headquarters for the army. That would have to change, and it was on his immediate list of things to accomplish. When he arrived, Kyran was there with a phalanx of men. His new commanders. He had gotten to know a few of them, but the rest Kyran had picked out over the past day. He had been forced to trust Kyran in this since he had no idea what he was dealing with. But he would. The mettle of these men would become apparent very quickly and he would know whether or not they were suited to battle as well as to leadership.

"General Dethan," Kyran said upon seeing him, his entire face lighting up as though with utter excitement.

"I think I have found the site we need for raising the barracks. It serves twofold," Kyran said, drawing a plan of the city and showing it to Dethan. "It's just on the fringes of the fairgrounds. There's wide-open space to be had and it's close to the center of the city, putting us between the wall and the fortress."

"A good choice," Dethan agreed. "You said twofold?"

"Yes. There's a line of vacant buildings just here"—he pointed them out—"that can act as headquarters."

"Good. We need a place secluded from this one to plan." Dethan looked at the fringes of the gathering, where guards were trying to hear what they were saying, some of them trying to glean that information for Grannish. He had no doubt that the jenden would pay well for such information. "What about training grounds?"

"Well, the fairgrounds themselves. They remain empty except during the winter festival and the summer fair. It's a waste of space otherwise. Surely we can use it at all other times and then just make way for the festival and the fair when the time comes."

"Perfect. Absolutely perfect. Well done, Kyran." Dethan clapped the man on the back. "You see? I was right in drafting you. You know far more about the comings and goings of this city than I do. But I promise you I am learning fast."

He had no choice but to learn fast. He needed a foothold here if he was going to make any progress. And he needed to win the hearts of his men if he was going to succeed in this endeavor.

He must succeed. Selinda's very life and future depended on it and he would not let her down. He would just need to be clever about it. Cleverer than the jenden of Hexis.

"We will rout the Redoe once and for all," he spoke up loudly. The men reacted with approval. "We will teach them they cannot take your farmlands any lon-ger." The approving sounds turned into heavy grunts of agreement. "We will show them the strong arm of Hexis and they will never come to our doorstep again!"

The entire room erupted in cheers. The men at the table banged their fists upon it.

"Come, Kyran," Dethan said, drawing the man close and speaking softly in his ear. "I need you to take me to the best black market runner you have in this city."

Kyran nodded. "That would be One-Eyed Jyo. He's not likely to speak with you . . . even if you could catch him. He's sort of the king of the lower swells—the poorest part of the city. He runs the black market and looks after the place with a gang of thugs. He strong-arms protection money out of the merchants in the bar-tering square, our commerce district. Of course in the end he's protecting them from himself."

"And the city guard does nothing?" Dethan asked with a frown. Then he rethought the query. "Let me guess. The jenden gets a cut of One-Eyed Jyo's profits, so the guard is instructed to leave him be."

"Aye, something like that. The jenden is the richest man in the city for a reason. Some say he's even richer than the grand."

"Very well. Take me to this man."

"He won't talk to you," Kyran insisted.

"That may be, but Tonkin said you wouldn't talk to me either," Dethan said, giving the man a grin.

That made Kyran chuckle. "True. You do have a way with words. And you get the men on your side. I'll take you to the lower swells. We'll see how close we can get to Jyo."

"Those are lookouts," Kyran said, pointing out the group of men sitting in a circle around a table, upon which sat a game that two of the men were heavily engaged in.

"We'll start there, then."

Dethan walked up to the men directly.

"I want to see One-Eyed Jyo," he said flatly. The men looked at him in surprise and then as if he'd gone mad.

"Lolly and I want to see the grand of Hexis, but neither of us is likely to get what we want."

"I can take you to the grand. Can you say the same?"

"Oya, Lolly, get your mind around this one," the man said to his gaming companion with a coarse laugh. "He's going to take me to see the grand."

"Get on with you," Lolly warned, getting to his feet. He moved aside his vest, just enough to flash the dagger at his side. A clear warning.

"You're going to take me to see Jyo," Dethan said quietly, "or I'm going to kill all but one of you and then let that one lead me to Jyo. The first way you all get to live. The second way ... well ... Who would like to volunteer for being the survivor?"

The men shifted nervously, laughing to try to cover up their sudden uncertainty. They didn't quite know what to make of Dethan or his threats. They were used to being the ones who did the threatening. They each sized Dethan up, trying to figure out if he could make good on his threats. In the end, they decided there was strength in numbers and gained courage from the idea.

"Get him, Lolly!" the first man ordered. The other men moved too. The whole lot of them—six in total— swarmed around Dethan and Kyran.

Dethan had learned his lesson from the assassin. He had since armed himself and would wear his weapons from that day forward. He had the daggers he had taken off the assassin and his god-made sword, which luckily he had retrieved his first day in the fortress. He knew if he pulled out the sword he could cleave through these men in a matter of seconds, but he chose the more up-close-and-personal daggers. They would, he thought, make far more of the impression he was looking for. He pulled one dagger and in an instant had jumped on one of the men, the weapon flashing in and out of his chest between heartbeats. The man dropped like a stone, shock clearly written on his face. But Dethan took no note of it. He was moving to his next target, grabbing him by the hair and slicing the man's neck open on the right side. Flesh parted and blood spurted forth.

He took a moment to check on Kyran. After all, he had yet to see the man in any kind of action. But he saw Kyran move like lightning as he elbowed one man in the face hard enough to smash his nose, an immediate spray of blood jetting forward as the man cried out and fell back. Then Kyran pulled his weapon—a short axe that had been tethered to his belt with a quick-release knot. In a mighty feat of strength and with a roar of power, Kyran planted the axe blade deep in the forehead of the next man.

Dethan took his third with just as much ease as the first in spite of his enormous build. The failing of men that big was that they thought their size made them strong enough to do anything, defeat anyone. Dethan kicked the man in the gut, making him double over, then cracked him in the jaw with the hilt of the dagger. The man hit the ground like a huge stone, and that was when Dethan made his killing blow, a dagger right through the man's spine at the back of his neck. When Dethan looked up, there was only one man standing. The man whom he had spoken with initially. His eyes were wide with shock and fear and he was literally shaking in his boots. Kyran jumped on the man, grabbing him by his hair and holding the wicked-sharp blade of his axe to his throat.

"It looks like you're the winner," Kyran ground out.

Then to Dethan he said, "Are you sure we can't kill him? He probably doesn't even know where Jyo is."

"No! I-I do! I know exactly where he is!" the man insisted in a panic. "I can take you to him right away!"

"Now see, why couldn't you have done that in the first place?" Dethan asked mildly. "It would have saved so many lives."

"I'm sorry. We're under orders not to let anyone get close to Jyo. I-I had no choice!"

"There's always a choice," Kyran said darkly.

"W-who are you guys?" the man asked shakily.

"That's not important to *you*. The only thing important to you right now is taking us to Jyo and then figuring out a reason why we shouldn't kill you afterward," Kyran said.

"Now, Kyran. That's not very friendly," Dethan scolded with a tight-lipped smile. "After all, we're all going to be friends here." Dethan leaned close to the other man's face. "Take us to Jyo, and if you value your intact throat, I wouldn't try to lead us into any traps."

Five minutes later, after being led through a maze of structures standing in six-inch-deep mud, they found themselves at the door of a dark building.

"They're with me," the man, who they had discovered was named Harro, said to the guard at the door. The guard narrowed eyes on the group, maybe sensing something wasn't quite right.

"Who are they?" the lumbering brute asked, his voice as deep as he was tall.

"That's not your business," Harro snapped. "They have business with Jyo. Now, let us past."

The guard debated with himself for a few seconds but then stepped back and let them enter.

Dethan didn't like being crowded into the tiny hall Harro led them down, but there was nothing he could do about it other than to keep his hand on his sheathed dagger. He noticed Kyran was in a similar mode, his hand close to his dangling axe.

They could hear some kind of ruckus, almost like the sounds of a party. It reminded Dethan of the common room of an inn during a celebration. Loud and raucous and full of shouts and laughter. The hall emptied into a brightly lit room and inside was indeed a party.

There were men everywhere with mugs of mead in one hand and plates of food scattered on the tables before them, and many were grabbing for the bare-breasted girls who were serving them. The women were pulled from one man to the next, their breasts being fondled constantly. They seemed to be laughing good-naturedly and enjoying the attention. One was even chugging back a bottle of wine while the men around her cheered her on.

Dethan knew Jyo the minute he saw him, even without the fact that his right eye was little more than a healed-over scar from a savage rending of the orbit. He was at the head of the room, in a large wooden chair like a king on his throne. The table in front of him was full of food and there were two women—one standing, one in his lap—touching and petting him with interest. He was thin overall. His hair was a long dirty blond that looked like it had not been washed in several days. He had a thick beard that protruded a good five inches from his face. There were little bits of food caught in the nest of it.

He noticed their entrance immediately and shoved the woman in his lap off him so he could stand.

"Oya! What's this, then?" he demanded, his voice loud enough to be heard over the din in the room. That din immediately quieted.

"Jyo . . . th-these men wish to speak to you," Harro stammered. "A-and I think you better listen."

"Is that right? You think I should?" Jyo came down from his dais, making his way over to them, pushing men, women, and furniture out of his way as he came.

He got right in Harro's face. "And what makes you think you can tell me what to do?" he growled.

Then, with a single movement, Jyo had a dagger in his hand and it was pumping in and out of Harro's gut in a flash. Stunned, Harro fell to his knees, his hand going to the wound.

"That's a warning," he said, his voice rising, "to anyone who thinks they can tell me what to do!"

The crowd behind Jyo burst out in raucous agreement. Jyo turned back to Dethan and Kyran.

"So who are you and why are you interrupting the party of us law-abiding citizens? Come to think on it, you don't look like the city guard."

"If we were the city guard, we would have arrested you for killing this man."

Jyo's laughter was loud and wild. "I don't know what city you're from, boyo, but in this one you only get arrested when you've crossed the jenden. Otherwise, they don't much care about anything else."

"Then why the lookout?" Dethan asked, nodding to Harro's body.

"There's competition, you know. For who thinks they should own this here mud-infested wallow. The swells are full of gangs or those who want to be one. So who are you? Just another man trying to take what's mine?"

"No. In fact, I want you to do exactly what you've always done."

Jyo raised his good brow. "Then be on your way and leave me and mine in peace," Jyo said dismissively.

"I hear you're the best black market smuggler in this city. That you can get anything, any supply necessary, through the siege line," Dethan pressed.

"Ah. So you want me to smuggle something in for you? That'll cost you."

"It always costs you!" another man shouted from behind.

"But you didn't need to see me directly for that," Jyo said wisely.

"Yes. I did. Because, you see, I don't want you to smuggle something in . . . I want you to smuggle something out."

"And why should I help you?"

"Because I have a long memory, Jyo," Dethan said. "And one day I'm going to remember I owe you a favor. And I'm going to be just the kind of man you want to call in a favor from, I promise you."

"I don't ask for small favors," Jyo said. "And you probably wouldn't like what I'd be asking for in any event. You seem too straight and law-like to do a man like me any good. And I don't know who you are or why it should matter to me what favor you owe me."

"I am the commander of the grand's new army," Dethan said quietly. "And I mean to change things around here. Now, you can either have a place in harmony with those changes or you can find yourself at odds with me. And trust me when I say that you do not want to be at odds with me."

Jyo took his measure slowly, then after a minute gave a brusque nod. "I can see how that's possible. But you're full of a lot of talk."

"I'm full of a lot of opportunity. Either that or I fall flat on my face and you're no worse off. But work with me and you'll have gold in your pocket and a favor due you. Work against me and . . . Well, ask your other lookouts for the result of that."

"Where are my other lookouts?" Jyo asked.

Dethan smiled.

Grannish was seething. His attempt to assassinate the thorn in his side had thoroughly backfired on him. Instead of ridding him of the problem, it had just created more of them. Now the grand was utterly paranoid that there were assassins around every corner. He hadn't been able to focus on anything else since Dethan had brought that body in to them, and so they had gotten very little work done. It also seemed Grannish's network of spies was failing him miserably. He had yet to acquire any intelligence worth anything to him.

"My lord jenden?"

The query came tentatively, a head peeking in the open door.

Tonkin. Just the man he wanted to see.

"Come in and shut the door," Grannish commanded him.

Tonkin did and moved closer to him. He was twisting his page's cap in his big hands so hard that it was a wonder the thing wasn't in shreds.

"You have something to tell me?"

"Yes, milord. I did as you asked, kept an eye out. I thought you should know . . . they plan on using the fairgrounds to train the men. And they'll be erecting the barracks close by."

"Come to the map and show me."

Tonkin did so, pointing out what he had seen Kyran show Dethan.

"Sor Kyran come up with the idea. Dethan approved of it. Then they left together to see a man about smuggling something in past the siege. I don't know who it was or what they wanted."

"When you find out you will let me know," the jenden commanded.

"As you wish, milord. Also . . ." He trailed off, clearly reluctant to be tattling on his master. But in the end Grannish knew greed would win out. This man wanted his farmland back. He would do anything to get it. Even things he didn't necessarily want to do. "My lord was alone in his rooms with the grandina earlier. It wasn't long," he said with a little haste. "Not long enough, I mean. Seems she tended to a wound he had. I wasn't there, but I was told there was an assassin . . ."

"Yes, I heard all about it," Grannish said with impatience. "And I heard about the grandina from the household staff as well. It's not unusual that she would see to the well-being of a guest of the household. I did not like it, but as long as it was only a short while . . . And believe me, she knows better than to go sniffing after him. I saw to that. She'd have to be a damn fool to risk it. Besides, I have him under watch now nearly the entire day in one form or another. Especially thanks to you."

"Yes, milord." Tonkin said, looking miserable.

"Is there anything else?"

"Yes, milord. The men . . . they are deserting."

"What, already?" Grannish released a scoffing laugh. "Why does it not surprise me? How do you know this?"

"Just by watching. Faces seen one day are not there the next. If Dethan has noticed, he ain't saying nothing about it. But they *are* going."

"So much for their supposed loyalty to him. Good. Very good. Anything else?"

"No, milord."

"Then go. Get out of here. Keep an eye on him every minute. Tell me what else you see."

"Yes, milord. I will." Tonkin gave him a short bow and then hastened from the room.

Grannish was left to stare at the map as he tried to figure out how to thwart Dethan's placement of the barracks.

No, he thought then. *I will encourage it. To seem as though I am very much on Dethan's side and behind the cause against the Redoe.*

He had been naysaying too much, he realized. It was giving Dethan power over him. He had to at least seem to be on the right side of this. At least enough to keep a comfortable hold on the grand. It infuriated him that after years of having the grand completely dependent on him, completely under his sway, now, in a matter of days, he was struggling to stay on top of things.

True, in a way he was finding himself enjoying this. It had been a long time since he had faced any true challenge. He had dismissed Dethan as not being worthy in the beginning, but it was quickly becoming clear that there was mettle there. Mettle and intelligence. Perhaps enough to actually pull off a good show against the Redoe.

It irritated him that Dethan had discovered the undermining. It had made him and General Firru look the fools.

But there was no changing that now. He simply had to see to it that there were no more advantages won by the so-called general of the newborn army. General. Grannish scoffed. So the man was able to fight off one assassin. That did not make him a warrior. Grannish would simply have to find a better grade of assassin. And while he was at it he was going to get his gold back from the failed assassin's accounts. True, it was only half the agreed upon price, the other half due upon completion of the job, but the man hadn't come close to making Dethan even half dead . . . so therefore had done nothing to earn the coin. He would see the coin returned or he would see that the go-between paid the price.

As for Selinda, he was satisfied that he had gotten his point across to her. She had remained silent, called a mem to heal her, and had sufficiently covered any visual evidence of their altercation. In fact, she was so good at it maybe he wouldn't hold his temper in check with her as much as he had been. Until yesterday he had never laid a mark on her that she could show her father as evidence of his cruelty to her. For that was what she would deem it: cruelty. When the truth of it was that she needed to be kept in check. Left to her own devices, she, like her father, would run the city into the ground. No. No matter what she said, how much she complained or whined or wept, she needed him. She needed his structure and his discipline. She would do well to remember it.

And he would see that she did.

As for her being alone with Dethan . . . it had been, as he had said, of little consequence. She did not dare defy him. She may want to, may even consider it, but in the end she cared too much for the well-being of her family and knew too well what he was capable of. She knew how far his power stretched. There would be no way she could hide any assignations or flirtations from him. He had eyes in every corner of this fortress . . . this city.

Grannish moved to his desk, sitting behind it and relaxing for a moment before he got back to the business of running the city. This city, he knew, would fall apart without him. That was the simple truth of it. Only he knew the everyday workings of it. Only he had the relationships necessary to keep the cogs of it running smoothly. The grand knew this well and that was why the man trusted him so implicitly.

This was his city.

His.

And no one was going to get in the way of that.

CHAPTER
EIGHTEEN

Selinda walked into an alcove just down the hall from Dethan's rooms. She checked carefully to see if Hanit had distracted the lookout watching the rooms. She had waited until well after juquil's hour—nearly an hour past—before coming. She fretted that he would think she wasn't coming. Nothing could be further from the truth. She was looking forward to this night in a way she had not realized she was capable of. Her entire body felt as taut as a bowstring. Ever since she had left him earlier her clothes had felt too heavy . . . too confining . . . almost scratchy against the sensitive tenderness of her skin. She couldn't explain it, could barely understand it. It was such a new feeling to her. Logically she understood it was because she craved him, but logic did not encompass the actual feeling of it.

She saw the way was clear and she hastened to his door. She did not knock; she just swept into the room in a swirl of skirts, shutting the door tightly behind her. She exhaled a breath of relief. She could not be seen. It would mean catastrophe for her and her family. It was crazy to even do this, but here she was just the same and excited to be doing it. She must have gone utterly mad, she thought. It was the only explanation.

She felt and saw his hand covering hers where it laid against the door, his body moving up against hers and radiating incredible heat. She turned to see him dressed in spite of his burns. He'd had an hour to heal already and it showed, but he still must be in pain.

"I thought you would not come," Dethan whispered softly as he touched his face to her hair and breathed deeply of her. She had no idea how good she smelled when all that had been in his senses previously was the smell of burned flesh.

She wore her hair loose, the shining black curls falling down her back. It was so rich and beautiful and he had no choice but to touch his fingers to it.

But he was burned still and did not want to touch her until he was healed, so he immediately withdrew from her.

"Come," he said, taking up her hand. "Come to bed. It has been a long day for us both."

She followed him, and when she reached the bedside, she turned and sat him down. Then she dropped the cloak from her shoulders, revealing her dressing gown. She had not wanted to come to him armored with all her clothes. She had put on the thin, nearly transparent gown with its intricate gold embroidery and scarlet color and had hoped he would like it.

"By the grace of Weysa," he breathed fiercely upon seeing her, "you are beyond tempting to a weary soldier's eyes."

"Thank you," she said, flushing prettily for him under the compliment. Gods, how he wanted to grab her and throw her down on the bed right then.

Softly. Easy. There will be time for that, he chided himself.

"Come to bed," he urged her. He needed to feel her in his bed beside him, if nothing else.

"Not yet," she said firmly. "First, we address these burns."

"They will heal," he said dismissively.

"They heal faster when I tend them," she pointed out. It was the truth and he could not refute it. Plus, her ministrations made him feel better.

He watched her move as she worked, the very sight of her agony, never mind the feel of her. Every time she bent forward he got a glimpse down the front of her loose, deep-necked gown and he could nearly see the whole of her pretty, lush breasts. It took every ounce of his self-control to keep from pulling her toward him, putting his hand down the front of her gown just to feel her, and then lifting the weight of her free of the clothing, raising her to the hungry drift of his mouth.

He grew hard just thinking in those ways and he had to grit his teeth against the subsequent pain of it.

"You need to disrobe," she said to him once she reached the edges of his clothing.

"No. This is enough," he said hastily.

"You will disrobe this very instant," she said firmly, her tone telling him she would not be moved on the matter.

Slowly he took off his shirt. When he reached for the drawstring of his breeches he hesitated.

"Go on," she urged him. "I have seen you before."

And she had seen him in an aroused state as well. But then she had been reluctant and shocked. Now . . . now she was different, so it made the experience different. He could not execute anything just yet, but the promise of it was right there, hovering close to them. It made him long for her in a way he had never longed for a woman before. But he would heal in a few hours and then he would have her, he reminded himself fiercely. He *would* have her.

Slowly he drew his pants from his body, the relief of having them off so profound.

"Do not do that again," she scolded him softly. "Do not dress. I know how much it hurts you and I do not wish to see you in any more pain than you already must suffer." He saw her glance at his aroused penis, but she made little note of it as she went about the business of dressing his wounds.

When she was done she gingerly climbed over him and settled in the bed next to him, drawing the covers around herself but not around him. She snuggled down and laid her head on her pillow.

"I am so very tired today," she said with a yawn. "It was a busy day for me."

"Me as well," he said.

"What did you do today?"

"Mostly prepared to build the barracks. It is a huge undertaking."

"I can imagine it would be. Where will you be doing it?"

"Just outside the fairgrounds. We will use the fairgrounds as training grounds, since there is no other use for it once the fair is done."

"The fair is done as of today. It only lasts a week."

"So I was told. All the better. The newly drafted men can focus on the task of building the barracks."

"But where will you get the lumber?" she asked. "The Redoe . . ."

"There is a full row of vacant, run-down houses in the swells. Even more in other places. We will tear the houses down and reclaim the wood for the barracks."

"Why not simply use those houses?"

"They are in a bad location, too deep into the swells and too far beyond the fortress. I want the army to stand between the city walls and the fortress. When this is over and we have access to more supplies, I will see to it a new home for the royal household is built back behind the city, in the mountain. It will be impenetrable, unlike this so-called fortress with its open bailey and not so much as a moat to stand between it and an invading force. No. You need to be behind stone walls, with a moat of pikes and water, and anything else I can think of."

"Pikes and water?"

"An old trick I've used before. You dig the moat, and before it is filled with water, you bury metal pikes in the bottom of the moat in a dense amount, then fill the moat so they are covered by water. Then if anyone decides to jump into the moat to get to the walls, they will find themselves run through on a pike."

"I see," she said with a little shudder as she envisioned just such an act. "And what of children who think the moat will be fun to swim in?"

"That's for their parents to warn them," Dethan said, but reading her worried expression, he added, "If it will make you feel better, I will build a wall around the outer edges and put spikes along the top of the wall. That should discourage anyone from taking a dip and add a little extra difficulty for anyone with a nefarious intent."

"Thank you," she said with a smile. "That does make me feel better. But all this building of walls and moats . . . it feels as though it will distance us from the people. I do not want that to happen. I do not want us to sit up here in our spiked cage while the people lose touch with their rulers."

"Then we will make certain to keep the drawbridge down and the bailey open as long as there is no immediate threat beyond the city walls. I will set up a strict guard, though, to see you and your family are protected.

Just as I will see to it no one like Grannish will ever hold sway over your father again. It is time your father is rudely awakened to his blindness."

"I know it is," she said softly. "I wish it did not have to be a rude awakening, but all my gentle prodding has done nothing, so I see there is no other choice."

"I am glad that you see that."

"It is what I have wanted all along," she assured him. "I want my father back. I want him to rule his own land instead of leaning on others."

"I do not think that is possible," he told her gently. "Your father leans on Grannish for a reason. He uses him as a man with a limp uses a crutch. Take the crutch away and the man cannot walk. There is something flawed within your father that makes it impossible for him to rule without a crutch. I mean to make you his new crutch. You and me. Us," he said, meeting her eyes firmly. "Me with my strength and you with your connection to the people. Together the three of us can run this city. I have complete faith in that."

"As do I. Even crippled we would be far better than Grannish is. He rules with an iron fist. A cruel one. He rules using fear. I mean to rule using love and kindness."

"Yet stern, like a disciplining parent," he injected.

"Yes. I suppose we are a little like parents and the people are our children. They need guidance and caring for."

"Yes." He paused a beat. "Along with the fortress, I mean to raise temples to Weysa. I must win this city in her name. I must bring the people to her faith."

"You can do whatever you wish to do," she said quietly. "After all, the city will be yours. We would not be worth our ruling blood if not for your strength behind us."

"You will find your own strength," he assured her. "And once you do . . ." He trailed off.

"Once I do, you will leave me," she said.

"I have no choice," he said fervently. "I wish it could be otherwise, but I have no choice. I must conquer in Weysa's name. But as I do, it will bring riches to Hexis. The wealth of the other cities will be ours as well."

"I do not care about the wealth of other cities," she said bitterly, looking away from him.

He caught her chin in his hand and turned her face back to his. "You should care," he told her firmly. "I have a feeling that Grannish has been robbing the coffers of this city for years. If that is true, you will be near destitute. It is part of the way he holds sway over your father, I believe. The Redoe have hurt the city's profits for years now. You have to imagine just how badly this city is ruined financially because of it."

"Because of him," she said tightly. "Why can we not just kill him and be done with it?" she asked him.

"That may be the only way," he agreed. "But if I run Grannish through before gaining your father's trust and his promise to your hand, then all will be lost. I must play this game with your father and Grannish smartly . . . not with impulse. I will win you," he promised her. "And I will protect you in the process."

Selinda did not respond to that. She did not want him to know that he had already failed to protect her. She did not want him to know just how much danger she was in. She was afraid he might react rashly, in spite of his words of acting with methodical patience.

"Once I take care of the Redoe, then I will kill Grannish. And quickly too because once he knows he has lost you, he will act with haste and vengeance."

"I know."

"But this is not to be worried about right now," he said then, rolling in bed and gathering her close to him.

She could feel the incredible heat coming off him and wondered if it was because of the burns on his body. Was he burning even now? Did it never truly stop?

"Sleep, Selinda. I will wake you in a few hours."

Selinda met the startling green of his eyes and knew, just as he knew, what that would mean.

"Do not forget. Do not let me sleep too long," she said.

"Do not worry," he said softly. "I won't."

With a sigh, Selinda closed her eyes and fell asleep.

Hours later, Dethan was looking down on her, watching her as she slept, her features soft and quiet. He touched her face, the barest of caresses, with the very tips of his fingers. She was sleeping on the scarred side of her face, so all he could see was perfection and unblemished beauty. Not that it would have mattered to him otherwise, but . . .

Something caught his attention. She was wearing makeup, he realized. Heavily, by the look of it. How strange. He would have thought she would have washed it off before retiring for the night. Perhaps she had simply forgotten. He smudged it with a finger.

She woke with a gasp, some kind of instinct making her strike his hand away from her. Her sleep-dazed eyes went wide and she shied away, sitting up and turning her face away.

"I-is it morning?" she asked, looking to the window. It had not even begun to grow light.

"Not quite yet," he said sitting up. "Selinda, are you afraid of me?" he asked.

"No!" she cried, immediately turning back to him, her whole body coming toward him, her hand resting on his bare chest. Her fingertips brushed against scarring, but he could feel them just the same. The smallest touch and it did amazing things inside him. It stirred him, drew him. He had stripped away his bandages an hour ago and was well into the healing process . . . but he was not certain if he was healed enough that she would not be repulsed by him.

"I am still not healed," he said, withdrawing from her before her touch made him feel too good . . . made it impossible for him to think clearly about what would be best for her.

"That doesn't matter to me," she said, catching him at his shoulder. "You are remarkably healed for so short a time . . . and even if you weren't . . . it does not matter to me."

She proved it to him by leaning toward him and touching her lips to his. She had never instigated a kiss before, so she was a little unsure, but that slipped away the moment their mouths meshed together.

Oh, but she was like the sweetest sugar on his tongue, he thought passionately. There was absolutely nothing sweeter in the world and he had tasted confections from many lands. But she was all the confection that was needed. There was no craving for anything else. Had he ever wanted another woman? Right then he could not even recall. He did not wish to recall.

He cradled the back of her head, her silky hair filtering through his fingers, and held her mouth to his. The sweet taste of her quickly turned erotic and he felt an instant fever in his blood. Oh, he knew, he absolutely knew, there would be a fire here to rival what he suffered every night. But unlike his suffering, this fire would bring bliss.

He let his big body crowd her smaller one, raised himself over her until she was fully beneath him, right where he had wanted her to be for what seemed like ages. Had it only been a matter of days? How can something feel so intense with so short a prelude?

He did not care. He threw himself into the feelings, pressed his naked body all along the length of hers, the silk of her dressing gown sliding against his hypersensitive skin. Was it a curse that the process he went through made him so raw to sensation, or was it a blessing?

A blessing, he thought as he felt the soft contours of her body against his. Oh, what a blessing. He broke from her mouth to tell her so but found he could not speak. He simply stared into those magnificent teal eyes, one hand pressed into the bed and the other hand in her hair, both clenching as he tried to rein in his fevered emotions. *Gently,* he told himself. *This is her first—*

The thought was interrupted when he felt her hand touch his hip, caressing him over the pronounced bone, her fingertips flirting with his backside, her wrist coming into contact with the part of him that was already heavily aroused by her.

"I will not break," she encouraged him on a soft voice. "*You* will not break me. I know this," she said with an utter confidence he did not share. "You would never hurt me."

"By the gods, I don't know whether to think you amazing or addled," he said fervently. Then he was back on her mouth, his bigger body pressing hers down deep into the bed. It had been so long since he'd had to care about a woman's feelings, her sensitivities as a lover. In an army camp there were camp followers and whores to be used with perfunctory need, not with any great care for how they felt in the matter. And even so, he had rarely availed himself of such things for many reasons, not the least of which was disease and general distaste. Those women were dirty and coarse. This one was fresh and refined.

"I am going to make my way through your body, Selinda," he promised her against her lips. "And then I believe I will do so again."

At that, her eyes widened with surprise.

"Again?" she asked, pulling back from his mouth and blinking at him.

"Yes. Think you once will be enough for me?" he asked her, amusement and intensity sharing space in his voice. "I plan to use you well, Selinda. I insist you do the same."

She thought about that for a moment and then she gave him a slow nod. "I think I would also like to use you well," she said softly.

Her words made him instantly harder. The full weight of his erection pressed between their bodies, a loud pronouncement of his intentions.

Curious for some time now about this part of a man she had never seen, before she had first seen him naked, she pressed her hand low against his stomach, urging him to lift up and away from her just far enough so she could look at him. And then, with a bravery she didn't know she had, she touched him.

"No!" he cried out, making her pull sharply away.

"I'm sorry. Did I—?"

"No. No, of course not. I just . . . I fear if you touch me there, it will turn me rough and desperate. I wish to be gentle with you. I need to keep control of myself to do that, and your touch . . . It makes it easy for me to lose control."

"But I have to touch you," she argued with him. "There and everywhere else. It is what will make us lovers. A sharing of such touches. Not simply me receiving yours."

He hesitated, the war inside him all too clear. "I want to share everything with you . . . I just . . . I am a coarse man, Selinda. It takes effort for me to be soft with you.

The feel of your hands on me makes the effort nearly impossible."

"How do you know? I have hardly ever touched you."

"I just know. Gods, just looking at you here beneath me, how lush and fine you are . . ."

He reached to run his hand down her chest and over the swell of her right breast, finally putting the full weight of it in his hand, feeling it through the silk of her gown. He brushed his thumb over the silk covering her nipple and she drew in a sharp little breath.

"Do you see what I mean?" he said, bending his head down to her, his breath penetrating the silk of her gown and coating her sensitive breast in heat. Then he extended his tongue and laved her directly through the fabric. The muted wetness of it was dynamic and she released a surprised little cry. Then she moaned as he took her into his mouth, his teeth biting at the silk in gentle, erotic slides.

Quickly he grew tired of the fabric barring his way, and he reached for the neck of the gown and pulled it, trying to expose her breast to him. The delicate fabric tore and she gasped as he tore it even more in his frustration. Then her chest was fully bared to him and he was on her with the full force of his passion. He took her nipple in his mouth and sucked at it until she literally felt her toes curling. Her head fell back and her chest lifted up as her spine curved with need. She fed herself to him eagerly, her hand stabbing through his hair and then gripping it tightly.

She couldn't possibly know how much it aroused his passions to feel her doing that. It spurred him on. It was *her,* something about her—whenever she did something that felt like a raw invitation, he simply went mad in his effort to take up the gauntlet.

He grabbed the front of her gown with vigor then, tearing it from her body, ripping it in two straight to the hem, making her utterly naked before him. He knew very well it meant sending her to her rooms stark bloody naked under her cloak, but he could not help himself. Nor did he want to. It was this heedless feeling he had been trying so hard to get her to be wary of. But now it was out. Unleashed like a wild beast, and he could not help her any longer.

He devoured her . . . her breasts, her nipples, her mouth, her neck. Anything he thought of he covered with open-mouthed kisses and the laving of his tongue and the scraping of his teeth. He bit at her nipple before he could stop himself and was surprised to hear her cry out . . . and then moan with pleasure. Then her hands were both in his hair and pulling him to where he must be in order to repeat the process on her opposite breast.

His body was hard with distended muscles, but his skin was soft under the frantic touch of her hands. Selinda knew he had asked her not to touch him, but she could not help herself and must defy him. She drew her hands out of his hair and down his neck. She felt the flexed strength of his muscles at the base of his neck and then the rounded, rock-hard power of his shoulders. Skin, both soft and scarred, ran beneath her hungry fingertips. Each patch of it was different, but each was warm and covering the undeniable power of a very strong man.

Her hands moved to his back and he made a low, pleasured sound as she touched him, his body rocking forward, his erection pressing into her now naked skin. He was hot all over, but there . . . there he was burning like a fiercely hot forged metal. Or so it seemed. She wondered then if, when he put himself inside her, she would be burned to ashes. It certainly felt as though that were possible. He was fire itself. He owned it. Held it to himself like a lover. Burned her with it. Every touch of his body, every stroke of his tongue.

And now that tongue was running down her belly, below her navel, coming so close to—

"Wait! W-what are you doing?" she demanded of him, her hands rushing to stay him. He looked up at her through his lashes, a devilish sort of smile toying with his sculpted lips.

"I am making love to you, Selinda. Every way I know how."

"But you cannot mean to . . . to kiss me *there*."

"I mean to kiss you and more," he told her intensely. "Now hush and let me love you."

She lay there tense and resisting, afraid of what she did not understand, but he pressed on in spite of her, his mouth drawing hot streaks down her belly and then beyond her pubis. He worked his shoulders between her thighs, spreading her open wide for his mouth. When his tongue first touched her, she squirmed under the sensation of it, still determined to resist the strangeness of it.

But after a moment her resistance cracked, when she began to feel the dance of his tongue, sure and hot, against her most private of places. After another moment she felt a frisson of pleasure wend through her tense body. And then that frisson multiplied once, then again, until she was lying under the onslaught of a wave of pleasure. Her body melted in his grasp and against the play of his tongue.

Dethan was thoroughly aware of the fact that her body was not experienced in taking pleasure this way. In any way, really. Everything was brand-new to her. So it was up to him to build a roadway for her to follow. To wake her body to this kind of indulgence.

His fingers drifted over her as he momentarily lifted his mouth away. She made a little mewl of disappointment. Untried she may be, but she had such a passionate nature. She may not know exactly what she wanted, but she knew she wanted it.

And he gave it to her, finding her entrance with the touch of his fingers, breaching her tight body for the first time.

She was wet. So very wet. And the readiness of her body had a twofold effect. One, it made it easier for him to slide his finger inside her. Two, it drove him utterly, wildly mad. His desire for her seemed to magnify exponentially. He ached to breach her body in the most intimate of ways. He wanted to know what it would feel like to work himself inside her, feeling all the wet tightness every step of the way.

His fist clenched atop her breast, but then he forced himself to open his hand, to stroke over her breast gently, to pull her nipple in synchrony with the stroke of his tongue across her clitoris.

Her hips lurched upward, the onslaught of pleasure almost too much for her to bear. Selinda didn't know what to think . . . what to do . . . how to breathe! Her body simply lost all regular function as it focused on the pleasure of his touch inside her body and his mouth outside it.

It was such a crescendo of building pleasure and she let herself fall into the music of it. She sang out with it, harmonizing with it, the unique song completing her in a way she had never conceived of.

Her body suddenly replete, she exhaled in a burst of breath, everything relaxing. He withdrew from her then, moving his body up along her, his mouth seizing hers. With wonder, she realized it was herself she could taste on his lips. She would never have thought something like that could give her satisfying pleasure, but it did.

He invaded her thighs with his hips, holding the hard heat of himself against her as she panted for breath and tasted his tongue. He too was drawing hard for breath, and his big body was tight with strength and tension.

"I must have you, Selinda. My little juquil. You sing so prettily . . . and I must hear it again."

He reached to grip himself in his own hand, forcing himself to wait, trying to squeeze patience into himself. But it was no use. He wanted her much too badly to force any semblance of logic or thoughtfulness onto himself. It almost made him pull away from her entirely. He could, *should*, wait for another time. Should wait until he could exercise more control.

But he realized that time would never come. He realized this wasn't just about him not having had a woman for hundreds of turnings. It was about Selinda. The woman herself. Sweet to the touch and sweeter to the taste, she was incredible. Undeserving of a beast like him. But beast that he was, he did not have it in him to pull away from her.

"Please," she whispered then, her hands coming to frame his hips, her legs falling wide open. She dug her nails into his buttocks and urged him forward. Unable to resist so perfect a lure, he set the head of his erection at the crucial entrance to her body. He pushed forward and had to grit his teeth because it felt so amazing to breach her like this, the warmth of her pressing over and around him, the tightness of her beyond anything he could have imagined. It didn't take long for him to lose control over himself, to go from gently making his way into her to pushing harder through impossibly tight muscles. He needed to be inside her . . . completely inside her. To have her wrapped around him with perfect heat and tightness. He got his wish quicker than he should have, but thankfully she gave way to him easily. If she felt pain, she didn't reflect it to him, didn't let him see it. Perhaps that was why he felt no compunction about thrusting fully into her. He filled her until their lower bodies connected perfectly. And then he stopped, took stock, simply enjoyed the feel of her. He looked down into her face and saw a gamut of emotions and thoughts there. Wonder. Curiosity. A little fear, he knew, as she understood the gravity of the action they were taking. There was certainly no turning back from this now. And for a moment he feared she regretted it.

"Are you . . . ?" He couldn't ask. What if she wasn't all right? What if she wanted him to pull away and leave her be? He didn't know if he would be able to do such a thing. Not now. Not after he had finally claimed her.

"I'm fine," she said on the softest breath. "Please, don't stop. I want this. I wouldn't be here if I didn't want this," she assured him.

"Good," he said fiercely, "because I want this too and I am not going to let you leave me until I am ready to let you go."

After that the entire tenor of the encounter changed. He no longer held back, no longer worried about her delicate nature. He remembered she was stronger than that, and she was proving to be even stronger than he was right then. She had made up her mind and was completely invested in it. It caused a level of excitement to wash over him that he had never felt before. Actually, she was responsible for a lot of things he had never felt before.

He withdrew from her, almost completely, his hand moving down to where their bodies had been joined, slipping between the most intimate folds of her body and touching her as he returned to her. He did this for several strokes until she was moaning . . . then several more until she was crying out in lusty passion. It didn't take long for her to reach orgasm and he gritted his teeth as she came around him almost violently, her body clamping down tightly around him.

"Gods, you were made for passion," he swore to her.

"I've never seen a woman so unused to it take to it so easily."

"You've had many virgins, then?" she asked, a twinkle in her eyes.

"I've had my share," he said, putting both hands in her hair, resting his weight on his elbows, and looking down into her eyes. "But none like you."

Selinda wondered if he was just saying that to make her happy. Then it didn't matter to her because he was moving inside her again. She was floored. "You mean there's more?" she asked dumbly.

"Yes, little juquil," he said with a chuckle, "there's more."

And just like that, the tempo changed. He began to thrust increasingly harder, increasingly faster. "By all the gods . . ." he hissed, "it's more than a man can stand."

She didn't know why, but the comment pleased her no end. Now this, she thought, she believed. There was something frenetic about what he was doing to her just then. He reached back with one arm, hooking her leg into his elbow and drawing it up nearly to her chest. Muscles unused to flexing like that twinged, but not enough to make her want to stop. She would get used to it, she told herself. Because she would do this thing as often as possible with him. She had never felt anything like it. It was by far the most joy in one span of time she could ever remember feeling in her whole lifetime. Oh, she'd had a happy enough childhood, but her adulthood, starting with the deaths of her mother and then her brothers, had been overshadowing that. Now here was something new and wonderful, a desperately needed bright spot in a life fully in the dark.

She threw herself into the moment, lifting herself to meet him as best she could from her position, working hard to please him as he had pleased her. She didn't know much about any of this, but she did know he hadn't come close to feeling those brilliant moments of pleasure that he had made her feel . . . and it was very necessary that he do so. At least it was to her mind. She wanted to do anything she could to make him happy. She desperately wanted to make him happy.

In the end she didn't have to work that hard or that long at it. He devolved into short, hurried, slamming thrusts, sweat shining on his skin, his breathing ragged. He released a mighty groan, thrust into her hard and gritted his teeth through the savagery of his orgasm. He held himself to her, everything seemingly suspended, and then suddenly he released, collapsing on her, gasping for breath.

On a growl he said, "Gods, that felt good!" More good than a man like him deserved, he thought heatedly as his pleasure-saturated body grew more and more lax. He rolled away from her, not wanting to crush her under the weight of his heavy body. But no sooner had he done so than he was ringing an arm around her and hauling her up and over, using her like a blanket to cover his sated body. She was warm and sleek and beautiful with her tousled hair falling all about her pretty face. Sex looked very good on her.

"Oh no! Look at the sky!" she gasped suddenly. And just like that she was off him and on her feet, her hair flying. He watched her naked body move as she scrambled for her cloak and covered herself with it. "Hanit said the boy who watches your rooms would be back at first light. I must go before he returns."

He knew it was true, that it was dangerous for her to linger, but he was loath to let her go. He moved out of the bed and came up to her, drawing her slowly into his arms, bending her back as he caught her tense mouth against his. He kissed her until she relaxed, until she melted into his arms. Then finally he lifted his head and gazed down at her wet mouth and dazed eyes.

"I had to do that. I needed it to take me through the day. Now, let me make sure the boy isn't there and then you can go."

He reached for his pants, pulling them on quickly. She watched as he left the room and then waited with hurried breaths for his return. If Grannish were to find out . . .

He came back shortly. "The way is clear. Hurry, now," he said, knowing as well as she did what it would mean if they were caught. She jumped up to give him a fleeting kiss, then ran from the room, naked save for her cloak. Luckily she did not have far to travel and the household was still asleep. In the future he would remember to be kinder to her clothing . . . provided she didn't look so damn good in them.

Gods, he thought heatedly, what kind of trouble had he found?

CHAPTER
NINETEEN

It was a slow time coming, but Dethan could feel Selinda's trust of him mutating from a trust of necessity—meaning she had no choice—to a genuine trust. An understanding within her that she was safe with him. The proof of it was in the very nature of their lovemaking. It seemed to run a wide gamut of types, from something tender and gentle . . . to something wild and uncontrollable.

Nothing made that clearer than the night she did not come to him at the appointed hour and did not send Hanit with word. It worried him more than he could possibly have expected from himself. It made him wary of his growing attachment to her, made him aware of how dangerous attachment for either of them could truly be. They did not have the luxury of fanciful feelings.

Not that he was capable of such things. No one had ever been able to accuse him of being the fanciful type. Certainly not if they wanted to keep all their essential appendages.

Dethan was left to assume, then, that Selinda had developed one of her headaches and had simply forgotten to send him word. It worried him, how often she succumbed to these things. It worried him that they were so bad she was crippled by them, unable to move from her room. He would have to discuss with her going to see a mem from one of the healing temples. Or perhaps she did call on mems and these headaches continued in spite of them. Now, that was certainly something to worry about.

Left at odd ends, he had no choice but to go to sleep, letting himself heal once again from his brutal nightly torment.

It was two hours before dawn when he heard the door to his room open. He jolted out of sleep in an instant, flying out of the bed with a dagger in his hand, gained from its hiding place beneath one of his pillows. It was dark and he was poised to strike, barely stopping himself in time when he realized who had entered the room.

"Selinda! For the sake of the gods!" he ejected. "I nearly ran you through! What are you doing skulking about at this hour of the—"

His tirade jerked to a halt when her hands suddenly shot out and caressed him hard up the front of his body, starting at the tautness of his belly and running over the wall of his chest. Her fingers were splayed wide, the touch fast and hungry. She leaned in and he instinctively brought his hands low on her back, catching hold of her as she rested against him. It felt as though she were somehow desperate . . . or maybe just famished. In any event, her need was overpowering as she dropped her mouth to the skin of his warm chest, her breath exhaling hotly against his nipple.

"Touch me," she breathed, her lips damp against his skin. She inhaled shakily and kept her lashes lowered so he couldn't see her eyes, couldn't fathom what was driving her to come at him out of nowhere like this.

"Has something happened?" he asked her, trying to

keep himself above the reactions he was having at the feel of her nearness and her touches.

"No," she said, finally lifting her lashes and looking up into his eyes. "I only wanted . . . wanted you."

"Why did you not come to me earlier?"

"I thought to let you rest. Let you be free of me and my demands of you for a night. Only . . . I failed. I couldn't stay away."

He couldn't help but smile at that. He drew her forehead to his lips and kissed her, inhaling the fine scent of her. He had missed her. Day after day he could not touch her in public, not like he might have wished to. So that left him only the nights. Nights when he could do whatever he willed . . . and she always let him.

And here she was, telling him she was just as addicted to the drug of their lovemaking as he was. He caught her head in his hand and fiercely brought her mouth to his. He kissed her fast and hard, deep and wet and needful. Kissed her until they were both drawing hard for breath.

"I do not need to be relieved of you," he said huskily. "In truth, you are my relief from the pressures of the day."

"And you mine," she admitted before lifting onto her toes in order to catch his mouth again.

This time as he kissed her he dragged her up hard against his body. He could then feel the looseness of her clothing and the freedom of the body beneath. She wore only the thinnest of shifts beneath her cloak. It made him tense even as it aroused him to have such free access to her lush young body. She had moved through the castle dressed like this. True, it had only been a short distance, but still . . . anyone could have come upon her. Could have been able to see through the scant material to the treasures beneath. The idea made him clench his teeth a brief instant . . . but then she was back to demanding kisses from him, dragging him into the act of paying attention to what was truly important in that moment.

He pulled the tie of her cloak, sending it sheeting back off her shoulders and down to the floor in a pile near her ankles. It left her standing barely dressed in that thin white shift with only delicate touches of lace on it to provide any sort of protection from his devouring eyes.

"You will not come to me dressed like this again," he said gruffly as he ringed a hand around the back of her neck. "Anyone could have seen you."

"I . . . I was careful," she said. "I'm sorry. If you do not like me like this, of course I won't—"

"No! I did not say I didn't like you like this," he said, giving her a squeeze and a shake as he tried to rein in emotions he couldn't seem to get control of. He took hold of her hand then and brought it to the thrusting heat of his erection, wrapping her fingers around his naked state. "Tell me again I do not like it."

"But . . ."

"What I do not like is the possibility that another might see you and like you just as well."

"Oh. Oh!" she said, finally grasping his meaning. His jealousy. In the dark he saw a sly little smile slip across her lips. "I see," she said. Then her hands grew active . . . hungrier . . . as they coasted over his naked flesh. She stroked his engorged staff with a great deal of intent. Her thumb circled the head of it again and again at the end of each such stroke. He groaned and found himself blindly thrusting into her hand, his own hands gripping at the thin cotton and lace on her body. It took every ounce of willpower he owned to keep from ripping it from her, destroying it in its entirety and, along with it, any possibility of her making it back to her rooms in anything other than her cloak. Again. The idea of her

moving naked through the halls of the fortress only en-
flamed him further.

He gripped her wrist, removing her torturous touch
from his body just long enough to strip her of her flimsy
clothing, exposing her to the room and his eyes. The fire
was not lit and he felt deprived without it. Not that
he needed or desired the heat of it, but he needed and
desired the sight of her in firelight. Instead he had to
make do with his hands, shaping them to the curves and
valleys of her body in wide sweeps in order to recon-
struct her in his mind, to help him remember the fine
softness of her skin, the fullness of her breasts, the lush
curves of her hips as they flared out from her narrow
waist. She was perfect. In light or in darkness he had
never known such erotic perfection or such unmitigated
craving as he felt when it came to her.

He suddenly turned her hard about, pulling her back
to his chest, dragging her backside into the lee of his
hips. The weight of his erection came to rest against her
and he pressed forward until he was perfectly nestled
against her behind, drawing wetly into the small of her
back, where the tip of it touched her. He dragged her
hair off her back and over her shoulder, baring the line
of her neck and shoulder on the right side to the play of
his mouth. Within moments his teeth were scraping
along the exposed skin there and he heard her gasp in
a small breath. Then he felt her pressing back against
him.

No. Rubbing back against him. She was using her
body to touch him where her hands were not. Then she
thrust her hands between their bodies and used them
as well. The fingers and palm of her left hand crawled
down his thigh and the fingers and palm of the right
cupped the sac beneath his rod and molded the mallea-
ble flesh.

Dethan growled against her neck. She was determined

to be bold and forthright, and he would not gainsay her. Then he was equally forthright and took the sweet flesh of her breasts into his hands. Oh, how he needed her, needed to feel her like this and more. His craving for her nearly overwhelmed him.

But he denied any emotional aspect to this and focused on the physical. She was utterly delectable and he must have her. Must have her before her wicked hands made an overeager idiot of him. As it was, he could hardly think straight. When, he wondered, had she gained the upper hand in the physicality of their relationship? Oh yes, she had been too quick a study by far for the peace of his mind.

He coasted a hand down the soft plane of her belly until his fingers were crawling through the thatch of curls hiding her wet, heated flesh from him. But he found her easily enough and quickly enough, and she moaned softly as he did. He unerringly found that sensitive button of flesh hiding within her folds and slowly and surely swirled his touch against it. Her moans grew louder, her body active. She stood on the tips of her toes and pressed back into him harder. He persisted—his touch against her clit and her nipple, tugged between his fingers, while she turned her head, reached back and engaged his mouth in a wicked kiss.

She cried out into his mouth, and feeling fevered with lust just from hearing her, he tore his mouth from hers, turned her toward the nearest wall and bent her forward at the waist. He nudged her feet apart, widening her stance, and placed her hand against the wall.

Selinda followed every action willingly. He had shown her much in their time together, and though this was new and strange and unpredictable, she knew he would show her pleasure. He always did. She felt herself becoming open and exposed and knew instantly how he planned to take her. And in the next instant he was, thrusting into her hard from behind, filling her so full she could only gasp for breath. Her knees went weak at the raw pleasure of it, but he was there, holding her, seemingly with ease, seemingly not half as affected as she was.

But that thought was belied a moment later when he released a guttural sound of pleasure, as if he had been waiting so long to be where he now was and had finally found relief.

"I mean to take you hard," he ground out in warning . . . or was it promise? She didn't know and didn't care. It was more than welcome either way.

He kept to his vow, rushing into her so hard her toes were barely clinging to the floor. She heard his hand hit the stone of the wall above her head and his other gripped her hip. All she could do was brace both hands against the wall as well and let him ride her as if she were a wild mare in need of breaking. All the while pleasure swirled and grew inside her, so much so it was all she could do to keep from crying out too loudly. Even surrounded by stone as they were, she still did not trust they would not be overheard. But instead of hindering her pleasure, the idea of getting caught, as terrifying a prospect as it was, only added to the racing of her heart and the keenness of her nerves.

She flew into orgasm and forgot to keep her voice down. She didn't care. She had never known such pleasure and could not contain herself. But once was not enough for Dethan. He kept on until she came again, filling her again and again in an endless sea of thrusts, his stamina the stuff of legends, until finally she had to beg him for reprieve. With a chuckle, he bent to kiss her shoulder briefly.

"As you wish," he said, a smile in his voice.

And yet he drove her up once more . . . one last time,

this time losing himself in her even as she was lost around him again.

She was absolutely boneless and exhausted. She couldn't have held herself up a single moment longer. So it was a good thing he was there to sweep her off her feet and carry her to the bed. He snuggled down under the covers with her, refusing to let so much as an inch of air come between them. And still he touched her, his hands running over her skin again and again.

"Now rest, little juquil," he said softly against her ear. "I will wake you in an hour and maybe love you once more before I am forced to let you leave me."

"Mmm," she said. Then she yawned fiercely. "That sounds nice."

"Oh, it will be," he promised her as she drowsed toward sleep all too quickly. She had spent hours so keyed up, in need of him, and now at last there was relief and reprieve, and she was right where she needed to be.

She had never known such happiness.

It frightened her. It scared her to think it might all somehow disappear tomorrow. She didn't know how exactly, but she feared that unknowing more than anything . . . even more than she feared Grannish's fists and temper.

The thought troubled her as she fell asleep.

The days passed quickly after that, each one seeming to fly by . . . the nights between Dethan and Selinda seeming to fly by even more swiftly. Because of his curse their time as lovers was so very short, but the hours when he was healing allowed for them to learn about each other more thoroughly. She learned that, like her, his mother had died on the cusp of his adulthood and it had profoundly affected the course of his life. In his rage over her death, he had joined an army—any army—so he could kill with impunity, venting his fury on his enemies ruthlessly. Before he knew it, he had moved up in rank, and even though his rage had long ago been spent, he found himself marshaling his own army, conquering city after city in Weysa's name.

Both his wives he had wed for the same reason: to gain a foothold in the government of their city. It turned out that he was just as willing to conquer in peaceful ways as he was with a strong arm and fist. Selinda thought that showed remarkable intelligence and benevolence. He scoffed at that and said it was more that peaceful ways cost less in both coin and lives.

Dethan worked hard on his army throughout the day, training his recruits and testing the mettle of his new commanders. Some he kept on; others he let go. Kyran remained, having proved himself invaluable as his right arm time and again. Dethan began to trust him more with responsibility and with the plans he was making.

He also rounded up the city guard for practice sessions at the fairgrounds, pitting them against his greener soldiers, only to find out half of them were just as green and untrained. Soon all of them were swinging swords whenever they were not on duty at the walls or in the streets. All the better, Dethan thought. The city guard would be just as important in the skirmish to come as the army would be.

Day after day the Hexis army swelled in numbers. The barracks were raised and found to not be enough to house them all. So more barracks were raised. Soon there was a ring of them entirely around the fairgrounds. When not training, the soldiers were not allowed to be idle. They were assigned to either make rounds with the city guards or help forge weapons. For they were very short on swords, bows and arrows, and long spears. To say nothing of shields. There were large metal sculptures of the ruling monarchs past and present in the center of the fairgrounds and Dethan had them torn down, using the metal to make the weapons they needed. There was not enough to make shields, but they would have to make do. Some of the men found wood and began to make strong wooden shields for themselves. They had four experienced blacksmiths and four apprentices. They in turn began to teach others, or at least use them to help with the simpler work. The forges were going all day long and into the dark hours of night.

Dethan also commandeered every horse worth its weight. Much to the protestations of the wealthy noblemen who owned them. But in a surprising turn it was Grannish who silenced them. And that was another thing. Grannish seemed to have become quite helpful. Dethan of course did not trust his motivations.

It was nearly harvest time before Dethan felt everything was at the ready. But harvest time, he knew, would mean nothing. The majority of the fields stood between the city and the bulk of the Redoe. They would no doubt be destroyed in the battle.

It had been a race. Could he get the army ready before the Redoe could undermine the walls? On his side had been the fact that the city was lying on the bedrock of the mountain behind them. That meant the Redoe had to chisel their way through just about as often as they had to dig their way through. Had he been in command of the Redoe, he would not have even bothered with such a near futile task.

Dethan had searched the ranks of the Redoe time and again for their commander. They lived in tents made of waxed fabrics, most of them pieced together like quilts. No doubt the remnants of old clothing. It seemed the nomadic Redoe used everything they had wherever they could in order to live and survive. But that meant no demarcation of rank, no real banners or other symbols to indicate who was in charge. He watched the activity closely. He could tell from what he was seeing that they were preparing for action. It was only a matter of days before they attacked the city, in his opinion.

It was time to take advantage of the situation . . . before the Redoe were actually ready. The citizens of Hexis would never realize just how close to being overrun they were, but the grand had been kept more than apprised of it. His gratitude toward Dethan had grown exponentially with every passing day. Dethan had quietly cultivated that gratitude into an all-out sense of trust. Luzien had thanked the gods for Dethan on more than one occasion, and had also made his disapproval toward Grannish and his former general more than clear when it came to matters of the Redoe.

Those were the days Selinda dreaded. For on those days Grannish would come to take his resulting temper out on her. He had made it a regular habit, releasing his fury on her and getting a perverse pleasure from it as well. That much was very clear. His threats against her family deepened the closer Dethan got to her father.

Mem Josepha became a regular visitor because of this. She would heal a desperate Selinda. Dethan could not know. Not under any circumstances. Not until after the action against the Redoe . . . after he had completely won her father's trust and could then prove Grannish to be the violent, deceptive man that he was. It would do no good for Dethan to find out now. There was no sense in both of them feeling helpless to do anything about it.

The mem's visits had another purpose. Josepha came to help Selinda exercise her mage ability too, helping her to gain some kind of control over the fire and its connection to her emotions. The progress was slow, sometimes seemingly insignificant. The only time she could reproduce the large flame, it seemed, was when she became irritated or outright angry. Luckily she had not accidentally set fire to anything during the mem's teachings. Josepha said this was because Selinda had had so much practice controlling her emotions and suppressing them, which allowed her to control and suppress the flame. In fact, that skill was probably why it was so hard for her to access the fire. She did not know how to let go of it, just as she did not know how to give her emotions free rein.

All the while she came to Dethan most nights. They were by far the best moments of her days. The only time she avoided him was after Grannish took his fists to her. She was too afraid he might discover the truth. Thankfully he never questioned her or complained about it. He simply took it in stride and took Hanit's excuses at face value.

Dethan walked into the fortress and went in search of the grand. He strode into the grand's offices and found him, as usual, in conference with Grannish. There were scrolls of information lying all about them and Dethan wondered about it. He wondered just how difficult it would be to take over the reins of this government. Grannish was so deep into it, his roots reaching far and wide. The damage could be unfathomable. But he would not worry about that. If he had to tear it all apart and rebuild it from the ground up, it wouldn't be the first time and it wouldn't be insurmountable. In fact, he would prefer doing things from scratch. It would help him get a better handle on the workings of the city.

"Your most honorable," he greeted Luzien, as usual ignoring Grannish. "Your army is ready for action."

"Finally," Grannish said. "It has taken you nearly two wanings of the moon to get them ready."

"Armies are not built overnight, or easily. Even with the time taken, it is not enough. But they have heart and we are out of time."

"You mean you are out of time," Grannish said, just this shy of snide. "The agreement was you had until turntide. It is nearly upon us."

"I am aware of the time," Dethan said coldly. "It grows very, very short."

Grannish was no fool. He heard the undercurrent in those words. It was a threat. It made him bristle, but he forced himself to remain calm.

"So we are to action, then. You will give me reports," the grand commanded.

"Will you not watch from the walls?" Dethan asked.

Luzien looked appalled. "And risk the leader of the city to some stray arrow? That would be most unwise."

"I see," Dethan said. And he did. Not only was Selinda's father a blind puppet, he was a coward as well. "We will begin at dawn."

"At dawn, then. Good luck, Sor Dethan."

"Thank you. I look forward to victory." He looked directly at Grannish. "And my prize."

Selinda was pacing her rooms anxiously, her hands clasping tightly and then releasing, over and over again. The news of the next morning's action had filtered down to her relatively quickly. Grannish was not the only one with household servants loyal to him. In fact, she had relied on those connections more over the past weeks.

When the door opened and the mem walked in, she hurried over to her.

"Mem, please . . . He goes to fight the Redoe in the morning. You must teach me how to help him! I am a magess! What if they have one of their own? What if their numbers prove too much?"

"He?" the mem asked, one fine-lined brow rising.

Selinda stilled. She had not meant to give herself away, but in her panic she had said the wrong thing.

"I only meant . . . General Dethan. He fights for us and so must I. You must teach me how to help him."

"I cannot teach you what you want in so little time. It takes years to become a practiced magess. Certainly to become one of use in a war. No, I am afraid you must be like the rest of us and wait and pray and hope. Perhaps if we pray to the goddess—"

"No! Prayer is as good as doing nothing!" Selinda snapped, pacing back and forth again.

"Prayer to the gods cannot hurt and it may actually help."

Yes, but which gods? They were at war with one another. And she would not call forth their attention. Not after knowing what they did to Dethan night after night.

"The gods are cruel," she whispered.

"Some are, it is true," the mem agreed, surprising Selinda. "Come, child, stop your pacing. You are making me dizzy."

The mem reached out in a rare moment of contact, surprising Selinda. She caught her by the wrist and pulled her to a stop.

"You must realize that we cannot—" The mem broke off, her eyes going suddenly wide. "You are with child!"

Cold shock and fear slammed into Selinda. "I am not!" she cried, jerking her hand away from the mem. "Th-that's impossible! You know I am chaste!"

"I know it is expected of you," the mem said calmly. "But if you are with child, then I also know it is not true."

"Stop saying that!" Selinda leapt for her dressing table, snatching the trimming blade off the table and rushing at the mem with it, holding it under her throat.

The mem leaned back a little, to avoid the bite of the blade, but she did not recoil from it. "Say it again and I will cut your throat!"

"And then you will be with child and a murderess," Josepha said.

In the face of her fearless calm, Selinda's fingers went lax and the blade dropped to the floor. She collapsed to her knees and her eyes filled with tears.

"Do not mistake me," Selinda said fast and soft. "I am glad of it. Truly glad of it. But to speak a word of it would mean the death of not only my child but me and all the ruling family. You must not say anything!"

"I have known for two wanings that you are a magess. Has it gotten back to you that I have said anything of it?"

Selinda shook her head.

"Then know you can trust me."

"I do not have the luxury of trust. Not as long as Grannish lives."

"I can see why that would be. But Grannish does not own me, however much he has tried."

"He's tried?" Selinda asked with surprise. Then she rethought the emotion. "Of course he has," she said with a sigh. "How is it that you were able to turn him away?"

"Because he holds no power over me. I am beholden to no one but my goddess. Luckily the other mems are of like mind and they did not pressure me otherwise. I am here to help you, my lady, however you need me to. Now, touch my hand again and let me see your child."

Selinda slowly placed her hand in the mem's. Josepha closed her eyes and concentrated. "It is a healthy child. Have no fear of that. Nearly a full two wanings old. You will start to show soon. Have you felt any sickness? Weakness?" She opened her eyes and looked at Selinda, who shook her head. "It is going easy for you, then. Good. You must be careful, though. The beatings you suffer could easily dislodge the child."

Selinda felt cold dread enter her soul. It was one thing to think she was the only one to suffer, but this changed everything.

"Oh gods," she breathed. "He must win. He *must*! I will not be safe until he does."

"So the father is the general, then?" the mem surmised wisely.

"Please, I beg of you . . . My life's in your hands. This information will mean my death if—"

"I can only reassure you so much, my lady. Besides, even if I were a spy, it would already be over, now wouldn't it? Unless you are willing to kill me, the minute I walk out that door I would report to Grannish."

Selinda swallowed. "What else do you see?" she asked. "Do you know if it's . . ."

"A boy," the mem said with a laugh. "It will be a son. Firstborn of the grandina of Hexis and a fine young prince if ever there was, yes? You and your fierce general will see to that. I have heard much of this man. He has the respect of the people." The mem leaned in and whispered, "They want him to win so he will have your hand and not Grannish."

"They want their lands back," Selinda said quietly.

"That as well. But the people love you and despise Grannish. Is it any wonder they wish you to be with the general instead?"

"A son," Selinda said, a sudden soft smile running over her lips. "I will give him a son."

"Yes. But the beatings must stop, Grandina."

"After the battle . . . they will, one way or another." Her tone was fatalistic.

"It is clear you do not have much faith in your man." The mem tsked.

"I have faith in him, but I know Grannish. I know this will all get worse before it will get better. I know I may be as good as dead right now."

"Do not spend your time expecting the worst. If you do so, it will be easier for your expectations to come true. Now, let us focus on other things. Let us practice your magery and discuss what you will name your son."

CHAPTER
TWENTY

Dethan sent word to Selinda, via Hanit, that she was not to come to him tonight. After he healed enough from his burning he would need to be among the men, readying for the battle to come.

He had no idea it would spark her instant appearance in his headquarters. She walked into the room and every man in there fell over themselves to get to their feet and bow to her with respect.

"General," she said briskly, "I wish to speak to you alone."

Dethan raised a brow at that. She was always so afraid of them being seen or suspected of being alone together. And here she was, in front of witnesses, demanding the very same.

"Kyran, take the men to the training yard. Come back to me in an hour. My lady, where is your pagette? Is this not unseemly?"

"She is just outside. With your page, no doubt. I believe they have begun quite a flirtation. This is all seemly, I assure you. The door will remain open and there is a barracks full of men just beyond. I think my honor is . . . as safe as ever it was."

That made him smile, but he waited until they were

alone in the room before chuckling and coming around the desk to her. She stayed him with a hand and a look, then moved to the door and closed it as far as it would go without the latch actually catching. Then, as soon as they were sealed away as safely as was allowed by propriety, she rushed across the room and into his arms. Taken by surprise, he caught the headlong rush of her body against his and wrapped his arms around her tightly.

"Here now, what's all this?" he asked, feeling the desperation of her emotion.

"I couldn't let you go without seeing you," she said, her words nearly sobbing out of her. "I am trying to be strong. I really am! But there is so much at stake and I fear for my family!"

"Do not be afraid," he said soothingly. "I told you, I will not let anything happen to them." He hugged her tightly once more before setting her away from him. He did not want someone to come into the room and catch them embracing. They still needed to be careful until this was all over. He would not be foolish and endanger her any more than he already did by calling her to him at night.

"I am . . ." She hesitated, unsure if she should tell him or not. But after all, hadn't he said this was one of the desired outcomes he had hoped for? Still, he was about to go into battle and did not need details clouding his mind. "I am proud to be your woman," she said softly, her hands reaching to brush across the width of his chest. "I cannot wait until I can be so publicly. I only regret that we cannot have this night together."

He chuckled at that. "You have come to have quite an appetite," he teased her.

She flushed and smiled. "It is true. I admit it gladly," she said. "You have done as you have said and proven yourself an excellent lover. I will be happy to have you to husband, now that I know what I am getting."

"Well, that is good to know, since I will be winning your hand by the time this is over. But Selinda," he said, falling suddenly serious, "watch the battle closely. Once you see it turn entirely our way you must go to the fortress and secure your brother and father. Take them somewhere Grannish will not look for them, and make certain they stay there until I can get to your side. Grannish may lash out the minute he realizes he has lost you. However, I believe he has spent so long manipulating things that he will still believe he can find his way around my victory. One thing I can say is that I have not seen him have fits of rage or temper. He is quite in control of himself. He thinks about the overall picture and not satisfying his immediate emotional whims."

Selinda blanched. She had to tell him! She had to tell him he had it all wrong!

"My lady!" Selinda started and looked over her shoulder to see Hanit standing there, a panicked look on her face. "The jenden is coming this way!"

Dethan saw her pale and he reached to cup her elbow in his hand, afraid for a moment she was going to pass out. He went to support her further, but she pushed herself away and out of his hold.

"I must go. Please . . ." She looked at him and a world of fear and desire was in her eyes. "Please be safe. I would keep you safe if I could, but . . . I am not strong enough."

"I do not need you to keep me safe," he assured her gently. "And you are strong in your own ways. Now go. Do not let him see you leave. Leave from the rear of the building."

She nodded and she and Hanit hurried off. The jenden was entering the rooms as Dethan watched from the windows and saw her hurrying away, undetected.

There had been something, something in her behavior that had concerned him. Almost as though she had wanted to tell him something but had not had the power or time to do so.

Whatever it was, it would keep, he thought. It would have to. He had many preparations to make.

"General Dethan," the jenden snapped when Dethan didn't respond to his address of him right away.

Dethan turned to him. "What can I help you with, Jenden?"

"When exactly is this action beginning?"

"Why do you need to know that?" Dethan asked absently, looking back out the window.

"I wish to be on the walls to watch."

"At dawn," Dethan said.

"Will you be on the walls as well?"

Dethan frowned and looked at him. "I'm going to be where I should be. On the battleground with my men, a sword in my hand and armor on my back."

"No, of course you are . . . I meant where . . . that is, what is your first move?"

Dethan forced himself to be more present in the moment, putting worries about Selinda aside. "Do you really think I am going to tell you that?"

Grannish demurred. "Now, I know we haven't always seen eye to eye, but we are for the same cause here," he said.

"Are we?" Dethan asked coldly. "I am not for the same cause as you are. Your cause is for yourself. It always has been. I can safely say that makes us very much on opposing sides."

"Very well," Grannish said, turning a moment to shut the door. "Since we are being so candid . . . I think you should know I have no intention of allowing the grand to simply hand his daughter over to you. He will, in the end, listen to what I say. He always does. So if you do this, know it is for nothing. Save maybe some compensatory gold. But that is a lot for someone like you." He all but sneered the last.

"Someone like me? What am I, in your estimation? Let's, as you say, be candid."

"A grasper," Grannish hissed. "An opportunist. Lowborn filth that has somehow managed to talk his way into a high position. If you think I am simply going to hand Selinda over to you without fighting you tooth and nail, then you are underestimating me."

"Then we are each underestimating the other, aren't we?" Dethan surmised. "It seems to me that you are seeing quite a lot of yourself in me. You think I am nothing more than filth and I think you are a coward. Let us see who is more correct, shall we? Ride into battle tomorrow . . . for the sake of your *cause*."

Grannish blanched, then recovered himself with a chuckle. "I will not let you bait me into some foolhardy action. I admit my forte is not with the sword. My strengths lie elsewhere. I think I will remain with the grand, tucked safely behind walls, and let the foolhardiness be on your head. Maybe if I'm lucky you'll die straightaway and put an immediate end to my troubles." He leaned in with a wicked smile. "But I do hope it takes longer than that. A nice slow death."

Dethan smiled. "So be it," he said before moving around his desk to get face-to-face with his enemy. "But let me caution you. If anything happens to Selinda or her family, I will be holding you responsible. You say you do not think much of me and that is fine, but I know you have had me watched and I know they have told you that my strengths *do* lie with a sword . . . and I will turn that sword on you if so much as a single hair on their heads is bent."

"You'll have to survive through tomorrow first," Grannish sneered. "And as good as my spies tell me you are, you are still outnumbered and your men have no armor on their backs to protect them."

"Luckily neither do the Redoe," Dethan said. "Now, if we are done trading insults and threats, I have a battle to plan."

Without another word, Grannish turned and left.

"Tonkin!"

Tonkin was at the door in a heartbeat, entering the room.

"What did he want?" Tonkin asked distastefully.

"To wish me well. Do you still have that page at the fortress whom you think you can trust?"

"Blummy. Yes. He's got no love of Grannish. Grannish had his father killed right in front of him."

"Tell Blummy he's to keep Grannish in sight at all times tomorrow. If he thinks something is even the slightest bit crucial for me to know, tell him to come find me. No matter what and no matter where. Think he's brave enough to wade through the chaos of a battlefield?"

"I think he is. Hard to tell. Half these men here won't know until they're out there."

"True. Go on. Find him and ask him if he'll do it. From dawn to dusk, he's to have no other task."

"And after dusk?"

"The day's fighting will be long over by then. No one makes war in the dark." Dethan could not make war in the dark. He would have to be elsewhere come dusk. It was a dangerous limitation, but there was nothing he could do about it.

"Do you think this will be over in a single day?"

"It is unlikely. War is not always won in broad strokes but in small, vicious stabs. If luck is with us and the Redoe are as vulnerable as we hope them to be . . . then perhaps. But I will not work in hopes, only in cold realities. We do not have a spy from the heart of the Redoe, however much I tried to find one. All I have are observations from the wall." Dethan frowned thoughtfully. "Much is riding on this. For you and yours and for me and mine."

"My lord . . . tell me what to do to help you and I will do it."

"I know you will, Tonkin. That is why I do not want you by my side tomorrow."

"My lord!" Tonkin protested.

"I want you to watch over Selinda."

Tonkin quieted but was still obviously agitated. "Sor Dethan, my place is with you. I am not afraid to fight. Grandina Selinda will have the whole of the fortress guard to protect her!"

"Believe me, Tonkin, she is not safe. There is much you do not understand, much I cannot tell you . . . but she is not safe."

"Very well. What do you need of me? Just to watch over her?"

"To protect her from Grannish."

"Sor, I know he is a cruel man and not to be trusted, but what makes you think he'll go after the grandina?"

"Because she is to be my prize should we win. Once he feels he has lost her, he will lash out. I have seen you on the training field. You have improved much these past weeks. She would be safe with you . . . though I'd send a phalanx of men if I could. But we need every man here."

"That's the truth of it, to be sure. Sor . . . why did you ask for the grandina? Is it strictly for the power of marrying the heir of the city . . . or is it more? Do you . . . do you have feelings for her? I mean, it wouldn't be a wonder. She's a fine woman. Kind. She cares about this city and us lowborns far more than . . . well, more than anyone else does."

The edited sentiment was obviously that Grannish and the grand did not have the city's best interests at heart. Dethan admired Tonkin's bravery for saying so aloud. But then the man had been outspoken from the very start. Just as Kyran and his men had been. It was a whole different sort of bravery than that which he had seen them display when swords were flying in the training circles.

As for feelings toward the grandina . . .

Dethan had not asked himself that question on purpose these past weeks. It would not serve him to become sentimental where she was concerned. This must strictly be a business arrangement between them. He had not been brought back above the hells to do something as foolish and time-consuming as fall in love. Weysa would never allow it. He feared for Selinda if Weysa thought for even an instant that she was an impediment to his task.

No. He did not love her. But he did not want to see her risked either. He was putting her directly in the path of danger, just as he had been every night he had asked her to come to him. If he loved her, he would not have asked that of her. He would have protected her.

But he had grown close to her in other respects. He had come to learn who she was. The things that made her such a magnificent creature. For instance, she was not overproud or vainglorious. He had seen many a princess in his time who had been quite full of her own importance and her opinion of herself. His Selinda was far more grounded than that. And, as Tonkin had observed, she worried chiefly for her people's safety and well-being . . . even when she should be worried for herself instead. Oh, she feared getting caught by Grannish, coming or going from Dethan's rooms, but she feared even more Grannish's effect over her people should he become grand one day.

Then there was her beauty and grace. Over these past weeks he had seen a new sort of confidence bloom within her. More acceptance of her own beauty and power as a woman. And the more she accepted her flaw matter-of-factly, the more others accepted it as well. He had watched her grow more beautiful every day, until the fine lines of her face and the shining curls of her ebony hair swam in his vision every time he closed his eyes. He had grown hungrier and hungrier for her with each passing night. Even now, at that very moment, when it should be the last thing on his mind, he craved her nearly violently.

Realizing Tonkin was still standing there awaiting a reply to his query, he dragged his thoughts away from the memory of her soft curves filling his hands, her long legs wrapping around his hips . . .

"You are right. She is a fine woman and deserves to be protected from Grannish. That should be reason enough for you. Now go find Kyran and help him see to the organizing of the men. Help him however you can before heading back to the fortress, where you will watch over Selinda."

"And where will you be, sor?"

"I have something I need to do before this battle begins," he said.

Dethan was moving through the halls of the fortress at a fast pace. The sword at his side was swinging with the speed of his stride, and his breath was coming swiftly. His chest was tight with a feeling he could not identify. All he knew was that things did not feel right and they would not feel right until . . .

He found her in her sewing lounge. He had found her there so many times, sitting serenely stitching, Hanit and other ladies surrounding her as they held soft conversations. Only she was not sitting peacefully now. She was pacing anxiously back and forth, her hands tightly gripped in front of her. Hanit was watching her mistress with an equally anxious expression on her features. Otherwise, they were alone.

She stopped suddenly, almost as if she had sensed his nearness, and looked up to see him. Heedlessly they hurried toward each other, and before he could stop himself from the recklessness of it, he was kissing her, devouring the sweet, hot taste of her. It was as though he had just come home, the battle already won. Only the desperation in their connection made it clear they were dancing in the swing of a sword, the cut of it heading straight for them.

He devoured her as a man in a vast desert might devour a drink of water. His hands locked around her ribs and dragged her tightly up against the lean of his body. He felt her fingers crawling through his hair. *Yes,* he thought fiercely. *This is what I need. I cannot go into battle without this.*

The feeling was so unlike him that it took him by surprise, but it did not stop him in his quest to conquer her. Recklessly he dismissed all his surroundings, dismissed Hanit's presence, and sought the laces that held her tightly bound in her corset.

"No!" she cried then. She pulled away but grabbed his hand and hastily led him to the storage room directly connected to the salon. "Hanit, watch for us please."

"Yes, my lady," Hanit said reassuringly.

Selinda pushed through the door and pulled him into the small, dark room. There were no candles and no windows, but the moment she shut the door there was utter privacy. The instant she was secure in that, she dragged his hand to her body, using it to stroke herself from waist to breasts and then to the ties laced tightly between them. He pulled at the bow just as their mouths crashed together once more. Her tongue was strong and sweet in his mouth, and the fever in her blood was radiating from her so strongly that he could feel the heat of her body.

Then her hands were at the ties of his breeches, one pulling them free and the other cupping his erect shaft through the fabric. The feel of her hand had to be straight out of one of the eight heavens, he thought heatedly. And as soon as she was able to push his pants down below his hips, she did, her hands and nails dragging up his bare backside before leaving him so she could gather up her skirts. He had barely loosened her corset enough to give him access to her breasts and he cursed the conservative line of the thing. But he could not be worried about that, because he was catching her bare legs in his hands and helping her wrap them around his hips. The feel of her thighs around him was just what he had needed, the feel of the moist heat of her most intimate flesh even more so.

She slid her pussy up along the length of his cock with the clenching of strong thigh muscles and he had to slam her back against the closed door because it made his knees go so suddenly weak with pleasure. She had learned much these past weeks, during their nightly assignations, not the least of which was how strongly the feel of the wet heat of her drove him instantly mad.

He hastily reached between their bodies to grab hold of himself, then brought his erect flesh right to the cusp of her body. He hesitated only long enough to hear her sibilant *"Yes!"* before thrusting himself hard inside her.

It was not pretty or sweet, this coming together. It was hot and dirty and it needed to be exactly that. She gasped when he thrust hard and to the hilt inside her. Her fingers and nails dug into his shoulders; her teeth scored his bottom lip.

"Yes," she breathed into his mouth. She kissed him madly, thoroughly, then once again said, "Yes!"

He growled low in his throat, unable to help the animalistic sound. She was so hot and wanting, so hungry and needful. He wanted nothing more than to fill that need, so he thrust deeply into her again. Then again. Then again. Soon he was driving so hard into her so quickly that her whole body shook. She was pulling herself forward, her mouth leaving his so she could bite at the fabric of his shirt at his shoulder. He quickly realized it was to keep herself from crying out with her pleasure. That left him with nothing to focus on save the feel of her tight, wet body around him. With incredible speed he felt himself reaching a razor's edge, the sharpness of it cutting deep. He gritted his teeth to keep from shouting out as his orgasm ripped through him.

Moments later they were standing there, clutched tightly to each other, panting so hard for breath that the sound of it filled the small room. After a long moment she said "Thank you" on a soft, breathy whisper.

He chuckled. "I think it is I who should be thanking you," he said.

"Then we are both grateful," she said. She slowly released the clenching of her thighs and he slid free of her body as she dropped her feet to the floor. He did not want to leave her, felt bereft when he did, but he realized, as she did, that to dally with her any longer than they already had would be utter madness.

She smoothed down her skirts and then adjusted herself a little before retying the bow of her corset strings. He pulled up his pants and did likewise.

"I'm sorry," he said then. "I had not intended to use you so brusquely." He reached to smooth back a strand of her hair that their vigorous lovemaking had caused to come free of her tightly wound design.

"No. Please," she said, grabbing up his hand in both of hers, "don't apologize for giving me something I needed so badly just now."

"Did you?" he asked her.

"Yes," she breathed. They were still in the dark, still barely able to see each other, but he felt as if he could see her so clearly just then.

"I needed you," he said softly. "Once I saw you, I realized that I needed you." Then, realizing what he sounded like, realizing it might make her think things . . . apply emotions to this thing between them that he did not have the luxury to spend, he said, "It is the best way to send a man off to war." He tried to lighten the mood with a chuckle.

She did not laugh. Instead her grip on his hand tightened. "You must come back to me," she said fiercely. "I couldn't . . ." She seemed to check herself before saying, "The future of my people rests solely on your shoulders. I pray it is not too heavy a burden for you to carry. Strong as you are, it is too much to ask of anyone. I am sorry I had to ask it of you."

He frowned. "Then you are sorry we have begun this?" *You are sorry for having chosen me?* he thought.

"No. Even if I were, it would be too late to change it. But no, I am not sorry. Not for any of it," she said to him, making sure he was looking directly into her eyes in spite of the darkness they had since adjusted to. "Most certainly not for you. Choosing you was the wisest action I ever took."

"It was a daring choice. But you had no other options," he pointed out, wanting to make himself see that in the cold light of reason, but flinching away from it. However calculated this had been at the beginning, they had both found a measure of solace in each other. Of that he was certain.

"There is always an option. I could have accepted my fate and married Grannish willingly."

"That isn't a choice. That was a dictate handed down

to you by"—he bit his tongue to keep from insulting her father—"others. At least this was truly *your* choice. I shall endeavor to be worth your faith in me, my lady," he said, bringing their clasped hands up so he could kiss her fingers.

Just then there was a hurried rap at the door.

"My lady!" Hanit whispered urgently.

Selinda hesitated, then said quickly, "Fight well, my lord. I will be awaiting you." Then she leapt up to kiss him hotly . . . starkly . . . before hurrying to swing herself out of his reach and out the door.

Selinda rushed out of the salon after Hanit did a quick inspection of her to make sure she was fit to be seen. She and her pagette made their way down the corridor at a rapid clip until Hanit chuckled, drawing her attention.

"Hanit," she admonished, trying not to smile and failing miserably.

"Did you tell him? About the babe?" Hanit asked.

"No. I'll not burden him with it. He must have no distractions if he is to win. I will not be the reason that he fails."

"I think it would take more than news of impending fatherhood to make him fail," Hanit said with a tsk.

"That may be, but I will feel better this way. There will be plenty of time later . . ." She trailed off. What if there was no time later? What if he died? He was able to heal from extraordinary wounds, but what if he was beheaded? She had heard tales of men who could take the head of another man with one blow. There were no guarantees he would come back to her. He could be captured. He could be tortured. He could—

"Now, now," Hanit scolded, gathering Selinda's hands in hers. That was when Selinda realized she had stopped.

"Don't go fretting about him, my lady. He's a strong man. Strong as ever I saw. And he has his wits as well. You're right. There will be plenty of time to tell him later. Come along, now. Let's get you ready for the eventide meal."

Selinda nodded and followed Hanit's lead, but the rush of pleasure from moments earlier was now gone.

CHAPTER
TWENTY-ONE

~~~

Selinda's body trembled as if it were a bow and an arrow had just snapped free of it, leaving her empty and without purpose. She was sitting beside Dethan, her father having seated him closer to him at the table that night—to gain comfort from Dethan's sure presence, she supposed. She was so close to him but felt so far apart from him. She reached for her wineglass, but withdrew her hand quickly when she saw how badly it was shaking. That was when she felt his hand upon her thigh, beneath the table, the warmth and pressure of it penetrating her skirts. He pressed into her, a calming, staying touch.

It worked. This time she was able to reach for her glass. She drained the contents and signaled for more. Despite the reassurance of his touch, she felt as though she could not breathe. How was it that the closer she got to freedom, the more oppressed she felt? It was only a matter of a single night. Just one night. All she had to do was make it through tonight and tomorrow, and then, the gods willing, it would all be over. One way or another, it would all be over. For her. For Grannish. For Dethan. For her people. For all of them.

"Daughter, you are very dull tonight," her father said to her from what seemed like a great distance. "I think women have little stomach for war," he said with a chuckle. She looked at him and saw how animated he was. He was excited about this. Of course he would be. It was not his neck on the line. Whatever happened, it would be others spilling their blood.

For the first time she was well and truly ashamed to call him her father.

"Men will die tomorrow, Father," she said tightly. "I see no cause to celebrate that."

"Have a little faith, daughter. This is for the good of the city."

"Since when have you cared for the good of the city?" she snapped at him. "If you had a moment's care for this city you would run your own affairs! You would not be standing behind a corrupt snake"—she glared at Grannish—"or another general! You would be out on that wall where your men could see you and gain strength from you, leading your people to victory! But you will not do that, will you, Father? But I will do that," she swore to him. "I will be on the wall, and for whatever good it does, I will make certain the people see me!" She stood up, shoving her chair back. "Sor Dethan, I wish you all the luck tomorrow. There is nothing I would like more than to see you victorious and to become your prize!"

The whole time she said that last bit she was glaring at Grannish. She didn't give a damn what he did to her when he caught up with her later. She would let everyone know exactly how she felt. And this time if he struck her, she would not hide her bruises. She would shove them beneath her father's nose and force him to see what he had allowed to happen.

But she heard her father chuckle as she stormed out of the room.

"Women do not understand the way of things," she heard him say. "They romanticize these things far too much. She does not understand what it takes to run a city, or an army."

Feeling nauseated, Selinda ran for her rooms. She barely made it there before grabbing the basin and vomiting up all the wine she had imbibed. Hanit, bless her heart, was right beside her, rubbing her back and soothing her with soft sounds and words.

"There, there. 'Tis just the babe kicking up a fuss. Though I must say it was good to see someone speak the truth of things out in the open for a change." But after a moment she fretted. "Grannish will come after you for it, though."

"I think he has other worries tonight," Selinda said, praying she was right. She never knew what would set him off. Usually it was when she dared to show any kind of bravery. It made her sick again to think she might have foolishly endangered herself and her child because she could not control herself.

"Oh, what a fool I am," she whispered before sinking to the floor on her knees.

"No, my lady. You are very brave," Hanit told her.

"I do not feel brave, Hanit. I feel the coward. Like my father. Oh gods. That's what he is, Hanit. A coward. He hides behind others. Let's another man rule in his stead while he . . . he fornicates with his mistress and . . . and . . . I do not even know what he does! Usually he hunts, but with the Redoe here he cannot even leave the city! If not for the snows, the Redoe would probably stay camped outside and simply claim the farmlands as their own! A city right on top of our city! Dethan is right. The Redoe are only a breath away from taking these walls down and taking Hexis for themselves. We are a weak city led by a weak man. A puppet king with a vicious puppet master's hand up his ass!"

"My lady!" Hanit gasped. Then she tsked and shook her head. "But you are right. You are only speaking aloud what everyone in this fortress and city knows is the truth. I only fear the reprisals you will face for it."

"As do I," Selinda breathed.

Grannish was not angry about Selinda's little outburst. It actually amused him. She could really be a little spitfire when she wanted to be . . . for all the good it would do her. Her father didn't listen to her now any more than he had before. He never would. All that Grannish needed right then was for Dethan to fail . . . and he had that quite taken care of already.

By this time tomorrow he would have his city safe and securely his again. Dethan would be dead and this time Grannish would insist on being married to the little bitch immediately. He didn't know why he hadn't done so sooner. It was his only secure way of ever becoming grand. But it had been a bitter pill, the idea of hooking himself up to that sniveling, scarred whore. The idea of having to fuck her to get his sons on her . . .

Well, he wouldn't make that mistake again. Especially now that he knew he could beat her into submission and she was quite adept at hiding it. She would do anything he asked, so long as the well-being of her father and brother could be brought to bear against her.

He considered seeking her out . . . paying her back for her little display. But the fact of the matter was he was in too good a mood. He might consider it later, as a way of blowing off steam while he waited for darkness to fall.

He walked into the belly of the rearmost part of the city wall, an old rusted gateway that had long been shut off and disregarded by the city guard. And even if the guard were there, he would have seen to it that his men were on watch. The gateway was blocked by a rockslide for the most part, but there was a small gap that allowed for a single man to work his way through with a little effort. Two such men, tall and red-skinned, had done just that as Grannish approached.

"Kru Mods," he greeted the Redoe equivalent of a general. "Are your men prepared?"

"Yes. They have trained hard and we have made much armor for them. It is heavy and weighs us down. We do not like it."

"But trust me, it will be for the best," Grannish said. "It will give you the advantage over these farmers. I just wanted to make sure we are very clear. When you overrun the city you are not to harm the ruling family. The citizens will not follow you willingly if you harm their grand and his family. But once you have put me in charge of the city, we will, as I have said for these past months, all prosper in the end. You will have a city to sack and all the grain and goods you want. Just leave the gold and the government to me when you are through. Am I understood?"

"I do not understand why you help to ruin your own city," Mods said, his dark eyes judgmental.

"My motivations are my own. Just remember you wouldn't have gotten this far without me. You are *my* army. We have been planning this for months. Just because there is an army does not change things. They are nothing but a bunch of inexperienced mud farmers. You will lay waste to them easily.

"This city will be mine again when you are through . . . and we will have our agreement that every year you will be given a stipend of grain after the harvest. All I need is for you to soundly beat back the army, as you have done so many times in the past, and see to it their leader, General Dethan, is killed. Feel free to do it slowly and painfully," Grannish said with a smile. "But I want his head by the end of the day."

"We will do this," Mods agreed. "With this agreement you will be free to tend your fields and we will not encamp upon them. If you break this agreement, we will return and we will overrun your city again, and this time we will keep it for our own."

"I have made the agreement and I will abide by it. It benefits us both that I do so. Now remember, they are planning to attack you at dawn. You must attack the city before then, when they least expect it. When they are asleep in their beds. It is unfortunate that you failed to tunnel through to the city walls, but that makes no difference. Knowing when they are going to attack gives you the advantage. The moment they open the gates to release the army, you will attack them from all sides. Keep your forces under the cover of darkness until the very last minute. Do that and you will be victorious, and then you will have the run of the city."

"And what keeps me from taking the city and keeping it for myself?" Mods asked dangerously, his entire presence, with its inked tattoos and its piercings run though with bone, trying to intimidate.

"Because you don't know where the gold is and your people have no interest in staying here when the cold comes."

Mods laughed roughly. "True. You northers are insane, staying in your stone and wood buildings and in the stark white of winter. Too much longer and we would have broken camp already and made for the summer lands."

"You mean the desert," Grannish scoffed.

"It's warm and arid, beautiful and golden. If only we could grow grain there to feed the people . . . we would never leave."

"You'll have your grain. Just do as we agreed and you

will have a summer campground any time you like as well."

"We will do as agreed. We will kill your general. We've seen him on the walls . . . always staring down. We will make him fall from his high perch and onto our waiting spears."

"Good. Now go. Make ready. I will see you by day's end tomorrow."

Grannish watched the leader of the Redoe leave, a smile toying at his lips.

After this, he would have that little cunt to wife and would be grand shortly after. No one would stand in his way.

No one would dare.

CHAPTER
TWENTY-TWO

Dethan went among the men as soon as his face was passably healed so that no one would question the level of his scarring. It was only two hours before dawn and the men had prepared all the night through.

"Are we ready?" he asked Kyran once he found him.

"As ever we will be. So it's still dawn, then? Because we are ready now if you wish it."

Dethan thought about it a moment. "No. We go as planned. Are they ready at the wall?"

"Awaiting your word, General."

"Good. Let me address the men, and then we will see what these Redoe are made of."

"Yes, my lord."

"Yes, *General*," Dethan stressed to Kyran. "I am no lord."

"You will be once you claim your prize," Kyran said, his smile almost impish. Dethan moved to cuff him, but Kyran ducked out of reach. "Come now, *my lord*. It is time you face facts. One night in her bed and you'll be royal."

"I can promise you this, Kyran. I will be no more royal then than I am now."

Kyran chuckled. "If you say so, General. Go on. Speak

to the men. Some are scared and can use the—What's this, now?" Kyran had moved to the window and was looking out into the fairgrounds. The men had been milling about, loosely assembled, awaiting direction from Kyran and Dethan, but now they all seemed to be in a single press of bodies, all their attention rapt in one direction.

"What is it?" Dethan asked, coming to the window.

"I don't know," Kyran said.

"Let us go find out, then."

Dethan pushed past Kyran and strode out of the room. He had armored himself of all but his breastplate, putting off bearing the weight of it against his still-raw skin until the last moment. As he went out into the brisk, dark air and headed for the gathering of his troops, a single voice could be heard in the vastness of the night.

"You do me great honor," she said loudly, looking down on them from high on the dais, where she had been sitting at the time of his shivov fight. For so small a creature in the face of so many, she seemed strong and regal and powerful. "I have done little to deserve your loyalty, I know. All I am is the daughter of a king. You fight for your homes . . . your lands . . . and to protect me and mine. I do not forget that. I will never forget that. You men, you brave, strong men!" She raised her fist into the air, clenching it tightly. "You are my arm! You will swing my sword! You will fight back the beast at our gates!"

The men cheered her, a loud roar of approval.

"And there are none stronger and braver anywhere in this vast world of ours. I swear it!" There was another roar of approval. "For we have the fire of the eight hells in our bellies . . . and at our helm!" She pointed to Dethan, taking him by surprise. He had not realized she had taken note of him, that she could even see him from where she was standing. "There is your leader! Though not born from Hexis, he was belched from the hells themselves and sent among us to scorch the Redoe in their tents! To chase them back once and for all! To see they know never to darken our doorsteps again!"

The clamor of men turned into a chaos of noise, and Dethan could do nothing but marvel at her. It was just the sort of speech he would have made . . . only from her it was more powerful than he could ever have imagined. He had thought her courageous before, but now he thought she was simply stunning. She was still holding her hand out to him and the crowd of men parted between them, allowing him to come up to the dais, exactly as he had when he had first come to claim his reward from her. Only this time the prize was something he wanted far more than gold . . . far more than anything. Burning in the hells, he had imagined any number of things in his efforts to escape his torment, but never had he come close to envisioning something so perfect. So truly heavenly. If Xaxis had given birth to him, then surely Grimu, god of the heavens, had given birth to her.

"My queen commands me," he said, his voice resonant and deep. He did not shout. He did not need to. The sea of men had grown quiet, waiting expectantly for her to give him her blessing. "And I willingly obey."

"General Dethan . . . as they are my arm, let you be my hand, and together you shall crush the throat of the Redoe between our fingers!"

Enthusiastic cheers ripped through the crowd around him, bodies leaping up, weapons thrusting up into the air. Within a heartbeat they were chanting her name.

"Selinda! Selinda!"

But Selinda had eyes only for him.

"I will be on the walls at dawn," she said to him. "I will watch you win me."

"Know this . . . Everything I do come the dawn is solely for that goal," he said. "It has been all along."

"I know. That was our agreement," she said.

"No. This goes beyond that agreement," he said, all the while knowing that he shouldn't. "I do not wish to win you to gain a crown . . . though I will not pretend that is not my goal. But I could easily leave, get an army, defeat this city, and become ruler of it that way. I do not need you to do it. But I do need *you*. I do want to win *you*."

As he spoke . . . as he watched . . . he saw tears well in her eyes. She nodded and the tears skipped down her cheeks.

"I understand. And I do not want you to win me just to rescue me from a horrible fate otherwise. I could just as easily opt out of my life altogether."

"Do not say such things," he said darkly, moving closer to her and pulling her down from the dais. He drew her close the instant her feet were on the ground. The roar of the crowd around them gave them a sort of privacy and they felt encapsulated within it. He reached to touch gloved fingers to her face, wishing they could be skin-to-skin. She had the softest skin imaginable and he longed to feel it. "You must fight, Selinda. If for some reason I do not come back to you, you must promise me to fight Grannish. Fight him or leave. Before you consider simply taking your life, consider that there are a dozen new lives awaiting you beyond these walls.

"But I know you and know you do not wish to abandon your people. Be strong for them, as you are being strong right now. Listen to them call your name. They love you, fight for you, and would do so at any moment. Ask them to overrun the fortress and string Grannish up for you, and they will. They are your arm . . . I am your hand . . . we will not let you down."

"Please don't," she whispered, running her hand over

his broad chest, smoothing his shirt. "Please come back to me."

"I will. Do not be afraid."

"I am not," she lied, holding her chin up. "Now, where is your armor? Your breastplate?"

"Inside my headquarters," he said with a chuckle. "Never fear. I am immortal but not stupid. I may not die from many blows, but they can take me down and the army with me. I will not let that happen. And I like my head firmly attached, so . . . my only choice is to win and come back to you."

"Good." She moved away from him, as hard as it was, and went to her horse. He helped her into the saddle, and she looked around at the incredible force of men Dethan had put together. "I will be on the wall. I will watch from there."

"Be careful," he warned her. "If they have archers, you are to get inside immediately."

"I will."

She encouraged her horse and rode away slowly, reaching to touch hands with the press of men who followed her progress away.

They loved her, Dethan thought, marveling over her. But then again, she was easy to love. She had done much to gain their devotion. She had conquered this city in a fashion previously alien to him. He had always used force . . . but she had used gentility and kindness. She had not sat on the power of her birthright alone. She had given to her people everything she could in spite of the limitations Grannish imposed upon her.

He had faith that she would find another way, should something happen to him. He did not want her to have to fight anymore, but if she had to she would.

"Tonkin, my arm—"

There was a scream that cut him off. Then another.

The sound of whistling air and then solid thumps and clangs rose up all around him.

"Archers!" he shouted, knowing the sound all too well. The rain of arrows came faster and thicker. "Kyran! Get the men against the wall!" He looked up at the wall and saw city guardsmen falling, riddled with arrows, or fleeing away from them. "Tonkin, get Selinda inside! Remember, I am depending on you! Kyran, I want a contingent up on the wall immediately! I want to see what they are doing!"

Not that they could see much in the dark of night. But they would see what they could. The question was not so much what they were doing but why they were doing it. Why then? Why, after all these weeks of simply sitting out there, content to lay siege, did they just happen to attack . . . mere hours before Hexis was scheduled to do the same at dawn. Now the element of surprise had been lost and instead they were the ones taken by surprise.

The city was utter chaos within minutes. Civilians and soldiers both were running around in panic. The screams of women filled the air. Dethan rushed up the steps of the dais and shouted for the men's attention until he had a large portion of it, the immediate crowd calming. He issued orders sharply, splitting his forces—into those who would wait against the wall and those who would be at the gate—and calling forth his archers. He then ran for the wall. He thundered up the stairs alongside a group of archers. By the time he came out into the open air of the wall the initial panic had come to a halt. He could hear Kyran's voice and the voices of other commanders corralling the attention of the men below.

"Archers, make ready!" Dethan said, his voice booming out. The command was echoed up and down the wall, and the sound of fire catching was heard as the archers lit the ends of their arrows. The Redoe lived in tents made of fabric . . . fabric treated with wax to keep the rain out. Fire was their worst enemy, and Dethan was about to rain it down on them.

"Loose!" he shouted.

As a single entity, the archers closest to him released their arrows. The command echoed down the wall and one group of arrows after another went flying from the wall. It would have been better if they could have seen their targets, but that was not to be for another two hours.

"Ready again!" he shouted.

But before they could release, an answering wave of arrows came sailing over the wall. Before he could take cover, an arrow hit Dethan squarely in the left shoulder. He went down with the force of it and he cursed viciously from the pain. But he had suffered much worse, and he recovered quickly. The men could not see him wounded or perceive that he was out of the battle in any way. He grabbed the shaft of the arrow in his hand and with a mighty pull yanked the thing free of his flesh.

"Gods!" he hissed, taking the pain of it on his knees for a minute, throwing the arrow down. Then he was up on his feet and commanding his men once more. "Loose!"

There was a moment's hesitation as the men absorbed the sight of him shrugging off his wounds. But then, immediately after, a volley of fiery arrows left the top of the wall.

The two forces traded arrows like that for the better part of half an hour. The Redoe tried to send flaming arrows back at them, but very few made it over the wall, proving that they had no experience in shooting them. Flaming arrows were heavier at the head and required adjusting for the weight of them.

As the flaming arrows of the Hexis forces hit their marks, the Redoe encampment began to burn. One tent after another caught fire and soon the entire encampment was ablaze enough to light it as clearly as if it were a room being lit by braziers. It revealed that the encampment had very few people in it, the forces of the Redoe sitting hidden somewhere in the dark. Since there was only farmland beyond the wall, that left little in the way of hiding places.

Kyran was readying troops at the gate, preparing to set them loose on the Redoe the moment Dethan commanded it.

That's when Dethan realized where they were hiding.

"Kyran! Don't open the gates! Make certain they are well locked!" he shouted down to him. "The Redoe are lying in wait along the walls! We wait until daylight, when we can see them!"

"Understood!" Kyran shouted back.

The Redoe were counting on darkness as well as surprise to be their advantages, and already they were half right. But now that the initial shock of the attack was over, the men had regrouped themselves and were ready for whatever would come next.

"Fire down along the wall!" Dethan shouted to the archers.

The archers lit arrows, moved to the edge of the wall, and fired. Screams and shouts rose up to them from below and the fire of the arrows lit up the Redoe troops. Immediately they began to fall back into the darkness.

"Shoot again! Follow them!"

And so it went, the archers shooting into darkness, until Dethan finally ordered them to stop, letting the Redoe fall back to their torched encampments.

Dethan cursed as he came down off the wall, his shoulder hurting and bleeding heavily. But his temper was high and it kept him from noticing.

The Redoe had known they were coming. Someone had forewarned them. He would bet his immortal soul that he knew exactly who it had been. But he had no time or luxury to pursue that just then. He found a page and had him help dress him in his breastplate.

He had been caught off guard once already; he would not let it happen again.

By the time daylight came, the forces of Hexis were itching for action. The trading of arrows had stopped long ago, Dethan conserving what was left of their ammunition for when they could see their targets. Meanwhile, he had ordered the cauldrons of hot wax fired up, the liquid ready to be dumped over the walls in case the Redoe came again and tried to scale them. They would have been ready for the initial attack had it gone off at dawn as they had planned, but . . . there was nothing they could do about the mistakes of the past. They were ready now. That would have to be enough.

Once dawn arrived, he ordered the gates unlocked and the men, more than ready, poured out of the portal the instant it was opened, with a roar of anger lifting from deep in the bellies of furious men. These men had been raped of their crops by the Redoe again and again, season after season, and they'd had their fill of it. Finally, today, they would be able to fight back. They would fight back from poverty and fight back from starvation.

The battle was tremendous. Dethan was in the thick of it with them and so was able to see, with surprise, that the supposedly native, simple Redoe were heavily armored against the Hexis forces. But the armor that protected them was not the advantage they had hoped it would be because it was clear they were not used to moving under the weight of it. The Hexis forces, while more exposed, were freer to move, faster on their feet, and could swing wide without encumbrance.

Dethan had no trouble moving under his armor. The god-made metal was feather-light. Each time a Redoe blade struck, it glanced off or bounced back. There wasn't so much as a scratch to indicate the armor had been struck at all.

Dethan slammed his weapon into one man, pulled it out, and swung it into another. Both dropped dead to the ground as Dethan looked up at the walls of Hexis. True to her word, Selinda stood there. He could tell because she had dressed completely in scarlet red, a beacon to any man who went in search of her. They all knew their grandina was there to support them, that she was proud of them for fighting for their city. But Dethan also saw the danger of it. She made herself a target, easy to see and aim for. But he knew she would not care. He would have to have faith that Tonkin was watching over her, protecting her as best as he was able. Dethan focused on the battle at hand, finding himself somehow energized by the thought of her standing there. All exposed and in danger. The only way he could keep her safe was to kill . . . to destroy . . . to win. Dethan became a vicious machine of death, his sword flying in and out of bodies, his emotions for Selinda riding high within him. He should not let it. He should remain calm and focused . . . and yet he had never felt more focused in his life. She was the arm, he was the hand, and together they fought with vicious perfection.

The Redoe finally faltered around midday. The hot sun baked them in their armor, the relentless mud-farmer soldiers of Hexis throwing themselves into the battle with a fury the Redoe simply did not feel in return. The Redoe were not defending their home. The Redoe, in the end, had thought Hexis would be an easy conquest and were now discovering that was not the case.

They began to retreat.

Dethan raised the flag being held by the page near him and waved it furiously. He waited until he saw the same colored flag raised up on the wall, it too waving furiously.

And with a roar, over the hillside came a second force of Hexis soldiers, this one fully behind the Redoe . . . leaving them nowhere to run, sandwiched perfectly between the two. And with a new injection of fighting blood, it was clear the Redoe had no hope of victory.

It was clear even to the shocked eyes of the woman watching from the top of the walls. Seeing that unexpected troop of soldiers come over the rise to fight for Hexis had to be the most beautiful thing she had ever seen in her life. At first, upon seeing them from the wall, she had thought they were Redoe troops lying in wait. But it was quickly evident whose side they were on, as it became evident who was going to win the day. The war. By the end of the day the Redoe would be gone . . . for good.

Selinda turned and ran from the wall. She grabbed her waiting horse, Tonkin by her side every step of the way, helping her into her saddle and then mounting beside her. Together they rode madly for the fortress. Selinda raced through the stone corridors and into her father's offices. To her relief, Grannish was not with him. She had feared Grannish would be watching over him, ready to strike him down the minute he heard the battle was being lost.

"Father! You must come with me! Your safety is at stake!" she said.

"Whatever for?" her father asked. "Have you not heard? The battle is all but won! We are victorious against the Redoe. There is nothing to fear now."

"Father, I know you have never listened to a word I have said against him, but surely now you must see that Grannish is not the man you thought he was. He has failed you against the Redoe. Firru was his choice, his general. You can see now how useless he truly was."

"Yes. A poor choice," her father agreed. "But we all make mistakes."

"Mistakes? Is that what you call it? We were nearly overrun by the Redoe! That is no small mistake! That is a crucial and dangerous flaw! Father, he is an evil, horrible man. Why can you not see him for what he is? And now that Dethan has won, now that he will claim me as his prize, Grannish will know his last chance at becoming grand will have slipped away. He will lash out and he will hurt this family."

"Preposterous," her father scoffed. "Grannish has never had anything but this family's best interests in his heart. Now, I am tired of hearing about this! You are endlessly harping on this and I forbid you to speak of it any longer! I know you hate him, that you did not wish to marry him . . . Well, you have your wish. You will not be marrying him. I have given you your desire. Can you not be satisfied?"

"You have *given* it to me?" she echoed, completely aghast. "You *gave* me nothing! I fought for it! With my heart, my soul, and my body, I fought for it! You have been so blind! I am warning you, Father. Your life is at stake here. Come with me now until Dethan has returned and secured Grannish. Once he does so, we will be safe. Please. What can it hurt you to just come with me?"

"I will not come," her father said dismissively, shaking his head. "You are being dramatic as usual and I am losing patience with you. Now go to your rooms and wait for word that the battle is won."

"Father, please! Why is it so hard for you to believe me? Just once! Just this once will you not give me—"

"I said go!" her father thundered. "I have had enough of you!"

"And I have had enough of you!" she railed back. "You do not deserve to be grand! A ruler who lets oth-

ers do the ruling for him should not rule! A man so
blind he cannot see the evil under his own roof does not
deserve the care of the people. You are supposed to be
protecting them! Protecting *me*! Instead you offer us up
like sacrifices just to keep your life comfortable. Very
well. Remain blind. It is your life and you can throw it
away if you wish. I will not risk mine or my brother's!"

She turned hard on her heel and swept through the
door . . .

. . . and crashed into Grannish.

He was just as startled by the contact as she was, but
only for a moment. He reached out with iron hands and
grabbed hold of her arms. Then he shoved her with all
his strength until she was thrown back and sent sprawl-
ing across the floor. She fought off the shock of it,
scrambling to get back onto her feet, but Grannish was
there, and with a mighty kick he caught her in the side
of her ribs and sent her flying against the far wall.

She crumpled to the floor, coughing and gasping for
air, trying to force her now-bruised lung to work.

"Grannish! What is the meaning of this? Why would
you do this?" her father demanded, moving hurriedly to
her side. He turned his back on Grannish and bent to help
her up. She couldn't speak fast enough to warn him. All
she could do was shout out, "Father!"

At least, she thought in that sharp second of time, her
father had come to her. At least at the very end she knew
he truly did care for her in some way.

And then Grannish drove a dagger through her father's back, through his heart, and out past his ribs on
the front side. Shock registered along with pain on her
father's face. It was only a second. Just one second between heartbeats, but she finally saw clarity in his eyes.
Finally saw the veil of blindness lift from him.

But it was too late.

Her father fell forward onto her.

Grannish reached out to grab her father's body and haul him off her. Still, she was stained with her sire's blood and with the shock of his death. Grannish pulled her free and wrapped his hands around her throat, dragging her up to her feet and slamming her up against the wall.

But out of nowhere came Tonkin's fist, crashing into Grannish's jaw, knocking the other man back and allowing Selinda to crumple back down to the floor on her hands and knees, again gasping for breath.

"You! You answer to *me*!" Grannish spat at Tonkin, working his bruised jaw as he faced off with the page. "This fortress is surrounded by the city guard . . . the guard that works for me. The army, as we speak, is being locked outside the city walls. This fortress and this city are mine now! If you ever want to see your farm again—"

"I don't give a rat's ass about my farm," Tonkin spat. "I never have. I work for General Dethan and always have. Everything I told you was a whole lot of nothing. Things you would have found out anyway. You think you have this fortress, but I promise you, you don't. And I won't let you at the grandina again."

Tonkin stood between Selinda and Grannish, his fists up.

Then two fortress guards entered the room. Grannish turned to them and said, "Quickly. He means to hurt the grandina!"

"No!" Selinda rasped out. But the guard did not hear her. They charged poor Tonkin with weapons drawn. Tonkin bravely tried to fight them off, but he was outnumbered. He was fully engaged and there was nothing he could do to stop Grannish from grabbing Selinda by her hair and throat and dragging her from the room. She tried to fight him off, but as usual he was much too strong for her. He pulled her down the hall to his offices and threw her inside. There, she fell at the feet of a be-robed mem.

"Very well," Grannish said to the old woman. "Here's the bride. Marry us."

"No! I will not marry you!" Selinda said. "You cannot force me!"

Grannish grabbed a dagger off his desk, unsheathed it, and held the point beneath her chin so closely it broke the skin.

"I can do whatever I like. And once we are wed the forces of this city will have no choice but to follow me."

"You're mad!"

"I will be grand. They will have no choice but to protect their grand!"

"You will never be grand," she spat at him. "I am granda now, Mem," she said, addressing the woman whose robes marked her as being a mem for Xaxis. "I command this city now that my father is dead! Dead at this man's hands! If you try to wed us, when General Dethan returns and retakes this fortress—which I promise you he *will* do—I will see to it you and your entire order are ejected from this city once and for all! But if you listen to me, if you obey your granda, then you will have a high standing in my regime."

"You will have no regime," Grannish spat. "Marry us!" he commanded of the mem.

The mem stood there a moment, seemingly indecisive. Then she turned and walked out of the room.

Selinda sighed with relief.

"Come back here! I will have you caught and your skin will be flayed from your body inch by inch!"

"She is gone," Selinda said, her bearing proud, her tone strong. "Don't you see? This city is tired of your tyranny. They belong to me now. Me and my child, the baby in my body conceived by this city's true general! Your power is *at an end*!"

"Not if I kill your whole fucking family, it isn't! It will leave only me, the conqueror, to rule! And I'm going to start by killing you, you disgusting little slut!"

Grannish lunged for her. She scrambled back from him, fighting her skirts every inch of the way. But eventually he caught her and held the dagger at her breast while choking off her air at her throat.

"I should have known you were fucking him. I saw the way you lusted after him. Flirting and throwing yourself at him. Flaunting this mangled face of yours. And that's fine. If he likes to fuck a gnarled up husk of a bitch, that's fine. But right now I'm going to squeeze the life out of you slowly, like I have been wanting to do for months," he growled at her, spittle flying from his lips as his face mottled red.

He did as he promised, crushing her throat with his bare hand until she couldn't breathe. Then he released just enough for her to catch a breath before doing it again. And again. And again. All the while he glared into her eyes.

No. She wouldn't allow this! She refused to let this monster kill her and her child!

He will not win!

And with that fierce promise, an explosion of flame burst out of her. Grannish ignited instantly, his hair conflagrating and burning to a crisp, his clothes lighting up like dry tinder. He fell away from her and she cried out as her clothes caught fire. She rolled across the floor, extinguishing most of the fire, then scrambled to her feet. She whipped around to face Grannish, who was rolling across the floor, screaming at the top of his voice in a shrill pitch that cut through her . . . with satisfaction. Focusing on him, she called up her hatred toward him, and another burst of flame seared out of her and into him.

By the time she sent a third volley of fire at him he was

barely flopping around on the floor. But she would not be content, would not be safe, she thought, until he was ashes. The stench of burning flesh barely penetrated her senses. She kept him burning until he was mere bone on the scorched stone floor.

Panting for breath, she stumbled away from him, giving him a wide berth even though there was no reason to fear him any longer. She rushed across the hallway to where Tonkin had been left fighting on her behalf.

He was wounded and on his knees, still trying to fight one guard back, the other lying wounded on the floor.

"Enough!" she shouted when the one remaining guard went to lunge for Tonkin once again.

The imperiousness of her tone drew him up short and he wheeled around to look at her.

"I am your granda and I command you to stop this very instant! The man you followed is dead . . . by my hand! If you do not wish to face the same fate, you will heed my command and you will stop!"

The soldier looked unsure for a moment, so she extended her arm and pointed to a chair in the corner of the room. She was exhausted and did not know if she could do any more, but she recalled all her feelings and frustrations of these past months and threw it out toward the chair.

The object exploded, splinters of wood spraying everywhere, each one burning as it fell to the floor.

The soldier dropped his weapons with a clatter and sank to his knees, his eyes wide with shock and fear.

Completely drained, Selinda could barely keep upright. But she had no choice. Dethan needed her. He had been locked outside of the city with the Redoe. She raced through the fortress, commanding the doors be opened, ruling Grannish's men into submission with just the power of her voice and bearing. These men were good men. Men who had been beholden to Grannish out of fear or blackmail. All they needed to hear was that he was dead and she was granda, and they made way for her with total obedience.

Tonkin was with her the entire way, his arm hanging useless on the left side, but his right hand immediately there for her when she raised her foot toward the stirrup of her saddle. He hoisted her up and she took her seat. Looking down on him, she said, "Rest now, Tonkin. You have proven yourself a fine and loyal page. I will see to the care of your master until you are well."

She reined her horse around and kicked him into a run. Her hair had come undone and now streamed like a black banner behind her. She rode up to the gates, shouting at the top of her lungs. "What news?! What news?!"

She dismounted with haste and ran for one of the wall towers, taking the stairs madly, breathing hard by the time she reached the top of the wall. She rushed to the edge of the wall and looked down on the battlefield. What she saw made her heart stop. The Redoe were all on their knees, kneeling before the power of her army. Walking the line of the prisoners, still blissfully unaware of how he had been locked out of the city, was Dethan. She was so relieved to see him that tears burned in her eyes. Before she could stop herself, she screamed his name.

"DETHAN!"

And by some miracle, he heard her, looking up toward the wall, shielding his eyes from the bright afternoon sun. She waved to him with fierce strength, then rushed to the other side of the wall and shouted down.

"Open the city gates! Your granda commands you!"

News of the grand's death had not even begun to circulate, so they hesitated several moments, moments in which she held her breath. Then one of the men echoed the command, and the powerful winches and chains began to move and the massive gates were opened. Selinda was already running down the tower steps again and hurrying through the crowd of pushing and cheering people. People were just beginning to understand that the Redoe had been captured and their city was free of the grip of danger.

Selinda ran out of the city, through a field littered with dead and dying men, and straight into Dethan's surprised arms.

And then . . . *then* she began to cry.

"But how? How were you able to get all those men behind the Redoe?" Selinda asked him later.

They were lying on a pile of soft fur rugs, in front of a crackling fire. She was in his arms and wearing nothing but her shift. He was as naked as the day he'd been born. As they lay there her hand drifted over the dips and swells of his warm, muscular body. It seemed that through the last weeks of training he had grown more and more defined, sculpted into a fine male beauty full of power and strength, and every night he had healed into that definition. Lying naked she could see it all at once, a landscape of energy and muscle.

"Ah. Would you have me give away all my secrets?" he asked teasingly.

"Yes! Tell me," she insisted.

"I smuggled them out . . . one by one, over the past few weeks. I picked them from the strongest and most skillful of men and had them camp out in the woods beyond the rise, behind the Redoe. It was risky. They could have been discovered at any time, but they managed to succeed and came in just when they were needed. And I think, after all those weeks of waiting, of being away from their homes, they were ready for it. They were ready to go home and go through the Redoe to get there."

"Well, it was brilliant," she told him, sliding her body onto his, pushing him down onto the rugs. She straddled his hips, rising up like a beautiful goddess of fire with the backdrop of the fireplace behind her.

"What, this again?" he asked with a humorous glint in his eyes and a grin on her lips. "You've used me twice already, woman."

"And I'll use you at least twice more. No, wait . . . I will not put limits on us. I think we will spend all the day tomorrow making love. I am granda and I command it to be so."

"Is that so? Well, I have troops to see to and prisoners to manage. We have to decide what to do with the Redoe left living. There are many women and children, and what men are left are either wounded or strong bucks in need of taming. I have them chained together sitting in the fairgrounds under guard at the moment, but that cannot stand."

"Well, I was thinking we ought to make them work to repair all the damage they have done to the city and the farms. Then, with so many of their men dead or wounded, we should simply banish them back to their desert territories, warning them never to return again or they will face much harsher retributions. If we threaten them with a more severe punishment in the future . . . say slavery . . . I would think that would be enough to keep them where they belong. It is very unlikely they will pose any kind of trouble in the future."

"This is true." He looked at her in surprise. "I would have thought you would seek a more bloodthirsty or punitive approach after so many years of being abused by them. I'm certain such a course will not be popular with many."

"I am not out to make the popular choice . . . only the right one. Do not act so surprised that I would come up with a good solution," she said with a pout as she ran her hands over the hard planes of his chest.

"I am not. Not at all. You were made to be granda," he told her. "Unlike your father, you will be a ruler in touch with her people, in touch with the workings of her government. I know you will not let it slide into the hands of others. Your only flaw will be the gentle kindness of your heart."

"I will make one exception as far as letting others rule for me, Dethan, and that is you. Oh," she breathed, "I will need your help these coming months. My father was right. I do not know how the city is run on a daily basis. And with Grannish gone ... Who knows what damage he has left behind?"

"I will be here," he told her, his hand coming up, his fingers burrowing into her hair, and his palm cradling her cheek. She closed her eyes and pressed her lips to his palm with intensity. "But only for as long as it takes you to learn," he felt the need to remind her. The words felt cold and harsh even to him, so he was not surprised when she jerked a little and her eyes flew open. She drew a breath and opened her mouth, fear racing across her features. "I will come back," he told her hastily, hating to see her so wounded by his words. Hating the fact that she would be alone without him for months, maybe even years at a time. "But I have a promise to keep. A destiny to uphold. Weysa would never allow me the peace of a life in one city, safe here in your arms. And I must win her approval ... so perhaps one day she might help me to free my brothers."

"I know! I know the reasons why! I ... I cannot bear it. I simply cannot bear the idea of ... Dethan ... I cannot do this without you."

"Of course you can," he soothed her. "You must and you will. You are stronger than you think you are. And after the way you handled Grannish ... there is no one who would dare touch this city now. Already the city is abuzz with news of their 'fire queen.' It will spread even farther. Soon the entire continent will know that the mouth to the hells is guarded by a fierce queen of fire."

He pulled her down to him, his mouth touching hers in the gentlest of kisses. He took a breath and touched his forehead to hers. Oh, how he wished he could tell her of all the emotions for her that had driven him in battle today. How he wished he had the right to tell her . . .

But he did not have that right. It would be unfair to give her emotions only to take them away again.

So instead he gave her this. Physical love. He put his hands on her thighs, sliding them under the shift, running them over her skin. His fingertips brushed her belly, tickled against her navel, then drifted upward.

"But for now you are *my* fire queen," he said softly against her lips. "A fire you fill me with every time I touch you."

She drew away slightly before he could claim her mouth in a kiss again. "And . . . you are not afraid of me? I . . . You burn and suffer every night . . . To be so close to fire . . . fire I cannot always control . . ."

"I am not afraid of you," he assured her, drawing her to the heated kiss of his lips before breaking away and saying, "I have been burned by far worse than you. In fact, had I been given your fire as my curse, I would never have learned my lesson."

That made her smile in spite of herself. Her hands moved over him again, her fingertips coasting over the flat coins of his nipples, her nails scraping over them until he hissed in a breath and began to grow hard between the press of their bodies.

"I don't know why you insist on seeing me as strong. I do not see it," she said, shaking her head and looking away from him.

"That is a lie," he admonished her. "You have been nothing but strong today and you know it."

"Today . . . but all the days before . . . when Grannish was beating me . . . I was—"

Selinda gasped as she was whipped hard around, suddenly beneath him, her back against the furs and her body trapped by his.

"When Grannish was *what*?" he said, his tone very dark and very dangerous. His green eyes were shadowed with a storm of emotions. Emotions she couldn't begin to guess at, so she assumed he was angry with her.

"I-I-I didn't want you to worry . . . That is, you needed to focus on other things and I was afraid—"

"So you let him beat you? Rather than tell me and let me deal with it, you suffered in silence? What if he had maimed you?" He gave her a fierce shake. "What if he had killed you? You knew he was capable of anything."

"He would not have killed me. He needed me," she reminded him. "However much he hated the idea of me, he knew the only path to the throne was through me."

"So . . . all those times you did not come to me . . . were they because of these beatings?"

She didn't dare lie to him, so she simply nodded. He cursed baldly, then cursed again and shook her once more. "You little fool. Brave, brave little fool. And you dare lay there and tell me you are not strong?"

His mouth came down on hers with a searing, volatile heat. He pressed into her, his emotions coloring his kisses from top to bottom. He was unhappy with her, but knowing he could have lost her at any moment all along, it completely undid him. He devoured her, his body tense and taut and growing harder for her by the second. Her hands were on him in earnest by then and he returned the favor. Their kisses became torrid, the energy between them nearly violent as he yanked her shift up and over her head, flinging it almost angrily away.

Now her delicate body was laid out before him. She had bruises on her skin from Grannish's rough handling of her, and it only fueled his emotions of the moment. To think she had suffered even worse than this again and again . . . It was too much to bear.

He told her so with fierce kisses and ferocious caresses. He then left her mouth and made his way down her body with scraping teeth and a laving tongue. He bit at her nipples, each in turn, but not enough to hurt. If it were in his power, he would never see her hurt again.

He stroked his hands down the pale length of her thighs, rising up on his knees enough to see her but never leaving his perch between her legs. His erect staff lay intimately against her, the tip rubbing through her curls again and again until she grew so impassioned that she lifted her hips, seeking the hot feel of him. He found himself sliding through wet folds, his eagerness to have her multiplying exponentially at the feel of her.

He grunted softly, gritted his teeth behind the lips still tasting her fine, soft skin. If ever she knew how strongly she pulled at him, then maybe he would be lost. She would have total control over him. But as much as he wanted her, he could not let that happen.

He slid down her body, drawing his erection away from her, making her rumble out a sound of frustration. A frustration he would not allow to live for very long. He put his mouth on her in a fierce, fast swirling of his tongue. She moaned, her thighs clenching against his shoulders, her heels pressing into his back. She squirmed beneath him, her hips lifting rhythmically against his mouth until she was wet and panting and hot with the need to find release. But every time she came close he changed on her, either pulling back for a moment or drifting his kisses away from her clitoris and down closer to her vaginal opening. He thrust his tongue inside her and she cried out, writhed beneath him, begged him to give her release.

He did not. Not with his mouth. Instead he lurched up over her body and kissed her mouth as her drove himself deeply—oh so deeply—inside her. He ejected a sound of pleasure, a sound she echoed as her fingers and nails dug into his shoulders. He could come right then, just like that, within only an instant of feeling her around him.

He did not.

What he did do was move in and out of her with slow, long, aching thrusts. Feeling her wetness all over him, feeling the heat of her body and the muscles within clenching around him, it was more than a sane man could bear.

Selinda had made love with him more times than she could count, but there was something different this time. A quiet desperation ... one that outshone even the hasty, desperate way they had made love before he had gone into battle. It compelled her to soften her hands against him, to stroke them through his hair as if she were comforting a child. All the while, she was swept up in a maelstrom of passion. The dichotomy of it was breathtaking. It left her overwhelmed with sensation and emotion.

She orgasmed forcefully, the pleasure thundering through her like a violent storm.

"Ah gods!" he cried out as she clenched around him with power and heat. He couldn't restrain himself a moment longer. With a flurry of fierce thrusts inside her, he drove himself to his own release, his entire being ejaculating into her in a way that blinded him. Crippled him. Made him want to cry out for all that he could not have with her.

When he collapsed atop her he had wetness in his eyes and no breath left in his body. He gasped and burrowed his face against the furs until the telltale emotions were wiped away from his visage.

He could not love her. He would not. He had never loved a woman in all his life. Not either one of his wives . . . though he had become great friends with each of them. But never had he felt like this. This . . . this loss of control. This insane rush of emotions, which had no place in his life. Oh, he wished he were free to love her, but it just was not to be . . . so he must grit his teeth and move on with his tasks. He would see her safely ensconced in her rule within the city and then he would leave.

There was no other choice.

"Dethan," she whispered breathlessly in his ear. "I am carrying your child."

CHAPTER
TWENTY-THREE

Selinda watched out the glass window as the first snow of the winter fell. It was a soft snow, full of fat, lazy flakes that had only just now begun to stick to the ground and frost it over in a thin, white blanket. But the skies were heavy and dark and the temperature was dropping and the mems of Jikaro's temple were predicting the god was sending one of his fiercest storms ever against them.

Good, she thought. It made her feel safer. Contented her that Dethan couldn't possibly leave her if there was a storm stopping him. And with the winter setting in there was no sane reason to go campaigning around the world looking for cities to defeat. Surely Weysa could understand that.

She turned away from the glass and went to kneel before the beautifully crafted statue of Weysa, the marble smooth and cool, the goddess dressed in full armor with a sword in one hand and a wey flower in the other. The wey flower, named for Weysa, was the flower of peace. Weysa, Dethan had schooled her, was not just the goddess of conflict. She was also the reverse side of that coin, willing to extend peace as readily as she extended her sword. It was that wisdom that powered her husband's belief, that had shaped the man Dethan was.

He'd had this temple and others like it erected in Weysa's name, so that the temples of Weysa outnumbered those of any other god. The city had willingly begun to pay homage to the goddess who had sent a great soldier to free them from the tyranny of Grannish and the blight of the Redoe. And even though they lived at the mouth of the hells, they bravely turned their backs on Xaxis at the urging of their grand and granda.

She was granda in her own right upon her father's death and had not been required to wed Dethan . . . in the eyes of her people. But she had made a deal with him, had made him a promise, and so she had bound them together, with Mem Josepha presiding, and had given him the power to rule beside her.

Not that she had needed a promise to compel her. For it had become quite clear to her by then that she was very much in love with her husband. She cursed herself for a fool one minute, then reveled in it the next. She knew she was risking her heart as she made love to him, every time trying to silently convey how she felt, but knowing that to speak it aloud would only make it harder for them both when it came time for him to leave.

So every day since this temple had been erected she had come to pray to Weysa. She prayed to her not to take him.

"I am selfish," she admitted breathily. "I know that I am. He is a magnificent soldier and you need him by your side . . . but I need him by my side as well. Is it not enough that he suffers the flames every night? Must you deprive him of the small comfort I can give him as well? Are you not satisfied that he has learned his lesson? How can you be so cruel to so good a man? I know he has wronged the gods, but he must be forgiven eventually. Or is there no forgiveness in the hearts of the gods?"

She sighed with frustration, her hand going to her belly as their child turned over aggressively. A son, she thought. A fighter just like his father. At least now she could give birth and he could be there for the first weeks of their child's life.

And then he would be gone.

She would go to Jikaro's temple and pray for a long winter. Even though it would be hard on her people . . . she selfishly could not help herself.

"Please . . . Can we not find another way? A way to win your cities and yet keep him here with me?" But she knew that was not possible. Unless . . . "He has brothers," she said quickly . . . heatedly. "Each is a warrior in his own right. They could fight for you. Two . . . three times as fast if you but rescue them. They would take on his burden. I know it. Dethan has told me they meant everything to one another, and I know that in his heart he is driven to obey you in hopes you will somehow free them. Can't you please . . . oh sweet merciful goddess . . ."

Overcome with emotion and a wave of dizziness, she sat back on her heels. She had been praying to Weysa all day, with only short breaks in between. She was fasting, for the mems said it would bring her closer to the goddess. Her husband was at the site where he wished to rebuild the fortress, deep into the protective mountain. He knew that once the snow flew there would be no work done, so he was pushing until the very last moment for as much progress as possible. But like her prayers to Weysa, it would prove to be futile in the face of things.

Selinda struggled to get to her feet, her body ungainly with the child and weak from the rigors of her prayers. One of the mems came forward to help, but it was too late. Blackness swept over her like a fierce tide and she fell to the floor.

"You just left her here?" Dethan demanded, stripping off his gloves and kneeling next to his wife. The mems had panicked when the granda had passed out. Hanit had not been with her, so they had run to a member of her guard and had commanded him to fetch the grand to them right away. Afraid to touch her, they had left her on the cold stone floor. But at least they had rolled her onto her back and put a pillow under her head.

"Selinda?" he spoke to her softly, his hand touching her face, checking her breathing, then her throat to feel the rapid beat of her blood. He picked up her hand, chafing at it, trying to revive her. "Did you call a healer?" he barked to the mems.

"No. We waited for you, your most honorable."

"Foolish women," he spat at them. "She isn't made of glass! She is but a woman, not something too fragile to touch! Send for Mem Josepha from Hella's temple and have her meet me at the fortress."

Dethan scooped up his wife, her weight heavy in his arms. He adjusted her so that her head rested against his neck and he strode out of the temple. The temple was close to the fortress, thank the gods, so it was not far for him to walk. He arrived with his burden just as Mem Josepha was arriving on horseback. The two met in the fortress's antechamber and Josepha hurried behind him as he brought Selinda up to their rooms. The moment he had her in bed, the mem was hovering over her, touching her skin, hair, and lips. The mem tsked her tongue.

"She is very malnourished," she said. "Has she not been eating?"

"I . . . I have not shared her table these past days because I have worked through at the building site. But before it seemed she was eating constantly."

"Well, I can tell you she hasn't had a bite in well over two days . . . probably more."

"*Hanit!*" he roared out, calling the pagette to him with a fury.

"Your most honorable, she is not here," another pagette spoke up nervously. "Her most honorable gave her the day so she could see her family."

"Find her! Now! And bring her to me immediately!" he demanded of the pagette.

"Yes, your most honorable. Right away." She hurried off.

"There's no sense in blaming Hanit," the mem scolded him gently. "You should know by now that if Selinda sets her mind to something, she cannot be swayed. Let's make her a broth, feed her what we can. Some wine and water as well. I will heal her as best I can. For now, she is stable enough and the child is well."

"But she isn't awake," Dethan snapped.

"She will be. We will take care of her," the mem reassured him. "Come and sit. Pacing will not help matters. But send a page for some broth and wine first."

"I've got it, my lord," Tonkin said quickly, hurrying to leave the room.

Selinda opened her eyes hours later, surprised to find she was no longer surrounded by stone images of Weysa. She had spent so much time there these past days it had come to feel like home. Instead she was looking up into the worried and tempestuous eyes of her husband.

"Little fool," he hissed at her, his hands cradling her head and face in loving contradiction. "What did you think to accomplish, other than what you did?"

Selinda burst into tears, sobbing weakly and piteously. "I can't do it! I can't let you go!" she sobbed, gripping at his shirt where it lay against his chest. "She cannot take you from us! There has to be a way!"

"There is no other way," he said gravely.

"How would you know? You haven't even tried! You make this entire city pray their thanks and worship to her, but you have never once gone to her temples. You would just as soon leave me as not and think nothing of it otherwise! You don't even care about the fact that your son will grow up without a father!"

"That is untrue!" he snapped at her. Then he quieted. "I do not wish to leave you. I have said so often."

"No . . . you have said you have no other choice but to leave me. You never said you did not desire it."

He frowned. "Then I have been wrong to do so. Selinda, if I have led you to think . . . I just . . . I was trying to make it easier on you."

"Instead it has made me feel unloved and unwanted!"

"Selinda! You cannot believe that I do not want you! I spend every night in your bed!"

"Stop! Your words only hurt my heart. If you do not love me, then say so and be on your way. For I cannot breathe with loving you, and no matter what you say or do you cannot change that now."

He stared at her, speechless, unable for that moment in time to figure out what he should say . . . what he should do . . . what the right course of action should be. He had always been so decisive in his life. A man more of actions than of words. But here he knew only words would suffice. Words he feared speaking because it would only make it harder for them in the future.

"Selinda, if you think I do not love you, then you are so very wrong," he said softly. "I love you so much that it makes my entire being ache. But . . . but I am not free to love you, so I thought it would be unkind to tell you so."

"Dethan, I would much rather have you love me be-

fore you leave me than not. My heart would hurt either
way."

"Sweet . . . sweet Selinda," he breathed softly, lifting
her knuckles to the press of his lips. "You can never
know . . . My love for you is so strong that . . . I wish I
had known your love before I had made that vainglorious attempt at immortality. I would never have left you
then. I would have stayed by your side, in your arms,
and been content with nothing more and nothing less."

"Do you truly mean that?"

Selinda gasped as the powerful words filled the room
from all corners. Then, in a bright flash of light, a tall,
beautiful woman with hair like midnight and eyes bluer
than the sky appeared in the room.

"Weysa," Dethan breathed, a mixture of fear, awe,
and panic filling his features. He fell to the floor, onto
his knees, bowing to the goddess . . . but never once
did he let go of his wife's hand. Selinda tried to move to
join her husband on her knees, but the goddess stayed
her with a raised hand.

"You have spent enough time on your knees these
past days to satisfy me . . . for now. Remain where you
are." She then looked down at Dethan, took in his
strong, healed body and the way it shook in fear of her.
"What are you so afraid of? What can we do to you that
we have not already done?"

"You . . . you can take me away from her. Her and my
child. At least if I do your bidding I will see them every
so often. But if I displease you, you might take them away
from me for good."

"Did you mean what you said? That you would never
have gone to the fountain if you had known her love
first."

"I believe that I would . . . but I was a different man
then."

"Yes. You were. You were selfish and arrogant. But . . .

you had every right to be so. You had defeated many cities in my name. You were unconquerable. But from what you say, this woman has conquered you. Perhaps it would serve me best to kill her and the child so you will have no distractions."

And just like that Dethan was on his feet, his big body blocking Selinda from Weysa's view, tension and anger in every line and contour of his body.

"Ah, there he is," Weysa said before he could speak. "The fierce warrior. The man who conquered nations. And you will do so again. But I will make you a bargain.

"You say you would have gladly given up immortality to be with her? Then do so." Weysa drew her sword, the ring of the godly metal unlike anything either of them had heard before. "Let me cut off your head."

"No! No!!" Selinda screamed, throwing herself to her feet and against her husband's back.

"For there to be redemption, there must first be great sacrifice," Weysa said, her blue eyes never wavering from Dethan's. "Our faction must know where Kitari's loyalties truly lie. If I kill you and she wants us to rescue her, then she will bring you back to life, make you mortal again, and you can live your life here in this little city . . . campaigning in my name for only the summer months.

"But if she is not on our side, if she does not wish to be rescued from Xaxis's faction . . . then you will be dead, back in the eight hells, and there will be no coming back from it this time."

"No! Dethan, please! I-I will live with you being gone for as long as you must. Do not . . . no! Do not consider this!" she cried as he stepped forward and pulled away from her a little.

"How sure are you the Kitari wants to be rescued?" he asked Weysa.

"Not very sure at all. That is the point of all this."

"How will she know . . . ?"

"She will know. She is the goddess of life and death. She will know. Consider yourself a covert sort of message. She cannot overtly communicate with us against Xaxis's wishes, but in this little way she can show us where her loyalties truly lie. Will you do it?"

"No! He will not!"

"Have you not just spent days on your knees begging me to find some way to keep him with you?" Weysa snapped at Selinda. "This is the only way." She turned back to Dethan. "Have you the courage? You will be mortal again. A dagger in the ribs will do you in this time around. How long can you be there for your child when your life becomes so fragile?"

"She is right," Selinda breathed, gripping at him so hard her nails were gouging his skin.

"No. No, Selinda, you are wrong." He turned to face her, cradling her face in his hands, brushing the rise of her cheek with his thumb. "You cannot ask me to give you and our child the life you so dreaded when I can choose something else."

"But . . . what if Kitari is with Xaxis?" she said fearfully. "Then we will have nothing!"

"What you would have is as close to nothing as can be imagined, Selinda. I want better for you and our child."

"And your brother," Weysa chimed in.

Dethan whipped around. "What about my brother?"

"Well, I will need someone to replace you as my champion. Both of you have sworn to me your brothers would do so. I will give one of your brothers release from his eternal torment so he can become champion in your stead. Then again, either way I will be releasing one of them because I will need a new champion. So, have you made your choice?"

Dethan turned back to Selinda. "Selinda, my deepest love, if there is a way of saving one of my brothers . . ."

"Do you love your brothers more than me?" she wept.

"That is not the issue here and you know it."

"Do I? I cannot bear the thought of losing you. That has been my agony all along."

"I must do this. I must try."

She brought their joined hands to her lips, sobbing against his knuckles, her tears falling down the back of his hand. "It is because I love you that I know this already. It's just . . . I am afraid."

"So am I," he said. "Now kiss me before I go."

She sobbed once more before lurching up to his lips, kissing him as best she could when she could barely breathe. *What if this is the last time? The very last time?*

He pulled away from her just when she felt the salt of his tears touch her cheek. Then he pushed his way out of her grasp, stepped away, and turned to face his goddess.

"Must it be done here? I don't wish her to see . . ."

"It must. But it will be bloodless. Once the blade goes through you, you will simply disappear."

"Good," he said. "Then do it. And quickly before I shame myself and lose my nerve."

"So be it."

Faster than light, Weysa's blade sang out, cutting his head from his shoulders. In a bright flash of light, his head and body both disappeared before his head could part even two inches from his neck.

"Oh sweet merciful goddess, please!" Selinda crumpled to the ground, passing out cold from the shock.

"Selinda. Selinda . . ."

Selinda swam up from the darkness, afraid to leave it because she could still hear his voice calling her name, and when she woke she knew it would be gone. Cut away by the edge of a goddess's blade.

"Selinda!"

Her eyes snapped open, and to her shock, she found herself staring into beloved green eyes. A beloved face. A beloved pair of hands stroking her shoulders and arms.

"Dethan!"

He chuckled when she flung herself against him, grasping at his back and shoulders in desperation.

"God of dreams, Mordu, please. If this is just a dream, then do not allow me to waken!"

"It is not a dream. Come and kiss your mortal husband," Dethan said.

She did so in an instant, kissing him as though it would be their last time, and she vowed it would be thus every time from then on. When she came away from him she looked around the room and saw Weysa still standing there, bold and beautiful in her gleaming armor.

"Kitari is with us," she observed with satisfaction. "I had thought so and now we have proof. I thank you for your sacrifice, Dethan."

"No. It is I who thank you. You have given me a gift beyond measure." He looked back at his wife and kissed her once again.

"You may keep your god-made armor. It will no doubt save your life each summer as you wage battle in my name. The curse of fire is of course lifted. You have come far, Dethan. And now, one last gift . . ."

In a flash of light Weysa disappeared and a large man-size object fell to the floor with a smack in her wake. Dethan flew from his wife's side and over to the object, which looked like a large chunk of ice.

"Garreth! It's Garreth!" Dethan said, touching his frozen brother and hissing as his warmer hands nearly stuck to the ice. "Tonkin! Hanit! Come quickly!"

The two came hurrying over and Selinda slid out of her bed to join them.

"My youngest brother," Dethan said as he and Tonkin slid his brother toward the fire to warm him. "But why would she pick him? He has never led any armies. He has only ever seen me and followed me. I . . . I would have thought she would have chosen Maxum or Jaykun."

"She is a goddess," Selinda said bitterly. "She has her own reasons."

Dethan turned to her, reaching to touch a now cold hand to hers. "That goddess has just given me everything I could ever ask for."

"Except your other two brothers," she said.

"Except that," he agreed. "But otherwise . . . I am the happiest man alive."

"Alive," she breathed then, running her hands over him. "You're alive. And . . . we will grow old together."

"That will be my every endeavor," he promised her.

"Good," she said. "Because your son and I will need you. Now, let us tend to your brother."

"Not you. You go back to bed," he ordered her sternly. "You will eat something and then, when he is warmed, you will meet my brother. For now . . . let me help my brother as I could not help him in all these full turnings past."

Selinda turned to do as he bade but stopped when she saw a pile of metal on the floor. She quickly realized it was armor.

And there, on the breastplate, was etched the beautiful petals of the wey flower.

Read on for an exciting sneak peek
of the next book in

The IMMORTAL BROTHERS
series

CURSED BY ICE
BY JACQUELYN FRANK

CHAPTER
ONE

Garreth walked into the command tent and immediately dropped his burden on one of the cross-legged tables within. He wore full armor, so every time he moved the sound of metal striking metal was made. It was a sound he had grown to love over his lifetime. The sound of a man ready for whatever battles might come his way. A sound he once thought he would never hear again.

"Well, little brother, how goes things with the troops?"

Garreth turned to face Dethan. "Well, elder brother," he said with a tight-lipped smile, "they are bored out of their skulls."

"I thought you were sending out hunting parties."

"I did. And we've game aplenty now. But these men have come for a fight and they are itching to do battle. I cannot say I blame them. The summer wears on, and soon you will be returning to your wife and child, taking half our forces back with you to winter. They want to see at least one more glorious battle before they go."

"Outside this tent and a few strides away is that glorious battle to come." Dethan moved to the front of the tent, looking out the opening and toward the city they had chosen to sack in Weysa's name.

That was their part of the bargain, the deal that had freed the two brothers from their torments after they had drunk from the fountain. Dethan, Garreth had learned, had been thrust down into the darkest, hottest pit of the eight hells, cursed to burn to the bone over and over again, just as Garreth had been cursed to freeze. But almost a full turn of the seasons ago, the goddess had freed Dethan.

Weysa needed warriors to fight in her name. She and the other gods had grown weak as the people turned away from their faith and belief in them, for they needed the love and devotion of the people in order to gain power. And now that the twelve gods were at war, split into two factions of six, they desired power more than ever. Weysa's faction consisted of Hella, the goddess of fate and fortune; Meru, the goddess of hearth, home, and harvest; her brother Mordu, the god of hope, love, and dreams; Lothas, the god of day and night; and Framun, the god of peace and tranquillity. They warred with the opposing faction of Xaxis, the god of the eight hells; Grimu, the god of the eight heavens; Diathus, the goddess of the land and oceans; Kitari, the goddess of life and death; Jikaro, the god of storms; and Sabo, the god of pain and suffering.

However, Kitari, the queen of the gods, was being held by Xaxis's faction against her will, a fact they had discovered only last winter, when Dethan had traded away his immortality in order to discover her true intent. It had been a risky proposition, one that could easily have backfired and meant a permanent end to Dethan, but instead it had freed him fully from his curse, made him mortal, and allowed Garreth to be freed from his icy hell as well.

Somewhat.

For every night, between dusk and the juquil's hour, Garreth was cursed to freeze again. A reminder, he thought grimly, of what he had done and of the gods' discontent with him. Weysa had only freed him to fight; she had not been willing to release him entirely from his curse.

But that did not matter. All that mattered was that they and their army perform well. They had conquered one city already, this past spring, erecting temples to Weysa within its walls and filling its army with more soldiers. Now it was coming on the end of summer and out there, only a short distance away, was the next city.

The first city had been easy. Almost too easy. Dissatisfyingly easy. Garreth had wanted a pitched battle, a fight to vent his anger and frustrations on.

Both of which were great and many.

But more than that, he wanted to please the goddess. Not from fear of her, although that was most certainly present, but in the hopes that she would see what powerful warriors the brothers were, what great assets they were . . . and maybe it would compel her to find and release the remaining two brothers from their torments.

Garreth and Dethan fought and conquered just the same, in the hopes that one day their brothers would be free. Yes, most of all, that was what they both fervently prayed for.

Just then a courier ran up to the tent. He handed a pair of dispatches to Dethan.

"Ah! A letter from Selinda!" Dethan said eagerly, moving back into the tent and handing the second dispatch to Garreth, unread. Dethan clearly did not care what was in the other message. The letter from his wife meant more to him than anything else.

Rescuing their brothers was a very close second to that.

"Look! Look how he's grown!" Dethan showed a paper to Garreth excitedly. It was a very skillfully rendered and life-like miniature painting of Dethan's infant son. The child was nearly five wanings old, and Dethan had been campaigning for three of those wanings. Garreth and the army had conquered their first city alone before Dethan had joined them at the turn of summer, as was agreed by Weysa. Dethan's summers were hers, when he would fight, and the remaining months he belonged to his beloved wife, Selinda.

These months had been difficult on Dethan, Garreth knew. He had wanted to be with his wife and child, and the separation had often taken its toll on his mood. But Garreth had easily forgiven Dethan his surly moments. He would have felt the same had he a wife like Selinda and a child like Dethan's fine son, Xand.

"She writes that they are both healthy and well. That—" Dethan broke off.

"Yes?" Garreth prompted.

"Well, I cannot repeat this part," Dethan said with a wolfish grin, his eyes bright with amusement as he looked up at his brother. "She would never forgive me."

"Say no more, brother," Garreth said, amused by the besotted man.

He was amused, but he did not smile.

He had thought he would never live to see the day his brother was in love. Of all of them, Dethan had never professed to love a woman—even in his youth, when boys tend to be reckless with giving away their hearts. But he was completely around the bend over Selinda, his devotion to her rampant.

Garreth envied him that. He envied the warm home and squirming child that awaited his brother once the cold of fall came calling. Garreth would continue the campaign against the new city until it was defeated, however long that took, but Dethan would leave him to it the moment the weather turned cold.

Garreth left his brother to his letter and turned his eyes to the missive in his own hands. The paper was folded neatly and sealed with wax, which had been stamped with the intricate image of a dragon of some sort, its wings broad within the circle of the stamp. The letter was addressed:

To the Beasts at the Gate.

Intrigued, Garreth broke the seal and opened the letter.

You come upon our small city with aggression and numbers. We do not ask for war, and yet you bring it. We will not stand idly by while you rape our home of its innocence and peace. Consider yourself warned. End your folly against us now and we will let you leave unharmed.

The City of Kith

"Brother, I do believe we have been threatened," Garreth said with thoughtful amusement.

Again, without a smile.

Dethan looked up questioningly as Garreth handed him the missive. He read it quickly and promptly burst out in a rich, raucous laugh.

"Such posturing. They are weak and they know it. Once we lay siege and they begin to starve for lack of fresh game and supplies, they will be welcoming us with open arms. As it is, their mill and butchery are outside the city walls. We have already seized control of them, as well as the farmland and crops, which right now are ripe with growing grain and thick with orchards. They know they are doomed to fall to us. This is mere posturing."

"It has spine, you have to admit."

"It shows fear." Dethan scoffed.

"I think it's just the opposite," Garreth said thoughtfully. "They sound very certain that they are not the ones in danger. Perhaps the more important question is, how did this missive reach us? The city has been locked down against us since we arrived, no one in and no one out."

"There is always a way in or out, whatever the circumstance. There are always some enterprising sorts willing to risk running a blockade. For profit."

"Yes, but the Kithians are violet-skinned. Surely we would have noticed one of them in our camp who was not under guard."

There were Kithians in camp, all of them prisoners of the army. Mostly farmers and others who had been caught outside the walls of the city. But as Garreth had said, they were all under guard.

"That is a puzzle, it is true," Dethan said, a frown marring his features. He walked to the tent opening and yelled out, "You! Page! Where did you get this letter?"

The courier who had dropped off the missives stepped into the opening of the tent, leaving the conversation he'd been having with one of the command tent guards.

"A messenger from Hexis brought it only a short while ago," the courier said.

"No, not the one from my wife. The other."

"Other? I handed you only one missive, your honor."

"I'm holding both in my hands, page," Dethan said, showing the letters to the man.

"I . . . I only . . . But there was only one," the page insisted, looking flustered and very honestly worried.

"Never mind. Go and get yourself a meal," Dethan said. Then, once the young man had left, he turned back toward Garreth. "What do we make of this?"

"Altered perception? It must be some kind of magery."

"So it seems. If they have a mage with that kind of power, we will have to be more alert. It was foolish of them to tip their hand though. We will now be on guard against it."

"But what can we do against a mage? Especially one who can alter the mind. Your wife is the only mage we know and she is two weeks' journey away from here."

"My wife will remain home with my son," Dethan said darkly. "We will not even entertain the idea of her coming on a campaign."

"Dethan, she is a magess of fire, one of the most powerful of the mage schools—"

"Enough! We will not discuss it!"

Garreth knew by his brother's terrible tone that it was indeed the end of the conversation. Garreth's sister by marriage, however powerful she might be, would never be allowed from behind the safety of Hexis's walls. Not for anything, and certainly not for war.

"Then how are we to prepare for whatever tricks they have planned? This is clearly a mage of some kind of mindcraft."

"Perhaps. The best way to battle this is by using deception and great numbers. No mage is strong enough to fool an entire army, but they can do damage in small increments. It is most important that they don't know where you and I are. As leaders, we are the ones giving commands and we cannot allow ourselves to be tricked into giving false commands."

"Not an easy ploy considering your armor is black. It rather stands out."

"As does yours with its golden hue. We will have to wear other armor."

"But both of our armors are god made. And you are no longer immortal, brother. I do not wish to see you—"

"I was fighting wars without immortality for a very long time. Do you not trust that I can come away from this alive and well again?"

"Of course I do. I only meant . . . I would not wish to

take unnecessary chances. Not when such a valuable tool such as our armor is available to us."

"It is not ideal of course, but it will have to be. I will call a page to find us suits of common armor. You cannot be killed except with a god-made weapon, and since I am the only one with a god-made sword, you have little to worry about."

"I would not say that," Garreth said with a grimace. He moved toward the opening of the tent. "Dusk comes."

Dethan frowned, his clover-green eyes expressing his deep regret, his awareness of what his brother was suffering, and the guilt of knowing it was his folly that had led Garreth to it.

But Garreth had willingly followed Dethan. He had made the choice of his own free will to go on their quest for the fountain. He had been weak and was now paying the price for not being strong against his brothers' cajoling coercions.

"Brother . . ." Dethan began.

"Dusk comes every night," Garreth said quietly. "Will you flagellate yourself every time?"

"Yes," Dethan said simply.

"I wish you would not" was all Garreth could say. Then he left the tent and began to head toward the orchards that stood a little ways away from the encampment. He headed for the section of marjan trees that had turned from a healthy white to a sickly brown, the only trees in the orchards not bearing leaves or fruit. Both had fallen to the ground the day after they had first come to Kith. The day after his first dusk in the orchard.

He stood among those barren trees and slowly removed his armor. Piece by piece, he set it down onto the ground a few feet away from where he eventually stood waiting.

The moment the first touch of darkness bled into the

sky, the grasses beneath his feet began to turn white with frost. The frost crept outward in an ever-widening circle, overtaking the dead trees, climbing up the bark and into the branches. Had there been leaves left, they too would have frosted over.

He began to feel the cold seeping into his bones and he could not help but shudder. He tried not to brace against it, tried in vain to just let it come without his body resisting it and causing him even more pain in the long run. But he tensed just the same, his heartbeat racing as his breath began to cloud upon the air.

He dropped to his knees, falling forward onto his hands, as pain screamed through his freezing muscles. His body shuddered again and again in a futile effort to try to warm itself. He felt everything within him turning to solid ice, from bones to sinew to flesh. The insides of his ears, his eyes in his sockets, his scrotum and his penis. Eventually his lungs and heart froze solid and he could no longer breathe. When that happened he fell, a solid block of iced flesh, to the ground.

And after an hour he began to thaw . . .

. . . only to freeze again.

CHAPTER
TWO

They laid siege to the city the very next day.

The city walls had pots of boiling oil atop them, which would be dumped upon the soldiers who tried to scale them. The trick was to ascend where the pots were not; the pots were so large and so heavy that they were fixed into the battlements and could not be moved. Unfortunately the soldiers could learn their placement only by trial and error. When the first wave of soldiers attempted the walls, which Garreth had ordered to be attacked from every quarter at the exact same moment, the pots were dumped immediately upon them, scalding every man the oil touched ... and showing exactly where the pots were positioned and where they were not.

Garreth then pulled the men back, and the wounded and burned ones were cared for, the camp mems—priestesses who had the ability to heal—making their way through the injured ranks and giving solace wherever they could. Dethan had done likewise on the opposite side of the walled city, looking for weaknesses that could be exploited.

The city of Kith's walls were eight-sided, the octagon

large and protective of the inhabitants inside. They rose up at least a hundred feet high, making scaling them a true challenge.

But when the soldiers attacked again that afternoon, they brought in scaffolds, placing them beyond the reach of the oil pots, and began to scale them by tens and by twenties. Archers came into play, shooting from the city battlements down into the climbing men.

Garreth walked up to his best archers, a contingent he had set aside for this one purpose.

"Aim for every archer you see," he instructed them. "Make every shot count and take your time. Let them show themselves and get overconfident. Then pick them off one by one."

"Yes, my lord," they said in unison.

And so they did. Archers began to drop from the walls, their bodies falling into the ranks of the advancing men. Either that or they fell back behind the battlements. In the camp, Garreth watched everything with a steady eye and a magnification scope.

And that was when he first saw her.

She would have been hard to miss, standing openly on top of the city wall facing him. She did not duck and cover, did not dodge the arrows flying all around her. She was dressed in a brilliant jewel-blue, like the blue of a diri's egg. She wore a long scarf, which blew in the wind, trailing behind her like a banner—a magnificent plumage for a brave and fearless bird. Her hair was down, it too blowing in the wild wind, the fiery red of it a color unlike anything he had ever seen—deep and dark in some places, light and coppery in others. And of course there was her lavender skin, marking her as Kithian, if being on their battlements was not proof enough.

Then, like some kind of powerful goddess, she

reached her arms up high and wide, tipped her head back, and closed her eyes. She seemed to breathe in the world around her.

That was when a shadow, swift and dark, skimmed over their forces.